PARIS
IMMORTAL

Absolutions

S. ROIT

snowbooks

Proudly Published by Snowbooks in 2009

Snowbooks Ltd.
120 Pentonville Road
London
N1 9JN
Tel: 0790 406 2414

email: info@snowbooks.com
www.snowbooks.com

British Library Cataloguing in Publication Data
A catalogue record for this book is available from the British Library.

Paperback Edition 978-1-905005-96-3
Library Hardback 978-1-906727-00-0

Printed in the UK

For you who dare to be different—to be yourself.

Thou lovest me, thy soul is mine. Come to my heart, thou can'st not escape the spell my spirit has cast upon me. Why do you repulse—

The Vampire: A Phantasm
Dion Boucicault, 1852

Bang!
Jerk.
He falls.
Blood red flower blooming under my hands.
Bang!
Jerk, he falls.
Blood petals on my hands.
Except I never heard a bang. My brain was more than happy to betray me with the imaginary detail that should have accompanied the scene. Silencers are for assassins.
Hot sweat.
Assassins.
Next I knew I was gripping the counter.
Next I knew, I couldn't breathe.
Next I knew, there was a voice, a sleepy voice.
"Troy?"
I can't breathe.
I'm getting dizzy.
"Whoa whoa, hey," I heard. Then I felt hands, arms, someone holding me up. "Slow down, you're hyperventilating." I heard a barely breathed curse word. "Paper bag, let me see if you have one."
Gasp of words. "I'm…I'll be…"
"Slow down, man, shh, deep breath."
I'm trying, I'm trying.

Hey. Good to see you again. You remember me, right?

Crazy as things were last time, well…

That was nothing. I don't know if I can make it through this one.

But the coffee's brewing; if you come inside, I'll try it, friend.

Chapter One

JULY 26

Trey

It'd been a couple of hours since I'd run into Scott at by Le Parvis. I'd already stopped by the office and still had some time to kill before my date with Geoff. We were having a late date, since he was working an evening shift. I decided, or maybe once again, my feet decided, to head by their place.

You know, them. My newfound grandparents.

This was definitely turning into a habit, just like Loki chin scratching, along with stinky-rope-toy tossing and tug of war.

Loki hadn't barked at me in a threatening way since that time I first came by here during the day. Apparently, he'd realized I was part of the family before anyone else did.

So, after he left his slobbery calling card on my hand, I headed towards their front door, wiping my palm on my trousers. It wasn't quite sunset, but I knew that didn't matter.

I think, in truth, I was here because I needed a little

distracting from my thoughts. My worries. I was wondering how my first conversation with Scott after all this time was going to go. I was damned happy to see him in Paris, but there was so much—so much I'd done wrong. So many things that I'd done wrong and felt guilty about.

I reached the front door. There was too much time yet between now and my date. Being with Geoff would make me feel better, seemed like it always did, but I had about an hour left to occupy myself. Maybe less.

Still enough time for me to drive myself crazy. Heck, I can do that in ten seconds flat without breaking a sweat.

I lifted a hand to knock, but the door opened before I could connect with wood.

Another habitual thing, nearly.

"My darling boy, to what do I owe the pleasure?"

Michel's dazzling smile was contagious. "I just wanted to see you."

"Such is always the best reason for a visit." He opened the door wider and gestured me inside.

I moved past him, taking a moment to notice his dark red, velvet robe. After he closed the door, I grinned at him.

"Are robes the only thing you ever wear at home?" I held up a hand. "Not that I'm complaining."

He answered my grin with one of his own. "Generally I wear far less, unless you count Gabriel as attire."

I laughed. "Well hey, it's your house. I kinda like the walking around nude thing, myself, sometimes."

"You know what I say, hmm?"

Nod. "Why not?"

Impish grin. "Indeed." He gestured. "Make yourself at home, darling."

I headed for the living room, him right behind me, and opted for one of the wingback chairs. When I caught sight of him again, he was giving me a look that managed to mix tenderness with amusement.

Only he could pull that off, I thought.

"What?" I asked.

"That's Gabriel's favorite chair."

"Oh." I ran my hand over one of its arms. "Well, it's comfortable."

"You've chosen it before. I don't know if you remember the first time that you did."

I thought hard. "When I came to interrogate you."

"You do remember, how lovely. I thought perhaps you were too swept up in your thoughts that day to notice such a thing."

I moved my hand over the velvet again. "It's strange. It feels familiar more than anything else."

"How intriguing. I'm certain it's that you both like the feel of its placement in the room." He smiled once more, then headed for the built in liquor cabinet.

I definitely remembered that.

"Would you care for some wine?"

"No, I'm..." actually, "Yes, please."

I heard him chuckle. "Special vintage, coming right up."

Yeah. I may already be salivating.

"I have a date with Geoff, so I can't stay long, but one drink won't kill me, right?"

"I should think not. Certainly it prompts the opposite." With that, he turned, moving toward me with a glass in each hand. Stopping in front of me, he offered the one that was a little more than half-full.

Taking it, I said, "You said each time could change me in some tiny way."

"Yes."

"What about pure blood? I've had yours and Gabriel's both, now."

Head tilt. "How is your eyesight, Trey?"

I contemplated. "It was always good." I stared at the wine. "Is this the same as before?" I lifted my eyes to his.

"If you mean whether or not it's the same as what I place

in the black bottles, yes. It wouldn't do to have you too high before your date, I think."

I stared at the wine again. "Um, okay. It could be my imagination, but the color does seem richer."

I heard his low chuckle and glanced up in time to see him taking a seat in the other chair, crossing his legs after he settled.

"Not my imagination, then." Nod. "Oookay. So it hits my eyesight faster. Anything else I should know?"

He took a sip of wine. "Mmm, health wise, you're a more resilient, no doubt. Faster than you would have been."

I couldn't wait any longer after watching him drink, and took a sip of my wine, too.

Okay, Trey. Resist the urge to gulp.

"I don't crash anymore."

"I doubt such things as colds will molest you easily in the future, either," he said, having another sip of his wine.

Contagious. I drank more of mine. God, what a wonderful zing. I knew coming over here was a good idea. No more bad thoughts.

"Pure blood is more potent, of course, so many of the things I told you before have sped up a touch. Likely your hearing is bit sharper as well, though you may not have noticed, yet."

"I can live with that. No fangs yet, right?"

He laughed, and it was as if someone rang a string of small bells right next to my ear.

"I should think not. You may find yourself a bit more randy, however."

"Like I needed that." I chuckled and shrugged.

Oops. I also just gulped the rest of the wine. Do not lick the glass, Trey.

More bells. In both ears.

"Dude…I thought your eyes were crazy before," I said.

And giggled. "Um, in a good way."

"Oh dear. This mixture may be a tad stronger," he offered a shrug of his brows. "I believe you'll have an especially wonderful time with Geoff this evening."

"I would anyway, so there."

"Indeed, but…" he waved a hand and grinned widely at me. "In any case, shall you find yourself wearing him this evening, do you think?"

Pause.

Did I just blush?

No way. Must be the wine.

"Uh." Slow grin. "Well." Half laugh. "I hope so."

"Then you should make it so," he concluded.

"You're right. I should. I will." Pause. "Unless he says no."

Whoa. Those are freaking loud bells.

"I very much doubt this will be the case."

I pointed my glass at him. "Been talking about me again?"

His fingertips went to his chest. "Moi? Would I do such a thing?"

"Yes. You have."

"Ah, quite right, I have." He set his glass on the table between the chairs. I figured maybe I should set mine down, too, before I dropped it.

"Come now," he carried on. "You know that he wants you."

"Yeah, I think he does. But what did you say? No, wait. What did he say?"

"After blushing profusely, he managed to say a few words, after which, he turned a shade I thought impossible for a human."

Blink. "So spit it out."

Mischievous look. "He wishes for you to be his first."

I smiled.

"And his only."

My eyes closed and my breathing hitched.

"I'm so pleased," I heard him say. "I knew the two of you would fancy each other."

I opened my eyes.

"I knew all along."

I swiftly changed subjects, because as much as I loved what he just said, a twinge of fear silently stabbed me.

"I ran into an old friend earlier."

Michel studied me, his brows faintly knitting. But then they relaxed and he rolled with it.

"How marvelous. Will you be seeing him or her again?"

"Yes. In the morning, and it's a he...Scott."

He tasted the name. "Scott. You knew him in New York?"

"Yeah."

"I should like to meet him."

I laughed. "I figured you would. I'm sure we can arrange it."

"Splendid." His head cocked. "Gabriel will stir soon. Would you like to see him?"

"I'd love to, but..." I looked around. Oh right, no clocks. I fished around in a pocket and checked my cell. "I should probably go."

"It wouldn't do to keep the little angel waiting, no."

I stood up. "Tell Gabriel I said hello, and that I'm sorry I missed him."

He rose. "But of course, beloved."

He led me to the front door, cracked it open, and then gazed at me.

"Are you quite all right?"

I just can't win. But I didn't come here for that. I didn't come here for bad thoughts.

"Yeah, I am."

His eyes narrowed.

Ah, hell. "What you said about Geoff..."

"Yes?" His brows knit themselves.

"It...scares me a little."

"But why?"

"Because..." I rubbed my forehead and he gazed and gazed at me.

Finally, when I didn't say anything more, he spoke. "Your past, it has such a grip on you."

I lowered my eyes. "I know I need to get over it. It's hard."

He placed his hands on my shoulders. "We each have our own time frames. You're not the only one in need of letting go. You're not the only one with a past. Don't berate yourself for it, it will happen in your own good time."

I searched and searched his eyes.

"What is it that you need to let go?" Besides maybe Vicont.

He took a breath and turned toward the door. "I've a lengthy past, Trey. Several things I should let go, no doubt."

I let the subject drop. Neither one of us wanted to talk about any of it anyway.

I moved partway through the door, stopped, and kissed his cheek; easily enough finding a smile since I was a bit high and the cheek had felt incredible against my lips.

Then there was the way he smiled after I kissed him.

"Have a beautiful evening, darling."

"You too," I said, and set off to meet Geoff.

****

I gently laid him back on the bed. As I moved away to stand, the unadulterated adoration in his eyes almost melted me to the floor, and made me want him even more when I didn't think that was possible.

I wanted to be with him. To claim him. To merge with him.

I took a deep breath.

Another.

I felt a sense of calming try to take me.

I slowly disrobed as he watched, letting his eyes take in the sight of me, no shyness to be seen, not one shred. He moved to take off his boots even as I sat on the bed to do it for him myself. He not only let me unbutton his pants, his hands guided mine. Our eyes locked as I slid those pants down, along with his underwear, his hips lifting from the bed as I did. I slipped up between his legs, parting even as he sat up a little and pulled his own shirt off, eyes finding mine immediately after he pulled it over his head.

I worshipped his skin with fingers, lips and tongue. His beautiful, creamed honey, flawless skin. Flutter after flutter, soft little moan after soft little moan, and his hands explored me wherever they could reach.

Then I was mere inches from where I could join us into one being.

His first time, I thought. I didn't want to hurt him. But it would hurt, the first time always does. Even the second, the third, there's always a little pain as time goes on, though one might discover it's a welcome thing, something that is desired as much as the rest.

As I stared into his eyes, a little nervous and nearly overwhelmed with what was about to happen, it came to me how it could be easier, how it was best to take his virginity. As it occurred to me, I felt his touch. A touch that wasn't physical. Words couldn't accurately describe the feeling, but I knew, *felt*, in that moment it was coming from him.

What took the concern away from me, what shook the last of my nerves, was the sudden rush of feeling from him that he wasn't afraid. He wasn't afraid and trusted me to know what I was doing.

My arm extended, hand found the little bottle of lube. Fingers slicked, I softly kissed him, then watched his face as I caressed his cheek with the other hand before letting it caress his chest, tease a nipple along the way to his flat belly. His lips parted and his hands came to my face when I explored lower. There was a look of nervous anticipation in his eyes.

I brought him over with mouth and hand. God it was beautiful, and the moment his body was relaxing after the orgasm was the perfect one for taking him. When he couldn't tense up as easily, yes, the time to take him.

With a shaky breath, I positioned myself.

His eyes flew open, his hands tightened in my hair—but his legs rose up my back.

What I saw in his eyes brought the feel of hot tears to my own.

Want.

Need.

Love.

His breathless, arduous little words brought the tears to the corners of my eyes.

"Make me yours."

A half choked cry left me as I did so. We both gasped at the same time and I nearly fell upon his body, it was so *overwhelming*.

So hot.

So innocent.

So beautiful.

Before I could find my voice to tell him to breathe deeply, he did it on his own. I felt his body fill and empty of air.

"Hnh...uh...Trey..." the words caught in his throat and his back arched even as he gripped me harder. Another filling and emptying of his lungs and I was on my way.

Slowly, carefully, making him mine.

"*Dios mío...pequeño gorrión...*" it burst from me. I had to freeze, the feeling so overwhelming I might have come that second. I took several deep breaths then. Our eyes locked, his very wide, and he was liquid in my vision.

I think I felt myself suddenly smile.

My skin danced with flames.

"*Te amo, te amo*, yours..." his words squeezed, strangled my heart. His brows knit tightly and his mouth went wider.

I had to take several more deep breaths when his legs tightened around me as I attempted to move, soft whimpering sounds wavering in his throat. I wasn't certain at first if they were sounds of pain—regardless, his hips tilted and his hands raced along my back, fingers digging into my flesh. His face went into my neck, then his head fell back and his eyes...his eyes...

Such a perfect surrender. Such a beautiful and complete surrender.

I gave over to his surrender. More choked sounds came in the back of his throat, his face went back into my neck, his teeth found flesh, and every part of him gripped me so tightly I thought I would explode, literally explode from it all.
He was gone to the world and existed only here with me.

Such a perfect surrender.

The moment his body tensed, I knew it and mine responded in kind. The moment his skin raced with shivers and his muscles began to shudder with his climax, I knew, and mine responded in kind.
He sang my name in surprised ecstasy and no doubt, I sang something of a melody myself.
Breathlessness came and went.
Oxygen started to return.
The scent of his hair filled my nostrils.
And his skin.
His musk.
Taste of his tears.

I forced my eyes to open.
I wanted to see his face when he lifted it. I wanted—wanted to feel this feeling of his skin tingling against mine, the dew of

his sweat mingling with mine, the lingering sensation of our merged essences washing over and through us, the feeling of our hearts touching, wanted—just wanted to keep the feeling as long as I could.

Oh God.
I *love* him. I do.
My heart skipped with it.
I had never experienced anything so seemingly transcendent in my life, anything so powerfully moving.

How long we lay that way, I don't know. It came to me that the room was light. It came to me that he breathed deeply as if in sleep beneath me, but I knew he wasn't asleep. It came to me again, the taste of him. Nutmeg, honey and milk.
And then I burst out laughing in a release of another kind.
I felt his little chest shake with laughter, too.
And finally, his shining velvet-brown eyes came to focus for me. We looked at each other a heartbeat in silence, then started laughing louder. Giddy.
He absolutely glowed.

"Can we do it again?" he asked.

I had a full-on laughing fit for a few seconds, nodding like an idiot.
"Again, again, and again," I said and showered his face with kisses.
He giggled happily. It turned into a deep moan when I set about doing it again.

****

"Do you *have* to go?" I said, watching him dress as I came out of the bathroom and plopped back down on the bed. "Let me answer that. No, no you don't."

He smoothed his hair into a ponytail, grinning at me. "I must work!"

"No you mustn't. I'm good with being your sugar daddy."

He gave me a full laugh. I'd already explained that term to him a few times before.

"Maybe so, but I must to do something."

"Baby, I have a mental check-list of things you can do." I waggled my brows.

He flushed and smiled. "Work, I mean work!"

I sighed. "Yeah I know. But good to know having sex with me isn't work."

He giggled, shaking his head.

I sat up in the bed, hugging my knees. "Okay, so just make pottery, how about that?" Which would also eat up his time, but it made him happy and his creations were beautiful. Besides, he had a studio now. I could pester him there without guilt.

He seemed to consider this. "Maybe so." His brows lifted. "I still like my job. Maybe when I get tired of it."

"Okay, I have a maybe. I guess that'll do for now." I winked at him.

"You suppose to work, too. What I do, sit and wait all the day?" he said, perfectly straight-faced.

"Yeah. I like that idea. You can hang out here, never wear clothing, and cook and all that."

He grabbed my wallet (the closest thing) from the dresser and launched it at me. "Ooo, what that word…chau—chaven—pig! I no be barefoot pregnant all the time!"

I started laughing even as I ducked the projectile. Laughed more when it went *spack*! on the headboard and tumbled to the floor.

He started laughing too, but when he stopped, he said, "You know I like taking care of you."

"Yes," I said, soft. "I know you do, and I don't mind one bit." I didn't. I was less afraid of it with each day that passed.

At least I thought I was.

He gave me a bright smile. "So you are talking to Scott soon today?"

"Yes." I glanced at the bedside clock. "In fact, I suppose I should get dressed, too."

"He is coming here?" He handed me a pair of jeans after I stood up, and that made me grin. I took them, giving him a smile.

"Yeah, I figured it was the place to talk." I lost my smile. "There's so much to tell him, and I have no idea exactly how it's going to go."

I felt Geoff's hand on my face. I looked down into his eyes.

"It turn out good." He gave me a firm nod.

My smile returned. "You would know, I guess."

"That right."

Fucking adorable, when he went for stern. I had to kiss him. Somehow, he managed to put a stop to what I was intent on following that kiss with

Even *though* his words were breathy, unintentional seductions when he spoke.

"To go. You too. Scott coming soon, no?"

"At least *he* gets to."

He gave me a playful shove. "I don't go now, I never will."

"This is a problem why?"

He tried that stern thing again and failed miserably. He wanted me just as much as I wanted him.

"I..." he gave me a hot little grin. "I jump you after work."

"Ohhh, well, okay then. Anticipation, all that."

His grin grew, and I started dressing before I could get any other ideas.

Okay, to focus on something other than my other ideas.

"I like to meet Scott. You think he will stay a while?" he asked.

"I'll ask him. I'd love for you to meet him."

"Invite him for dinner, I cook!"

I grinned at him and nodded. "Okay, sweet cheeks."

"Hee." His head turned just when mine did, because the buzzer on my door sounded.

I really need to change that sucker to a chime, yeah.

I glanced at the clock again. "If that's Scott, he's early."

"They fixed access code thing on building," Geoff said.

"Yeah, but I gave him the code."

"Oh. I go see, you dress. Maybe I get to meet him now before I go," he said cheerfully and exited my bedroom.

I smiled to myself, and found a shirt to pull on. Decided to hell with shoes and socks. I much preferred being barefoot, and I was in my own home, after all.

I was coming out of the bedroom when I heard their voices drifting through the apartment. It was definitely Scott, and Geoff was as cheerful as ever, greeting him.

"Hi, I'm looking for Trey? My name's Scott."

"*Hola* Scott! I Geoff. Trey is inside. Come, come."

I heard Scott chuckle even as I chuckled. "Thanks a lot, Geoff." Then I heard him whistle low. "Wow, this is nice."

"He has good taste, no?"

"Yeah."

"I picked you as a friend, didn't I?" I said as I strode through the living room, reaching them.

"Which shows just how exceptional your taste is," Scott replied with a grin.

I gestured to Geoff. "You've already met my boyfriend, so was there ever a doubt I'd lost that good taste?"

Scott turned a smile on Geoff. "Ohhh. I didn't realize. Trey and I didn't get the chance to talk much before."

"That okay," Geoff replied. "It's good you're here. I must go, but I hope we meet soon again?"

"That'd be great, Geoff."

Geoff clasped his hands. "Good." He turned and moved closer to me. "See you later."

"You bet." I leaned and gave him a kiss. He caught his lip between his teeth as he turned back to Scott.

"I see you," he said to Scott.

Scott's grin formed again. "Have a good day."

"You too!" And then Geoff was out the door.

Oh, damn. So much for his jumping me when he got home.

Dinner invite, I'm supposed to invite Scott for dinner.

Hey, but he's met him now. That counts.

Shut up.

Scott's eyes moved back to me. "He seems really nice." He chuckled a bit. "And he's very enthusiastic."

"That's my boy, full of passion."

"Oh, I just bet, knowing you." He glanced at the door, then back to me. "You know, he looks a little like young Johnny Depp, but more ethnic...yeah."

"I know." I sighed. "How lucky am I?"

He laughed.

"Well," I gestured to the sitting area, "are you just going to stand there all day, or make yourself at home, man?"

"Hey, I was waiting for the offer, like any polite person would."

He'd never had to before, but then, we'd not seen each other for how long?

Yeah. For the familiarity of the banter the day before, this was like starting over in its way.

"Oh right. You have manners. Sometimes." I took a seat across from him after he chose the sofa.

Everyone gravitated to the sofas, it seemed. And why not? They were nice and comfortable, and I wondered occasionally if the chairs seemed too nice to sit on. They were antique style, though nothing like Michel and Gabriel's antiques.

The apartment I'd rented was fully furnished. Nicely furnished, but I'd been thinking I might change a few little things.

"This is a great apartment, dude," Scott remarked, looking around. "Most of it fits you." His eyes returned to me, punctuating what was beneath the statement.

Unless I'd changed, they said.

"It came this way."

"Wow, when they say furnished here, they mean it."

"Some of them." I smiled a bit.

We'd never really had moments of awkward silence before, so when it happened, it was more awkward than any I'd had in my entire life.

"So," we both said at the same time, and laughed a little.

"You first," I said.

His fingers twittered on his knee. "So, uh, you like it here?"

"I love it here." All right, Scott, small talk.

He nodded. "Job, boyfriend. Guess you're in for the duration."

"Guess so."

Another nod from him and a somewhat forced, nervous smile. "Well, whenever I come through, now I have someone to pester, right?"

"Absolutely," I said and leaned forward, trying to capture his eyes.

Another moment of silence, and I came to a decision.

"Scott, I'm sorry." I decided getting straight to it was the best thing. Clearing the tension first, this might get us back to something resembling normal a lot faster. Sitting here, having veiled small talk with someone who had been my best friend, someone I had left behind, just wasn't going to work, especially when he was having such a hard time with the small talk.

It seemed he considered asking me what I was sorry for, but he knew just as well as I did what I was talking about, and I think he was relieved in a small way that I'd been direct.

Direct, like I always had been before.

His eyes dropped to his hands and he started chewing on the inside of his lip, a habit he'd long had. He did it most when stressed, usually—tense, uncomfortable. Sometimes when he got embarrassed, that kind of tension.

He sure as hell wasn't embarrassed.

"Okay. Yeah, we need to talk. I guess maybe I'll go first and just start at the beginning, then." His eyes lifted. "I was worried as *hell*, dude. You weren't okay that last night I saw you, and I knew it." He hesitated, then added, "I'm pretty sure it wasn't pain killers."

Now I knew he'd let that lie slide.

"I imagined all kinds of things." He hesitated again. "Things you might be into. I told myself that was bullshit, but your parents didn't even hear from you, so then I knew it had to be bad."

He'd spoken to my parents. Of course he had. How many times, I wondered.

Did he know they were dead?

"What's the deal with that, Trey?"

"I hid from them too," I admitted. "From pretty much everyone."

He leaned forward a bit. "What were you doing? Your parents called me, asking about you, maybe a week after I saw you. That freaked me out."

Of course they called him. I'd figured they would. Another reason I didn't see him again.

"I turned into a junkie, Scott." Short and sweet, I'd start there.

He looked stunned. "Why man, why? You partied a bit, but never like that. You never got hooked on anything, you were stronger than that." A ghost of a smile tried to form on his face. "My Tyler Durden, in a way."

I would have laughed, but I couldn't. I started to reply, but he wasn't finished.

"That case. It fucked with you, but maybe I didn't see just how bad. Is that why you hit the drugs?" He had trouble looking at me for a second; his eyes flitted down and back.

This, and with way he said it, it seemed to me like he felt guilty. I gazed at him a second longer.

"Don't, Scott, please. It's not your fault. I wasn't going to be stopped and," I took a breath, "and it was more than that case, actually."

He stared at me in silence for a minute, three.

"But I *knew* you weren't okay. I wish I'd of tried harder to make you stay that night."

I closed my eyes tightly. "I managed to avoid about everyone, man. No one was getting me to stay. I would have disappeared another night, if not that one."

I could still feel his eyes on me. I opened mine.

"It wasn't just the case, you said." His eyes drilled mine as if they could find the oil of truth. Then he pushed his hair behind his ears. "I don't even know what to say or ask, first. You became a junkie, you said." He covered his face. "Damn, man." He looked at me again. "How bad did it get, Trey?"

I kept my gaze as even as I could. "The pinnacle of my self destruction ended in my overdosing on a street corner in the city."

"Fuck," shaken whisper. "Fuck, Trey. On...on what?"

"Heroin."

He gaped at me. "You...you never did anything that hard while I knew you," he said, grasping for words, any words.

My eyes dropped to my hands. I cleared my throat. "No. No I didn't. Not before that, either," I confessed.

"It was...it was an accident, right?"

I lifted my eyes and saw the disbelief and fear in his.

I could say yes, but I still wasn't certain I could say no. Or maybe I just hadn't admitted it, even to myself.

"Not exactly."

"What does not exactly mean, Trey?"

"I said I became a junkie," I began.

"So were you actually trying to kill yourself?" he cut in.

"Not...exactly."

He searched and searched my face.

"Escaping" and punishing myself "from...the pain," I said.

"That's what it was."

I felt like such a shit heel. I didn't know how much I could tell him. How much he really wanted to know.

How much I could say.

"Let's...okay, let's back up, Trey. If you were in some kind of pain, why didn't you call your parents?" he asked, sounding incredulous. He'd been out to our house more than once, Sunday dinners with my parents. He knew how close we were.

Had been.

"Because I couldn't have them seeing me that way, and I didn't want help...and...I just couldn't."

"Why didn't you call me?" he asked in a quiet voice.

I gave him my eyes with my reply. "Same reasons, mostly."

He looked at me, waiting.

Was it better or worse to say it?

I had to say it. He was hurt either way. "Because you're the one person that might have stopped me. Something I knew subconsciously and fully realized later. You might have been able to stop me, and I couldn't have that." I didn't deserve help.

He looked away. It hurt him, all right, me saying it. I knew what he was thinking, thinking it even harder than before.

If only I'd called him. If only, if only. If only he'd tried harder.

If only.

"I'm sorry, Scott. I'm sorry I left you that way. I'm sorry for everything."

I watched him take a swipe at his eyes before looking at me. "I'm damned glad you're alive. You look great; you really do, so everything's okay now, right? So uh, it's okay."

"No, it's not okay. What I did to you *isn't* okay. You can't say that it's okay, just like that," I snapped my fingers.

"Whatever you did to *yourself* isn't okay." He stood up, paced a little, and sat back down.

"You can be mad at me, Scott. I left you behind. I shut you out."

He shook his head. "Not mad, just worried out of my mind."

"No really, you can be angry with me." That thing, that seed inside me that had turned into a weed, grew. "I never called. I got my shit together, and I still didn't track you down."

He gave me a square look. "You sound like you want me to get pissed off."

I stood up, voice rising against my will, rising with conflicted emotions. "I do. I want you get mad, damn it! You should be pissed as hell at me." And I should have to *beg* for your forgiveness.

His expression was one of shock and confusion.

I took some steps away, keeping my back to him, biting my lip hard and hugging myself.

I felt him, then heard him behind me. "Talk to me, Trey. Tell me what it is."

I swiped at my own eyes and took a breath. Had to take another. "Someone needs to be angry with me besides me, damn it."

I felt his tentative touch to my shoulder.

"No one ever got angry. Not my parents, not Sean." Not my new family…

"Sean? You went back to Sean…after?"

A couple more ragged breaths and a head shake. "During. He kept trying to take care of me. No matter what I did, no matter how many times I'd go away then drift back by his place just to sleep it off, or something, he always—he didn't get angry, damn it." I turned, asking, not really expecting an answer. "Why? Why did he do that?"

"You don't know?" he asked, quietly shocked. His eyes held mine. They were misting over, but I didn't think it was just because of my question. "Because he loved you," he said.

I had to look away, because I knew that. I already *knew* that loving me killed Sean.

Then Scott said, "So Sean knew, but no one else?"

My eyes darted back to him.

His jaw set. He turned around, took some steps away, and then, after shaking his head, turned back.

"I tell you what," he tossed his hands out, "and I'm not just saying this because you want me to. I *was* mad, okay? I got angry a few times. Then I told myself I shouldn't. But yeah, I was mad at you. I'm a little angry with you right now. Here you are, fine and dandy in Paris for how long?"

"I couldn't have you see me that way before, Scott, and then—"

"Sean saw you!" He strode to me. "God damn it, you fucking left me to wonder about you for two and a half years! I'd rather have seen it, don't you get it? Sean knew, but not me?"

"And it killed him!" I blurted.

This shocked the fight right out of Scott. "Wh—what?"

My hands found my biceps, gripping. "He killed himself," I whispered.

His mouth hung slack. Eventually a word or four made their way out. "I'm...Jesus, I'm sorry."

I had to look away again. "I killed him."

"Wait, no, what?"

I managed to look at him again. "It's my fault. It's *my* fault."

He started shaking his head.

"It is!"

He grasped my shoulders and shook them. "Listen. Okay, I don't know the whole story, but," he sighed. "It's not...it's not your fault."

"Sucked the life right out of him, Scott. I would have done the same to you."

"Trey, stop."

"Would've killed you."

"I wouldn't have left you, damn it!" As soon as he said it, his eyes squeezed shut. "I didn't mean—"

"No you're right," I choked on the words. "He had to leave me, and it was the only way he could do it."

He put his face in his hands, shaking his head.

"I did that to him, Scott. I did it."

He kept shaking his head. "You...you didn't make him stick around." I barely heard him. He lowered his hands. "You didn't make him...make him keep trying, you...he did it. He ended it," he said, the words still quietly strangled.

I could only look at the floor, then.

"I wish you would have called me after he—that had to of fucked you up even more, and you're still carrying it I...more than once, I..."

He walked away yet again.

I stared at his back.

I scarcely heard what he said next. "I didn't try hard enough to find you. I didn't."

"No, Scott, keep yelling at me. I could have tracked you down before, many times. You shouldn't have to track *me* down."

He started to shake his head yet *again*.

"Don't cop out on me now, damn it! Finish it! Here I am, right as rain, and I didn't track you down, you stumbled across me."

"Sean..."

"Don't feel sorry for me!" I pushed the tears from my cheeks. "That's not why I told you! I fucked you both over!" And you're the only one still breathing from that time, the only one, the only one I give a shit about that's still breathing!

He whirled and it came back genuine, his anger, at least in the moment.

"Fine! You're a fucking prick, running out on me that way. I was your best friend! I could have helped you, you could tell me anything, you knew that, you stubborn bastard." His face got redder and redder. "And you're definitely a thoughtless, spineless, sack of shit for not finding me after you got out of the hospital, or whatever. You didn't even try then, you son of a bitch! Did you!"

I looked between his eyes. "No, I didn't," I whispered. "I wouldn't even let my parents try to find you."

He stared at the floor and then me. "Bastard. You *bastard*. Your best friend, and you didn't let me know if you were still alive out there somewhere."

"No."

"You didn't tell me about Sean. I didn't know him long, but I liked him. A lot."

"I know."

He rubbed his face. "How could you leave me hanging like that? I would have been there for you, how could you..." His voice nearly broke on the last words.

Another whisper. "I won't do it again, I swear."

"How could you do that to all of us, Trey? Everyone that loved you."

Everyone that loved me...

Everyone that loves me suffers.

Exactly, Scott. Exactly. They suffer either way.

"I hated myself. It made me selfish," I was barely able to say.

His eyes lifted. They were darker, full of emotion. "At least you admit it."

"I couldn't deal with it, Scott. I couldn't. I couldn't face... anything."

His lashes made a partial drop, and his voice grew softer. "So...you fucking happy now that you made me angry? Make you feel better?"

"Don't ask me to explain it, but in a strange way, it does." I searched his face.

"Jerk."

"I know. You feel better?"

"Not really."

"I can accept that."

A half-hearted, "asshole," from him.

"Yeah, I am."

He folded his arms, not saying anything for a long moment. Then he inhaled, slowly. "I didn't hear from your parents after the last time they called, looking for you," he said. "I had to take off to Alaska last year. Mom was sick, and they needed me there. I was finally able to call your parents, but there was never an answer." He took a step toward me. "You knew how to reach mine in Alaska. To be fair, we were in Seattle a while, but I couldn't find you; I tried. None of your phone numbers worked, and I sent letters to your parent's house, but..." His eyes drifted to the side. "After a while, I worried you were dead or something and..." They drifted back to me. "And if you weren't, then maybe you really didn't want to see me again, anyway. So then I thought, well, fuck you too."

"Oh, Scott." I closed more of the distance between us. "I didn't think I deserved help. I wasn't sure I deserved you, after what I did."

"Trey—"

I rushed on. "A while after rehab, I got a new job and apartment. My parents were all about taking care of me during that time, and I don't think they knew how to reach you in Alaska, and I begged them not to call anyone, anyway, like I basically said. And..."

"And?"

"There was no answer at my parent's house later because— well because Mom and Dad were killed in a car wreck leaving my apartment. I was clean five months when they died."

His expression fell. "Jesus Christ. God, I'm sorry. God, they were the best people, the best. I'm sorry, Trey."

I had to press on. "I was pretty messed up again. I didn't go back to drugs, but it messed me up. If your letters were at their house, I didn't see them. I couldn't stand going there. I didn't want anything forwarded, either, and I moved twice. Just... messed up."

He was doing his best to keep up, God love him.

"Sure. I mean yeah, you'd be...yeah," he stammered.

I couldn't stop now. He'd drilled the oil. "I ended up running away from New York." I almost shrugged, though I felt anything but neutral. "I haven't quite finished running away, really. I haven't been here that long. I swear I thought about you all the time, I did. I thought about trying to track you down." I closed even more of the distance. "I didn't know how you'd feel; I wasn't sure that I could face you. I wasn't sure what to do with my past. I wasn't sure I was the same person; it's still hard."

He gazed at me the longest time, his anger certainly sucked dry.

"It's not an excuse, and don't feel bad about getting angry. I'm just telling you what happened. How I felt. I guess I wasn't sure you'd want to see me, either, after so much time passed," I finished.

Suddenly, he grabbed my shoulders in a much different way. A guy's half hug. "I...of course I wanted to see you." He squeezed my shoulders harder.

I tried to smile. "I was going to track you down," I said. "I'd decided. And then like magic, there you were, walking by Le Parvis."

He gave me a bit of a smile, after a cleansing breath, that is. "Funny how that works, sometimes. I was thinking about you hardcore. I turn around and bam, there you are. For a minute I thought I was seeing a ghost."

"Me, too."

Funny how that worked out.

"You know, I realized I missed you more than I knew, when I saw you standing there, man," I said.

He shoved me. "Okay, let's not get all sappy, now."

It made me laugh. He got me to laugh, the way he said it with a batting of his lashes and moony look on his face.

Funny how friends can go through the ringer and back in a relatively short span of time, then have a release of laughter.

That's how you know they're the best.

"Hey, is your mom okay?"

He nodded. "Yeah, she's doing great now. So's Dad. But we can talk about that later. I'd still like to know what I missed in your life since you disappeared in the City. I want to hear the rest of the story, Trey. I've been waiting a long time."

My eyes moved over his face. Yes, he'd been waiting, and I owed it to him.

Too late to chicken out now, and besides, hadn't I already laid some heavy shit on him, begged him to get angry, and wasn't he still listening? Still here?

Big breath. "We should probably sit down for this." I need to sit down for this.

I hadn't meant to sound so ominous. He looked wary, but nodded, and we went back to the sofas.

Chapter Two

I told Scott about all the drugs. I told him how I ended up nearly penniless and homeless. I told him about the sexual favors for money.

The favors that I had to be nearly out of my mind on drugs to perform, that is.

I told him about sleeping in Central Park, sometimes. I told him about the cutting. The cutting I'd first started when I was seven.

I even told him that Sean tried to call an ambulance one night, because I'd cut myself so bad he thought I'd bleed to death. I wouldn't let Sean do it, because I was afraid someone would find out. I was afraid, too, that someone would toss me into an institution.

I threatened to finish it, if he called an ambulance.

Yes. I was that fucked up, and that much of a shit about it.

He found a guy with some medical experience, and then took care of me for the next few days, desperately trying to fight off infections.

A range of emotions moved through Scott's eyes, his

expressions, but that one hit him the hardest in the moment.

It was hard as hell to talk about it; Scott wasn't the only one seizing up during that part.

He couldn't believe I'd cut myself so badly without really meaning to. It scared him even more than my telling him I'd actually been clinically dead after I was peeled off that street corner, wearing nothing but fucked up leather jeans that were, by that time, too big.

I couldn't really remember cutting myself the night I scared Sean to death. I'd gone somewhere else entirely, in a manner of speaking, I guess, and had done myself real damage with a knife.

He hadn't been able to stop me. He had gotten a few cuts in the struggle, himself.

I hated myself more than ever, which was saying a lot.

I'd even stabbed myself at least once, for Christ's sake. The scars were faint because most of the cuts had been clean. You probably wouldn't know what they were if you did see them. After all, when most people see little white lines (more visible when I tan) and other marks, they don't ponder whether they were self-inflicted.

Besides, you don't get to see much of anything unless I'm nude, or at least partway there.

I suddenly wondered if Michel had noticed the scars and just not mentioned them.

Probably.

I refocused on Scott. I'd told him everything, really, at least up until my parents died. I did not tell him what I meant about the case not being the only thing that fucked me over. If he asked...

It took him a while to recover, all of it sinking in as best it could right now. His voice was a bit shaky when he finally said something.

"You were so intent on punishing yourself, Trey." He slowly shook his head. He swallowed hard. "I know. I know your sense of right and wrong. I knew the second you told me what happened in the courtroom, it wasn't something you were going to get over easy, if at all." He shook his head again. "But God damn, you didn't really dive that far off the cliff because of the case, did you? No, you said there was something else."

He was going to ask.

"What was the something else, Trey?"

He'd taken it so far.

Fuck. I can't, I can't. It had nothing to do with him. Nothing to do with my—

Disappearing, oh yes it did, and I said the case wasn't the only thing, why had I said that?

I looked away and tried not to push my hand through my hair.

"You can tell me the rest; you know you can," he said.

I nearly bit my lip. "I'm not sure you *really* want to know."

I'm not sure I can *really* say it.

"You're still my friend. I'm still worried about you."

My eyes shot to him. "I'm..." I was going to say I'm okay. Looking into his eyes, I knew that wasn't going to fly.

"It's nice outside. I've already laid a ton of bricks on you." I got up. "Let's go out."

He just stared up at me.

"I'm hungry anyway." I started for my bedroom.

"Hey," I heard him say. "Hey, don't. Talk to me, damn it." I felt him closing in on me. "You've had all this bottled up, just let the rest out."

I made it into the bedroom, headed for the closet. "Just let me get some shoes."

He grabbed me and tried to turn me. It worked, because I'd lost the strength, suddenly, to resist.

Concerned, compassionate, Alaskan-blue eyes met mine. "I'm here now, Trey. Let me help you, *please.*"

I stared into those eyes. "I..."

They kept gazing back into mine.

"I..."

His hand slipped around the back of my neck, his touch intimately reassuring. "Let me help you this time."

Those eyes, those eyes.

I closed mine and pressed my forehead to his, chest tight, thoughts swirling.

I *did* need to tell someone. I really did.

I could tell him. I could tell him before I could tell anyone else, right? I had always been able to talk to him, and I still could, he'd more than proven it. Full circle, we had come full circle; this was it.

Shaky breath. I moved my head back. His hand was still resting on my neck.

"It's the kind of case it was," I said. "It's because I felt like I had utterly betrayed those girls." He looked confused. Well, of course. That wasn't an explanation, yet. I was still trying to work up the guts.

"I felt like I'd betrayed them because I knew what they might have gone through before they died. I know what it's like to think dying might be better because then it'll be over."

His brows knit tighter. I could almost see the wheels turning in his head.

Do it like a band-aid.

Can't say it otherwise.

Band-aid. "I was raped just before my sixteenth birthday. The second girl he raped and killed, she was sixteen, too." Some of my skin left with the sticky side of the band-aid, and I flinched.

His fingers tightened on my neck.

I said it.

I said the word.

Dear God, I said the word, the words, words I'd never said to *anyone*.

I felt bare. I felt vulnerable. I wanted to take a step back.

Yet.

It was Scott. My best bud Scottie.

He couldn't speak. I could feel the tremor that ran through his body and flowed through his touch.

But.

He didn't look away, and there were questions in his eyes.

So I didn't look away.

Questions in his eyes.

I had to rip another band-aid or chicken out, because the intimacy of the moment, standing this close to him, was both unbearable and comforting. It left me near paralyzed.

"I'd gone to the dance, the pre-graduation dance. Billy and some of his college buddies attacked me on the football field. I still don't know why I was out there, how I got there. Maybe I've blocked it, but I remember what they did to me. How they held me down, how they bound my arms and legs and took turns. How one of them," I almost bit my tongue, "shoved something in me that was cold. I don't know what it was."

Abrupt halt. He didn't need those details, did he? I couldn't believe they'd made it past my lips.

Paralyzed.

Paralyzed by my own words, and the look in his eyes, his expression.

His hand lowered, and he nearly looked nauseous.

He was appalled.

He was angry.

He was hurting for me.

He was stunned.

His voice strained when he spoke. "No one...no one heard? Tried to help?"

I shook my head. I swallowed hard. "I screamed. No one came, no one—probably because of the music inside, and the field wasn't...wasn't close..."

Paralyzed.

Except—

Forces tried to pull me in five different directions, air sat like lead in my lungs, and flames tried to char my esophagus.

I fell apart. Crumbled, fell, a wall of bricks exploded. My eyes burned, I couldn't see Scott now. I couldn't breathe, and all I could hear were the death throes of some tortured animal.

No.

That's me.

What felt like agonizing years later, I realized I was on my knees. I realized someone had their hands on me, on my neck and the back of my head.

I realized my face was in someone's shoulder and I couldn't lift it, because when I tried, my brain turned black.

I realized I could barely breathe for the full nose, and I could barely see for the tear-swollen eyes.

Fingers walked through my hair.

"Breathe, Trey. C'mon, breathe."

Scott. Scott is with me.

A lungful of air that hurts.

"I got ya, c'mon, breathe," he whispered.

Another lungful, still hurting. "Scott." A squeak.

"Yeah, I'm here. I got ya. I'm here."

"I'm," lift head, Trey. "I'm," lift your head, Trey, "S-sorry, I'm," almost, almost lifting my head.

"Shhh."

"I," hiccup, "I," hiccup, "Ohhh, God," lift your head; wipe your nose on something, Trey.

His hand. It pressed to my cheek. I must have turned my head, at least.

"I got you, buddy, I got you."

Fresh tears, I actually have some left.

Chapter Three

Michel

"They will be hounding you for days," my angel growled, his back arching and his head tossing, his glorious hair scything a black arc through the air.

"Yes," I grunted, my nails piercing deeper the flesh of his lower back.

"And so every moment between, you are *mine*." He rocked forward, causing my head to slam into wood yet again.

"My...ass...is...yours?" My fangs punctured my lip.

Yet again.

"All of you." He struck like a cobra, latching onto my mouth, sucking greedily at the welling wound he'd just opened wider, his hair creating a privacy curtain around us.

I slammed into him again, tearing a graveled moan from his body, my fangs finding a home in his tongue.

As every inch of you is mine, *dove.*

Scalding trenches did he lay into my chest, his head dipping, and hungrily did he lap at the wounds.

I let go with another grunt, and then a snarl. *"Baise-moi, baise-moi!"*

He reared back is if yanked by his hair, eyes gone burning jet affixing themselves to mine as he set about ever more sincerely doing what I craved.

When I scarce knew my own name let alone his, and when my focus wished to shatter, still I managed to study him, the rippling undulations of his body, and his face, the pleasure etching and re-etching on his face.

I studied his face when black lashes fluttered before his eyes went wide, seeing nothing, though they sought the ceiling, his chin lifting, his head falling back as he nearly hyperventilated.

This told me that he was close.

His body then tensed and he lost sound, breath.

His mouth opened in a silent scream, and then sound returned, a long cry forming as if I were slowly turning his volume up, up and up.

His fangs shredded his lips and glittering crimson painted my flesh before exploding like fireworks behind my eyes, when I painted the walls of my inner sanctum, my cry vibrating flesh and bone.

He collapsed, melting on top of me, his cheek finding a home on my shoulder and his nose tickling my neck.

His purr, deep and slightly stuttered, it rolled over and through me, and I buried my fingers in the tattered silk of his hair.

Beyond satisfied and floating in the dream that was he, thoughts floated as well, and after several and several more moments, they began coherently to form. Thoughts such as the fact that Gabriel was ever more aggressive lately because of the memories that had broken through. He needed to vent, to lose himself in me, and some of our sessions had been quite violent as of late, but I was fine with this. I was fine with taking what he gave and giving him peace, not to mention that physically I did not find it a hardship. He was nearly back to himself, in any case, as this session was not the glorious homicide of nights prior.

There is a fine line between pleasure and pain, one which is often blurred.

It was the reason, some of the emotion driving the sessions, that troubled my heart, though that would pass as well, for unleashing the tension within him further paved the way for his happiness to spread. So taken was he with the discovery of Trey I could touch the place Trey held in Gabriel's heart, hear it sing.

Aside from this release, I was thinking of my love's agreement, however begrudgingly given on the one hand, that reclaiming my former position was a good idea. That he agreed in great part because he knew doing such would make me feel useful, and provide some amusement, was beside the point.

No, it *was* the point. Whatever kept me entertained and feeling important, he was for, not to mention he preferred my rules to anyone else's.

He merely didn't like sharing me more than necessary.

"You will take meetings soon," he murmured, sliding down to plant his cheek on my chest, winding his legs through mine and his arms around me, completely trapping me in his glorious web.

"I imagine, to paraphrase you, my love, several will be seeking audience soon enough."

His entire being sighed. "Politics, how they bore me."

I twined a few strands of his hair around my index finger. "You needn't be present; I know they do."

"I am all a-flutter wondering what customs, if any, the younger generation has these days. How could I possibly stay away?"

A laugh rolled through me at his dryly spoken words.

"I shall busy myself with Trey, perhaps; yes, this will do." I felt the smile contained within his words.

"A splendid idea, dove."

Gabriel then shifted the subject completely, as he so often does. "I would tell you where it is hidden, *mon lion*."

The chest. The treasure chest containing a pound of flesh, the piece of Vicont's heart.

"I don't wish to know, I told you."

"You did, *oui*. I merely wish you to know that I would."

I let my fingers glide through his hair. "I did not doubt it."

"I trust your decisions regarding him."

My voice, it softened. "And I thanked you for this. I thank you again."

"It will be as it should be."

I filled my lungs. I emptied them, nearly. "Eventually the location will be sought out. Eventually you will be high on certain people's list of those to seek."

"They will not gain anything in doing so." He lifted his head slightly and his eyes dove into mine.

"Yes, I know how well you keep secrets," I said.

"I do not fear any of them."

"I know this as well."

His cheek returned to my chest, and rather than reassure me I had no fear of harm coming to him from others, he shifted the subject once again, if only slightly this time. "I can picture it now. He spends his nights as an invalid, the old man that he is, his mind screaming in frustration."

Yes, I imagined quite well this being the one thing Vicont was doing.

"Yet only the rogues amongst them will go against his word to leave us be for now," he said, returning to the subject of reassuring me in some way.

"And those we'll dispose of," I reassured myself.

"Quite. You have your own loyal subjects, and more still to return, I am certain, thus, all will be well." His words were becoming languorous. Stillness, its shadowed fingers were walking their way through his limbs.

"Of course," I whispered.

"When you gain full control, Trey and…"

The sentence never formed, he went under before it could form, yet I need not hear the rest to know the sentiment.

Trey and those others he'd come to love, he worried more for them than for ourselves, which was another reason my Gabriel not only accepted, but also encouraged my taking charge.

It would hopefully direct things farther away from our little family.

That is, once I made it perfectly clear on a much larger scale that I was not one to fuck with, though of course there was no accounting for the logic of others.

To do otherwise in this community of vampires implied weakness, inviting more problems than taking over, however, and thus, I would make it exceedingly clear that I was once again keeper of France and Crusher of Souls, should I be crossed.

As I lay there, stroking Gabriel's fine hair, my thoughts wandered yet again, to a place I'd rather have avoided, at least for the time being.

I thought of Petrov spending his nights with a heart never healed, a heart slowly weeping black scarlet inside his chest, his vigor much lessened, and no doubt his ire, great.

Surely, he was in hiding. Surely, he was spirited elsewhere after we located his lair in Algeria. I had no idea how many safe places he might possess. Perhaps I should engage my own spies once again, I thought. Perhaps I should see what gossip there was on the night wind, and if I were being honest, I was curious for personal reasons.

Out of sight, out of mind. John Heywood had been foolishly optimistic when he penned that phrase.

I had bid Gabriel to hide the wretched sliver of that blackened heart and lock the location away in his mind, lest I do something stupid, such as gaze upon it, contemplate it, possibly regret it or alternately, destroy it in a snit.

As much as a part of me called for Petrov's death, I knew bringing it about would leave the rest of his minions and his still loyal associates thinking they had less to lose in the pursuit of me and mine.

A war. There would be war, this was never in doubt, and though I had shown Petrov I did not fear this, had attempted to slaughter him in his bed, it was better that such had not come to pass.

I had to recollect my power, first. I had to assess who and how many were still loyal to me, and I had to see how many I could sway to my side by force or charm, either was exploitable.

It went beyond France. He had allies outside of France.

This was all well and good, for so did I. If or when the time came...

I sighed. Regardless, my loved ones would always be at risk; it was merely a matter of degree.

No doubt, Vicont knew this as well as I.

Gabriel had been right to leave Vicont with his life, and it went beyond his deference to me. There were other ways to exploit Vicont's weakness, I realized, and as I thought of it, a smile stole across my face.

Perhaps it hadn't been such a terrible place for my thoughts to go after all. I felt my smile broaden. Gabriel, he would surely love the idea that was forming in my head; why, he could help me mastermind the affair.

I would not be surprised if he'd thought of it already.

Chapter Four

Trey

I made my way out of the bathroom after blowing my nose and washing my face. Scott sat on the end of my bed and his head lifted when he heard me. I sat beside him, and when I did, he rubbed his thigh, then placed that hand on my shoulder.

"I'm sorry I pushed. I didn't mean for you to get so upset."

"You didn't. Push, I mean."

"Yes I did. I should have left it alone."

I grabbed his hand. "You didn't push that hard. I—actually, I needed to say it. It's just I haven't said it to anyone for eleven years." I let go of his hand, rubbing my own thigh, eyes dropping to my hand. "I feel a little better now. I never really let it out like that before." I lifted my eyes to his. "You know, just, let it all out at once like that."

He nodded a little. He tried to smile a little. "Then I'm glad you felt you could do that with me." He started chewing his lip.

"What is it, Scott?"

"I was just…" he shook his head. "No. Never mind."

"You don't have to do that."

"You'd probably rather move on right now."

"I don't know. It's out there now. I had my breakdown, and I think I'm okay. If you want to say something, go ahead and say it."

A tear attempted an angry escape from the corner of his eye. "Just...what happened to you, just..."

Oh God.

"It's okay Scott. It's long past and—well it's long past."

"That's what I sometimes saw in your eyes," he whispered, a second tear making a sad escape.

"What?"

His gaze drifted. "How many photos do I have of you...I lost count."

I'd let him take many shots of me while he was in school; his major was photography, after all. I didn't mind posing for him. He meant it all the times he asked me if I wanted to be a model. He thought I had a unique look, and that I posed well.

I refocused on his next words.

"The candid photos. When I'd catch you completely unaware. Some of those, you're kinda far away, and there's this look in your eyes. There's this certain...vulnerability." His brows lifted. "Your eyes were haunted."

God. He often had a camera in my face. I remembered him asking once or twice—maybe it was more—where I was in certain moments. What were you thinking about, Trey?

I always evaded it.

Everything was in my eyes; just like Gabriel.

Scott's hand found my shoulder again. "That's what it was. That was your secret. Sometimes when you talked about high school—Jesus. Demons in your eyes."

"Well...yeah," was all I could say.

"You didn't tell *anyone*?"

"No."

"No cops?"

"No."

"Why?"

There was the question I'd never wanted to field. But it was Scott, so I tried. Legitimate enough question, after all, and the lawyer in me could list reasons.

"I'd slept with Billy before, in my own bed, no less. His parents were richer than God; their lawyers would have ripped me apart. Billy couldn't have that coming out. He'd have threatened me."

"But there was evidence." His eyes, they flashed disbelief. "They hurt you. That leaves evidence. Maybe the cops could have protected you. And I'm not, you know, trying to turn this on you, by the way. I'm just trying to understand."

"I know," I assured him.

"Okay. So what about the cops?"

Humorless laugh. "Maybe they could've protected me, but I destroyed most of the evidence, I got myself home in a daze. Burned my clothes, scrubbed." Wore jeans to bed so I wouldn't stain the sheets. "I couldn't stand the idea of being…being probed again, either."

I couldn't have anyone touching me there again.

Ever.

Scott's eyes squeezed shut. "But," he sighed and stopped there.

So I carried on.

"I didn't want Mom to know. She didn't know I was bi, remember? Everything would have come out, all my personal shit." I moved quickly past that. "I would've been raped again in court. I know what they would have asked me. Do you like it rough? Do you sleep with many men? You had sex with him before, was this some fantasy of yours? Do you like group sex, Trey du Bois? Did you ask him to do it? How many people have you had sex with, Trey du Bois?"

Scott pushed his hands through his hair and sort of nodded, his face tight.

He knew I had a valid point—thank God.

"A lot of people don't take it seriously if a man says he was raped," I said.

"You were just a kid. I don't care how smart you were, are; you were just a kid."

I looked everywhere but his face. "I couldn't. I couldn't face it. I just wanted it to go away. I wanted Billy and them to go away. Even if they had been convicted, they'd have been out in a pretty short time, and then—I couldn't, I couldn't do it." I managed to look at him again.

His jaw clenched. Relaxed. "You were scared. Like I said, you were just a kid." He gave me a soft look. "But your mom. I know what you told me before, but you were attacked, Trey. Don't you think that would have mattered more to her?"

He knew I was right, but here were the *real* questions I'd never wanted to answer.

"I know Mom loved me, she did. She wasn't a bad person. But I *couldn't* have her knowing her son liked boys, too. Maybe... maybe I didn't give her enough credit, but I just couldn't." Shit, so many things seized up in me over those years.

His words skirted at least three emotions. "You really weren't confident she'd care more about your safety? Really?"

My throat tightened. "I didn't want her to find out that way. I didn't want to discover there was a second of doubt in her, if it went to court. A second of doubt over whether I was telling the truth. All of their families had a standing around there, all in her circle."

God, it hurt to say it. But I spent a lot of time being scared after that night.

Ashamed.

Shamed.

Defeated.

"More my issue than hers," I added. "After the rape I just— my brain did its own spinning. It decided that of all the ways to tell her, that wasn't it by a long shot."

He nodded somewhat again, trying to empathize best could, from his own shoes. "I know you told me it wasn't th most open-minded community, either," he whispered.

"I couldn't face the idea of being laid bare in front of all of them. I really couldn't, Scott."

His head shook. "But how did you keep that from your parents? You must have been...well, you know."

"Told them I was sick. Wore long sleeves, long pants."

His fingers wrestled each other. "Sometimes parents know a lot more than we think they do."

Yeah. I'd thought of that. "I also told them I had a fight with someone."

I heard his long exhale, inhale. "God, you've been holding this in forever, all alone with it."

"Yeah."

"Trey I'm..." he stopped. He didn't know what to say. That was okay. I didn't expect him to say anything

So he hugged me best he could instead, and this time I started to move away. Uncomfortable.

But I also wanted to be in that safe little bubble where I wouldn't feel so naked.

Scott was a safe bubble, and it won out.

"They should have been punished. Still should be, some way," he said at last, going a completely different route.

Thank God.

Dry laugh. "Believe me, I've thought about that."

"Fuck." He let go of me, looking me in the eyes. "I'm not always a revenge person, but they, they deserve to be castrated or something."

"I wouldn't mind a little revenge." I waved a hand. "That doesn't do much for my moving past it, I suppose. Hating them takes more energy than not, that's what some people would say. Guess I'll just keep spending the energy for now, because I ain't over hating them."

It helped me get past the shame and everything else for a

while, getting a good hate on for them.

"No shit," Scott said. "I don't even know them and I hate them. Why the hell did they do it?" He shook his head. "That's not a real question. I'm just grasping for something to make sense, you know?"

"I know what you mean. I might know why."

"There's no reason that'll actually make sense, Trey, and besides, what did they do, tell you?" he scoffed.

Head shake. "No, but I have a theory."

His gaze did the asking.

Retreat to some kind of logic, no matter how twisted it is. Yes, we can do that.

"You know Billy was my first guy. I told you that he had a girlfriend, Millie."

"Hardly forget that rhyme."

"Yeah. He was a jock, real man's man. No one was ever supposed to know what we did. When school started back up, he acted like it never happened, flipped me shit as usual."

Scott nodded, mostly to show he was listening.

"Well, the next year when he went to college, Millie was a senior, like me."

"Yeah, you dated her, right? Good revenge for his dissing you, by the way."

I managed a half laugh. He was making this easier, my best friend, he really was. "I thought I loved her, though. Puppy love? Maybe, but I thought I did. I thought she loved me too; she said so. So when she dumped me to go back to Billy the college boy, I was pretty upset."

He gave me another nod.

"In the heat of a moment, I made a comment. I told her to ask Billy, when she saw him, if he still liked it up the ass."

Scott's brow arched. "So?"

"She told him. She hadn't thought much of it, other than me being hurt, angry. But Billy knew it was true."

Scott's jaw hung slack a moment.

"Wait," he said at last. "He seriously got some guys to come and," he couldn't say the word, "do that do you, because of that? Who does that?"

Retreat? Yes, I suddenly felt oddly detached from it.

No. I realized I'd started detaching from it in some way for several minutes, now. How else could I have said so much already?

Numb. I'd achieved numbness.

"I think Billy does. I think he thought I'd told his secret, and he got paranoid. I think he wanted to get back at me for a few things, and he wanted to put me in my place."

But I could just be trying to make sense of it.

"Dude," lines described disgust in his face, "those other guys are worse than him. Shit, he what, asks them to come and mess up some kid, and they do?"

"Seemed so. There was one of them who tried to say no, but Billy threatened him." I snorted. "The guy didn't try hard enough. Yeah, I hate them more than I hate Billy. I don't know what he told them, but I don't know how anyone thinks yeah okay, let's rape someone with our buddy."

He put his elbows on his knees and his face went wearily into his hands. "Dude...this is so fucked up."

I placed a hand on the back of his head. "I've dumped so much on you in a short time, and you just got here. I'm sorry."

He sat up, waving his hands. "I wanted to know, and you needed to say it. It's just so messed up, everything that's happened to you. I don't even know what to say. Sorry just doesn't cover it."

I gave him a half smile. "Don't be sorry. You didn't do any of it."

He tried to smile, then went back to serious. "It still messes with you a lot."

Be honest, Trey. "Yes. I have nightmares. I have other issues."

"You can tell me, you know, if you need to get more out."

Yeah. I do know.

"How about—I'll tell you maybe when you've had time for this to pass," I suggested. I mean, there was dumping, and there was overkill.

We were probably going to trip on the road kill, already.

He sucked in his breath. "Yeah. Yeah, hey, it's a nice day, just like you said. Why don't we go outside, go somewhere? You said you had time."

I had an easier time finding my smile. "I sure do. And I'm sure you could use a drink. I need to stock up, anyway."

He smiled back. "A drink? Yyyeah. So show me where you hang out." His smile faded. "And hey. Don't worry about me. The least I could do was listen. That's what best friends are for. That hasn't changed for me."

He forgives me.

I looked at him for a minute, my eyes wanting to tear up, and then quietly said, "Let's not get sappy again, you little fucker."

His eyes dropped with his slight smile, then lifted with his laugh. "Who you calling little, asshole?" He grabbed his crotch. "You know this ain't little."

Definitely forgiven.

I pursed my lips and arched a brow. "I'd have to get closer to say for sure. Are you finally offering?" I gave him a sensuous smile.

He got up. "Still dreaming and still full of shit, but at least you're consistent. Now get off your ass and let's go, girly-man."

I stood up. "Ooo, you know I like it when you try to be tough, little man. Abuse me some more."

He just bit back the laugh. "Stuff it and," he started waving his hands, "scratch that. Shut the fuck up, and lead on, Cochise."

I smacked his ass before sauntering toward the closet. "You got it, big boy. I just need to freshen up a little more, doll."

"Queen."

Just like old times.

Man, I dump on him and fall apart, we make some jokes, and anything else can wait for later.

If there's anything left, that is.

Yeah. That's what friends are for...and he was still the best.

Chapter Five

So we went out. We didn't go all that far when it came down to it, but you can spend an amazing amount of time exploring Paris block-by-block, let me tell you. Especially when catching up with your best friend.

I took him to Shakespeare and Company in great part because I was thinking of Gabriel at the time, and it's his favorite shop. Scott was duly impressed. He'd been to Paris before, heard of the shop, but he was usually too busy to explore, and he'd not be here that many days at a time, either.

We chilled on Île St. Louis for a while. I had to show him the place where Geoff's pottery sells. Scott was quite impressed with the warmth of Geoff's work, just like I'd been.

He got caught up in gazing at Notre Dame (saying for about the seventeenth time he should have brought his camera) and eventually we went across to Île de la Cité, and went inside the cathedral (where he said for the eighteenth time why didn't I bring my camera, I always bring my camera).

Another time, I told him. There was plenty of time.

I took him by Poe—P.K.'s shop—after that. She was about

to close so she could run some errands, but she greeted him warmly enough, and chatted for a while before taking off.

That is, right after pulling me in back and informing me I needed to tell her everything, including details on Geoff's extra special glow this morning when she stopped by Le Parvis.

Have I ever said she was pushy with certain subjects? I don't think so, but she's pushy. Okay, pushier since we've been through some shit, not so pushy before. Since I know it's because she cares and since she had a certain spark in her eye— along with a pretty smile on her face when she got round to Geoff— I let these things slide.

She also insisted I bring my best friend back again. I don't think Scott will mind, if you catch my drift, and I know you do.

Anyway. Scott and I talked about old times. Lots of healing and laughter there. We also talked about his mom. She'd been stricken with Hodgkin's lymphoma, and they'd spent a good deal of time in Seattle, because Juneau just didn't have the caliber of specialists Seattle did. He told me she hadn't been diagnosed early, which always lowers a person's chances. But, with the combined experience and expertise of the Seattle Cancer Care Alliance, Fred Hutchinson Cancer Research Center and UW Medicine, they'd saved her. He assured me she was doing great now, but that didn't stop my inner guilt gremlin from reminding me that I hadn't been there for him.

We talked about Geoff. Well, Geoff was in and out of the conversation all day, of course, and part of this conversation took place at Le Parvis 'cause—do I need to say why?

Didn't think so.

So anyway, Geoff got off work and we all ended up back at my place, where Geoff made dinner. Don't ask. Just know it was damned good. I think Scott made num num noises.

Yeah—so, dinner.

"So tell me more about this gig of yours," Scott said between bites.

"Like what?" I said. "That the pay's great," overly so, "the bennies are sweet," oh yeah, "and my bosses are cool?" Drink.

Swallow. Cool is a word.

"Wait, bosses? You said something about some Boocher whatever dude, and that he was an asshole."

"Yeah, he hired me, and he's an asshole. He's not my boss, though."

"He hired you, but he can't fire you?" Scott set his fork down, listening.

"Nope. I'm working on getting him to devise ways to kill me though, and it's going pretty well, since he can't actually do that, either." I grinned.

"Don't get too cocky there," he pointed his retrieved fork at me. "Wait. Look who I'm talking to."

"Whatchoo talking about?" I fired back. "I can back up this attitude, you know."

Geoff giggled.

Scott said, "Yeah yeah. All right, so these bosses, then. Your *real* bosses. Who are they, clients? Is that how it works in this type of law, too?"

"Yeah. Lecureaux, that's who I represent, by the way."

"You must be damned confident about them wanting to keep you around," he said.

"Oh, they love me." I grinned again.

"Aha. That's who you blew." He glanced at Geoff. "Sorry."

Geoff just laughed, so Scott smiled at him before looking back at me.

"I didn't blow anyone," not that I didn't fantasize about it, "I told you. Believe me, there were hella background checks, though."

"Because they're major accounts, or is that just France for you?" Scott asked.

"Dude, obscenely rich clients. I think it's mostly because of that." And people like Stefan.

He stabbed a piece of chicken. "Well hey, I know you're

good and all, but wow. You landed a major gig, sounds like."

I nodded. Yeah.

I had.

"I figured it would be harder to get that kind of job here," he said. "French clients, French firm." He shrugged. "But what do I know. Just, it sounds like you landed it fast, too."

"It's because I rock, like totally." I smiled.

Except I'd started thinking about that again, being hired so fast. That is, when other shit wasn't hitting the fan, and I wasn't discombobulated like when I met Michel and Gabriel the first time.

Times.

Fast. Maybe because they couldn't—swallow—keep attorneys.

And maybe—

Another question for Michel.

We all turned our heads at the sound of a knock on the door.

"I'll get it." I patted Geoff's hand and got up, made it to the door, and opened it.

Yeah, to reveal the Devil, soft black leather in the form of pants, boots, and a well-fitted front zip jacket, caressing his body.

He was holding a pair of black gloves in one hand, and when my eyes moved up again, I saw that his hair looked wind tousled.

His multi-hued eyes peered at me over the gold rims of his wine-tinted shades.

Yeah. He wears his sunglasses at night.

A smile settled on his lips.

"Hey, Michel."

"Beloved," he purred. "You have company."

"Yes, I do." Sure. Repeat him why?

He took off the shades, slipping them into a pocket, his head tilting.

"You want to come in." I backed up. "Okay come in."

As he passed me, "Hmm, why not?"

I shook my head and closed the door, chuckling to myself. Followed him as he made his way directly to the dining area and stopped less than a foot from Scott's left side.

Scott, who was kinda, sorta—well he stared up at Michel, a little stunned.

Yeah, even the straightest guy would have to admit 'Chel was beautiful, and Scott never had a problem acknowledging beauty in any form—a reason I like him—but I think Michel wasn't doing much to tone it down, either.

He could. He could tone down the otherness in a manner of speaking, I'd found out.

Consider it "glamour." Trick of the mind, making you see what they want you to see. Not as nefarious as fogging—he was quick to tell me that at the time.

Or at least, it didn't always *have* to be, that's what Michel had said.

Michel's eyes absorbed Scott before shifting to Geoff. "Little angel, so sorry to interrupt."

Geoff smiled bright. "It okay. How are you?"

"Well, thank you. *Et toi?*"

"*Muy bien.*"

"Splendid." Michel's eyes shifted to me. "Are you going to introduce me to this lovely young man with the beautiful, clear blue eyes?"

I resisted the urge to laugh—too much—or nudge him. "This is Scott, friend of mine." Before I could finish with the intros, Michel returned to studying Scott, then gave him a knee-buckling smile, extending his hand.

"*Enchanté. Je m'appelle* Michel."

Scott forgot to move for a second—or couldn't—then managed to glance at Michel's hand—barely tearing his eyes from Michel's—and sort of said, "Hi," taking Michel's hand.

"Will you be visiting long, friend of Trey?" Michel asked, giving Scott a charm-the-pants-right-off-you, smile.

Scott managed to reply on the second try. "A few days, I hope."

"Splendid. You have known each other long?"

Scott finally managed to blink. "Kind of."

"We were at Harvard at the same time," I offered, helping things along.

Michel's smile widened. "Another Harvard man. I'm thinking it wasn't law you studied, however."

"Um, no. Photography," said Scott.

"I was not aware that one studied such things at Harvard," Michel said.

"Yeah. I mean you can. They do. It's a good program, really."

Back of my hand to my grin.

"It meant a lot to my dad for me to go there," Scott managed to add.

"I am certain, then, that you made him proud," Michel replied. "I'd love to see some of your work, and I do hope we'll meet again, Scott, but for now I'm a bit pressed." Michel *finally* let go of Scott's hand and turned his gaze on Geoff again.

Meanwhile Scott took the opportunity to look at the rest of Michel, now that those jeweled eyes didn't have him captured.

"I shan't borrow him but for a moment, but I'd like to speak with Trey," Michel said to Geoff.

"Okay," Geoff replied. "See you?"

Guess I was being borrowed and lent out, if but for a moment.

"Soon, yes little angel." Michel turned to me. "Might I speak with you in the hallway?"

In. Out. Fine. "Sure."

I followed him back out.

After closing the door, I just had to speak first. "You might wanna tone it down around Scott."

"Pardon?" he said as if he had no idea what I meant.

His impish smile gave it away.

"I think you blew a couple of his brain cells," I said.

He laughed and it tinkled down the hall. "I should like to know more about this friend of yours, but another night. It wouldn't do to whisk you away for a ride, now."

"Ride?"

"On my motorcycle, of course."

Oh. Of course. "Bike, huh? Cool. Ah, but no, I shouldn't leave right now." I grinned at him. "Besides, that's not why you came over here."

He went for innocent. "It's not?" His lips moved into a pout.

"Okay, not the only reason."

"Well, I do have something to tell you, beloved."

"Other than the fact you had an idea Scott was here *and* you just *had* to lay eyes on him, if but for a moment?" I smiled.

He answered that with a smile of his own. It slowly faded.

"Is something wrong?" I asked.

"No, not really."

I moved closer. "You had something to tell me, though."

He sighed. "Yes. I thought it best to inform you I've made an official declaration that I've reclaimed my position."

"That was fast."

He lightly shrugged.

"Is that all you had to tell me, Michel?"

"Oh, it's part of it." He placed a hand on my shoulder. "I may not be able to see you quite as much in the next nights. I have things to attend."

"Oh. Well, I appreciate you telling me."

He smiled a bit. "I couldn't have you thinking I didn't care."

"I know you do."

His hand came to my face. "Yes. Now, there is one more thing. There may be lingering unrest since the events in Algeria. I wished to wait until you were more yourself, before mentioning it."

I felt my brows knit. "Should I be worried?"

"We'll keep track of you. Mostly, it may be a matter of

dissenters, and they'll aim for me. But I do have something pressing to ask you."

"Anything." I looked between his eyes.

"*Pour moi*, promise not to leave the city alone. Can you do this, Trey?"

Immediate. "I promise, Michel."

He smile unfurled. "*Merci*." He leaned in and inhaled. "Mmm. You scent thoroughly of Geoff." He leaned back, catching my eyes, his sparkling.

Let me guess. He smells the sex, too. I didn't shower after.

Would that even matter?

I laughed. "I should." I waggled my brows.

"Perrrfect." He kissed my nose, then gazed into my eyes, some of the sparkle in his leaving. "Are you well?"

Blink. "Yeah, I'm good. Why?"

That gaze went deeper. "Everything is all right, truly?"

Breathe...look down. No use, he sees something. I looked back into his eyes. "I haven't seen Scott for a long time, and there was a lot to talk about."

He traced the line of my jaw, the touch soft. "Your past, how it haunts you."

I could only nod. He'd seen it before, sensed it.

"He is a bright spot in this past however, no?"

"Definitely."

He nodded. "Then all will be well, beloved. He still loves you, I sensed it."

Quiet laugh. "You sense all kinds of things."

He caressed my cheek. "That I do."

I lifted my hand, touched his. "I laid some heavy stuff on him today. That's probably what you were seeing in my eyes."

"And he is still here," he said, taking my hand in his.

"Yeah...he's still here."

"Then all *is* well, no?"

Simple as that, he summed it up the important part, I supposed. I smiled. "Yeah."

"Then I shall return you to this wonderful friend of yours, now. I'll see you soon as I'm able, beloved." He placed a kiss on my knuckles and released my hand.

"All right then. Have a good evening."

"I always try." He grinned and turned, walking away.

I watched him walk—okay, I watched his leather clad ass until I couldn't see him any longer.

I gave one of my neighbors (I didn't know his name, those on this floor seemed fairly private) a smile as he walked by, going the opposite direction Michel had, trying to pretend he wasn't puzzling over—whatever it was that puzzled him about me.

I might have had some guesses.

He sort of smiled back. Oh well.

I stood in the hall for another moment.

Try not to worry about the dissenters, Trey. Well, hell. Worrying never stopped anything anyway, right?

Right then.

Go see if Scott can speak.

Back at the table.

"Who. Was that?" Scott asked me.

Good. He can speak. "Michel."

"I know that, he said so."

Just checking. "One of my bosses."

His brows shot up. "*That* was Lecureaux?"

"The one and—well not only. There's his husband Gabriel."

He sat back. "Dude. I'll say it straight out. I've never seen anyone who looked like that."

"Beautiful, isn't he?" I said as I took Geoff's hand.

"Yeah. Dude, and young, too. Rich and beautiful."

I gave Scott a smile. "He's really cool, too."

Geoff agreed with a nod.

"Yeah? I mean he seemed nice, but it was a damned short visit," Scott said. "He's never a snobbish asshole?"

I shook my head. "Nope." Not that I know of.

"Well that's good. But does he always just drop by like that?"

I couldn't help laughing. "He does whatever he wants, really."

"Doesn't that get annoying?"

"No." Um.

No.

"What'd he want, anyway? If it's okay to ask."

I could make up something.

Nah.

"To give me a ride on his motorcycle, but he saw that I was busy." We'll just leave the rest out.

Scott's brow arched.

"Hey, I said he was cool," I replied to that.

"I think you blew him."

I laughed. "He and Gabriel are very together."

"Yeah, I get it, the three of you, together," he winked at Geoff, since Geoff was laughing, taking it well.

"No really," I said. Fantasies aside.

Scott held up his hands. "Out of respect for your boyfriend, I'll drop it."

I smiled, shook my head, and took a drink.

"You think he'd let me lense him?"

I grinned at Scott. "That always did sound dirty."

"Heh. But really, you think?"

"Hmm. He doesn't mind being admired," I said over the rim of my glass. "I could ask him."

"Let me know, 'kay?"

"Sure."

"So what's the husband look like?"

I glanced at Geoff.

Back to Scott. "The ultimate sin sometimes disguised as a dark angel?"

Scott started laughing in that way that made him snort. "Dude, when did you get all flowery?"

Since I met them, Scott.

I shrugged and chuckled. "So," I said. "Did you really mean you're gonna be around a while? Because Michel's, well he's busy right now, so if you want to lense him…"

He looked at Geoff. "Well, I've got a shoot to finish for L'Uomo Vogue—"

"Woo woo, la ti da," I interrupted.

He looked at me. "Yeah that's right; I'm good, they love me." He looked very pleased with himself. "Anyway, if you guys don't mind me intruding on the honeymoon, I can stay past that. I never get to see enough of Paris, anyway."

"You must stay!" Geoff pointed to the proverbial heavens and out rushed the next words. "You best friend and should no stay in hotel." He shook his head emphatically. "You should stay right—" he cut himself off, looked at me, and dropped his eyes.

I slid my hand over Geoff's thigh. "You should stay here, Scott. I have an extra bedroom." I smiled at Geoff, who was giving me the sidelong look through his pretty lashes, his own smile coming back.

"Oh." Scott held up a hand. "I dunno, man. I mean, if you're gonna be making noises all night when Geoff's here, I just don't know."

Geoff blushed.

Scott covered his grin by drinking some water.

"He does have a nice singing voice," I said.

Geoff gave me a blank look.

Then understanding hit and his face went into my shoulder with a small sound. Cross between a giggle and a kind of, *no you didn't*, sound.

"Oh dude, now look what we did." Scott set his glass down and he grinned at me wide, then mouthed the word *cute*.

I nodded and mouthed *precious*.

Chapter Six

JULY 27

I shook hands with *Monsieur* Chomette, the investor I'd had to meet with today.

"My attorney informs me everything is in order, *Monsieur* du Bois."

Amicable smile. "I should hope so. I'm very thorough."

He returned my smile, and I have to say, it was genuine. "You represent well, your employers. I hope you'll choose to remain in their employ, my young man. I like you far better than some of your predecessors." He leaned in. "Vincent was competent, but ah, such a bore. It's good to have fresh blood to keep us in this century." He laughed, patting my back before letting go of my hand and stepping away.

Fresh blood. Hah.

No, he is not a vampire. He's decent looking, though. A trim, maybe 5'9" frame, intelligent, clear grey-blue eyes, with a fashionable modern Caesar cut for his dark brown hair accentuating and softening appropriate angles of his face.

But let's see, Vincent made the third attorney he'd mentioned by name during this meeting, another being Stefan.

I nearly asked more about Stefan, but decided Chomette's demurring after saying the boy apparently lost his wits (and he meant it literally), it might be best to let it lie.

Lost his *wits*. Mmm hmm.

"I'm not planning to leave, sir," I said to *le Monsieur*. Not *planning*, nope. "I like this job."

"Wonderful." He glanced at his attorney. "Yes, Marcus, we have other appointments, I know." His eyes returned to me. "Enjoy the remainder of your afternoon, *Monsieur* du Bois."

"You as well, *Monsieur* Chomette, but please, feel free to call me Trey." 'Cause I like you.

"In this case," he said, "in future meetings, address me as Renaud, if you please."

Inclination of my head. "*Merci*."

"*Au revoir*, Trey." He inclined his head as well, and then left with Marcus.

Whom I didn't mind, either.

I gathered up the papers, tucked them away in their files, and headed out of the conference room, going down the hall. Along the way, I passed Robert.

Well, started to pass him, but he gave me the hairy eyeball, hesitated, and stopped.

So I stopped.

Apparently Michel had told him to let me handle meetings alone, that I didn't need a damned idiot looking over my shoulder (idiot being my word, but Michel would have said it, I'm sure), and that Robert bored most he met, anyway.

Mental smirk.

Robert was seething on the inside over this; I knew he was. This and other things, like me being unreachable for a few days with an explanation he didn't buy.

Like he'd buy the truth. Snort.

Then again...

"I trust things went well?" Robert gestured toward the conference room.

"*Parfait*," I said.

Slight grunt from him.

He could be the poster child for the perpetually constipated, I tell ya.

"Well," I said, "see you." He wasn't getting anything else out of me, since Michel told him to back the fuck off anyway, and besides, it annoyed him when I did this. Do I need to say I enjoy that? Probably not at this point.

"*Attendez un moment.*" He looked me up and down. "This suit..."

Dior, this suit. "What about it?"

"I'm not certain it is, mm, appropriate."

Brow arch. "This," I gestured to myself, "is a damned *nice* suit."

"*Oui, oui,*" he said, nodding. It irritated him to say the next words. "You look more like a client than their attorney."

Big.

Big.

Grin.

"Oh, I see. I shouldn't out-dress the VIP's. I'll keep that in mind." I lightly slapped his shoulder. "But you know what? Renaud *loved* my suit." I shrugged. "Anyway, gotta run, ciao."

I left him grunting in the hall, his face having exploded in shock when I used Renaud's first name, not to mention the comment.

Well, I *tried* to leave him in the hall. He stopped me yet again. "*Attendez!*"

I contemplated walking on, then thought *fine, what the hell*, and turned around. "What?"

He composed himself, lowered his voice. "This cousin of yours."

Cousin, oh yes, the one I'd made up for the explanation of

my absence. "Yes?"

"She is well, now?"

"Yes. There wasn't any permanent damage from the stroke."

He studied me. "Seems so young, to have a stroke."

I shrugged. "Some people drop dead jogging, and they're only in their twenties."

He contemplated this, and nodded. "Still, you seemed not quite yourself when you returned."

As if you know what me being myself is truly like, Robert. "It was startling. I was still shaken."

He attempted a sympathetic look. "I imagine so. But ah," he gestured, "it seemed you were limping the one day."

I couldn't lie for shit. But even if it was a lie, he was being rude.

"I had a fall while I was gone."

His eyes narrowed.

Right. You know what? Fuck it.

I moved in close, looked around to see if anyone was watching, and placed a hand on his shoulder, whispering, "Okay it's like this. I was kidnapped and then I was tortured by a monster."

His eye twitched.

I carried on, trying not to laugh and doing a good job of it. "He looked human, but I'm telling you, he wasn't, and he knew some scary magic." I touched my chest. "Thankfully, even monsters sleep, so I got away, but then I had to run through the Sahara, and let me tell you, that'll take it out of a person."

His other eye twitched.

"I was then rescued from the desert by two beautiful angels; you should have seen them. They were *amazing*." I leaned back. "That's the short of it, anyway."

He snorted.

"But don't tell anyone, okay? They'll think I'm crazy." I let my eyes dart around again, like some nervous schizophrenic. "Besides, *they* might hear you."

He couldn't help himself. "Who?"

"The monsters," I whispered even lower. "They're *everywhere*, man. Everywhere." I gave a firm nod.

He took a step back, and another. "Trey…"

"Yeah?"

"…you're…"

I sagged. "Crazy? Fired?"

He grumbled something unintelligible and swiftly walked away.

And I started laughing.

After checking on some things in my (sometimes) office, I decided it was time to go. I made my way to Odette's desk.

"Hey, sweets." She whistled. "Nice suit. I didn't see you come in before."

"Hey, doll. Thanks. Looking pretty fine yourself." In that few-inches-above-the-knees skirt, high heels, and flirting-with-being-too-low-cut blouse.

Meow.

She batted her lashes at me, then laughed that whiskey laugh. "Something for me to do?" she asked, her eyes moving to the folders.

"Yeah, if you don't mind. Just copy and file. I've got the discs."

"Okay doke." She reached for them before I even started handing them over.

Okay doke. Close enough. I smiled. "See you later, then. I'm heading out." I patted the desktop.

"*À plus tard!*" She smiled, turned, and set about her work.

I made my way outside, checking the watch I remembered to wear for once. 4 p.m.

Scott was still working his shoot, so I decided to call P.K. and see what she was doing. Sometimes she closed early on Fridays, she'd said, so she could go out and have some fun of her own. I hit speed dial, and she answered on the second ring.

"Hey there, handsome."

"Hey there, beautiful. You busy?"

"Not at the moment, but are you going to change that for me soon?"

Laugh. "I was thinking about it."

"So stop thinking and just do it."

Grin. "Where y'at?"

"Home, and Lucien *must* be rubbing off on you."

"'Long as it's not literally, I suppose I can live with it."

Light laugh from her. "Come on over. You can tell me how it went with Scott."

"All right. I'm by the office, so give me a bit. I'll hit the Metro and be there soon."

"I'll fix some tea, sound good?"

"Sure. See you in a bit."

"Okay handsome."

"Ciao."

"Ciao."

Shut phone, deposit in pocket, and off to the nearest Metro station.

****

A short distance from the Metro and I was at the corner of rue des Ecoles and rue du Cardinal Lemaoine, where P.K.'s apartment building stood, in the heart of the Latin Quarter. Besides having a great view of Notre Dame, particularly with her being on the sixth floor, and being fairly close to her shop, she loved her apartment because she was also close to the famous *Place Maubert*, a traditional Parisian market with fresh produce and the like. There were several movie theaters and music shops on rue des Ecoles too, another perk.

It was the first time I'd ever been to her apartment.

What? Is that so strange? You tell me when I had time for house calls with all the shit that's gone on in the last, oh, not quite two months. Okay, and with my other obsessions in the last two months. She always found me, anyway, and I've only been to Geoff's three times as it is. Besides, he likes my place.

Anyway, once she buzzed me in, I took the elevator and found her door, which she opened just as I was going to knock.

"My, my, don't you look elegant. Do come in, sir." She stepped back.

"Don't mind if I do, madam." I entered a small hallway that led to the living room.

"It's not as big as yours by far, but it's cozy, and I like it," she said as she closed the door.

I turned and looked at her, pretty in an ankle length sundress of soft yellow, with a halter-top bodice. "I'm sure it's very nice. Size isn't everything."

"We both know that's a lie."

I grinned. She grinned. "Right this way," she gestured, and I followed.

The living room was comfortably small. There was a small light brown sofa, a plush dark chocolate chair, and a square coffee table, black. There was a black T.V. stand with modest television not far from the well-placed French doors, which opened to a small balcony.

Her walls were almost brown eggshell, just lighter. Her floor, light colored hardwood, and there was a deep cream throw rug with caramel edging in the center of the room, under the coffee table.

"I like it," I said. "It's clean and simple." My eyes moved to the artwork on the walls. "That's cool, that mosaic."

"That was done by an African artist I once met."

I took in the riot of colors a moment, found them pleasing, stimulating in some way. I looked at her. "I bet there's a story to that."

Her pouty lips curved mischievously. "That I might tell you one day."

Laugh. "I see, I see."

My eyes darted around, catching the pottery here and there. Some of it seemed familiar.

"Let me show you the rest. It won't take long." She laughed and gestured for me to go on ahead down the hall. I snapped to and did so.

"Don't you love these built-in shelves?" I said as we passed her row of books and magazines.

"Completely, utterly, and in all other ways, love them."

I laughed as we passed a door on each side, but for now, moved forward.

"Oh, this is really nice." I stepped into her kitchen. The countertops, cabinet doors, they were blond wood, the appliances, stainless steel. The floor and part of one wall were brick tiles, and the wall over the sink sloped, a window set in it.

"I do love my little kitchen."

"It's so tidy and bright." I smiled at her. "I can only judge from yours and Geoff's places, but it sure seems like the French know how to utilize even the smallest space."

"Doesn't it?" she said. "This was a selling point for me, this adorable kitchen."

Nodding, I said, "Yeah, I can see why."

Next was her airy, lovely bedroom. More creams and light wood, with a dark accent here and there in the form of African sculptures, as well as Native American art, and an iron bed frame. There was a giant vase on the floor filled with dried pampas grass. It was close to a large window that nearly took up an entire wall.

I refocused on the vase. "Hey...is that one of Geoff's?"

"It sure is. Good eye."

I studied the crackling chocolate, creams, and burnt oranges of the glaze. "I think I'd know his anywhere. There's some in the living room, yeah."

"He's so talented. I had to have this one, especially. Would you believe the little darling insisted on *giving* it to me? He refused to let me pay him for it."

I turned a smile on her. "He did the same thing to me. Gave me a pitcher on our first date."

"Oh, I see. A detail you neglected to give me before."

"Yeah, well, I have to keep a few things up my sleeve, don't I?"

She folded her arms. "Oh, I suppose."

"Hey," I pointed at her. "You've still never told me about this girl you went out with in high school."

"Yes I did, I remember very clearly indulging your fantasy life while you were recovering."

"You skipped some good parts, I know you did."

She gave me a sly smile. "So you have a point. Titillation factor, you know how it is."

I laughed and looked around her room again, walked over to the large window. "Hmm, I bet I could see some interesting things if I stood right down there, looking up." I turned to her. "With a telephoto lens, maybe, and I happen to know someone who's got one of those."

She sighed. "I love that window. I sometimes lie here and soak up the sun, like a cat." She tossed me a wink. "And if you want nude photos, you only have to ask."

"Good to know." I winked back.

A brief stop in the small bathroom revealed a nifty built in washer/dryer, and we were back in the living room after another stop in the kitchen.

She set the tea mugs on the coffee table, and sat next to me on the sofa. She pulled her legs up under her, facing me.

"There you have it, the five-second tour."

"With the high ceilings, it doesn't seem so small." I glanced around. "And the coloring. I like the colors." I nodded. "It feels like spring, just not in pastels, you know what I mean?" I looked at her. "Fresh, airy."

Bright smile from her. "I know what you mean. I don't need a lot of space anyway. I'm out a lot. Just a nice spot to call my own and I'm happy." She laughed. "Besides, I'd rather spend my money on other things."

"It's not exactly cheap to live here, either. Not if you want a decent neighborhood at all, especially."

"True. I'm doing okay, though. The shop does pretty well, and I've saved over time."

"Good girl."

She laughed. "That sounded almost fatherly. Or like my mother."

"If she told you to plan for your future, she was right."

She held up her hands. "Plan some things, yes, like how you're going to get food on the table. Other things, be open to the flow of the universe."

I let my eyes move over her face. "Free spirited, yes I knew that about you. So they encouraged it?"

She nodded. "I consider it a blessing. My folks weren't the type to plan my life out for me, insist on this school, or that career, any of that. As long as I was happy and could take care of myself, they were happy. I have to say my mother was pretty happy that I followed in her footsteps, though."

"What, does she have a bookstore or something, too?"

"Mm hmm. Bookstore slash occult shop."

Grin. "Pretty cool." I laughed. "My mom never would have gone for that."

"What did she go for?"

I studied my hands a moment. "She always envisioned me over-achieving. Her father had practiced law in England. She definitely saw that as my future." I rediscovered her face. "Dad was more the free spirit."

"Then you got the balance, right? This isn't a bad thing."

"It wasn't exactly balanced. But I pushed myself, too." I shrugged. "I had this big ole brain, and it made her happy, made her proud."

She touched my arm. "Did it make you happy?"

"Oh, I was fine with it. I wanted to be a lawyer. I liked

learning, and it wasn't difficult for me, school." I laughed. "And really, when she pushed, it was probably because she thought I'd get bored and get into trouble if I wasn't occupied."

Soft smile from her. "Idle hands are the devil's tool."

"She never said that, but I suppose." I paused. "She didn't know half the stuff I did as I got older."

Her eyes moved over my face. "Parents know a lot more than we think they do, sometimes."

"Scott said that the other day, and yeah, they do." I'm sure they did.

"Speaking of..." she prompted.

I sighed.

"That bad?"

"No...well." I ran a hand through my hair. "We're good, he and I. We're cool."

She smiled wide. "He forgave you, of course."

I smiled a bit. "Yeah." I started shaking my head. "I just dove right in, though. God, I dumped so much shit on him all at once."

She took my hand. "The questions are, did he take it well, and do you feel better?"

I looked at our hands. Gave hers a squeeze, and looked into her eyes. "He needed to know where I'd been all that time, what happened to me. I know he did, sure. He took it pretty well. Just..."

"Just?"

Another sigh. "I still think some things could have waited. He says no, but..." I wasn't ready to get specific again just yet. I wasn't ready to say these things again. "Well it was a lot."

Her gaze deepened. "You don't have to tell me what you talked about. Just tell me, do you feel better?"

I looked into those lovely dark eyes, warm eyes. "Some weight's gone." True. "At the same time I'm...I don't know." True. "I told him something I didn't think we'd be discussing any time soon." If ever. "And I feel..." I feel "I feel...I think

79

I'm still slightly shell shocked, and I hated how it hit him." I closed my eyes, leaning back. "And that's hella cryptic, I know, but I can't say the things I said again. I just can't, not yet."

I felt her squeeze my hand with both of hers. "Like I said, you don't have to."

"It's a lot for him to digest and I know it's rolling around there in his head, and he probably doesn't know how to act, now. It's weird." I opened my eyes and looked at her. "On the one hand, we banter like we never spent time apart, but on the other, I see it. I see it in his eyes; I read it in the little ticks I know so well."

She caressed my face. "I'm sure he wishes he could change it for you. The past."

Nod. "That's a good deal of it." Head shake. "He can't change it. No one can." I closed my eyes again. "I kind of wish I wouldn't have told him the one thing."

"But you did. You can't change that, either."

"Nope." I sat up, finding her eyes again.

"But you said kind of, that you kind of wish. That means you're also kind of glad you got it off your chest, hmm?"

Dry laugh. "I had a fucking breakdown, so I guess you could say I purged something, all right."

Another caress to my face. "Then you needed it."

"Yeah," I whispered. "Yeah, and that's what he said. That I must have needed it."

"I'm certain he's glad he could be here for you, Trey." She gave me a soft smile. "He loves you, after all."

I pulled my hand away. "This time. He could be here this time. I left him to wonder and worry, and…shit." I rested my elbows on my knees, leaning forward.

"Another thing you can't change. But he's here now. You can start over."

I leaned on my hand. "Start over, without a clean slate. It'll never be clean, P.K."

I heard her breath. "Not strictly clean, but you're forgiven, and from here on out, the two of you will write over that slate and move on to a new one."

My eyes snapped to her. I smiled a little.

"So tell me more about this friend of yours, the photographer," she said, and smiled more.

"He's a *fantastic* photographer." I smiled more. "He's doing a shoot right now for L'Uomo Vogue."

"That's the magazine? He must be good."

"He's done other work, too. Travel photos, some celebrities. He's mostly freelance."

"How did you meet?" She got a little cozier. I got a little cozier.

"At Harvard, his first year, my second." I chuckled. "Out on campus. He was standing there when I was getting some girl's phone number, and after she walked away, I went over to him and hit on him. Teasing, really, I was teasing him, but hey, you never know, right?"

She laughed her warmest laugh. "Never hurts to take a chance."

"I knew he was straight. I'd seen him around, so it was cool he took it in stride. We introduced ourselves, and we just hit it right off. We were friends that day forward."

"You have to tell me what you said to him, you know." She gave me a nudge.

Grin. "The first thing I ever said to him was: 'It must be my lucky day. Dark hair, blue eyes and a pretty mouth times two, and one of each gender.'"

Her laugher floated over me. "So you, so very you."

"Yup." I laughed. "He stood there and chewed on the inside of his lip, like nervous, so I told him not to worry, that I knew he was straight. He didn't even ask how I knew, just laughed, said his name, and we were cool."

"It's a nice story, Trey."

I tipped my head. "We'll all have to get together, so you can see how nice he really is."

"I'd love to, just say when."

"Groovy. Know what else? He's currently single." I winked.

She lifted a brow. "That so."

"He thought you were hot."

She lifted the other brow. "Did he now."

"Maybe you can distract him from some of those bad thoughts, for me." Shoulder nudge.

"Setting up your friends already, I see." She nudged me back. "He's cute. I'll try not to monopolize all of his time."

Another nudge. "If it's the right kind of time, I won't bitch."

Feigned shock on her face. "Are you suggesting I take him to bed?"

"As long as I get details."

She shook her head. "Nice girls don't kiss and tell."

"Good thing you're not a nice girl."

She did a neck roll. "I know that's right."

I started laughing, she started laughing, and next I knew we had our arms around each other, but it was sibling-like. Yes, definitely sibling-like, and it felt so, so good.

I still think she's hot, though. Incest wouldn't be that bad.

"Now about that girl..."

"Would you rather know about her, or my new friends Charlotte and Emil? They had me over for dinner the other night," she said. "They have an open relationship..."

"Spill."

Chapter Seven

Michel

I leaned back in the chair and sighed, making it dramatic, I admit. Kar's eyes, the irises like jet marbles, shifted in my direction.

"I shall inform the rest that the Prince will grant them audience another night."

I wearily waved a hand. "You do that," and with a lift of my brows inquired, "Just how many *are* left that seek me this evening?"

Travis, standing to the left of my desk, replied, "About twenty."

"Not as bad as I thought."

"That's just the ones present," he said.

I fired him a look, and he smiled a bit, making with a light shrug. "Sorry?"

I tapped my nails on the slick ebony desktop.

"Several merely wish to pay tribute, my Lord," said Kar.

"Which for the most part has been lovely," I admitted.

"Though tell me, when did video games become a proper tribute?"

Travis' laugh warmed me, despite my impatience with the time the formalities of my position took. "Well, it is 2007."

I looked at him. "It surely is, but what is the proprietor of *Tainted*, all of twelve?"

"He is fourteen," Kar informed me.

"Oh for God's sake, are you serious?" I asked, not waiting for an answer, for I knew that he was. "Are we turning them this young these days?"

I heard Travis clear his throat. "Well, as you know, in your day one could be King at a much younger age. Or Emperor, eh, Kar?"

I gazed at him a moment, then began to laugh. "So someone else might pull the strings, yes." I leaned back once more, and Travis' lovely amber-hued eyes met mine. "However, I thought by now our kind might learn this was a new century, and that they should allow them to mature more before turning them."

Travis gazed at me, expressionless, delivering a perfectly smooth faced reply. "We both know you're just bent because it wasn't the new Devil May Cry."

I felt the smile forming. "When *is* the new one coming out? I tire of waiting, though no doubt Gabriel is pleased that it fell behind."

"Next year," Travis said. "Spring, I think."

I sighed once again. "I should buy the company that makes it. Look into that, will you, Kar?"

Kar gave me a rather blank look. I chuckled, and then waved a hand. "What the hell is Katamari, and why should I love it?" I asked.

Kar burst out laughing, rare when he was on the job, and Travis spoke through his own grin. "Near as I can figure, you're this thing that rolls around and...collects other things."

My reply was dry. "Sounds absolutely titillating." I looked to Kar, whose expression was now serious.

"This is for Play Station Two," he said, eyes moving over the game, still wrapped in plastic as it was. "This is not proper."

I feigned offense, adopting an airy disdain. "That's it. I'm starting a war and taking over his little club. How dare he give me something this old and this," I glanced at the box Kar was holding, "ugly. Good gods, what is this, this crap on the cover?"

"Your PS3 is backwards compatible," Travis offered. "At least he observed tradition, right?"

"I will give him credit for that." I waved a hand once more. "I'm going to prowl my city with Gabriel, now." I made to stand. "To think I'd forgotten how tedious this all could be." I arched a brow. "Oh no, I didn't forget, that's right. It's a reason I quit giving a damn." I winked at Travis before making for the hidden back exit.

"My Prince," Kar spoke, his tone asking me to wait. I looked across my shoulder at him, and he was looking down at his little contraption, an iPhone, they called it.

"There is an emissary just arrived who states it is urgent he see you."

"If his hair isn't on fire for my entertainment, I'm not certain that I should care," I replied.

Kar's eyes lifted to meet mine as I turned to face him. "He comes from Belgium."

I took a breath, contemplating this information. "Belgium belongs to Elise, unless something has changed." Someone I had once known rather well, Elise.

His eyes moved over the iPhone again. "'Tis on behalf of Elise he comes." His eyes lifted once more. "It appears she requires assistance on a matter."

"Why didn't you tell me this hours ago?" I snapped, or nearly did, yet it was not Kar who caused my irritation.

He bowed his head. "Forgive me."

This was all that he said. Kar was not one to make excuses, whether I was in the right or wrong.

"No, my apologies. You've not made a misstep. He just

arrived, yes?" I returned to the large antique desk and sank into the smooth leather chair. "Show him in."

Kar crossed to the double doors, opened them and stepped through.

"Michel," Travis began, and when he called me Michel, I knew he was about to speak to me on a more personal level. "Elise is the one who dragged you into the mess that..." he trailed off, not wishing to speak the rest aloud.

"Yes." I looked up at him, letting my eyes move over his handsome face. "Curiosity, I suppose, demands that I hear this emissary out."

He began to say more, and then thought better of it.

"Travis, *mon fils*, you may speak your mind to me, you know this."

His expression, it softened. "I remember that time. I remember the bitterness and pain. We were all very worried about you. I was very worried."

My own look to him was tender. "Don't worry now, beloved. History will not be repeating itself in any way, shape or form, on this one."

He shook his head. "I'm not worried about that, not at all. Only the feelings it may bring up."

I began to smile. "Have I told you lately how much I love you?"

His own smile bloomed, bright and sincere, and sat a moment on his soft lips, before his reply followed. "Yes."

"Good, good. Perhaps I should also show you." I reached for the video game, and held it out to him. "There we are."

His laugh, full and like heated gravel rolling over brushed suede, filled the room, warming me as he took the box. "Gee thanks, Dad. It'll make a great Frisbee."

My own laughter danced with his, until the door opened, Kar returning with Elise's emissary.

The fresh-faced young man, his blond hair clipped short, stopped just short of my desk, and made with a bow.

"Greetings, Prince Lecureaux. We thank you for the audience." He straightened, his pale grey eyes meeting mine.

I gave a slight nod and observed certain pleasantries. "Greetings. How fares your Mistress?"

"Well for the most part, your Lordship, and may I relay to my Princess that you fare well?"

"You may."

"She will be glad of it."

Debatable, I thought. I was already tiring of pleasantries, though this was no fault of his.

"For the most part, you say." I gestured to that which he was holding. "Which part, then, is not going well?"

Kar, to the emissary's left, took the rolled parchment from the young man, his eyes moving swiftly over the words once he removed the ribbon and unrolled the paper. He then moved around the desk and handed it to me. After skimming it, I returned my gaze to the young man in the deep green suit.

"I am not a lawyer," I commented, still absorbing certain of the words written on that parchment, attempting not to display the emotion they had, of a sudden, fanned. "Why then, does she come to me with this?"

"Forgive me, your Lordship; I am only the messenger in this," said the young mortal.

"What is your name?" I asked.

"Phillip, sir."

"Phillip." I allowed my eyes to traverse his baby face, and surmised that he had no inkling of the true history betwixt his mistress and me. "There is nothing in this missive, Phillip, which compels me to Belgium."

He bowed his head. "I am only to relay your reply, sir. Shall this be the message?"

He had not read the missive, either. Trained well, he was. "Come now," I said. "Surely she must have given you a few more words for me, boy."

He boldly met my gaze. "Only that she prays you would

deign to speak to her in person, at which time all will be made clear."

My eyes were wont to narrow with my slight smile. "I see." I had not spoken to Elise for years, had not wished to speak to her for years, in fact, had not wished to even think of her, for years.

Once like a sister, a confidant, a good friend, she then became a backstabbing, conniving, lying hussy that I—

It could not all be laid at her feet. I hated her as much for what she reminded me of in myself, as for what she'd done, perhaps.

"Sir?"

My eyes snapped back to Phillip, even as I felt the subtle, so subtle shift in Travis, he no doubt having felt something of what moved through me.

"You may tell your Mistress that I will consider meeting with her, and that I will send word of my decision soon."

"Very good, your Lordship. I shall return at once and let it be known to her." Phillip bowed once more. Kar moved to escort him from my office. If Kar was as surprised as Travis at my even considering a meeting with Elise, he did an admirable job of hiding it.

I sat, contemplating the situation as they made their exit.

"What does she want?" Travis asked.

I handed him the parchment.

"And what do you make of that, then?" he asked after reading it.

"Mmm." I rose and stepped away from the desk, requiring movement.

"News of Vicont spread like a bad rash," Travis said. "What if it's merely an attempt to take advantage of the situation?"

"I thought of this." I pivoted, sparing him a glance. "And some of you are worse than—what is it, the Enquirer?"

He did not smile.

I dismissed it with a wave of my hand, coming to another

turn in the path I'd soon mark upon the floor. "Such news, of course it travels like the plague." I paused to look at him. "They fell out years ago, Vicont and Elise."

"So she said," he replied, echoing my thoughts exactly as he set the paper on my desk.

"So I heard, yes, though she never legally dissolved their business partnerships." I made yet another turn. "Of course, why lose money simply because you had a spat of biblical proportions, she might say."

"Because if she had, he'd have no leverage, no power to tangle up her affairs."

I spared him a longer look.

"I know, it was a rhetorical question," he said.

It was easy to spare him a smile. I resumed my stroll. "She's a bit greedy and a bit lacking in business skills."

"Maybe she needs an attorney like Trey, let them sort it out."

"There's only one Trey, and she can't have him." My steps paused. "This Randolph that's supposedly threatening her, I can't find memory of him anywhere in my mind."

"Alias, new flunky or fresh upstart, maybe."

He knew I thought of such things. He also knew that having certain discussions outside of my own mind often helped, soothed me. Occasionally one needs another to state the obvious in the event one is looking too hard for the forest in the trees.

"In any event, it appears I may be going to Belgium."

Travis folded his arms, not speaking all of his thoughts aloud. "Shouldn't she be coming here? She's the one seeking help."

"True enough, but I'll not have it seen as fear or weakness, refusing to leave my own sanctuary after being so politely invited." Nor would I have her in my territory.

His brows made an ascent. "So you *don't* think it's just to do with business, do you."

I bestowed a larger smile upon him, my shrewd one. "Of course not, just as you don't believe it is."

"If it's some sort of trap, you'll waltz right into it."

"Yes, though not unprepared, although I don't believe it's the type of trap you likely have in mind."

"Subterfuge it is, then," he said.

"If I know her, and I certainly did, she wants something else, and perhaps I can more easily convince her to be honest from the comfort of her own home."

He studied me. "Now can I ask the *other* reason you're considering going to Belgium? You haven't spoken to her for years."

I returned this studying. "I'm not exactly leaping at the chance to see her." I crossed my arms as thoughts kept forming. "However...I still owe her a little something." Perhaps it was time to start paying her back. "And as I was saying, the best way to get to the truth of a matter is through its heart."

Yes, through its heart.

"*This* is what you were saying. I see," Travis replied. He gave a short nod. "When you decide, I'll be ready."

I stopped in front of him and placed a hand on his shoulder. Delayed were my words, when the door opened and rather than Kar, my devastatingly delicious Gabriel glided in, dressed like sex incarnate, which he was in any event.

"Belgium," he began. "How very." He crossed to where Travis and I stood, dropping a kiss on each of Travis' cheeks before attempting to find my toes through my mouth.

He often succeeds, and I mean this sincerely.

After having my attitude most completely adjusted, I turned back to Travis with a smile to match his own.

"Now where was I? Oh, yes. I'd like you to remain in Paris, should we go, *mon fils*."

Travis made to shrug. "Kar's better with formalities any rate."

I knew that beneath this easygoing reaction lie a measure of disappointment, if only because he would prefer to be with me should things go awry.

"I don't know, Travis, you have your own certain regality." I placed a hand on the side of his neck. "However, there is a very special favor I wish of you should we leave the country."

"Name it."

I smiled. "Would you be so kind as to look after certain precious mortals?"

"After everything you've said of them and what I've seen, I'd be honored."

I caressed his face. "Even if you knew nothing of them, you'd still do this for me."

He offered a nod. "Of course I would, Father."

Chapter Eight

JULY 28

Trey

"When will Scott be done with his work today?" P.K asked from the counter.

I looked up from the book I'd (not) been reading. "Eager to start distracting him, are you?"

I'd had more business to attend today, and Scott took the opportunity to check out of his hotel and gather his things while I did, bringing them to my apartment. He still had his shoot to finish up too, and when we did see each other for lunch, it seemed we were letting certain things slide by at this point. We stayed in the now.

For now.

He also took to wandering the city with his camera while I was busy and he wasn't working. He said he was going to do some shots when it got dark, last I'd called him.

P.K. walked toward the table after finishing at the register. "Well, I am doing you a favor, right? I may as well pay it forward as soon as I can, that way you'll owe me sooner."

Chuckle. "I think he'll be free in another couple of hours." I closed the book. "I can tell him to give you a call."

She flowed into a chair. "You can do that, yes. But I have a few errands after work, and really, you should spend another evening with him alone before I take all his attention."

Brow lift. "All of it, huh?"

Sensuous smile from her. "The right parts of it, anyway."

"Yeah, since I never got that far." Grin.

"I bet you've seen him naked, though." Her eyes held amusement.

"Oh yeah, a few times. He's certainly seen me nude." Laugh. "The little shit even took pictures of me in the shower more than once."

"Like you mind!" She laughed. "When are you going to share, by the way? I offered, after all. We can make a trade."

"You'll have to ask Scott. I don't have them."

Quirk of her lips. "I don't know that I believe that."

"No really, I don't." I spread my hands. "I'd have already shown them off, otherwise."

"Mm, okay, that I buy. I'll make certain to ask if he has them on disc, or something. Maybe he's got them in a file, on a laptop he was good enough to bring with him."

Laugh. "Probably. Some were digital. But he still likes developing film, too. He's real good at it."

She leaned on her hand. "I wonder if he has any life sized nude photos of you hanging about."

"Don't think so, and I never saw any. I teased him enough about the shower pics and what he might do when he was looking at them as it was."

She started laughing. "But he's straight. Hmm."

Shrug. "He never had a problem telling me I was a beautiful

man." Smile.

"I like men that are secure enough to say such things, appreciate such things." She sat up and smiled. "I understand more and more why you're friends."

"Yeah. He's very open-minded."

"My kind of people." Her smile grew. "I'm positive I'll enjoy taking his mind off certain things."

"I know he'll enjoy it."

"Then what's that look in your eyes about?"

"Huh?"

"Trey…"

Almost an eye roll. "I just can't win around any of you, I swear." Slight laugh. "I was just thinking that I hope no more shit hits the fan. I mean, I've already run him over with my stuff, the last thing we need is for a steam roller to come through and squash him on the pavement."

"What do you suppose he'd make of," she lowered her voice, "vampires and dead people and marks, oh my."

I leaned on my hand, contemplating. "That someone dropped acid in my cereal?"

"I could see someone thinking that. But he's your friend. Do you think he'd believe you?"

"I…really don't know."

"You said that he was open-minded."

Incredulous laugh and a whisper. "There's a difference between being open-minded about humans, and believing in vampires and ghosts and marks, oh my."

"Is there?" She grinned a little. "Still, you knew him well before, right?'

"Oh yeah."

Her brows lifted, pushing the question.

I contemplated some more. "I never lie to him, he knows that." Uh. Well, just the one time, and he knew it. Hmm. "I think he'd *want* to believe me." I sat up, waved my hand. "But right now, it's just too much. Someday. Maybe."

She gave me a short nod. "Yes, he's already been given a lot to think about, I agree. I was just wondering."

"He used to like to read about what he called oddities."

"Oddities?"

"Ghosts and UFO's, the unexplained, stuff like that. And he's open to other's spiritual paths. In fact, he read a book or two on voodoo, now that I think about it."

"Then maybe he wouldn't think you were crazy."

"Reading is yet another thing, babe. Really believing is *still* another." I gestured. "Look at me. My brain was debating the truth when I met Michel and Gabriel. It took me a while."

Tilt of her head. "But it was more because you'd lost confidence in your instincts, because of that court case, wasn't it?"

I sat back. "Well. Yeah. I did realize I'd known all along there was something very different going on with them. Still, who jumps to that conclusion? Even if you had told me straight out what you knew, I don't think I would have just gone…oh yeah! That's it! Isn't that part of the reason you *didn't* simply tell me?"

She laughed. "Yes. And no, most wouldn't immediately believe it. But then again, you're not most people, Trey."

Warm smile. "Well thank you."

"You're welcome." She leaned on her hand again. "If Scott's that open-minded, and knows you that well, believing you will be easier."

I waved my hand again. "Maybe, but I'm still not dumping it on him this trip."

"Of course not. Another time. I'm just saying."

"Well okay. We've got that sorted out." I leaned forward. "But now I have to ask you something. You knew about Michel and Gabriel. Michel said he'd been somewhat acquainted with you for three years." I paused.

"Mm hmm." She lifted a brow in question.

"How is it you didn't, I don't know, get closer? Michel seems to like you well enough. Unless of course I'm missing something here, you all didn't seem to know each other *as* well as I'd think you would after three years."

"Well, it's like this. I'm very open-minded myself, as you know, but my family is also superstitious."

My turn to lift a brow.

"There were stories passed in my family about such creatures."

"Scary stories?" I cut in.

"Some. But the most common moral of the story was this. Admire and appreciate certain things from a respectable distance. For many reasons. Much like you would a wild animal."

"Ah."

For the first time since I'd known her, a sheepish sort of smile formed on her face. "Some things just stick with you when you hear them over and over growing up. I'd want to get closer, but then I'd hear my grandmother's voice. Watch out for dem old men, dey cain't be trusted."

I nodded. "I understand. But you didn't seem afraid of them."

She shook her head. "I wasn't, not really, but I was wary at first. I believe they knew I was keeping a certain distance, and so they respected that. Michel consciously did, anyway, so I believe. Gabriel—you know him far better than I do. He shields himself most of the time as it is, so he was already distant, for the most part. Michel paid me more attention all along."

"So how do you feel about losing some of that distance?"

She gave me a much better smile. "I'm fine with it. I like them, and they're your family. They really love you." She smiled more. "And everything happened when it was supposed to."

"Meaning what, exactly?"

"I was waiting for you to come along and test the deeper waters first."

I grinned at her. "And then drag you into them?" I winked.

"Yes." She winked back. "No, you know better than that. I agreed to everything. I'm here to help you. It's all as it should be."

As it should be…

"You did more than agree, you prompted me where I needed to go, which reminds me. I still need to burn the bracelets."

She reached across to touch my arm. "I haven't forgotten. We'll burn them very soon, now that you're feeling better."

"I'll find something to occupy Scott so we can do it. Will it take long, doing it right, like you said before?"

"Only as long as it needs to," she said.

I nodded, and then both our heads turned toward the door after hearing the bell.

Whoa.

Okay, first: man did the day slip by.

Second: it was Travis.

"My, my, speaking of handsome, *hopefully* available men," P.K. said under her breath.

Which he probably heard, though his expression gave nothing away. When he saw me, he gave me a killer smile.

I took him in as he approached. Y'know, since this was a much better situation than the last time I saw him.

At least 6'2".

Broad shouldered.

And I say God damn; judging from the fit of his trousers and the way he walks, those be some nice thighs.

Very well dressed and it totally suits him, those midnight blue trousers, the matching three-quarter length (and very well tailored) suit jacket, open, with a pale blue silk shirt beneath. No tie, a few buttons undone. Black belt for the trousers, with an elegant silver buckle, oval.

Yeah. I got all that in the short time it took him to cross the room to us.

Detail man here, remember?

Yeah, well *then* I got a closer look at his shining, warm brown hair, which was kinda shaggy; you know, longish on top, waves combed back, wavier at his neck, just going over his collar.

He actually passed for human far better than say, Gabriel or Kar. What I remember of Kar, messed up as I was. Travis wasn't so pale. Just a human with awesome hair and what was probably a killer body.

Except for his eyes.

Backlit, almost translucent amber, and not just one shade, that amber.

Still, I suppose most wouldn't immediately point at him and yell *vampire!*

It wasn't just pure Michel in my veins that night. Travis was damned good looking. Add another to the list of hot vampires. Geez.

"Hey, Trey," he said.

Ooo. Yup, that's a sensuous sound, all right.

"Hey. Didn't expect to see you so soon, or see you here," I said. "But that's cool, man." I smiled.

"You know one another," P.K. cut in, and looked at me. "You've been holding out."

"That's Travis."

"Ohhh." She turned a fully flirtatious smile to him. "I'm Polly. Definitely a pleasure."

Hmm. Now that she was in the deep waters, was she ready to *swim?*

Wonder what her grandmother would say to that.

His eyes swept her as she rose, and it managed not to be lecherous in the slightest. "Good to meet you, Polly." He took her hand, giving it a firm shake.

"In the market for some books?" I asked.

Or something else? Heh.

After smiling at her yet again, he let go of her hand, turned to face me, and folded his arms behind his back.

Almost as if he'd just gone "at ease."

"I do love books, actually."

"As you can see, I have many," P.K. said.

He turned a warm smile on her. "It's a wonderful shop. As warm and inviting as Gabriel's said."

Her smile was girlish pleased. "Feel free to browse all you like."

His eyes swept her yet again. "I believe I will."

Great accent, by the way.

"Can I get you a tea or something? My number?" said P.K.

Travis turned an earnest smile to her. "No tea, thank you. I promise to consider the number, though."

"Well, it's a start," she replied.

I looked back and forth at them. "I could get out of the way. I'll just spy from over there," I gestured to some back shelves.

Travis grinned at me, winking right after P.K. said, "Voyeurism. One of my favorites."

Yeah. I kinda like that one myself.

"I bet if you sat down, she'd just bring books to you, Travis." I grinned up at him.

She shot me a look. "I've done that for other people." She looked at Travis. "Admittedly I'd bring more for you."

He laughed, and it was so warm I almost wanted to take off my shirt. "You don't have to bring me books, but maybe I'll sit for a bit."

She made a sweeping gesture. "Oh please do, you certainly add to the appeal of the place."

Another warm laugh, and he took a seat by me.

The bell rang again. "Excuse me," said P.K. She headed for the customer, greeting her warmly. I got the impression it was a regular, for sure.

"So how are you?" asked Travis.

I took to gazing at him. "Much better now."

"Good to hear."

"You just in the neighborhood, or what?"

His brow arched sharply. "I can't just stop by a local

bookstore? Your tone suggests I have other motives."

I sat back. "No, no. I mean, just...you're the last person I expected to see. You can go anywhere you want, and I'm sure you do."

He burst in to laughter.

Dawning came. "Oh, dude. You got me. The Aussie got me. Damn, that was straight faced, stone cold serious."

He laughed a little more, crossed his legs, and leaned an arm on the back of his chair. "To be honest, I was looking for you."

"Ut oh. Am I in trouble?"

"Not yet."

Stone cold. This time, I laughed. He remained straight faced, and for a second I wondered. I went with it. "So what's the scoop?"

"I kinda liked ya last we met. Thought I'd come around."

Brows, lifting. "Oh." Smile. "Cool, 'cause I was hoping to see you again anyway." Pause. "Under better circumstances."

"I hear you." He smiled. "You look and smell better this time, that's for certain."

"Hah. I'd hope so."

His expression became somber. "You're one hell of a resilient man."

"Oh..." I shrugged. "People can do amazing things if there's enough adrenaline, all that."

Slight shake of his head. "Nah. It's more than that with you. I can tell."

"I made a promise," I whispered. Cleared my throat.

"You kept it."

Well. Sort of. "You'll understand if I say I hope I don't have to test my resilience like that again."

"We're going to do everything we can to make sure you don't."

Brow lift.

"All of us."

Soft smile. "Looking after me. All of you?"

"You bet, mate."

Just then, P.K. returned to the table. "See anything you like yet?" she asked Travis.

He studied her face. "A thing or two."

"Maybe one of those things will leave with you; one never knows," she said.

His smile to her was warm, very warm. "One might. The other, I'm afraid, won't."

"Really guys, I can go over there," I cut in.

P.K. looked at me. "Or join in."

Travis held up a hand. "I'm really a skirt chaser, thanks."

And that's why they call it a fantasy. Oh well. I swear, if I meet one more hot male vampire (or human, for that matter), I may have to rethink the bi in my sexual.

Mmm. Nah.

"Trey is rather pretty though, don't you agree?" she asked Travis.

He performed the same sweep of me with his eyes that he had her. "Absolutely."

"Well then, if you ever expand your horizons, let me know. I'd love to take notes, if nothing else," she said.

Travis laughed—it sounded like suede felt, I decided, and so did his speaking voice, come to think—and shook his head. "I don't know about that, but far be it from me to ruin your fantasies. Have a go at it."

Her lips curled in satisfaction. "I like you even more already."

"And I like your vibe, darl."

She got coquettish, catching her lip. I arched a brow at her, not that she saw it.

He looked at me. "Can you spare some time, mate? I need to move, walk. Maybe you'd like to come along."

I looked between them, catching P.K.'s slightly disappointed expression. "Yeah, I can spare some time."

"Cool," he said, and rose from his chair. To P.K., he said, "It was great meeting you."

I got up while she gave him the appreciative eye and he returned the favor.

"Promise to come back by, handsome, and I'll lock the door so you can browse in peace." She gave him the full on, stop-you-in-your-tracks and give-you-whiplash, smile.

But he said, "I can see my way to a hello. The rest will have to be covered in my own fantasy life, I'm afraid."

I shot a look to P.K., who lightly shrugged. "Isn't that just my luck lately?" She sighed and moved off to help the customers.

I looked at Travis. "Excuse me, but are you nuts?" Not to mention he seemed to go for her. "Or playing hard to get?" A grin began to form.

"I don't play games." His eyes left her, found me. "Not that sort, anyway."

Well. Maybe she *wasn't* his type, and he was just being nice. No way, that was genuine interest, and he didn't strike me as less than genuine.

There was the whole human-vampire thing.

Yeah, maybe *that* was it. But still, couldn't he...

"Well anyway, probably a good thing you want to go. She said she had errands to do after closing. You're too distracting," I said.

He grinned. "Best get on with it, then."

"Yeah, I should check on some things anyway." We headed for the door.

"Work, or Geoff?" he asked.

"You know about Geoff because you're, you know, you, or some other way?" I couldn't help asking.

"Michel speaks of you both." He tossed me a smile. "Very fondly, he speaks of you."

My eyes dropped with my smile. "Good to know." I looked up. "Anyway, I like to see Geoff at work at least once in a day." I shrugged. "Even just for a second, see that he's fine. And a friend of mine, I should probably see how he's doing."

"All right then, no more dawdling."

So out the door we went.

"Polly's a good looking woman to be sure, by the way," Travis offered as we walked along. "She's fair dinkum, don't get me wrong."

"Eh, what the hell is a fair dinkum? Something obscene, I hope."

He chuckled. "She's the real deal, good stuff, that's what I mean."

"Ah. So why *not* ask her out, then?"

"Can't do."

I fell into his pace. Stalk.

Nice stalk, yeah.

"Why not?"

"I don't date humans," he said.

Ahah, it *was* the vampire-human thing. "Is this some new rule, or just another that gets broken, because I know about Gabriel and Michel's meeting."

"My rule. Some vampires do, some don't. Me, I can't cross that line."

"Can't? Why?"

"They'd end up dead."

Oh.

Nope, not the best way to end a relationship.

Or even a one-night stand.

"Uh, why dead?" Stupid question, maybe, but I like clarity.

"I'm a beast, mate," he stated.

I cleared my throat. "Not just in the bedroom, you mean? Or is that bad enough?"

"There, too." He grinned. "I'm a great lay, though."

I nodded. "Cool. We got that out of the way." I didn't need to know that.

'Cause I believed him.

Sigh.

He chuckled.

"What's the heart of the problem, then?" I prompted. "I might have guesses, but I don't like to assume, vampire or not," I whispered the last.

"Good way to be, non-assuming. When I say beast, I mean it fair literally. It's close to the surface. I often have trouble leashing it. A human couldn't handle it."

Mental flip-flopping.

I heard, felt his laugh. "I don't think you'd much care for it. Even vampires have run off screaming." He gave me a square look. "Strong image, by the way. I wasn't trying to nose about."

I shrugged. "I'm starting to get used to it. Sorta." Grin. "No worries. Do you mind me asking these things, by the way?"

He stopped. Gave me an even look. "If I minded, would I keep answering you?"

Breath and laugh. "No."

He smiled. We started walking again. "I'd tell you if I minded," he said.

"Cool."

"You're like that, aren't you? Direct."

"Most of the time."

"Then you should have known that." Half tilt of his lips.

"Ahhh, yeeeah, but I find myself being extra polite around new vampires."

He chuckled. "That can be wise, but no worries here, and you'll get used to me soon enough, I reckon."

I tossed him a glance. "Does that mean I'll be seeing more of you?"

"Think you can handle it?"

"Oh, I suppose I can try, though it's *such* a hardship."

Another chuckle from him. "Now then, that's sorted. There is another reason I found you this evening."

"Le gasp." I touched my chest. "You mean it wasn't just because you kinda liked me?"

He stopped walking, I stopped, and he turned to me. "No, but it doesn't mean I like you less."

"So what's up?"

"Michel and Gabriel may be going to Belgium. They may be there a few days, maybe not."

Eyeballing him.

Not a hardship, let me tell you—

Again. This group makes me terribly redundant, I know.

Sorry?

"Why aren't you going with Michel and Gabriel?" I asked. "Since you're one of his Guards, I mean."

"Michel asked me to look after you. I wanted to get you out of Polly's shop so I could talk to you about it. I'm your bodyguard, mate."

"Aren't I special?" I frowned. "Do I need guarding?"

"No worries, I'm sure things will be fine. He just prefers someone look after you while he's away. Geoff as well, of course."

"Makes him feel better."

Travis gave me a more serious look. "Yes, but I won't candy coat it, either. There's likely some spoiling for a fight since Algeria, and there are those that will see this as a great opportunity."

Michel sort of told me that.

"Opportunity for what?" But not that part.

"Such as getting to Vicont through Michel, or to Michel through Vicont. Hide behind them, shift the blame."

"And possibly using me for something, again? That's why you're guarding me?"

"Maybe. It depends who really knows anything about you and Michel, anyone that matters, anyway. Someone might just want to pester you for information, what have you, nothing more. But like I said, no worries." He gave me a reassuring smile.

"Right. Hah, no worries." I shook my head.

"I'll take care of you."

I looked back into his stunningly confident, beautifully lit eyes. "I'll do my best to let you, then."

He broke into another smile. Another beautiful thing.

"Still, I'm surprised you're not going with them," I said. "Being so close and all."

"Kar's better with the emissary shit. I get a little too hot headed sometimes." Beat. "This is a much better assignment, anyway."

I just looked at him.

"I get the pleasure of your company."

I laughed.

He glanced around, gestured to a bench, and took a seat beside me after I settled.

"Any rate, you mean more to him than business in Belgium. He trusts me with you."

I gave him a soft smile. "I see."

His following smile was eager. "This could prove to be more fun, staying here."

I lifted a brow. "My fabulous company?"

"I might get to kick some ass."

He sounded very eager for that.

Beast, huh?

"Well, uh, I hope you get to? Then again, kind of not... mate." I gave him another smile.

"S'alright, I get you."

"So what's with Belgium? Can you tell me?" I held up a hand. "Michel told me he officially reclaimed his position."

He nodded. "It's to do with that. The leader of the vampire community there, she's seeking his help on a matter."

"What does she need help with?"

"I can't really say, sorry."

I held up my hand again. "No problem." I glanced around. "Probably shouldn't be talking about these things out in the open, anyway."

"No worries, no one's listening. It's vampire politics, and honestly, I don't know all of the details."

I almost glanced around, but I figured he'd know if someone was listening. "Guess everyone has their politics."

"They do at that." He leaned back. "Anyway, I figured I'd let you know I was going to be around, so you wouldn't think I was just stalking you." He winked. "Which in a way I am, really. But Michel said you're kinda sensitive. I wondered if you'd notice I was, and certainly if I kept popping up, you'd wonder why."

I shrugged. "Fair enough. So if we're going to be hanging out, can I just get straight to the third degree that will be littering our time together?" I smiled.

"First let me say that I don't need to be at your side to keep an eye on you, really. No need to get in your way, unless I have to."

"Oh." I shrugged again. "I don't mind if you show yourself. I'm always up for another interesting friend." And maybe that was his way of saying he *did* mind a third degree.

He shot me a wide smile, then leaned back farther, elbows to the back of the bench. "In that case, fire away on the questions if you like."

"Really?"

"I don't mind you asking, no. It's other people's stuff I keep quiet when I'm supposed to."

Groovy.

"Okay…how did you meet Michel?"

He smiled to himself. "I ran into him in Père Lachaise at Molière's tomb, right after New Year's rang in." Beat. "At least I thought it was random at first, but it soon became clear it wasn't. He'd been watching me."

"I'm not surprised."

He smiled more. "Well, I was making a spectacle of things. But he was curious about me, very much so."

"Spectacle?"

"That beast thing."

"Oh. Which you'll elaborate on later, right?"

He just arched a brow.

Which he does wicked well, by the way.

"So what was that first meeting like?" Back to the original target.

His eyes shifted away, then back, softness there. "Of everything he said, what I'll never forget the feeling of is this: 'I know you're lost. But I've found you now. You don't have to be lost any longer, Travis.'"

His expression. I had an *insane* desire to touch his face.

Did touch his face. Started to pull my hand away because gee, I barely knew him—but he rubbed his cheek across my palm.

Like a big cat.

"I don't know where I'd be, what I'd be, without Michel," he said.

And I just had to run my fingers through his hair, which he didn't seem to mind, either.

Silk.

He certainly wasn't a beast right now, Travis. "I'm glad he took you in, for lots of reasons. Right now, I'm glad because maybe I wouldn't have met you, otherwise."

His following smile nearly dazed me. "We'll see if my luck holds."

My brows wanted to knit, but faced with that smile, they couldn't. So I just ran my fingers through his hair once more.

He purred.

It was deep in his chest and far different from Michel's.

"What kind of cat purrs like that?" I asked in a whisper, still stroking his hair, because it kept the purr going.

Well. Until he answered, though the purr lingered on the edges.

"Fastest one known to man." And with that, he rose. "You had some people to check on. I'm guarding you, not disrupting your activities, as I said." He grinned. "I'm not supposed to, any rate."

I looked up at him.

The cheetah.

I rose. "I really don't mind the disruption."

"Be careful about that. I can be *very* disruptive."

I started laughing. "Yeah, be careful what you wish for?"

"Something like."

He gestured for us to go on, so we started walking, and I felt the subject probably needed to shift. "I bet you're good at your job."

"Too good, maybe."

"Is there such a thing as too good? No one sends me these memos, damn it. I would have scaled back if I'd gotten the memo."

A laugh trickled through him. "Depends on your point of view, I suppose."

I very seriously stated the next thing. "Everything depends on that." I cleared my throat. "By the way, Polly knows what you are. She's like—*sensitive*." I glanced at him. "And I didn't say it outright, but she wanted to know what happened to me in Algeria, so…"

"It's fine," he cut in. "I've known about her for a while and they trust her." He looked at me. "I know you wouldn't give up secrets, either."

So he trusted me too? "Known of her just through them, or what?"

"Through them, and I've seen her a few times; she just hasn't seen me until tonight." He smiled. "Not a hardship, keeping an eye on her."

I laughed a little. "Spying on her is probably interesting. Maybe you have some good gossip, eh?" I nudged him with a shoulder. Yeah, I felt that relaxed around him. Even with Michel in my veins and teetering on a precipice the first time we'd met, I'd felt he was on my level.

"Kar will give me an ear bashing."

Not literally, I hoped.

"A good talking to."

"I'm gonna have to catch up on my Aussie slang, I see." I grinned at him.

"Reckon so." He grinned back. "Just keep in mind I may be out of date, and haven't lived there for some time, now. I've been surrounded by foreigners." He winked.

****

We soon passed Le Parvis. I saw Geoff at the edge of a row of tables, picking up some glasses, so Travis and I caught him before he moved away.

"Hey, baby."

Geoff turned, his eyes lighting up. "Hi." His eyes darted to Travis.

And away, and back to Travis.

Uh huh. Someone else thought Travis was handsome.

"*Hola*," Geoff managed to say.

Travis gave him a bright smile. "*Hola*, Geoff. *Cómo estás?*"

Geoff gave him a shy smile. "*Muy bien.* You?"

"*Muy bien, gracias.*"

Geoff smiled a bit more.

"This is Travis," I said.

Geoff's brows shot up. "Oh!" His smile was a little less shy. "Trey say something about you."

"Oh, really? And what did he say?"

Geoff giggled. "That you nice."

"Oh yeah, everyone thinks I'm such a *nice* boy when they *first* meet me." Travis' look caused Geoff's smile to get shy again, and he said, "That's a lovely smile."

Sure, make Geoff blush some more. Madly batting his lashes, Geoff thanked Travis, and attempted something conversational. "You are, um, visiting Trey?"

"Yes. He's about to show me his apartment, as it happens."

"It's very nice," Geoff said.

"I've no doubt of it," Travis said. "He dresses well and he has a lovely boyfriend, so I imagine his taste extends to his home."

Shy giggle from Geoff.

And, I noticed, a flash of something tender in Travis' expression before he smiled at Geoff again.

"I um, must be back to work."

I turned my smile on Geoff. "Okay. I just wanted to let you know we'll be seeing Travis around a bit more. I'll explain later."

His eyes bounced between us. "Okay."

"Nice to have finally met you, Geoff," Travis said.

Geoff caught his lip in his smile, nodded, then went back to work.

I looked at Travis. "Well damn. I might have some competition," I teased.

Travis laughed as we started walking again. "He's very cute." He looked at me. "Don't worry, though. He's still a human male." He winked.

"Have you watched him before, too?"

"Yes. I've seen him countless times."

"Oh, you *have* to give me details."

He laughed again. "I can see my way to that."

"Even if Kar bashes your ears?"

"Ah, what he doesn't know won't hurt me."

"What's the deal with that, anyway? Is he stuffy, strict, what?"

"Old fashioned in some ways."

I had to ask. "How old is he, anyway?"

Sideways look. "He was born in 1577."

My next footstep, okay, it might have paused a little. "A little older than them."

He nodded.

"Wow." And Vicont was so old his blood type had expired. "And you?"

"I'm a joey compared to them."

I gave him a square look while we waited to cross a street. "Hey, I'm not ageist."

His smile slowly reformed. "Born in 1936."

"Still a lot older than me." We started crossing. "How old were you when turned?"

"Thirty-one."

"Where were you born?"

"Alice Springs. Northern Territory."

"Groovy."

He shot me an amused look. "I'm likely what you Americans think of as a typical Aussie in some respects. I spent a lot of time in Never-Never." Beat. "That's the Outback."

"I knew that one. So what, beer swilling, croc fighting, shrimp on the barbie, you mean that kind of thing?"

Another chuckle. "Beer, yes. For the record, though, Foster's tastes like shit. We let the rest of you think we like it, because we can. That and it's funny, Americans buying it because they think ooh, Aussies love it."

Full laugh from me. "Is it even brewed there?"

"Used to be. I think it's in Texas now, and has been for a long time."

"Well, that makes perfect sense, sure."

"Doesn't it? And let's see, I don't think me or anyone I knew ever said to throw a shrimp on the barbie. It's *prawns*, mate."

Laugh.

"Anyway, croc wresting, well. I may have done that a time or ten."

"I faced a gator once. Okay, so I didn't wrestle him. Anyway, such a tough guy, you."

We neared rue chapon. "Rugged as the land I came from," he said.

I just resisted singing *I come from a land down under*.

He laughed. Guess he caught that. Jeez, I'd never need a coat again, if he hung around and kept laughing like that.

"Vegemite, everyone has it growing up, I think."

He definitely caught that. "Some people are crazy for Nutella, here. Everyone's got their thing," I said.

Nod from him.

"What does Vegemite taste like, anyway?"

"Vegemite."

"Makes sense." We reached my building.

"I don't quite remember the taste of some things," he said.

I punched in the access code. "Sorry. I mean, if it bothers you."

He shrugged as we went through the door. "Sometimes I miss it. At least I think I do."

"Can you drink anything besides blood? I've seen Michel drink. Well, there was blood mixed in."

He nodded. "I can do that. I can a little without blood in the mix, but I don't much like hemo-free drinks." He looked at me. "So can Michel. More than me." He gestured. "I like stairs. You?"

"We can do stairs. Keep me in shape. Somehow I doubt you need to worry about that."

As we ascended. "Still nice to stretch the muscles."

"Yeah, that rugged thing." I smiled.

"I was quite active. I still like to move. Some of it's habit."

"What else have you done besides beat up crocs?"

"Rock climbing, sky diving, bungee jump, did that. I quite like motorbikes."

"Thrill seeker."

"That's me."

"Bungee jumping. I think I could try that."

He eyed me as we reached my door. "Only if I supervise."

His expression was very serious, so I said, "Your job."

"It wouldn't do to have something stupid happen to you on my watch."

"Hey. I wouldn't want to get you in trouble."

"It's not that. I'd hate myself, mate."

I studied his eyes. "Hey. No worries. Someone has to supervise anyway. So, night jumping it is, if I ever do it. Right?"

He broke into a smile. "Night jumping's a rip snorter."

"Bigger thrill?"

"Even more thrilling for you, since you can't see as well as I can in the dark, now."

I sighed as I opened the door and let him in first. "I really envy some of your senses."

He turned to look at me. "Some of them are pretty cool, yes. Would you want to trade other things for it, though?"

I found I couldn't reply right away.

His nod, slow. "Yeah. It's a lot to think about, alluring as it seems."

I took a step closer. "Did you choose?"

"Yes, I did."

"Do you regret it?"

"Not these days. Besides, that gets ya nowhere."

Yeah.

Regrets didn't get me anywhere good.

Then again...

I wouldn't be here if I'd taken another path. Wow, that's a heavy thought.

I felt his hand on my shoulder, then.

"Things manage to work out in the end, if you let them."

I looked into his eyes. "Yeah. I'm learning to let them."

"It's a step." He smiled. "Right then. Show me around your place?"

Mental shake. Smile. "Yeah, right this way."

****

He didn't just check out my place, he *checked out* my place like he was filing details of all possible exits/entrances, how best to defend them, where the safest place in the apartment was to hide, that sort of thing.

Yeah. I could tell he was doing his job.

"Nice place," Travis said when we came back to the living room, and he settled on the sofa next to me at a polite distance, instead of sitting across from me.

Okay. That's fine.

Scott wasn't back yet, so I thought it was a good time to keep drilling Travis.

I mean ask him questions.

I know. That's not where your mind went.

Mine either. Damn, he's sexy. I usually went for the pretty boys, not that he wasn't pretty in his way.

More fem boys, I went for fem boys. I don't mean totally fem, not girly, just…pretty and not so butch.

Travis was *not* fem.

Must be that animal magnetism.

"Can I ask about your Sire?" I started.

"What would you like to know?"

God this was great. A non-cryptic person. "I'll start with; who was he?"

"Her name was Clarice."

"Ah…she."

His smile, it was one of those between-guys kind of smiles. "Very much a sheila. Very French, too."

"Is that how you ended up in Paris?"

"She brought me here, turned me, and dumped me."

Blink. "Dude. You mentioned abandonment before, but shit. Harsh much?"

"Harsh, yeah. Never saw her again. It was two, three days after my change."

"Damn. I don't guess you know why."

"I didn't then." He lifted and dropped a shoulder. "I think I do now."

"Why?"

"She wasn't prepared for how I turned out. Neither of us was. Neither of us knew what happened, and I think she got scared. She didn't know what to do with me."

"What do you mean, how you turned out?"

"A facet of my nature neither of us knew about."

"What is it?"

He arched that brow.

By the way, besides having an expressive face, he gestures a lot. I had the impression if you tied his hands, he wouldn't be able to talk.

Nice hands.

Mental shake. Focus, Trey. "So, she didn't know what to do with you."

"I don't think so," he said. "I didn't know what I was, really. I knew I was a vampire, but I wasn't exactly like her. Michel recognized this other facet." His look was very steady. "She couldn't have known. I wondered after he told me, if she thought she'd made some kind of mistake in the turning."

I took in his expression. "You seem pretty okay with all this. I mean your past."

He lifted and dropped that shoulder again. "No use wallowing in it. Get'cha nowhere fast."

He had a very good point.

"Do you have any idea what happened to her?" I asked. "Where she went?"

"She's dead," he said it with little emotion. No wallowing?

Still, I said, "Sorry." Was, he said her name *was* Clarice, yeah. Keep up, Trey.

"I felt it before I heard the stories," he said.

"Felt it?"

"It's like," his eyes seemed to search for the words, "there was suddenly this absence. A small void where there used to be something else. Something I didn't fully understand, really feel, until it was gone. When I heard about her dying, I realized that's what it was. The absence of her."

I let out a breath. "That's...profound. I'm still sorry."

He almost smiled. "Thanks."

"Do you know how it happened?"

His reply was not so flat. "She was murdered."

"Do you know who did it?" I quietly asked.

"Yes." Beat. "I know him, and you've met him."

My brows must have shot up again. "Vicont?"

"Vicont," he nearly spat. I'd found a chink in his easygoing personality.

More like a thorn. Yeah, a thorn in his armor.

"He's a real bastard," I said. "Why? Do you know why he did it?"

His brows furrowed. "They'd been acquainted. I figure it's because she didn't fall for his bullshit charm. He couldn't manipulate her." His eyes glinted. "She didn't deserve that. She wasn't a bad person."

I could only look at him, not knowing what to say. I'd found a big, big thorn, whittled from a two-by-four.

But then his face relaxed. "I knew she was trouble when I met her. The kind of trouble I found sexy. She was a spunky one." He nudged me and laughed. "I knew she'd leave me one day, but I asked her to turn me." Again, the one-shoulder shrug. "So maybe I didn't reckon she'd dump me that fast with no direction in my new life, but I think I understand why, now."

I could only shake my head and smile. "You've got a pretty healthy outlook on things."

"I think Australia grows us different than you."

I laughed.

"I have to say, I always felt she might come back," he said. "Maybe I was only hoping, but that's how I felt. Vicont killed her here in France; it was about two years after she left me. I've wondered since if she was coming to see me when it happened. Now I'll never know." His brows re-knit themselves.

"That's what you hate him for most, isn't it," I said low.

He stared straight ahead at nothing. "Yes. I'll never get to tell her it wasn't her fault, me turning into a monster. I'll never get to tell her I don't hate her for leaving."

I took a breath, and another. "Why do you say you're a monster?"

His eyes snapped back to me. "Because I was. When Michel took me in, I was a feral thing. I had no control. I still have problems sometimes, but I have solutions, now. Most of the time."

"Feral."

He chuckled. "Michel's given me several reasons why he spoke to me, and one of them is that he was getting tired of cleaning up my messes. I was going to blow everyone's cover eventually, he said."

Did I want to ask? Yeah. Did I actually need to? Probably not, but clarification was always good. "Messes?"

He gazed at me. "You know what I mean, but all right. Bodies. The bodies mate, or what was left of them. He told me I either needed to hire my own cleanup crew, or get a handle on that shit."

Mental shake. "Okay wait. First, cleanup crew? Or is that just a joke?"

Sly look from him. "We all have our place in life."

"Riiight." Visions of people—vampires? carrying mops and body bags and, I don't know, bleach and acid? danced through my head.

Travis started laughing, and that laugh felt like warm fingertips sliding *under* my skin, for sure.

"Fire works well," he said. "It's Rosh's preferred method." He made a motion with his hand. "Blow torch."

I sort of sagged. "Do you literally read minds too?"

Shrug of his brows. "Sometimes. Really, I'm just very good at sensing, catching the vibe."

"Like an animal."

"Exactly like that."

I leaned closer to him. "Big cat, just like I said."

His lips slowly spread into sultry smile, and I don't think he was even trying. It just happened naturally, like it did with many of his smiles.

"Me*ooow*," he…meowed.

"I've heard Michel purr, and Gabriel. They can be feline too, sometimes. It's why I asked before. But you probably knew that."

He nodded. "Mine's closer to the surface, as I said before."

"Your cat. But I'd always heard cheetahs were the easiest to tame, you know?"

"Yes, but it's not just that, what I call the Beast. We're not all like cats, by the way, and cheetahs aren't total kittens, you know."

"No, they're not." Beast, back to that. "You still have trouble with things now, you said."

"Yes."

"Is it because you're younger than Michel and Gabriel?"

He started shaking his head. "Maybe a little, but really it's to do with the other facet of my nature. One at a time, I could likely handle. The combination is what did me in. Michel and Gabriel," he paused. "Well, they aren't like me."

"What's this other facet?" I was fascinated.

Yeah I know. I tried asking before.

He looked at me a good long time.

"Never mind. It's private." I leaned back. "I understand."

He looked at me a moment longer, then said, "They trust you. If they trust you, I can trust you." His nostrils flared. "I *know* I can trust you."

I started waving a hand. "Wait, wait. This is reminding me of a conversation I had with Michel. On the one hand, I'm really honored he told me some things, and I wanted to know, but on the other—"

"I know what Vicont tried to do to you. That he tried to invade your mind."

I just sat there looking at him.

"I was damned impressed when Michel told me how you stopped him. I was damned impressed with how you handled the entire ordeal, really." He held up a hand. "But I understand. Knowledge can be a burden. I don't want to burden you with more than you want to carry; it's why I hesitate, mostly." He leaned in, and I watched the softness move through his eyes. "Keeping certain secrets can get lonely, though."

Eyes, almost dropping, as I thought of my own secrets, not so secret now.

I gazed into those lovely eyes of his. Those friendly, understanding eyes. "Now I feel like...I *want* you to tell me if you want to say it. If it's a burden, if you feel alone, I'll listen. It touches me that you'd consider sharing with me."

At first, he only smiled, a gentle sort of smile.

"I'm honestly still curious, too," I added.

He smiled more. "I'm beginning to like you quite well, you know that?"

"Aww shucks. I like you, too."

He placed a hand on my shoulder. "I believe I will tell you. I know I will, or I wouldn't have mentioned the other facet to begin with. Not just now, though." He leaned back.

I nodded. He studied me. Reading the vibe?

"Someone's about to buzz," he said.

Bzzzt.

Or he was...yeah.

"Oh, it might be Scott," I said. "Though I gave him a key."

He closed his eyes. "Dark, curly hair, about 5'8", big blue eyes?"

"Dude. That is so cool." I started to get up. "Yeah, that's Scott."

"Good. I'll get a good look at him, keep an eye on him, too."

I paused. "Really?"

"He's your best mate, right? I sensed it when you mentioned it earlier."

I was touched yet again. "Thanks."

"No problem." The buzzer sounded again. "Best get that. He buzzed in case you were occupied, but he's not going to wait much longer."

"Yeah...and then think of how to explain you on the way."

He laughed. "I won't stay long, and I'm just a new friend, ay?"

I headed toward the door. "Well, that's true enough."

****

"How do you know him again?" Scott asked, settling in a chair, O.J. in hand.

Hey—someone does like the chairs.

"Through Michel and Gabriel." I sat in the chair next to him.

Feels weird, now.

"Just how well do you know these bosses of yours, again?" He lifted a brow.

Well. I've been naked in a shower with Michel (okay more than naked), and he's bitten me.

Drank my blood.

While he was naked.

For starters.

Nope. Not gonna say *that*.

"Oh, pretty well."

He took a drink. "They get friendly with their previous attorneys?"

I'm not sure they got *this* friendly, but what do I know?

Stefan suddenly came to mind, as he seemed to be doing more of lately, but certainly that qualifies as friendly in a not good sort of way.

Still needed to ask about that, obviously, since I couldn't obliterate the thought.

"Yo, Trey."

Mental shake and shrug. "They like me, what can I say?"

His brow lifted again. "Maybe you did more than blow one or both of them."

"Hey."

He bit back a laugh when I pointed my finger at him. I laughed and dropped my hand.

"Kidding aside, you seem really into Geoff anyway. Besides, I don't remember you ever denying getting down with someone, especially if they were hot in your estimation."

I leaned back in the chair, crossing my legs. "No, not too shy about that."

"Not shy at all, man. Anyway, Geoff's really got it bad for you, I think." He smiled.

"He loves me," I said, soft.

He smiled wider. "I'm glad you're with someone. You didn't waste any time, did you?"

Chuckle and shrug. "Happened as it happened."

"Do you love him?"

Eyes, drop and lift. "I think so, yeah."

"Ooo, you *must*, because that was what you call coy."

I realized I'd even caught my lip in my teeth, so I didn't bother to protest, just laughed.

"Have you told him?"

Smile, falling. "Um…no."

"You're really not sure, then?"

"I'm…my heart is." There was no denying it.

Tilted smile from Scott. "Waiting for the perfect moment or something?"

Eyes, falling.

"Trey?"

Eyes, lifting. "I know that tone. I'm fine. Just thinking. I guess I'm kind of afraid to say it."

"Why?" he asked, sincere.

Lengthy sigh. Volume close to mute. "Sean, mostly. First person I really loved, and…" Shrug.

"I'm…I'm not sure what you mean."

"I'm still trying to get over the feeling that I hurt everyone I love. So maybe if I don't say it…" hand through my hair, trying to laugh as I move on. "I think I'm afraid it'll all go poof when I say it, yeah."

Even though Geoff probably feels it. Does he feel it? Still, it's nice to hear it confirmed, right?

Right.

Scott looked sympathetic, too much so.

I waved a hand at him. "I'll figure it out." I gave him a smile. "I'm okay, really. I just haven't felt this way since Sean. I haven't been this close to someone since—all that."

"So...was it difficult, reintegrating after rehab?"

"That's a perfect word to sum up a lot of it, Scott. It's like... you're the same person, but then again, not."

His nod, slow. "In a bright, shiny new world?"

"Yeah, and suddenly you have to relearn how to relate to people as a clean person, except you have all this baggage, and there's always the chance you'll fall off the wagon with it."

He studied my face. "But you didn't," he said low.

I studied his face. "No."

"And you won't."

"I don't want to be in that place ever again, no." I searched his eyes.

"I'm proud of you. You've made it this far already. I think you'll make it the rest of the way."

I gazed at him a second longer, then smiled.

"So anyway," he said. "I like Geoff. He's cool, he's nice. I hope that all works out for you, too." He fiddled with the label on his bottle. "It's good you're not alone here."

"No, I'm not. You're here."

He smiled a bit. "We gonna get sappy again?"

I measured with my fingers. "Just a little."

"Well okay, if it's just a little. But no more than that."

"I'll try to save some for later, then." Breath. "I wish I would've been there for you when your mom was sick."

"Oh," he tried to shrug it off, "you had your own problems." He cleared his throat and shoved that away. "They mentioned you last time I called. Maybe we can go see them together again sometime."

An immediate, "Sure."

His eyes brightened, sun hitting a clear blue lake. "I sent an email, telling them I'd seen you. They were excited about the news."

I'd met them twice. Adored them immediately.

"Maybe you could pop your own message off to them," he added.

"I can and will do that, just give me the addy."

His boyish smiled erupted. "Cool, I will." He fiddled with the denim covering his knee.

"You're kinda fidgety there, Scottie boy."

"Huh?" He flattened his fingers on his knee. "Oh, yeah."

"C'mon, what is it?"

"Just, it's just uh," he sighed. "Okay, I can't really stop thinking about all the stuff you told me."

"I should have at least broken it up over a few days, huh?"

He gave a little shake of his head. "You held it in and it finally blew up, and I'm glad I was here for you." He set his bottle on the side table and looked at me. "I just can't help feeling like, I don't know. Like I'm gonna say something wrong."

"Wrong?" I scooted to the edge of my chair, reached and touched his hand. "What do you mean, wrong?"

"The way we always teased each other. Some of that stuff…" his eyes rolled to the ceiling and back.

"Oh, hey." Shaking my head. "I missed that, you don't have to walk on eggshells. And what happened to me at school, that was there before, and our banter never bothered me."

He met my gaze. "You could probably tell these last couple of days I was being weird, huh?"

"Well. Yeah."

"See, and I don't want to make things awkward like that. And then I don't want to bring any of it up, in case it makes you uncomfortable."

I gazed at him a moment, then broke in to a smile. "Dude, don't make this more complicated than it has to be. That's *my* job."

He gaped at me a second, then laughed. "You're right, I am."

I grabbed his hand. "Really, though, I don't want *you* to be uncomfortable, okay? It's over, past."

"But you said you still had issues."

I felt my brows knitting.

"I guess I'm afraid if I don't know what they all are I might step on one. So I should ask things, but then I'm back to worrying about your comfort level. Big circles."

"Okay listen, Scott. I have nightmares, like I said, and I can't stand to be pinned, especially my arms and legs. Occasionally I even get claustrophobic."

His smile formed, if only a little. "I won't follow through on those plans to wrestle you any time soon, then."

I returned his smile, but bigger. "You mean I'm not getting the chance to have you under me this trip?"

He shoved my hand away, laughing. "Keep dreaming."

I sighed and scooted back in my chair.

"I wouldn't mind being under Polly, though."

Slow grin. "I don't think she'd mind, either."

His expression perked at this. "No?"

"Nope."

"So tell me something about her."

"Like what?"

He shrugged. "How about where she's from? I can't place it and I forgot to ask before."

"Georgia."

"Really? She didn't sound that southern."

"Once in a while she does. She just has one of those ears, picks up the sound of a place."

His elbow went to his knee, his chin to his hand. "Like you. Except you're not sounding very French."

I chuckled. "I can when I want to."

"You're not sounding so nasal-ass Upstate New York, either."

"What do I sound like?"

"Mmm, I dunno exactly. But it's different."

I thought of what P.K. said about me picking up Lucien's patterns.

"Well, if it comes to you, let me know."

He sat up, shrugging. "Sure. So back to Polly. What's her background? I mean ethnic. Just curious."

"African American, Cuban, and Native American."

"Wow, quite a mix. Makes for a good lookin' babe, I'll say that."

Another chuckle from me. "Sure does."

"No offense to Geoff, but I'm surprised you didn't go for her."

I set my left ankle on my right knee. "Oh, I did. Then I met him. Then I was sorta stuck in the middle."

"Ehem. Literally?" Wag of his brows.

"Hahah...no. Geoff would die of embarrassment, I think."

He grinned. "Geoff doesn't seem like he's into girls, anyway, but I didn't want to assume."

"Nope, he's not."

He nodded. "And you're totally into him."

"I think we covered that."

"Just making sure." He smiled.

I grinned. "Don't worry, no competition from me. Good thing, too, or you'd lose."

"Pff." He waved me off. "Actually...I was getting used to that. I'm not sure I know what to do with a girl that's interested in me instead of who I know.."

"Ahhh, c'mon, lots of girls liked you."

"Right. Like a friend, lots of them."

"So they're stupid."

"So they all wanted mister bad boy over there."

"Hey, I was working on your bad boy-ness."

"Can you finish reforming me, now?"

"Shore thing." I leaned forward. "But c'mon, now, I happen

to know you can be the kind of bad boy chicks dig."

He tossed his hands up. "If I could keep their attention, maybe they'd find out."

"Dude." Laughing. "You didn't want those girls anyway, trust me."

"Hmm…maybe not beyond a night or two, some of them."

"Which you had."

"Which I'll never get to hear you say in front of someone else."

Head shaking, shaking. "Never."

"I like you why, again?"

"'Cause I'm sooper kewl."

"In your mind, anyway." He stood. "I'm hungry, you?"

"I could eat." I rose. "What are you in the mood for?"

"You tell me, you live here."

Chuckle. "Geoff's been feeding me, either that or I hang at Le Parvis, and I think we know why."

"Dude, still. You're in Paris and you haven't tried more places? Not that I blame you when it comes to Geoff's cooking."

I stretched a little. "We can walk around and see what smells good, and where there's room. It's like there's two main dinner times here and if you miss them, your choices get narrowed down, because all the places are full. No reservation, no go."

"Well, I'm sure we can find something. Just let me put on some shoes again."

"Yeah, I need to do that, too."

"Hey," he stopped me before I headed for the bedroom. "Does Polly stay open late? What time is it, anyway?"

"She's closed. It's way after ten. But *she* might be open this late."

He put a hand in my face. "Do not speak so of the woman whose figure I love, sir."

Laughing, we both set about getting those shoes.

Chapter Nine

Gabriel

I devoured the space between Michel and myself. I laced my arms about his waist and set my chin upon his strong shoulder, pressing the front of my body into his, reveling in the feel of his brawny back, his well-developed gluteus, his powerfully built thighs. It had always been as if our bodies were created to fit together this way, this and any other way.

"So we are going. You have ignored her for years," I said, my fingertips pirouetting on the satin flesh across his ribs. "Are you certain that you can gather enough information whilst we are there by speech alone?"

He reached back, moving his hands over my buttocks, and this melted me further. Difficult it was to be irritable when he held me so.

"She's not as shrewd when discussing business." He shifted against me, which nestled me nicely in the cleft between those firm muscles of his. "I rather think she'll be so surprised to see me in her home, she'll not be at her most guarded."

"Perhaps not. She has lied very well in the past, however."

"I know you've no wish to see that woman, *mon amour*. Though you agreed this was an opportunity to gather information, I'll do my best to keep it brief." His fingers massaged that which they coveted and a purr roiled through me. "Thank you for agreeing to accompany me, my darling."

"Being separated is less enviable than seeing her," I said, feeling like damp cotton at the prospect of Belgium, all the same.

"Wretched, it's a wretched thing." His thoughts flashed on the past, I knew. I sensed it, and it caused the volume of his voice to flee.

A sigh moved through me sans sound. "As much as I love where your intentions lie, are you certain you wish to suffer this, *mon lion*?"

He turned in my arms, which nearly caused me to protest. However, he slid his hands up under my hair, a favorite gesture of both mine and his, and he placed a soft kiss upon my lips. "If you can, I can."

I searched his bejeweled eyes, deeply did I search. "Little I may care for her, but you, you still bear a wound that does not always remain sealed." A wound I could trace far too well.

His forehead came to rest against mine. "She can't touch it, now."

My hands, they roamed his back at will, both soothing and, unable to deny my fingernails, arousing to him, I knew. "I hope that this is so." How I hoped that it was so.

My vision was flooded with glittering particles of gold, miniscule facets of jade, and sections made of sliver after sliver of sapphire and cobalt, a circle of jet set at their center.

"She will not have the opportunity, as she should be tiptoeing around that subject if she desires my help," did my angel say.

"Help that you do not intend to give." The bit of satisfaction at the prospect of him succeeding in his plans, it grew, and I became aware of the arching of my lips.

"I only have to convince her I'm open to the possibility." I knew the moment his own lips curved without aid of seeing it, though I could envision it crisply enough.

"This should not prove terribly difficult, I suppose, as she has been dreadfully eager for you to forgive her," I replied, wearied by the very thought.

A snort left him. "I read less than half of her missives, as you well know, but yes. *Dreadfully* eager."

A cold front moved within me. "The messages through others, I thought that they would never cease. As if I care whether or not she holds regret. As if I care what her reasons were." I stepped back. "She is a liar and a common whore."

He merely nodded. He knew quite well how I felt. A few of those messengers had never returned word to Elise, not because neither of us would answer, which was also accurate, but because several of them were incapable of speaking after what I considered a tiresome trespass.

I made quite certain that it was the last thing they ever did.

"Kar will accompany us. You need not linger whilst I speak with her." He pushed the hair away from my left eye and watched it cascade back into place. Another favorite gesture.

"Kar is fine company; this suits me." Yes, it did suit me. "Perhaps we will stroll through Brussels; it will bore me far less."

"Irritate you far less," he corrected, tracing the line of my jaw with a near nacreous nail.

I moved into the touch, as I moved into every of his touches; there was nothing for it.

"At the moment, bore would be the word." I ran my tongue under his chin and then lower, across the carotid pulsing beneath silken, tawny flesh, the taste of him, the anticipation of tasting him more, and the thickened breath of a moan that left him, pleasing me immensely.

"Speaking of her bores me," I murmured into his neck, and then allowed the tip of my tongue to trace the artery once more, whilst my hand forced itself between us, finding that which it coveted most at this moment.

His desire grew. The flame of it settled in my tailbone, poised to coil, to wind, to lick at my groin as it fed my own need.

"You're so wickedly distracting, *mon ange foncé*." His words were naked flame, and his nails scored shallow lines across my hips, a tease, merely a tease, this. "As is no doubt your intention."

Truth there was in his last words, heedless of the fact that I always desired him. I knew that he had well loved that woman once, that they had been close. I knew well that he had trusted in her, and I came to know much later, just how deeply she had sliced him. I also knew that he had not truly forgiven himself his part in the play she wrote. He was an unwitting player, this I came to know, had suspected before we parted those years ago.

Yet gone I had, for his lost faith, this had sliced me acutely. This most of all. I forgave him, though he never quite believed my reasoning. He never quite believed that he deserved my forgiveness.

"Yes," I whispered in reply, just before piercing through the fluttering flesh at his neck and losing myself in the waves of his ocean, an ocean whose depths echoed endlessly his heart.

Chapter Ten

JULY 29

Trey

"So he's keeping an eye on us," I said to Geoff, keeping my voice low in case Scott was awake and happened by my bedroom door, even though I'd closed it.

"There are people after us?"

"Probably not. Travis said not to worry." And I didn't want Geoff to worry.

"He keeps a good eye?"

"I would have to say yes."

Geoff—reclined between my legs, back to my stomach—nodded, scrubbing my chest with his thick and currently somewhat tangled hair.

It was possible Scott was still asleep, since we'd been noisy last night. I'd been happy to find out Geoff forgot to be shy when I had him properly distracted.

He's a hot tamale, let me tell you. Quick learner, let me tell you that, too, because I know you were wondering, and I'm good like that.

I readjusted my back on the headboard, mostly to feel him move against other parts of me.

"Travis seem nice," he said.

"Maybe we should let him see your apartment."

"What for?"

"Maybe he'd like to check it out the way he did mine."

"Oh. Um, okay, I don't mind."

I slid a palm down his creamy chest. "He won't bite. Unless you ask him, maybe."

"Hee...um. No."

"You were awfully shy around him, sweetness." I grinned to myself.

He didn't reply, opting to keep tracing the veins on the back of my hand.

"I dunno. I think you've been fantasizing."

He slapped my thigh. "No!"

Chuckle. "Methinks the boy doth protest too much."

"I...no." Shake of his head. Mmm. Love, love, love the hair.

"C'mon, you can tell me."

He craned his neck, trying to look at me. "I only want you."

The way he said it, I grew serious. "Hey, now. I'm only teasing."

"Okay, but I just need you. I'm happy this way."

I gave him a quiet smile. "I'm happy, too. But you know, fantasies are normal. It's okay to have them."

He relaxed his head. "Okay. It's okay you have them, too. I never have a boyfriend before. I just want...I don't want you to think the wrong things. I want you to feel safe. No, secure. No, both things."

"I –" love you "– agree. It's important to communicate. In the interest of that, did it ever bother you about Polly?"

"Polly? Oh, you mean flirting. No. Flirting is okay." He smiled up at me.

I returned his smile. "And you know you don't have to worry now, right? It's you that I want." All flirting aside, I wanted him the most. "I'm just one of those people that can't help flirting."

He smiled more. "I know. I always know you want me."

I felt my brows lift. "Really?"

He grabbed his lip. "Mmm, uh huh."

I ran a hand over his hair. "I guess you would, little sparrow."

He grinned up at me.

My insides warmed.

"So, since fantasies are okay, tell me more about Travis," I said.

He craned his head around again, smiling shyly. "He is handsome."

I began to smile. "Yes, he is."

"Probably he is very like you say, fit."

I smiled more. "Definitely."

"Probably he would look good in short pants."

Laugh. "I agree."

"Hee. Probably...no, I can't say."

I nudged his side with a knee. "You can say it, it's just me here."

"Probably he have..." he covered his face.

I dipped my head closer to his ear. "A big cock?"

Mad giggles from him.

"Yeah, I'm thinking you're probably right, Geoff."

He moved his hands. "But not as big as yours. No way no one's is."

"Hah! Oh, you just scored *major* points, *bonito*."

He twisted and squirmed (mmm, nice) until he was straddling my thighs. "Yours perfect, so pretty."

Half laugh. "Ooo, it's pretty and perfect, too?"

Nod and nod from him.

"You just keep stroking my ego, I don't mind one bit."

He reached down. "Like this?"

My next words rasped on my breath. "That'll work nicely."

"Who wants coffee?" I then heard.

Scott was up.

But so was I, and I planned to be up longer than it took to brew coffee.

"We'll be there in a while!" I called out, before I moaned and captured Geoff's mouth.

"Yeah, yeah, more like coming in a while," I heard after that.

Of course. That's what I meant. But I was now ignoring everything outside my bedroom.

****

Deigning to dress after all and not leave Scott to fend for himself, Geoff and I made our way to the kitchen, where Scott sat at the little breakfast table.

"And they come up for air," he said, lifting his mug in salute.

I glanced at the coffee pot, which was perking. "You already drank a pot?"

"Hey, it took you a while to come."

Geoff stifled a giggle and headed for the cabinets.

I slipped Scott a smug smile. "It always does, but still, you're hopped up on the equivalent of ten cups. I'm not so sure I want to hang out with your hyper ass today."

"I'm stuck with you just being yourself, give me a break," Scott countered.

"At least I have a brain. Caffeine does nothing for your ability to converse intelligently; in fact, it lowers your chances considerably and makes you sound like a three year old on a sugar binge. No wait. That part's normal, never mind." I took the chair across from him.

"At least I have an excuse. What's your excuse for having your thumb up your own ass so much of the time?"

"It feels good, you should try it. Middle finger's better

though, being longer."

Geoff laughed. Scott chuckled because Geoff laughed.

"Is he already corrupting you?" Scott asked Geoff, turning in his chair.

Geoff gave him a blank look, then a frown. "You are saying I'm tainted?"

"Um, no, no. It was a joke."

Geoff's laughter bubbled out. "I joke too."

Scott laughed, looked at me, and jerked a thumb in Geoff's direction. "He's got excellent cover in that naïve thing."

"True, but I know when he's teasing. I laugh every time, but I generally know." I glanced at Geoff, whose brows had lifted. "I know better *now*, and I know he's not completely naïve." I winked at him, and he went back to rummaging around, deciding what his masterpiece of the morning would be.

"He corrupt me nice," we heard Geoff say.

"Yeah," said Scott. "I was getting lessons before. He promised to finish that." Scott threw a wink at me.

Geoff turned. "You," he pointed back and forth at us, "you?" His brows shot up.

Scott lost it.

Once I stopped laughing, I cleared that up. "Not like that, no."

"Oh. I didn't think so, but maybe I was wrong, so I ask." And back to the counter turned Geoff.

"Scott's the only one to stupid enough to say no," I quipped.

"Trey's still dense enough to keep trying," Scott retorted.

Geoff walked over and set a mug of coffee in front of me, then looked at Scott. "This is not possible. Trey, he could never be serious wanting you; it all pretend."

Scott looked up at him. "Never, huh?"

Vigorous shake of Geoff's head. "No. Because you are nothing like me." He folded his arms. "I am much more pretty. I bet you no cook, either. You probably burn water." He pointed at Scott. "Also, you would gag on it. This no attractive, and I do not gag," he finished in a matter of fact way.

"Ooo. *Ouch*. He guessed my secret, too, shit." Scott put a hand to his chest and sniffled, that is, after he could stop the laugh.

As for me, I'd nearly sprayed coffee through my nose.

Once I recovered. "Well done, baby. Bravo," I said through the lingering laughter, clapping my hands together. "You definitely learn fast."

Geoff beamed at me. "I make omelets?"

"Sounds great."

"Absolutely," Scott agreed. "I need to find a happy place again, damn. Food might work."

Geoff patted his arm. "There there, you still nice." He smiled and turned, setting about spoiling us.

"So what should we do today?" I asked Scott.

"Definitely no dick sucking."

"I already scratched you off that list. You probably wouldn't swallow, even if you didn't gag."

He jerked his head toward Geoff and lifted his brows.

I nodded yes.

He does *now*, anyway.

He grinned at me and shook his head, as in, *you lucky bastard*.

"I see that!"

We looked at Geoff. "Be proud," I said. "Very proud. You know *I* was proud."

"I don't think that the word," Geoff said over his shoulder.

"No, but it's on the list."

He giggled and cracked eggs into a bowl.

"Anyway," I looked at Scott. "I've been thinking about the catacombs. That's one thing we could do."

"Oh yeah, that sounds cool. I'd love to take pictures there. That's allowed, right?"

"Far as I know. But I wasn't just thinking of the official tour."

"But the rest is off limits, isn't it?"

"Yes, but that doesn't mean people don't explore them. There's still spots that aren't sealed up."

He leaned back in his chair. "Wouldn't it be better at night, less chance of being seen? Do you even know where to go?"

"I was looking stuff up before I ever moved here." I leaned forward. "I think there's a place or two not far that we could slip into."

"But it's easy to get lost, right?"

"I'm just talking about small areas, like with rooms, not going deep into tunnels or anything. No entrances requiring ropes, whatever. We can just walk in and out, well... mostly."

He stroked his chin. "Hmmm."

"C'mon, just a small adventure. It's better to find cataphiles for the serious stuff; I'm not completely crazy."

"Cataphiles?"

"That's what they call themselves, people who go down there, explore the catacombs a lot."

He smiled. "Cool." He lightly slapped the table. "Okay. I'm up for it."

"You be safe!" Geoff said.

"Don't worry baby. Like I said, nothing dangerous. Just a peek."

"Okay. But no get caught, you get in trouble."

"I can be sneaky when I have to be." Scott and I grinned at each other.

"Hey," Scott said to me. "How about the crypt under Notre Dame, too. Well it's under the square in front, right? But you know the one I mean."

"Totally. Yeah, let's do that, too."

"Day of the dead." Scott smiled.

I decided not to say, even in jest, that every day could be considered a day of the dead for me.

It just wouldn't have made sense to him, not even in jest, and I was still not about testing that water, yet.

Chapter Eleven

BRUSSELS

Michel

Kar preceded us into the grand salon, quietly regal in his modern Asian-styled suit of maroon silk, complete with mandarin collar and 'frog clasps.'

Elise's home was a beautiful study of Art Nouveau, the salon a combination of Victor Horta and Charles Rennie Mackintosh.

The room was a blushing pastel palette of sunset peach, pink, lilac and white, with touches of peacock blue and green, actual representations of the feathers themselves on a handful of vases. The wall next to the elegantly curved staircase, tastefully done in stylized flowers on curving, elongated vines.

More color in the stained glass of umbrella-shaded tiffany lamps accented the soft palette.

"Michel! How long has it been?" She crossed the room, her

hands held out, and her sapphire evening dress slithered with her body, the slit parting as she walked, revealing an alabaster thigh.

"A few years, certainly," I replied, taking her hands, willing to go right along with her as she more than obviously chose to pretend the past was nonexistent at the moment.

"You haven't changed." She kissed each of my cheeks. "Still so radiantly beautiful."

I feigned laughter at her poor attempt with sarcasm as well as the implication beneath the sarcasm.

"And you, still so uninspiring," said Gabriel from a few paces behind me.

She did not so much as spare him a glance. Instead, her crystalline golden-green eyes held mine. "So good of you to come on such short notice."

"Curiosity and a cat, as is said."

Her throaty laugh filled the room. "I shouldn't think you'll be losing any of your lives over it."

I should say not.

One of her hands smoothed a non-existent wrinkle at the waist of her dress. "I really am pleased to see you."

In her eyes, some spark of hope flared. I could surely guess what manner of hope.

"Well, the weather was nice, and we haven't seen Belgium for quite some time," I replied. "Also, I had other business to attend, so there was no reason not to kill two birds with one stone."

Her chin lifted slightly. "I'm pleased it wasn't such an inconvenience, then, stopping on your way through."

I refrained from telling her it most certainly was. "As you said, it's been years. It was time to say hello to an old friend."

A first she merely studied me. Her expression then broke with a pleased smile. She gestured to the plush sitting area with its gently curved chairs and couch upholstered in flowered fabric, the flowers dainty tulips and lilies. "Let's be comfortable, shall we?"

My eyes moved over the hearth with its cast iron hood and white tiles with inlaid silver and semi-precious stones, as I moved to a chair.

I forced myself to soften a bit. I had once held love for this woman, could still hold love for this woman, if only…

It seemed everything Vicont touched became tainted.

Gabriel's hatred ran deep. Stiffly, he moved toward the offered chairs and sat, just as stiffly, in a chair to my left.

Kar remained standing at the closest entrance to the room.

Elise perched upon the settee to my right. "Would either of you like a drink? I've procured a lovely AB-."

"I will pass," Gabriel replied – stiffly polite.

I waved a limp hand. "*Non, merci*. Shall we just get to it?"

Her ruby-painted lips curved seductively. "You are still not one to waste time, I see."

"Why waste time? I'm here on business, *oui*?"

She flicked her gaze to Gabriel, "Yes of course, though there is no harm in some pleasure."

Gabriel did not rise to the bait. Try as she might in years past, she could not snare Gabriel with common innuendos, much to her disappointment.

She resumed gazing at me, smoothing a hand over her copper Veronica Lake hair. "Won't you let me be the good hostess, first? I've planned for your visit."

"If you don't mind, I'd rather speak first, and depending how this goes, perhaps I'll suffer your niceties." I bestowed a sugary smile upon her.

She sighed. "Very well, to the point. Randolph Dumont has found a clause in one of my contracts he can exploit, and if I don't cooperate, he'll do more than exploit it."

I leaned back, crossing my legs. "Your emissary already informed me of this, Elise. Ruin your good name and take away your precious little company by force unless you hand it over quietly. Not much of a choice." I waved a hand. "I'm not an attorney. Perhaps if you'd trust a few, you'd not be in this situation."

She sighed. "Give me one I can trust, perhaps I would."

"That's the least of your problems," I said. "What do you want from me, a recommendation, or for me to throw my weight around?" I leaned forward and spoke again before she could interrupt. "I'm certain it's the latter."

"He doesn't take me seriously," she pouted. "He believes women have no place in business, much like his employer."

Gabriel interjected. "He is not without a point," he baited.

Her eyes narrowed as she looked to him. "I am not a helpless, mindless woman."

"Ah, then I concede the point," he stated simply. "It has nothing to do with your gender."

Her chin lifted as she looked back to me. She'd learned before that verbal sparring with Gabriel could often leave her brain hemorrhaging.

"That's just it," I said. "You're not mindless, and you're certainly not helpless. So let us cut to the chase." I leveled her with my stare. "There is no Randolph. What is it you've asked me here for?"

She feigned surprise. "Of course there's a Randolph. I can put you in touch with him shortly, if you like."

"I'm certain there's someone you know who will say they are this person, and that they will also back up your little story. I say again, helpless you are not, and if this were merely a matter of business, I'd not be here."

She held my gaze a moment in silence. "I don't like being threatened, and he is threatening me. I don't like losing, either. That company is mine."

I laughed. "You're really going to dance with me? I am no idiot, Elise." I had to appear resistant and still somewhat bitter with her, which was an easy task. After all, too nice after these years of ignoring her, why even in her desperation she'd not purchase belief for a penny.

"I will hand it over to him, you buy him out," she stated with a slight toss of her hair.

My laughter grew. "Buy him out, and then give it back to you?"

Her brows made to lift. "Don't be ridiculous. I'll purchase it from you."

I arched one of mine. "Are you certain you could afford to?"

Her hand fluttered to her bosom. "You'd not give me a fair price?"

I had wonder as to why I should, and so should she. "As far as stories go, this is without doubt one of your weakest, Elise."

She did her best to seem as if she were attempting to keep her dignity with her next words. A ruse, though there was some truth to her admission.

"I've been losing a lot of money on everything. Investors are pulling out, particularly as of late, since they heard about Vicont."

"You are not about borrowing money from Michel," Gabriel said.

"No, you're not," I concurred. "Who is it that you want me to threaten, to kill, perhaps?" I leaned farther forward. "Vicont himself, perhaps, so that everything reverts to you? Ah, but no no, that can't quite work, as I know his tactics. I'm certain he's added very particular clauses in the event of his premature death by murder. It's a reason he still lives, after all, for there are many who have fantasized about killing him."

She smoothed the line of her skirt. "Fine. I didn't think you'd come if I told you all of it."

"I was given a ridiculous enough premise as it was, yet here I am." I presented her with a winning smile. "I've come all this way to see an old friend, for we were, we were such good friends, so for me, come clean, hmm? My mood should improve exponentially if you do."

She studied my eyes carefully before proceeding. I must have learned a bit about acting from Gabriel after all, for she capitulated, and with a smile hinting at more than a little slyness.

"Very well, but first, since we're coming clean, I have a question. Is it true you hold a piece of Vicont's heart?" Her eyes flicked between Gabriel and me.

"He likes to say that I do, but he and lies are longtime bedfellows," I replied. "He doesn't know the meaning of love."

She let go with a sound of exasperation. "You know that's not what I mean."

"Is this the rumor of late?" I inquired.

Her gaze drifted to Gabriel as she spoke. "They say a pound of flesh, placed in a chest…" her gaze snapped to me. "You have the upper hand, now."

"If I do, this has what to do with you?" I asked.

"If I had it, I would have the leverage to negotiate with him."

I felt my brow arch more sharply. "As if he will give an inch when it comes to business, particularly to you, after the falling out you had."

Her brows rose. "You know about that."

"Yes. He was quite happy to inform me of it," I stated with little enthusiasm.

"Of course," she whispered. "Yes of course." The volume of her voice returned. "You of all understand, you see? It's why I asked you to come."

"What are you after, Elise?"

"You have means to threaten him. I'm willing to purchase it," she said somewhat excitably.

I glanced at Gabriel. "Do we, *mon amour*?"

"I am at a loss as to what she could be referring to," he replied.

"Ooh!" Fluidly, she rose. "I know you have it. Name your price."

I leaned back as I spoke, bored with it all. "Even were I in possession of such a thing, I thought you were going broke."

"There are other things I can do to sweeten the deal."

"What could you possibly have that I'd want?"

146

"Art, homes, slaves, name it."

Gabriel let go with a snort. "Slaves. Have we not evolved?"

She remained focused on me. "Information."

I waved a hand, certain she had no information that made a difference to me, for it would not be the information I was seeking.

"Your price for the piece, name it!" Her arms folded across her ample bosom.

"Such a petulant child," Gabriel remarked.

"The piece?" I spread my hands. "Are we speaking art again?"

"If you won't give me the leverage, then go in my behalf, I beg you." She moved to me and dropped into a near kneel, eyes searching my face. "Please, Michel. I despise him, and I know I should have taken care of it years ago, but you know how impossible he is."

I nearly gave off my own snort. "Prostrating yourself at my feet will not get you far, for I know how impossible *you* can be."

She pushed her lips into a pout. "You're still angry with me."

I feigned ignorant surprise, my fingertips fluttering to my chest. "*Moi*? Still angry? I can't think *why*."

Her delicate hands balled into loose fists. "I apologized over and over, but you would have none of it. I didn't mean for it to turn out that way."

"You never mean anything, now do you?" I countered.

Her chin dipped and her fingers laced through each other there on her knees. "I've regretted it for years, Michel. I always cared for you and now you hate me, not that I can blame you."

"I should say not," Gabriel offered.

She lifted that utterly feminine face, the face of a *femme fatale*, her large eyes finding mine, more sincerity there than I had seen in decades, perhaps.

"I thought perhaps you coming meant…" she paused and started over. "There are things I never got to tell you about—"

"I'm not interested in the past right now, Elise. We're discussing business, remember?"

She drew a slow breath, and then one more.

"Someone is making threats on Vicont's behalf, Michel." Her hand drifted to her neck. "He threatened to have Omar killed."

Her words struck a chord in me, for they tasted of truth, and I knew what such threats could do to one's heart.

"Why didn't you send word of this to begin with?"

Her gaze wavered. It then fell. "I wanted you here, looking me in the eyes, so you'd believe me when I said it. I truly didn't think you'd come if Vicont was mentioned directly. Honestly, I'm surprised that you're here now."

I closed my eyes, taking a breath. "I've been a bit bitter, you might say." I opened my eyes and reached out, touching her hair. "Bitter and angry, yes."

I would play the game; I came here to play the game.

Slowly, she lifted her gaze to meet mine once again. "You've not forgiven me," she chanced a quick glance to Gabriel, "nor has he, but…" She grasped my hand. "As long as Vicont lives, I'll not feel secure. I'll always worry. I don't even care about the companies anymore, Michel, not really. I just need these ties severed, and I need some assurance he won't carry out his threat. I realize nothing short of death truly ensures this."

My hand, reflexively it tightened. I had no wish to voice the thought; the truth was I still hadn't been able to bring myself to end Vicont's life.

Upon looking into her eyes, I understood that I had no need of voicing it.

"Elise, killing him will only anger others even more." This, it was just as true.

"Then I say again, perhaps some sort of bargain can be struck," she said. "On my behalf, would you do this? Will you try? I have no one else to turn to in this."

"He is not known for keeping his word."

"I know this well, but if there's a chance..." her eyes did the pleading.

I gazed and gazed at her, all the while feeling Gabriel's thinning patience crackling along the edges of my nerves.

"Allow me to think on it," I quietly said.

The green in her eyes brightened. "It's more than I could have hoped you would offer." She rose, pressing her palms together. "Please, stay as my guest a time. I promise, no pushing, only allow me to make some manner of remunerations for the past, however insignificant they may be to you in the end."

To Gabriel most of all, she meant.

I could feel the weight of his stare when I made my reply to her. "We accept, and I shall give you my answer before we leave."

She clapped her hands as if in call for servants. "Wonderful."

The humans that filtered into the room were not servants, at least, not in the traditional sense.

They were there to serve dinner, however. It was then I felt Gabriel's disgust. It was not that he was disgusted with the idea of willing donors, it was that some of them sensed as being less than willing. Even that would not always have mattered, but it was Elise doing the offering, after all.

When all was said and done, he preferred taking his own prey on his own terms in any event, willing or no...as did I.

I gestured in the group's direction. "Elise, there's no need to enrapture on our behalf. Let the unwilling go."

She gave off the vibe of one stunned and confused. "Well, you don't have to kill them."

"Of course not, but at least two of them don't find the idea of being bitten the slightest bit appealing, I can sense it through your flimsy hold on them. Send them off with no memory if it, like a good girl, if you please."

She gave a toss of her hair, whilst I could not help but grin. She had never enjoyed my referring to her as a good girl in that particular tone of voice. Desperate for my agreement to her proposal, however, she did as I asked.

While she busied herself with this, I met Gabriel's stare.

We are staying because she capitulated so easily, there must be more to it; I passed to him in thought. *We did not suffer coming here only to leave with less than we brought, mm? I must have more information on their companies.*

Yes of course, my love, we do have a plan to execute. However, I needs must walk; it has been ten minutes too long already; he passed back, retreating from my mind and rising.

I watched him move toward Kar, nod, and then move past him, leaving the room completely.

Leaving me to it, for now.

I sighed as my eyes travelled back to Elise. She turned, offering me her best hostess smile.

"There. Now would you care for some *hors d'oeuvres*?" Her eyes jumped to Gabriel's retreating form and back to me. "He's leaving?"

"Come now. Are you surprised that he opts to walk rather than sit here?"

She rubbed her arms as if chilled. "I shouldn't be, no."

"Those are the truest words you've spoken thus far this evening."

Her chin rose.

I rose and took a step toward her. "If you tell me the lot of it, I'll be ever more inclined to help you." I took another step. "Many years have passed now." Yet another. "I did care for you, woman. I simply cannot abide more subterfuge." Two more and I could have touched her.

She gazed up into my eyes. "No, I don't want to lie to you again." With a snap of her fingers, a non-human servant appeared, whisking away the remainder of the humans. "Now we can speak."

PARIS

Trey

"Dude, what a cool day," Scott said as we entered the apartment.

"That's the third time you've said that." I grinned, closing the door. "Glad you had such a good time."

He made his way to the first sofa and plopped down happily. "Are you kidding? That's some of the coolest shit I've ever seen, and it was nothing compared to the real depths, you said."

I plopped down beside him. "I saved some pictures I got online. I'll have to show you."

"Did I ever show you the ones Nadar took in 1861?" he asked.

"I don't think so – who's Nadar? You can't possibly mean Ralph."

"Heh, no, not that one. This Nadar was one of the first guys to use artificial light in photography, down in the catacombs. He's the first to take aerial photographs, too. When you were working, I went to his grave in Père Lachaise."

"This sounds like something you told me a few years ago, but I didn't recall that name."

"Maybe I said his real name, Gaspard-Félix Tournachon."

"Ah, that rings a bell."

"No surprise. You remember the complicated handle. Anyway, I don't know the location of all the underground shots, but one had a pile of bones in it. It'd be cool to follow his footsteps."

"That's probably on the official tour, a pile of bones. As I understand it, there aren't really that many bones in the rest of the system."

"Oh. Think it'll be open tomorrow?"

"I don't know. I guess they don't always keep set hours. It's been closed for months at a time, before. But we'll get you in there sometime."

He kicked his feet up on the coffee table. "Cool."

Geoff did not allow that when he was here. I grinned and kicked mine up, too.

"Dude," Scott said. "Fun as it was, I thought we were busted when we came out of the last place."

"Shit." Chuckle. "You got so paranoid. What, did you think he was some undercover member of catacomb special forces or something?" I gave his shoulder a push. "The look on your face cracked me up."

"Well hey, they might kick me out of Paris or something, never know. Maybe you, too."

"I know and I take that seriously Scott, really. But it was funny. Besides, they'd probably just fine us—the first time, anyway."

"Cool he turned out to be one of those cataphiles. How about that?"

"Serendipitous," I agreed. "I'm not sure I could hang with him in some of the places he talked about, though."

"Some of it sounded treacherous, yeah. But I'd give anything to photograph it, at the same time. Maybe."

"Reminds me. He said he had his own photos online, remember?"

"Oh yeah. What was the site?"

I dug into a pocket, fished out the paper. "He wrote it down with his email."

"Awesome. I'll check it out. Kinda surprised they do websites, though."

I shrugged. "They don't list the exact locations, generally. I don't know if the police here really comb the internet trying to catch them, either. If we talk to that guy again, I'll have to ask."

Scott nodded and leaned his head back. "That one room, it gave me the chills."

I knew which one he meant, I was sure I did, because that room with its arching bricks was pulsing with ghostly activity. I'd felt the fingers up my spine, literally. I'd heard the loud whisperings, and it took me more than a moment of down-dialing. I'd been practicing, though, and I managed it. Scott merely thought I was getting the same creep vibes as him.

Well, I was, just on a much grander scale, though I realized I was starting to get more used to it.

It was intense just being underground, whether far in or not, especially knowing the history of the place.

At first it seemed like all sound was absorbed, but when you stood still, when you were quiet, the beat of your own heart seemed to echo.

The juxtaposition of carefully placed blocks with free form tunneling, all its bumps, grooves and curves, was a natural wonder all its own, too.

I thought of Algeria more than once while we were down there. The mountain, the fortress inside the mountain. All things considered, I'd not seen much, but it had to be a mini-fortress at the very least, I figured.

But back to the Paris underground.

Even though the official tour housed most of the bones in the catacombs, that didn't mean all the spirits attached to them had moved there, too. The absence of bones in other places didn't clear away the psychic energy, the residuals of those who utilized the underground network of arteries. Not all the bones from the cemeteries and arteries of the catacombs had made it to that one spot, not *quite*.

They say that the Resistance and the Nazis passed each other without knowledge during the war, so complex were the catacombs, so huge.

Yeah, well I'm here to tell you, there was still a run in or ten.

I realized Scott was gazing at me, probably wondering where I'd gone in my head.

"I should take Geoff to the second place we went," I said to him.

"It was like being in a different kind of cathedral or something, know what I mean?"

Nod from me. Slow smile from me. "Sex in an underground 'cathedral.' I like it."

Scott laughed and gave my knee a slap. "Such a one track mind."

"I'm making up for lost time, that sort of thing. And he's, you know, pretty. I can't help myself."

He held up his hands. "I'm not criticizing, no, not me." He nudged me. "Say, is Polly interested in the catacombs?"

Another slow smile. "She's the one who told me about that tunnel."

"Wicked. Maybe she'd like to go spelunking with me."

"That always did sound nasty, you know it?"

"Are you kidding? Isn't that what sex is, spelunking?" Another nudge from him.

"Heh. It's one of the things sex is."

Chapter Twelve

JULY 30

"Now just close your eyes and relax."

I did what P.K. said as we sat there crossed legged, facing each other, knees touching.

"You're so connected already; what we need here is to help you master your control," she said.

"Okay," I said after another slow breath.

"*And*, for you to stop resisting the other side. It's part of your very nature."

"Papa will guide me, right?"

"Yes, if you pay attention. You're not consciously resisting help so much anymore, but subconsciously you are, which is understandable."

"In self defense."

"Pretty much, yes. It's so foreign right now, that instinct sends danger signals and you self protect. Eventually you'll know on every level that it really is part of your nature, just like I said – this Mark, this destiny."

Breathe in, breathe out. The scent of frankincense and the low, soothing melody she created with her words were nearly entrancing me.

Earlier we'd gone to Montmartre cemetery, found a quiet spot (not so difficult to do, actually) near a cherubic statue, and burned the bracelets. The ceremony wasn't complicated; we didn't need a bunch of tools or anything else I'd imagined.

Mostly it was a matter of me releasing the bracelets' hold on me. Releasing the negativity, and replacing it with positive energy, or at least making the space for it.

Sounds simple, anyway. Well, it's not so simple, this mind over matter, but if you have someone with you that knows exactly what to say, how to say it and how to walk you through a visualization until you literally see it, it's not impossible.

I actually felt the weight leave me at the time.

"See the Roads, Trey." Her voice lulled me further. "See the trees, the moss. Can you smell it?"

"Yes." I did. And I saw the sudden clearing, the roads in the center, edged by dark sentinels of the natural variety, some darker than the night itself, but I knew they were there. Hardwoods, a cypress or three, maybe, and I could smell the pungent water in the air.

I could also see the old black man with white hair standing where the roads crossed.

"Dis you," he said, lining a circle around himself in the dirt with his twisted cane, looking to pivot in place on one foot.

"Me?"

Wizened brown-black eyes latched onto mine, pulling me in. "You da place between. Da balance."

I thought carefully before opening my mouth again. P.K. had said asking the right questions meant getting the right answers.

"It's true then? Souls pass through me?"

"Yes'm."

"Will I always feel," I shook my head, "no, wait. I don't

156

always feel it, I know I don't. So many die in a day. Why don't I feel it?"

"Some is distant, only a breeze you give no notice."

That was fine by me.

"Okay." What else did I most need to know right now to help me understand this? "Not everyone practices, or even believes in this... this path. Do others go somewhere else?"

He smiled. "In a way o'speakin'. Dey sees what dey knows, like you see what you know."

I felt the knitting of my brows. "But I didn't really know this before. I didn't believe in things like this, not really. I've never been religious."

A patient and amused look was in those depths he had for eyes, even a laugh. "Yous born to it. Even so, you believe in dere some where's afore dis. Nevah did ya disrespect it in you heart."

I contemplated that, then only said, "Fair enough."

He made a sweeping gesture with his cane. "Dis be your domain."

"What's my purpose?"

"A man, he may have more den one."

I gazed at him for a moment.

"What does it mean for me to be marked? Do I have a specific task?" I asked.

"Be da balance."

I felt myself frown. "Just be the balance. Somehow I think it's harder than it sounds."

"Easy can be made hard, if you makes it hard."

I decided not to make a stupid, probably wish-I-hadn't-made-it, remark.

No disrespecting Papa, nope I wasn't going there.

"Yous da path. Da way between."

"The way between..."

"All be clear soon," he said and started walking away.

"Papa?" Questions, questions he will answer, let's see. "Am I the only one?"

"No. But dere are few who dance with death da same as you, in da world."

Dance with death. "Do I...judge?"

"Not da way you mean." He kept walking.

"Please, wait." Quick, next question, Trey. "I'm the path...do I help them move on?"

I saw him nod. "Yous learnin'." He kept walking. "You da Roads."

"I'm totally in charge?"

"Yous da way. I guard da way." Pausing, he looked back at me.

"How do I send them on?"

"Each different, chile. Each different. You know soon."

I contemplated a second. "I'll have to learn as I go...each person."

He gave me a smile. "Each dat need you." With that, he started walking again.

And then I was looking into a different set of brown eyes. Lighter, but with their own wisdom.

She smiled. "It's fascinating how your eyes literally change color when you're channeling."

Blink. "I was channeling?"

She nodded. "Papa said a few words to me. He didn't *completely* take you over, so I opted to say channeling. I think the word 'ridden' still startles you, anyway. The idea of it."

Uh, yeah. Just a little.

"Oh...I didn't...I thought it was just him and me," I said.

"He had a separate message for me."

"What did he say?"

Her lashes dropped and lifted with her smile. "That it's good I found you when I did so I could help guide you."

I felt myself smile. "He gave you his blessing."

"Yes."

"Well, I'm glad you found me, too."

She smiled wider. "Right place, right time, all for a reason."

I smiled wider. "So fate's not always a cruel bitch."

Her laugh caressed the air. "Nope." Her hand then caressed my cheek. "And you know, most of the time she doesn't give us more than we can handle."

I placed my hand over hers. "No?"

"You're still here, aren't you? And stronger for it."

I knew she didn't just mean Paris.

"Yeah. I'm still here."

"So," she lowered her hand, "did you find some more answers?"

I couldn't help the wry laugh. "Yes and no. As far as my purpose, mostly he said to be the balance."

"Everything must be balanced, Trey. Everything has its opposite."

I spread my hands. "That's deceptively simple sounding, and I can't be the balance and the opposite at the same time."

"You're the very between."

"Why do I get the feeling this is one of those things I'm supposed take at face value and just go, oh, okay, I'll just…go with the flow."

She laughed somewhat. "Some things are what they are." She took both of my hands. "A necessary thing in the universe, like a stillborn child beyond the veil mirrors the live birth on this side, and so it goes."

I just studied her face, not certain what to say.

"Papa opens the way for the living to reach the dead, and you open the way for the dead to reach the living."

"But—it's not truly opposite; you could just as well say that the other way around."

"Exactly."

I fell back on the floor, laughing. "Fine, fine. Guess I'll just *be*, for now."

"That could work," she half quipped.

"Some guide you are," I teased.

"I've got to admit, you've taken me out of my realm a bit.

I've never met anyone claimed in the womb by Papa, before."

I sat up. "Ah, you're doing great. You're sounding less cryptic to me, while Papa's sounding more and more cryptic."

"You just have to learn his language," she said.

"He said all would be clear soon." Slight shrug. "Guess it's a learn through experience thing."

"So many things are, Trey."

"He did say—well actually he just nodded and said I was learning when I asked if I help the dead move on. I asked how and he said each was different."

"The Dead are just as individual as the living," she said.

"Kinda noticed that, thanks."

The door opened before that went any further.

"Hey, guys," followed Scott's voice soon after, and he made his way to us in the living room. "Smells kind of good in here."

I sat up as P.K. turned her head to shine a smile up at him. "Well hello there, cutie."

He gestured to himself. "Cutie? What am I, eight?"

"I've wondered that more than once since I've known you," I cut in.

"Hey," he pointed at me. "No one was asking you." Humor danced in his eyes.

P.K. stood up, facing him fully. "Now, I know you men prefer handsome, or hot, or stud, or some such over cute, but I happen to like cute. Is this a problem?"

Before he could reply, I butted in again. "Face it, Scott, you ain't getting past cute with that baby face. You're done maturing."

He stuck his tongue out at me, proving my point, then said to her, "I don't have a problem with your liking cute, not at all."

She tipped him a grin and put her hands on her hips. "I'd imagine not, because what most cute men don't admit, is that they know damned well many women fall for that cute thing, so they work it hard."

I burst out laughing, while Scott just looked at her a second.

"Damn. I should have thought of that years ago," he deadpanned. "I hope you don't mind cute but not too bright."

P.K.'s head tilted with her next words. "Hmm. I'll have to explore your education before I come to a decision. There could be a stud lurking under all that cuteness, after all."

"Sounds fair. It's better to have an informed decision, after all," he said, giving her one of his best smiles.

He really does have a great smile.

I looked at him, then her. "Just remember, all the best lines, he learned from me."

They both looked at me then, and P.K. said, "Did you teach him anything else that's useful?"

Scott held up his hands. "I didn't need any help from him, thank you."

"So he says. He learned a few things with his ear pressed to the wall," I said.

"Yeah," he said "Like how to make sure they lose your phone number on purpose."

P.K. held up both hands. "You two were sent to different homes at one time, weren't you?"

"I ran away," I said. "He wouldn't stop wetting the bed, and we had to share. That was the last straw."

"Thank God he did, because if I'd've had to watch him pick his nose and eat it one more time, I was gonna snap," he volleyed.

She looked between us. "I must be insane, agreeing to hang out with both of you today." She threw us both a smile. "As I never claimed to be fully sane, it all works out."

I shrugged. "That's how it is in Trey-land. Leave your sanity at the door."

Scott laughed; meanwhile P.K. and I shared a more meaningful gaze at the reference.

"So are you guys done with your meditation or whatever?" He looked between us.

That's what I'd told him, that P.K. was into meditation and

I was giving it a go. Hey, it was true enough.

"I think I've had enough ohhhm for today. I'll just grab some shoes." I stood. "Let's paint the town."

"Red or pink, girly-man?" said Scott.

"Plum red," P.K. said. "He's more a plum red kind of guy."

****

We strolled through the Jardin du Luxembourg, first, or *Luco*. It used to be the private garden of the Palais du Luxembourg, but was now the largest public park in Paris.

I loved the central octagonal pond as much as the locals, and the puppet theater, too. (Punch and Judy, still going strong.)

Scott had to take photographs of that, as well as some of the statues in the park, especially the first model of the Statue of Liberty. He then insisted on photos of the famous fountains, like the *Fontaine de Medicis*. Couldn't blame him, they're gorgeous.

Having an interest in certain histories, I told Scott as we were leaving the park, that it was where Michel Ney had found death by firing squad, for treason. He'd joined up with Napoléon in 1815.

Obviously that didn't fly. Scott thought it was cool.

We had to hit up the Musée Maillol, then, because it housed a large collection of modern art, including Rodin.

Scott loves Rodin.

Finally, deciding all this touristy stuff was working up our appetites, we managed to snag a table at the popular café Conti in Saint-Germain's bohemian neighborhood.

And here on the terrace is where we sat now. It'd been a great day overall, I was thinking, while the two of them talked about Scott's mother. My two friends had hit it off well, and the conversation had flowed all day, from mine and Scott's college days and clubbing nights, to her run ins with cops in Alabama.

It might've had something to do with green plants, but I'm not saying anything else.

She'd handled our juvenile bullshit with great aplomb, too. It was kinda Three Musketeer-ish there for a while. Very cool.

My attention was brought more fully to the here and now, when P.K. brought up the first words I'd said to Scott. I had to shake my head and smile. Should have known she'd ask him about that. He was nodding and confirming what I said, laughing, but when she asked him what it was he liked about me back then, the laughing stopped, and what he said, well...

It really touched me.

"What I liked about Trey?" He glanced at me, then directed his gaze at her. "He was like James Dean in a way. He was direct, honest, and he seemed like a caring person. He was loyal, had integrity, but he also had a wild side that I lived vicariously through." He took a longer breath, his gaze steady. "I thought he was funny and beautiful. Seemed like all the girls wanted him," he almost laughed, "and lots of the guys." He shrugged. "He was just so *real*."

P.K. beamed a smile at him, and then turned it on me. Scott looked at me, too. I gazed back at him, thinking I should say something, but he wasn't finished.

"All the things I liked then, well, I think he's the same now. I wasn't sure what I'd see if I ran into him again. A shadow of his former self? I couldn't stand the idea. But I when saw him again, it was like, forty-foot screen in Technicolor for the first time after only black and white." He put a hand on my shoulder.

My lashes dropped. "Damn, Scott." I reached up, placing my hand over his. A very different thought sped through my mind. I shoved it aside, not wanting to taint the moment.

I lifted my eyes, and very sincerely said, "I love you, man."

He gave my shoulder a little squeeze before letting go. "Ditto."

"I could just eat you up," P.K. said to Scott. "What a

perfect, wonderfully detailed answer." She flashed him another bright smile. "I'm so glad you found each other again."

He smiled back. "So am I, but can we get back to this eating me up thing?"

Chuckle from me, sultry grin from P.K. "Trey has definitely rubbed off on you. Not that I mind." She offered him a wink.

"Hey, why don't you guys go on ahead, do something without me being third wheel," I suggested.

They both protested, saying I certainly wasn't a third wheel.

"No, no," I waved them off. "You two go bond some more without me." I got up.

They looked at each other. "Well," said Scott. "He's offering."

She nodded. "He sure is."

"Better take him up on it before he changes his mind," from Scott.

From P.K., "You never know when these offers will expire." They both looked at me.

"Good, it's settled." I gave 'em a small wave. "See ya later," grin, "maybe. Break him in slow, P.K." That prompted a good laugh from her.

"Dude, seriously, are you sure?" Scott asked. "I mean, I want to spend time with you, too."

I gave him a nod. "I know. But it's not like I won't see you later, right?"

"Of course you will," he said.

"So have some fun, and I'll see you later."

He smiled. "Okay, cool."

I turned and strolled away, deciding I'd walk and enjoy the night air.

I meandered along rue de Buci and cut over to rue Dauphine, heading toward Pont Neuf. I had a nice, warm feeling in my chest, all because of Scott.

Even if I didn't think I was as wonderful as he said. At least not for a while, now, and he was better off not living vicariously through me. Hell, I should've been more like him, some of the time.

These thoughts were a reason I decided to make my exit. I didn't want, inadvertently, to start giving off the wrong vibes. Even if Scott didn't pick them up, P.K. would, and I wasn't out for sympathy, or a reminder that I was not the sum of my issues.

Damn. I wasn't always this pathetic.

Anyway. I was betting Scott might get freaky tonight, and what are best friends for, if not for getting out of way of that? This also meant I could pump him for details, later. (How cool am I? He shows up, I set him up, and bam. I was always an excellent wingman.) Hey, if he can live vicariously through me, it's only fair I get a turn.

My darker thoughts weren't holding me too hard and fast when I started listing all the positives in my head. I had myself a sweet Spanish boy that loved me and I—yeah I loved him. I just needed to get over the fear of saying it, as if it would jinx things when I did.

Enough of that nonsense.

I had cool bosses—relations—and they were groovy vampires that cared enough to assign a bodyguard to me.

Yeah, I was feeling all right with my world even *though* I had a bodyguard, but hey, better than not having one, yeah?

Right. How many people can say that? Okay, a few, but how many regular-but-totally-hip guys like me can say they have bodyguards.

Count. I'll wait, 'cause it won't take long.

So I started feeling chipper again – that is, until the old fart popped into my head.

Bein' stalked by dat weird-talkin' mass o' muscle.

"Yeah, I know. Thanks for the news flash. And look who's calling who weird-talking."

How many o' dem bloodsuckers you plannin' on gettin' friendly wid, anyways?

"None of your business. Besides, I thought it was okay with you guys over there."

Din mean yous got to be dat damn close. When you get so perverted, boy?

"Look who's calling who perverted, mister peeping disembodied. Mister let's talk about oil and P.K. in my head in the middle of something a lot more important." Shudder.

Disem wha?

I noticed a guy and his girl looking at me as they walked by, laughing. Sure, 'cause for all they knew I *was* talking to myself.

"You, you're the disem wha," I said under my breath. "Even *I* wouldn't be trying to score through someone else's body, you dirty old man."

You try bein' dead a while, see how you likes it.

"Well…" Was I really thinking he had a point? "So find yourself another nice disembodied over there."

Been tryin'. Ain't quite da same, tho'.

I so did not want to know. "Gee, with that sparkling personality and handsome face of yours, I can't imagine why you aren't getting lucky."

No respect.

"If you'd stop barging in like this, maybe I'd be nicer."

Fine, doan wan' my help, jus' say so.

"You're helping me with what, right now?"

Nuthin'.

"Exactly. Now go away, mmmkay?"

Yous my grandson. Mebbe I jus' wan' talk.

Eye roll. "How sweet. Maybe later, okay?"

No respect.

"Try knocking next time; I might be more receptive." I stopped, spreading my hands. "Just because I've invited you lately, you know, trying to get you to say something *useful*, that's not an invitation to pester me whenever you feel like it."

Is it?

No. I'm supposed to be in charge, right?

I reckon not.

"Finally, we agree. So anyway, it's been nice. I'll give you a call sometime."

Silence. I waited a little longer, just in case.

More silence.

"Well how about that?" I smiled to myself and started walking again. I hadn't gone far when someone fell into pace beside me.

"Hey, mate. I was wondering when you were going to show yourself." I looked at Travis, and he gave me a smile.

"Just like Michel said, you're sensitive. It's definitely a good thing I told you up front I'd be around," he said.

I shrugged a little. "I can't really take credit for knowing you were there."

"I don't follow."

I looked at him again. "I had some help."

He just lifted his brows.

I stopped. He stopped. I faced him. "You said you could trust me. I'm sure I can trust you too, so here's the deal." I paused, considering. "Of course, you may already know a lot about me."

"Michel's told me several things about you, yes. Whether or not it's what you're about to tell me, well I can't say, unless you tell me." He broke into a smile that I returned.

"Flawless logic, yeah. First I want to say that I don't mind about him telling you things."

His smile grew. "They're all good, like I said before."

I laughed. "Still nice to know." I nodded. "Okay, so, my dead grandfather told me you were following me."

He didn't bat a single lash. "I knew you could speak to the dead. It's the dead that helped you with Vicont."

"Oh right. You said that Michel told me about it. I didn't know exactly *what* he told you, so. Well, now I know." I could laugh now that I had distance. "It was wild, all that with Vicont."

"It sounded like quite the display. Michel wishes he could have seen it."

"You'll understand if I say I hope he doesn't get another chance at seeing it, right?"

"Abso-bloody-lutely. He said the same thing."

"Good that we're on the same page. Anyway, Lucien, that's my grandfather, it wasn't like he was telling me anything I didn't already figure." I leaned in. "Apparently he's just bored."

Travis laughed and placed his hand on my shoulder. "I'm getting a vibe from you that suggests you'd rather he'd find something better to do."

I shrugged. "Oh, he's not so bad. He just doesn't seem to understand that my head isn't some swinging door he can walk through when he feels like it."

"This gives whole new meaning to the term dropping by."

I started nodding, laughing with him. "Shore 'nuff." After the laughter trailed off. "You don't think it's weird, huh?"

He studied me. "What, your connection to this other side?" He shook his head. "No. Why should I think it's weird? There's stranger things in the world, mate. I'm one of them." He winked.

"When you put it that way…" I grinned. "I don't think you're so strange, though."

"And that's one of the reasons we like ya." He winked again. "However, if you insist on wandering about in caves and tunnels, I might need to hurt you myself."

Blink.

Um.

Oh. "So you found out about the catacombs. Hey, I didn't go that far."

"I'm just giving you shit, mate."

"Yeah?" I considered. "But you're right. I don't suppose that makes it easier to keep me safe at all." I glanced at him. "But you can't come out in the daytime, right?"

"Not full light, no, but I have back up, so no worries. I don't expect you to stay locked up, after all."

"Back up?"

He smiled a bit. "Yes. I have back up."

My brows lifted. "So there are humans watching me, too?"

"Indeed there are."

"They must be good. I hadn't noticed."

He arched a brow, his tone was flat. "Do I strike you as the sort that would employ anyone less than stellar?"

Contrite. "Um, no."

He broke into laughter.

"Shit. I need to learn when you're taking the piss out of me. You're too good an actor."

"At least you're getting better with the slang. That's something, even though I wasn't close to really taking the piss out of ya." He arched a brow. "I heard you were likely rather worldly, though." The wink was in his eyes.

"I've been dealing with serious business and lawyers for a few years." Head shake. "Still, you'd think I'd get it. Scott and I give each other crap all the time. Not exactly the way you do, but still."

He gestured for us to start walking. "I'm better at it, but take heart. It's not your fault that you weren't born Australian."

I tossed him a glance. "I'm working on it, and you've got to admit I'm pretty good for an American, yeah?"

"I'll give you that."

"There's no hope for Scott, though. He's never been good at it, and it wouldn't matter if he *had* been born in Australia. He'd still be hopeless."

Travis was still laughing as he reached into his pocket, pulled out an iPhone, and put it to his ear.

Short conversation. Not that I was trying to eavesdrop, I swear. But he was right there, after all.

He slipped it back into his pocket and said, "Feel like taking a ride? I need to go to the Fall Out for a bit."

"Sure. Um, Geoff's safe, right?"

"Extra eyes. Besides, I can see him when I need." He tapped his temple.

"Huh. Another nifty trick."

"Handy one at that," he said as we detoured. "I'm parked this way."

"Hey," I said as we reached his car, having, I thought, an epiphany. "Scott and I ran into a guy who said his name was Marc when we were coming out of a tunnel, and he just *happened* to be a cataphile. He's your back up, isn't he? One of them, at least."

Travis merely smiled and unlocked the passenger door for me.

****

We pulled up to the side of the building and down a private drive. Well, more a hidden path that was just wide enough for the Mustang.

A 1965 fastback, oh yes. Rich blue with a black hood, or bonnet, as Travis would say. Black leather interior and tinted windows, and does this baby *purr*.

On the way, he'd told me that he just wanted to check up on the club, see how things were going without him there. That was when he told me he was head of security at the Fall Out, amongst other things.

After that, however, he got to talking about his car, then his motorcycles, and let me tell you, this vamp loves motorcycles and muscle cars.

It was definitely an education.

"You can wait here if you like; I won't be long," he said.

But I was still curious about other things and replied, "I've only been here once. I wouldn't mind getting another look. The last time I was here, I didn't exactly get to enjoy it."

He gave me an even look. "I heard about that. Don't worry, we've tightened security since then and reinforced some old rules, as well as made some new ones, since Michel restated his position."

"Hey, I've got my own personal bodyguard this time around. I'm not worried."

He tossed me a grin.

"So you work here sometimes, too?" I asked him.

"Often."

"Doesn't surprise me. I don't remember seeing you that night, but that doesn't mean you weren't here."

"I wasn't here," he said. "I'd've been in the fray if I'd been here. They never would have touched you."

I gave him a smile. "So...just how much have you been watching me, by the way? Without my knowledge, that is."

"Since Michel took an interest in you, really."

"Why?"

He shrugged. "Whenever he's interested, I get interested. Partially because I can't help wanting to be certain I have his back, just in case, and partially because he's met some cool people over the years, so when he speaks of someone several times, I pay extra attention."

"Have his back. You're very loyal to him. I was about to say you don't need to worry about humans, but then I remembered torch-bearing mobs and all that."

His grin was wry, and he nodded.

"So you've been around, which makes sense, since you're also his son, basically. But what about the rest of the Guards?"

"Some scattered when Michel stepped away from his position, but a lot stayed close, too. They like him, respect him, and wanted to be around even if he never took up the mantle again." He reached for his door handle. "It hasn't been difficult, then, to reassemble them, and word's gone out to our travelling brothers. A few have already returned, and I'm feeling fairly confident that the rest will, eventually."

"Just how many are in this, uh, army of his?"

"Oh," he gave me level look, "enough, mate. Enough." He got out of the car.

I nodded to myself and got out of my side, catching up to

him as he strode toward the building.

"You stuck around for however long Michel wasn't in charge, right?" I asked.

"I took some side trips, but mostly, yes."

"So tell me, did you watch Geoff from the beginning too, then? Did Michel talk about him early on?"

His smile, soft. "Yes, he did. Gabriel even mentioned him early on, which really made me sit up and take notice. It's rare for Gabriel to do that." We made our way around to the entrance.

"Michel told me how he is, yeah."

He reached for the door and opened it to let me through first. "The times I spied Geoff, I could see why they paid him attention—and he stirred some memories for me."

Before I could ask, he closed the subject by moving on.

"Any road, you know you were also a special case, since Gabriel spoke of you as well."

I gave him a sideways look as he drew up to me, letting my first question die. There was a reason he'd moved past his earlier statement, and I wasn't going to push. "Gabriel—do you know that we're..."

"Related? Yes." He lifted a hand and squeezed my shoulder. "It's fantastic, him finding you. He's very happy about it."

I felt my own smile break free with that, and then lost myself in looking at the, well, doorman I supposed. There hadn't been one the last time I was here.

I wasn't one to assume, but as I looked him over, I couldn't help thinking he seemed the least likely person to intimidate anyone trying to force their way through.

I was looking at a very young man with straight, long, pale hair to go with his pale skin. He was maybe 5'10" and willowy. Downright fairy-like, that's what came to mind with his delicate features and violet eyes.

Of course, the violet eyes and skin coloring alone told me he might be a vampire, so surely he could handle acting as a bouncer, or whatever.

Just, damn. Talk about fragile beauty.

"Hi," he said to Travis, and even his voice made me think of fairies, elves. They gave each other a hug. When the young man (barely a man, at least to my eyes, but who knows with vamps?) took a step back, I noticed his shirt, and I grinned. It said *Satis-FUCK-tion* in chromed gold and silver letters, spaced out vertically, on the black.

He greeted me and I smiled more. "Hi. I like that shirt," I said.

"Oh, thanks. I can tell you where to get one. They have other cool ones, too. Fam'House, that's the designer." He gave me a bright smile, pointing to where it did indeed say Fam'House in smaller letters at the bottom. "I'm Shane, you must be Trey, we heard about you from Michel."

I couldn't refrain from laughing. He talked faster than Geoff did at his most exuberant. "Great to meet you, Shane, and I might check into this Fam'House thing, thanks."

"They're online; you can browse the site. Just Google them and they'll come right up. All the coolest clubbers and DJs wear their stuff!"

I grinned.

"I DJ here sometimes, you know," he swiftly added.

Travis cleared his throat, getting Shane's attention as I stood there thinking *how cute is that*, while having a lot of trouble imagining him putting the smack down on anyone. Maybe he talked them to death.

I mean that in a nice way.

"Dane's inside then, watching the floor?" said Travis to Shane.

Shane nodded at Travis. "Yes, but probably dancing more than watching." He gave Travis a big, big smile. "You know how it is."

Travis planted a kiss on Shane's cheek. "I know how the *both* of you are."

Shane beamed at him and yanked the second door open. Music poured up the stairs, pulsing techno music. He looked at me. "Have fun, and maybe we can hang out sometime; Michel says you're really cool."

I gave him a grin. "Is that so? Well, I can hardly say no to you, so we'll see about hanging out sometime soon."

"Great!"

The door closed behind us and Travis said, "Just wait until you get the two of them together; you'll be racing to keep up. Sometimes I have to tell them to downshift."

"The two of them. You must mean Dane."

"Twins."

Full laugh. "Shane and Dane, of course." I glanced at him. "Is Dane a vampire, too?"

"He certainly is."

"Well, well. Twin vampires… "

Travis' laughed echoed off the walls. "Fantasy of some, no matter what the species, eh?"

"I didn't say a word."

"You didn't have to." He looked at me. "Even I think they're too pretty to be ignored."

"Ahah. Exceptions to the skirt rule?"

He gave a slight shake of his head, followed by a nod.

I nudged him with a shoulder.

"I had a little fun with them once, but it didn't go very far. I'd hurt them anyway, and I can't stand the thought of that," he said.

There he went again, talking about hurting people and distracting me from other questions. "Even though they're vamps?"

"Even though they're vamps." Once we reached the bottom of the stairs, he gave me a square look I could only catch because of the way his eyes stood out in the darkness. "Like I basically said, I'm different." He started walking again, and I followed. He said something else, and it dawned on me that even with the volume of the music, I could hear him.

Nifty trick; he wasn't even in my mind, at least, it didn't seem like it.

"They're too sweet to be hurt that way," he said.

Before I could say anything else, we ran into Shane again.

No, no wait. Dane. Must be Dane. Had to be Dane. Same clothes, but Shane hadn't passed us on the stairs.

Dayum, even between the strobes and red light, I could see they were identical twins, and I mean identical, because when he spoke, he even sounded just like Shane.

"Uncle Travis!" He gave Travis a hug.

Ehem. Uncle?

"Hello, Dane. How are things going lately? Your dad's going to want a report from me."

Dane giggled. "Right, right. It's been great. We've been taking care of everything, don't worry, but still, we miss having you out here."

Travis gave him a charming smile. "I haven't been absent that many nights, you."

"Yeah, but still, we miss you."

"You're a darl. So everything's fine, really?"

Dane nodded and nodded. "We're okay, I promise, and we can handle it."

Travis ran the backs of his fingers over Dane's cheek, which Dane thoroughly enjoyed. "I know I can trust you. Wouldn't have put you charge otherwise."

This pleased Dane even more. Then his eyes shot to me. "Hi! You're Trey, right?"

My reputation was preceding me everywhere, apparently. "Yes, and you're Dane."

"That's me! Are you having fun with Uncle Travis?"

"You could use that word, sure." I lowered my voice, realizing that out of habit I'd done that bar yell thing, which was unnecessary with these two. "I like your Uncle."

"He's the best," Dane said.

"So where's my gift?" Travis asked him.

Dane's eyes shifted to Travis. "In your room."

"Perfect." He kissed Dane's cheek. "Keep Trey company." Travis looked at me. "Back in a quick."

Speaking of quick, I'd finally just caught up on their conversation. I looked at Dane. "Gift?"

His look became coy. "You could use that word, sure."

I had to laugh.

"He won't be gone long; it never takes long."

Brow arch. "That could be a bad thing, depending."

He touched my arm as he laughed. "No, no, not that. That's never short, I hear." He then laughed at what he said. "And neither is that."

Had I really thought, mere seconds ago, that the two of them looked innocent?

My laughter joined his. "Oh, now I know we're going to get along really, really well."

He moved completely into my personal space and spoke into my ear. "He won't let us find out first hand, though." He moved back, a bit of a sly smile on his innocent face.

I wasn't certain I should make the first comment that came to mind, so I said, "He's pretty straight, yeah." Even if the two of you could easily pass for women, I thought.

Dane shook his head. "That's not the only reason and besides, we like girls too, and he'd probably be okay with a girl there, but I should probably shut up." He smiled.

Maybe I could make the comment, or something close to it. "He sort of mentioned, mmm, having problems with restraint."

Dane nodded.

I stood there for a minute, debating. It seemed I'd been accepted into this world, their vampire world, completely, all because Michel had spoken of me. This not only told me they must truly respect his word, think highly of his opinion, but also that I could speak freely amongst them, ask them things. It didn't mean they could answer every question, but I doubted they were this open with someone their Prince hadn't taken under his wing.

"He said something about the beast. Is it so bad?"

Dane's expression smoothed. Maybe I had gone too far. Or maybe he was thinking. He was completely still, Dane. Gabriel looked like a statue when he did that. Dane wasn't far from it.

Then his features animated. "It can be bad, yes. He's very fierce sometimes." He gave me a smile. "But that's okay. He's a sexy beast."

I contemplated him, and rather than ask more, since it felt too much like going behind Travis' back, and Travis had already said he'd tell me some time, I smiled back, and agreed. "He definitely is."

Dane's head snapped to the side, his attention obviously yanked to something on the dance floor. "Uh oh. I think that guy's had too much to drink already." He took off and like liquid, disappeared into the crowd.

Blink.

Too much to drink? Yeah, that could go either way in here.

I looked around, debating a drink myself since he brought it up, eyes landing on the long bar. I headed that way, found a stool to sit on, and ordered a scotch and soda. The bartender got it to me in pretty short order, and I was about to take a drink, when I felt someone's stare boring into me.

I glanced over and found the ugly mug those eyes were set in, and mentally groaned when he moved closer.

"How about a dance?" He smiled. "Or a drink?"

Shudder. The few teeth left in that God-forsaken smile were honed to sharp points.

Okaaay. There *are* ugly vamps, unless he's a wannabe.

"I've already got one, thanks," I whispered.

"But I don't," he replied. "I promise I'm gentle." He smiled wider.

Not a wannabe, I guess, because he heard me. So okay, he has fangs, but for the rest, does he gum people to death?

"I already donated, sorry."

"You seem healthy to me. I'll treat you good, what do you say?"

I say I want to vomit.

I supposed someone somewhere thought he was handsome, but I had to wonder what that person looked like as I stared at him as if I was looking at a train wreck.

Which I was. He had the worst skin I'd ever seen, I mean damn, those are some…pocks, and his face just isn't formed right. Did someone slam him into a brick wall when he was born?

Repeatedly?

Not to mention he should have gone on a diet before he was frozen for eternity. It might have helped a little. I kinda felt sorry for him, actually, being stuck this way.

"I say I'm spoken for."

He leaned close.

Ack, he stinks. Related to a vambie in some way, by any chance?

He inhaled me.

This is Trey, thoroughly disgusted.

He moved back.

I am halfway to rejoicing, but it might be too soon for that.

"Sorry. Don't mention it to your master, okay? Please?" He asked, sincerely worried, it seemed.

I must still smell like *them*. Thank *God*.

"Eh…I won't, if you go away right now. Deal?"

He nodded and said, "Thanks," and proceeded to do just that. Go away.

I am rejoicing.

I couldn't help tracking his retreat (that train wreck thing again), but then my eyes betrayed me and swung around to the black curtains at far end of the bar. The ones I'd run through, trying to get away from those vampires that night.

Had Travis gone through those curtains? I'd ended up in

a room. No, that couldn't be his room, could it? What kind of room would he have here? An office?

The curiosity was gnawing at me. I let my eyes sweep the dance floor. Not seeing Dane now, they moved back to the curtains, and next I knew, I was moving in that direction, yup, feet moving in that direction.

No one said I couldn't go back there.

I had this urge to get a better look at the place I'd run through. An urge to get a look at the place the vamps cornered me, the place Michel saved my ass.

Yes, and still the urge to see where Travis was, what he was doing, even though I hadn't paid attention to which way he'd gone. Should probably stay right where I am, right? Dance, have some fun, sure. Stay out here, wait for Dane.

Whoops. I'm through the curtains, too late now.

Hall, yes I remember the hall. Cold, concrete. Is that the door I went through? It seemed a lot farther down the hall last time, and I was running. Of course, a few vampires with unfriendly intentions chasing you could make any hall seem three times as long.

Shit. There's another path. Now why didn't I see that last time? Maybe I wouldn't have ended up at a dead end with a locked door.

Like it mattered with vampires after your ass, Trey.

I should probably turn around and go back.

Yes'm, you should.

"Who asked you?"

Jus' confirmin' you thoughts.

"I don't need your help on this, thank you. Besides, you realize that now I really want to go that way, just because you said that. You're in my head; you should know better."

Fine den'. I woan tell you ta look out.

"Huh?"

Oh now you wan' listen.

I stopped walking. Yeah, I'd still been walking. Long passage. "Rrrr, fine. What're you on about?"

Best back up, er sumpthin'.
"Back up? Why?"
You gone repeat ev'ting, or do's I say?
"If you'd tell me why—"
Nevah mind, too late.

Something whooshed past, knocking me into the concrete wall and punching the air from my lungs.

I scrambled up, trying to get my bearings, about to run back the way I came.

'Cause okay, Lucien wasn't fucking with me!

But I couldn't.

I froze.

I freeze when I hear stuttering growls.

Freeze when I see little more than blurred shadows as my eyes re-adjust.

"Who sent you?" I hear a growl-laced voice that my body tries to tell my brain—or my brain tries to tell my body—should be familiar.

Hissing.

Snarling, lots of snarling.

What the fuck is that?

Chirping?

Not like any damned bird I ever heard.

Warm wet spray on my face.

"Fuck...me." I start to lift my hand.

And step back.

Well. Sideways.

Flash of claws and two men.

Claws?

Men!?

I step forward.

Fall back, stumble.

I want to look away.

Can't look away.

—*Déjà vu*—

Crunch.

Crackle.

Fuck, this is excessively up close and personal, why don't I just leave?

Gurgle, snarl and slurp and—

Ohhhh what did I just see, give me a second to digest—

Not!

Jesus—

And Christ—

And—

SHIT!

Waiiit, waiiit, give me a moment to—

Whoa, whoa, whoa!

GAH!

Fangs in my face, shit are there four, shit are the bottom ones *hooked* or some—

Shit, pale, pale eyes with slit pupils, oblong slits.

Wait. Wait.

GAH!

Wait!

"T-T-T…"

Pressed against the stone, fuck yeah, that's a solid build, and I don't mean the stone.

Snarl in my face.

Shit. Shit, shit you're supposed to be protecting me, not eating me!

Find some guts—bad word, man.

"T-Travis it's—"

He's dipping his head, oh why do I just KNOW it won't feel good if he bites me right now?

Cool breeze.

Peek.

Open the other eye, Trey.

He backed up, I see.

Okay. Okay.

Ohhhkay, now he's—he's—it's like a dog (cat?) shaking water from its fur but not as violent.

Shaking his muscles, tendons, and I don't know what else. Just rolling right through his body. Like wow.

"Trey."

Check myself.

Yeah, I'm Trey, but you still don't sound like Travis, quite.

"Sorry about that, are you okay?"

Um.

Well.

"Yes?"

He sounded more like Travis the next time he spoke. "I was having a bit of fun, and he ran this way. I was lost in the kill for a minute."

"No..." my eyes moved to the, er, remains. "Problem?"

Jesus. Did he chew through the guy's neck? How did his head get over there again?

And does he carry a rib spreader in his coat, Travis?

My eyes shot to my bodyguard. "Um. You have blood..." All over your face and—

Stuuuuff in your hair. Chunks.

He reached into his jacket, pulling out a handkerchief.

But handed it to me. "Got a little your face, mate."

I took it from him. Silk.

"Weren't you supposed to be out there with Dane?" he said, cocking a brow.

"Uh...yeah. My bad."

He started to smile.

"That was uh. So was that the beast?"

"That," he pointed, "smelled like Vicont. I don't like *anything* that belongs to Vicont."

And he winked at me.

"Got it," I said. "Crystal clear."

He glanced at the remains. "We can go back to the main room. Shane and Dane will take care of this, and we'll just get in the way." His now normal eyes moved to me.

Swallow. "Blow torch?"

"Roast pig, mate."

"You just put me off pork." I wiped my face. Some of the blood just flaked away.

Vamp blood.

He chuckled. "It's better than picking up all the pieces, and makes for a complete clean up."

Nod. Kind of. "Sure thing."

He chuckled again. "They're not going to use a blow torch. They will light him, though, and I'm figuring you've seen enough."

Nodding, sort of.

Travis' hair and shirt were still fubar-ish. "Maybe you'd like a shower," I said.

"Do I smell?"

"Well...no, but..." wait. He's teasing. "Never mind."

"C'mon, let's get you home," he said, putting his arm across my shoulder.

"So was that...that your gift?"

"No, that was an unexpected present someone else let through the back door, since I was here."

Took a few steps before I found some more words. "That's... nice?"

Fuller laugh from him. "Most everyone that works here knows what I like."

I then realized Shane and Dane were coming toward us. Both beaming at Travis. "Your lucky night," they said in unison.

Any other time, I might have laughed and made a comment about...

I have no idea.

"Seems so, luvs. Sorry about the mess."

"No you're not," they said and smiled.

"No, I'm not." He patted each of their arms. "See you later. I think this one needs to go back home."

They looked at me. "I turned around and you were gone," one of them said.

That must be Dane. They were wearing the same clothes, but Dane's the one that I was supposed to stay with. Right.

"I'm...sneaky that way," I said.

They both laughed. "Well, see you soon I hope."

"Yeah, see you soon, I hope."

I lost track of who was who; they spoke too fast. So I just nodded.

Travis and I started walking again. Not long after, I heard some...noise. Forced myself not to look or turn back, keeping pace with Travis.

Like I *needed* to see anything *else* tonight worthy of nightmares.

That's it. Yup. My life really is part horror flick. How many sequels we gonna milk out of this, anyway?

Sigh.

Whoa, whoa, chest expanding, whooshing...whatever. Right through my pores, shit.

Familiar, that...

Oh.

No.

Way.

Was that? Was the vamp still...? When they started...?

Mental shake.

Okay. We have total confirmation. Vampires definitely have souls.

I checked my clothes for obvious signs of ick (there was a little), wondering at my capacity for seeing such things without tossing my intestines.

Death by vambie. Jim had looked like he showered in hydrochloric acid and then dried off with a cheese grater. Definitely puke worthy—but so was this. Gee, getting used it already, am I? Then again, this was Travis, and he hadn't turned the guy into....goo

Still, this, in a way, should actually be worse. I didn't throw up when Michel got medieval on those vamps here either, though.

Hey—Michel got beasty, so what's the big deal with Travis, and...I'm far too fascinated with this. Likely more accepting of this shit than is healthy. But they *are* vampires. I'm just considerate of their alternate lifestyle. Right?

Analyze yourself later, Trey. Just keep walking.

"What compelled you to come this way?" Travis asked as we reached the curtains.

"Guess I'm cat like, too."

I felt him pat my back. "Seems so."

"I've been back in this hall once before. I had an urge to see it when I wasn't running from psycho vamps."

"Got'cha."

I glanced at him. Gross stuff still in his hair. I looked ahead as we went through the curtains and into the main part of the club. "You're not reprimanding me."

I felt him shrug because he still had his arm across my shoulder.

"You were curious. No reason for me to get bent over it, and I'm not your keeper. I'm not your boss."

I almost smiled. Then I frowned. "It occurs to me how stupid that really was." I looked at him again, not looking at his hair. "You told me, basically, that you sometimes lose control. I almost got in your way and could have gotten hurt." Then I added, "Wouldn't have been your fault."

He stopped us not far from the bottom of the steps.

Placing both hands on my shoulders as he faced me, with a serious expression he said, "First, you didn't know what I was doing back there, right?"

"Well, no, actually I didn't."

"Right. Second, I would've made certain Dane kept you away if I were worried about it."

"Well—yeah okay, you're supposed to be protecting me, right."

"Third, I sensed you before I goaded him into running."

I gaped at him, three different things at least, vying to fly out of my mouth, none of them making it.

"Yeah that's right, I knew you might witness something," he said.

Gape.

"You've been curious. I reckoned you would either leave, or satisfy your curiosity," he said. "Now you know a little more about me."

"Some things can only be experienced." I was considering...

His head tilted. "That's like something Michel says. You wanted to see something, well, now you have."

"Yeah..." I was considering that I wouldn't have left, frozen or not.

"I'm not at the end of my leash, so I let you choose, and I want you to know that I wasn't so lost that I couldn't smell them in you. I wouldn't have harmed you in this instance, unless you did something stupid. But I don't think you're stupid, Trey."

My eyes bounced between his. He offered up a smile.

"I have to say, it's cool that you're not afraid of me, even now."

I shook my head a little.

"Shall we get you home?"

I nodded.

He led me up the stairs and out, me silent, considering a few more things.

Like the fact I remembered that at one point, the last time I was here, when Michel was ripping into that last guy...

Some part of me had found it darkly pleasing.

****

Travis stopped in the middle of the street in front of my building. "There's no parking right here; I'll have to go round a few times."

I opened my door. "All right. See you in a few."

I got out, shut the door, and watched him pull away. He'd complained about the stench of the other vampire on him during the ride back. I couldn't smell a damned thing, so it must have been a vampire thing. Or a Travis thing. Or both.

I'd said he could use my shower; he'd said that was nice of me, said okay.

That about covered the extent of our conversation, because I was still mulling some things over. He seemed to know this, and let me analyze myself in silence.

I turned and headed for the apartment building. Reaching the door, I punched the access code and someone tapped me on the shoulder.

"Aghh!" I jump-turned.

Shit, that was fast or I walked slow, or something in-between the two.

Hand to my chest. "*Dude.* Don't *do* that."

Travis spread his hands. "Sorry."

I punched in the code again, grabbed the door, went inside and checked the hall, then motioned him in.

He headed for the stairs.

Fine.

We made it up the stairs and to my apartment without anyone seeing us.

Great.

Once inside, I got a better look at him. Or really, decided I would now get a better look at him.

Yeah. That silk shirt ain't tan no more, and the suit-weight, camel-colored, trench-length jacket— a bit fucked.

A bit?

"I don't think dry cleaning is going to cover that," I said.

He glanced down at himself. "No. That's one of the reasons I have so many clothes."

"Don't you get hot in those jackets this time of year?" Going right past that, yeah. "Not that you don't look good." Sure. We'll just discuss fashion.

He smiled. "Doesn't bother me. I like heat."

"Must be that cheetah thing." I plopped onto a sofa and gestured. "Bathroom off my bedroom, you remember, right? Shower will make you feel better."

He chuckled, nice and warm. "I remember." He took a step. "I'll do my hair twice, just for you."

I waved my hand. "You do that while I retrieve my mind. I think I might have left it somewhere."

"I don't know, mate, I think I hear it rattling about."

"As long as it doesn't fall out."

He grinned and stalked off toward my bedroom.

Shortly after, Geoff burst in the apartment. In a rush, he said as he walked, "I work extra, need bathroom, hi," and he waved as he went past me.

Toward my bedroom, I saw as I watched. Yeah. Where Travis was in my shower.

"Hey, Geoff," I considered, "okay, see you in a sec."

Yes. I can still be devious after horror scenes and dark thoughts. I'm good like that.

Shortly after, I heard, "Oh!" and "Scuse!" and then saw a flaming red Geoff come rushing out, gape at me, then run to the other bathroom.

I, of course, started laughing.

Soon enough, Travis came out in a towel that in no way hid enough of that—oh fuck, yes—solid body of his.

Which was fine with me, but you know that.

We won't bother telling him I have bigger towels.

Dayum. He's bigger than Michel is.

Muscles, I mean. Other muscles. I couldn't see *that*. Damn it.

Travis took one look at me and grinned. "I see. Very much something I might do."

I smiled while not bothering to hide the fact I was trying to see more of his thick thighs. Not ridiculously thick, mind you. I don't like ridiculous muscles.

Rock climbing thighs, yeah.

"No wonder we get along so well. Geoff will be blushing for days. Maybe even weeks," I said.

He grinned, then flashed me.

"Oh. Oh, thank you. From the bottom of my heart, thank you."

My, my

"Your heart? Sure about that?"

I got distracted a second by his wet, curling hair and the beads of water clinging to the fine spread of silken chest hair. Just a little. Just right. (This from a guy who likes bare.)

Okay, so more than a minute. I also noticed the silver chain against his skin, bearing a pendant that looked to be a *fleur de lis* with a lion head in the center.

He laughed. "I should dress."

My eyes snapped to his. But why? "In what? I know nothing of mine's gonna fit you."

"My trousers are fine. The jacket is reversible. I'll just skip the shirt."

"You do that."

He turned, presumably to head off to dress. "We can talk if you need to after I'm sorted." He looked over his shoulder. "Let me assure you that guy had no designs on any of you, though. Just a stray. You hadn't asked yet, but you were about to wonder, I'm sure."

"Yeah, once my brain stopped rattling." I leaned back. "Good to know, thanks."

"Will it be too much for Geoff, by the way?"

"You, or talking about it?" I threw him a grin. Yes, almost naked wet men made lots of things better.

He tossed it back. "Talking. But now I have to wonder about the other. You should have seen the look on his face."

"Oh, I got a good dose of it, I think, when he rushed back out. Anyway, he'll be fine with talking. Though maybe not to *you*."

Another laugh from him. "Back in a quick." He headed for my bedroom.

Geoff came from a different direction and started getting red again even as he sat down beside me.

"You no say, um. Company."

"You rushed through so fast I didn't get a chance."

He stared at me, then shoved me with both hands.

Sure. I laughed again.

"You…you, you…" he gave up and laughed even though he shoved me again. "Why he in your shower?"

"Jealous?"

Another shove.

"We'll both give you the scoop when he comes back out, okay?"

"Um. Kay."

God that's a pretty shade.

BRUSSELS

Michel

Gabriel had gone for a walk, entreating Kar to accompany him, which left me to endure Elise's company. I made no objection, as I knew it was distasteful enough for him to be in her home, let alone in her presence. I had learned little else of use the previous night while she danced her dance, but this evening had proven more fruitful. I had decided we would be leaving when Gabriel returned.

"I'm afraid you'll have to charm your own way out of this mess, my dear. We shall depart this very night," I said, cutting off her incessant need to speak of years best left in their graves.

Briefly startled, she was. "But..." she quickly recovered a less harsh tone of voice. "But why? You have every reason to hate him, more than I, in fact."

I knew what she still most desired. "Indeed." I rose from the chair and walked a few paces away, speaking as I did. "Yet I am under no obligation to you, nor indeed, obligated to intercede in the business of Belgian exports, for that matter. It does not touch directly upon any of my assets."

"No need to save your own ass, so no need to help me, I see," she replied.

"That you can't properly handle your affairs is not my concern." I turned to look at her. She had risen and the green-gold of her eyes, it sparked with restrained anger.

"I told you that it wasn't truly about that. Besides, I'll survive; I have so far."

I offered her a smile. "*Exactement.*" Though I was not speaking only to her business affairs.

She made a quick move to me, her hands out, palms up, beseeching. "Give me the piece of his heart, give me the leverage to ruin him."

"I have no idea where it is," I said.

The sparks flashed in her eyes once more. "Of course you do. I know you do."

"No, I do not."

"Ohh!" She beat at my chest with her small fists. "You'll punish me forever, won't you! You willful—" She sagged as if suddenly claimed by weariness.

"Bastard? Yes, yes I am."

She took three steps back. "I'll never have peace."

Join the club, I thought. "If I knew where this pound of flesh was, if I were to give it to you, you'd only destroy it."

"And why not, I say! Why not destroy it?"

"Because, my dear, then he would have nothing to lose."

Her expression smoothed. "Then let it be done in his presence, and what remains in his chest, crushed."

"You would never get close enough," I said.

"You could."

I waved a hand. "He's certainly gone into hiding. I've no idea where he is."

"I have spies. They've heard whisperings," she reclaimed the distance between us, touching my arm. "We could find him."

"I'm not of a mood, currently, for a goose chase."

"You have one of the best hunters known on your side." She touched my other arm. "Travis Starke. We've heard of him."

A nerve in my jaw twitched. "He is otherwise engaged, and I'm quite fine with the situation Vicont finds himself in at the moment. It's an inventive torture, wouldn't you agree?"

"He's had his choke hold on both of us for too long, Michel."

"Speak for yourself. You have no idea what a true choke hold is."

Her eyes searched mine. "Oh but I do, I do. Let us help each other rid the world of him."

My eyes moved over her delicate face. "I'm not yet done letting him suffer."

"Then kill him slowly, Michel."

"And then what? Will you fight in the war?" I lifted my brows.

"Yes! I have allies, whatever you need; it would be at your disposal."

Whatever I wanted was going to be at my disposal one way or another as it was.

"Elise, Elise. Wait it out for a time, for as I said, I'm enjoying his predicament at the moment, and furthermore, I'm rather enjoying a bit of peace."

She slid her palms up my arms and to my shoulders. "For me, Michel."

I felt my brow arch sharply. "*Pour vous*? After what you did?"

She stiffened with my formal French. "If you would only let me explain…"

My patience was becoming much, much too thin at this point. "Why, so you may lie once more?"

She gazed at me a long moment, before executing a fluid shift. "Do you not remember those nights when it was just the two of us? I could be at your side again, if you wish. Anything you wish."

I removed her hands. "Elise…" I would not rise to her bait, I would not.

She lifted to her toes, lifted her face, bringing our lips closer together. "Those nights in each other's arms," was her honeyed whisper. "The hours spent whispering of the things we'd do to him, all the while bathed in—"

I slapped her. So much for not rising to the bait, perhaps.

From three steps away she looked back to me, her hand having flown to her cheek. She then lunged at me, fingers twisted into claws. I snatched her by the wrists, bringing them over her head and lifting her until her feet dangled. I threw my words into her face.

"I know the story! Could I hold such a grudge for anything less than a betrayal so complete, by someone I held love for?" I shook her. "You stabbed me deep, you whore! I could have forgiven you, might have forgiven you, had you told me the truth yourself. Did you really think I would *help* you, *putain*? Who is the gullible one now?" My expression certainly must have reflected my current disgust. "Stupid of you to speak of sex. But of course, you always turn to sex; it's all you know. You weren't as good as you thought, by the way. I've had better from my own hand."

Flashing, her eyes.

"You were nothing but a vacation, Elise. A cheap one at that, in the armpit of say, Mexico," I said.

Which was not *completely* true, not the latter half of the statement, if I were to be *completely* honest, but I knew it would stab at her ego, all of these words, and besides, I needed to reclaim my...composure.

She spat her own words at me. "You seemed to enjoy certain things well enough. Does Gabriel know how to make you moan like that?"

My teeth, gritting. Relaxing.

"I'm fantastic with faking when I wish to be. You should know a thing or two about that, so well did you fake love."

"I never lied about loving you!" She writhed to no avail.

"You blasphemy the sanctity of love. Only a woman like you could be so utterly conniving, so completely deceitful, and not feel a shred of guilt." My face, a breath from hers. "Did you think I would not sense it when I came here? Did you think I had no ears in the time since?"

She became rigid in my grip, her feet ceasing to knock at my shins. "Believe whatever you like, but just remember this." Her Cupid's bow mouth pulled up at the corners. "You're the one that crumbled in the face of the lies," she said, not bothering to deny it and very self-assured.

So self-assured because she knew just where to twist the blade.

"If you had been confident in your relationship, if you had believed in Gabriel, it never would have gone the way it did." She licked at the tip of my nose. "*You*, betrayed him. You are the blasphemer."

She pulled her wrists free, easily done as the strength had fled me, fled my intention.

"He was manipulated most completely by the two of you, you and Vicont."

I could not turn at the sound of Gabriel's voice. I could not quite look at him.

Stop berating myself for the past, this he had said numerous times since we'd worked through everything, but to hear him defend the worst of mistakes I had ever made—not believing in him, in us—this I could not make peace with.

I felt him move closer, and as he did, his silken thought caressed my mind.

It was yourself that you did not believe in.

I near closed my eyes as I stood there, still frozen for the moment, frozen in the guilt, the shame I'd opened for her to touch, particularly worsened as I'd told Gabriel she could not touch it.

Elise shifted her gaze to him. "Michel betrayed you. Vicont threatened me; I had little choice."

Gabriel's next words to her were made of ice particles. "I care not what atrocities Vicont promised to visit upon you. Michel was as brother, friend, loyal to you. He would have protected you with his own life, and as he would have, so too would I. The same cannot be said for you, coward."

She made no reply, and Gabriel spoke yet again, this time the words filled with the weight of his sincerity. "Michel did not betray me, not in his *heart*."

This...this was the true reason he had forgiven me, this is what he had said over and again.

I felt his phantom touch to my chest. I inhaled slowly and found my words. "We shall be leaving now, Elise."

I turned.

"Michel."

I walked on, ignoring her, Gabriel at my side. I heard the stomp of her heel on the flooring. "He still has those who will bring harm to me and mine!"

Gabriel took my hand. I saw Kar waiting just ahead.

"I. Don't. Care."

I spoke those last words before we left her.

"I've gotten enough information on the companies to give to Trey," I said once outside.

Gabriel caught me in his peripheral. "If there is a way to wrest the companies from them both, Trey would be one who could discover the means, I should think."

"I'll have them one way or the other. All of them." I glanced at Kar. "Did you book the hotel in Bruges?"

"Yes, my Lord."

"What was the word from Travis last you spoke to him?"

"Everyone remains safe," Kar replied, then added after a smile, "He's enjoying his assignment."

I found a bit of my own smile at this, shaking off a little more of my encounter with Elise. "I knew they'd hit it off. How are the twins handling the Fall Out with Travis and yourself otherwise occupied as of late?"

Kar's smile grew. "Shane and Dane are making me quite proud, to hear Travis speak of it."

I found a bit more of my smile. "No doubt having all the fun they can handle. I'll return you to them soon enough." I looked to Gabriel. "We leave tomorrow night after I speak to Miles in Bruges."

"Bruges, it is rather quaint, but I shall be pleased once more distance is placed between us and the harlot."

We reached the Mercedes, Kar opening the rear door. I stopped and took Gabriel's face in my hands, whispering. "I know you've forgiven me, but I need to hear you say it again. Forgive me even this, but I need to hear it."

His soul was in his eyes when he spoke. "I *forgive* you." He crushed his lips against mine, his hands gripping my waist. "You did *not* betray me in your heart," he said into my mouth, before slipping into the car and pulling me in after him, pulling me straight into his lap.

PARIS

Trey

Geoff huddled up to me. Travis was across from us on the other sofa, his jacket now dark brown since he reversed it. Had to admit, it looked damned good.

"Anything more you need to know about it, mate?" Travis asked me after we filled Geoff in on the event. Minus the totally gruesome details, that is.

"Well, you said he wasn't after any of us, and that he was a stray, so I don't know. How about—do you always off the strays?"

"Michel's given me free reign since Algeria. I can do whatever I want with them."

"I see." I glanced at Geoff, who was still having trouble looking directly at Travis. Other than that, he seemed fine. I directed my gaze back to Travis. "So does this basically mean you're ridding Paris of anyone not loyal to Michel?"

Travis nodded.

"That's some serious politics, man."

"We do what we have to do."

"Predators of the same disposition," I said. That didn't just cover vambies.

"With the power to carry out some of their worst desires," he said.

I let go of a breath. "Yeah. I guess the only way to get through to some people is by show of force."

"This is part of what it means for Michel to officially reclaim his status. Show he's serious, fears none, and will not tolerate crap from those who won't exist here peacefully."

Wry smile. "I was about to say something along the lines of that sounding like ancient times, but then I remembered. Humans haven't necessarily come that far."

A lift and lowering of his brows. "Not in some respects, some of them, no." He brought his wrists to his knees, leaning a bit. "Michel isn't truly interested in mass killing, war. All it takes is a few rumors to spread of a few death sentences, and a lot of them will run far away, or fall in line."

Short laugh. "Rumors. Immortal grapevine?"

He smiled. "Basically."

"With some of your kind's powers, I bet it spreads faster than poison ivy."

Rich laugh from him. "Michel would agree, and you're both right. We don't always need the telephones."

"I've figured for a while Michel and Gabriel shared thoughts. I know you said all vamps are different. Maybe you can't all read minds, but between vamps, is that different from reading humans? Special connection?"

"Some can lock others out quite well, and not all Sires and offspring read each other well. Some can't at all, I guess."

My brows lifted. "Really? I'd think that if anyone should have the connection, it'd be them."

"I agree, and that's likely why some have evolved, like Michel and Gabriel."

More evolving. Vampires never change? What a crock that was, except for the not aging thing.

"It's more the older lines that still have some gaps between them," Travis added.

"You guys fascinate me." Sudden grin. "Stating the obvious, there."

He smiled. "A bit."

Geoff managed a smile in Travis' direction.

"You're awfully quiet, baby," I said to Geoff.

"I like to listen," he said.

I smiled and looked back to Travis, who was giving Geoff the tenderest look.

"They're right about you," he said to Geoff. "Precious little angel."

Geoff's chin dipped, his lashes dipped, then he smiled. "*Gracias.*"

Travis super-beamed a smile at him, then looked at me. "It's a special bond you're forming with that one."

I could only smile more.

"Sitting with the two of you, it's a nice vibe," he said.

I hugged Geoff to me. "I think I can speak for the both of us when I say how nice that is for you to say."

Geoff nodded.

Travis smiled and shrugged. "It's true."

"That's why it's so nice," I said. I glanced at Geoff. "And I guess I'll have to keep speaking for both of us and say that we like your vibe, too." Geoff giggled and nodded.

Travis chuckled. "Thank you."

I couldn't help myself, then. "You must have a girl or five."

His head went back with his laugh and he sank back into the sofa. "I can't find a middle ground, mate." His chin dropped and his eyes found mine. "I keep thinking there's got to be one. Maybe I'm sniffing up the wrong skirts."

"You lost me."

"I get laid, but I don't have a steady girl."

Brows shooting up. "Really?"

"It's true."

"What are they, blind and stupid?" I noticed Geoff's eyes were on Travis now, too.

"What can I say?"

I shook my head. "Oh no, you have to explain that. I know, it's the job, right?"

"It does keep me busy, but that's not it."

"Fine, fine, just tell me it's none of my business." I winked at him.

"Don't you think I would?" he asked, straight faced.

He wasn't teasing. "Yes, you would."

"Right then." He leaned forward. "That something I said I'd tell you?" His eyes shifted to Geoff and back. "Do you still want to know?"

Did I?

"Yes, especially if it has to do with you being single." I glanced at Geoff, too, wondering if Travis wanted to tell me alone.

He nodded and looked between us. "I know that I can trust Geoff. Something that I have always sensed, but can't define."

I couldn't define it either, but I knew what it was. I said nothing, and waited.

"I'll start with the facet," Travis said. "You'll better understand if I do."

I nodded, and so did Geoff.

"I carry a rather special gene," Travis began. "When Clarice turned me, it woke up, you might say."

"Dormancy, it came out of dormancy." I knew something about that.

"Yes." He waited, gazing at me.

"Sorry. Go on."

He placed his hands on his knees. "I carry a gene from an ancient race of demons."

I *know* my brows shot up.

"But don't think biblical. Think of the Greek word," he said.

I nodded. I think.

"They weren't exactly human, but they could mate with humans in their own way."

I think I nodded again.

Did I say fascinating? Oh yeah.

"Now you see, the Demon in me can reason, and he can be reasoned with. Well, some of the time." He smiled. "The Beast, it's all instinct. The Demon feeds off the Beast, and vice versa. Together, they send me right off."

Brain, racing through questions. Pluck one, Trey. "Are they actually separate things in you? The way you worded that, I mean—you know what I mean."

"No, I just tend to speak of it that way. It's all me. But

sometimes one carries more sway than the other does, and sometimes I don't know what I'm doing when I'm doing it. Not consciously."

Questions, absorbing, questions. "What kind of demon? I know races are diverse, but... Am I making sense?"

"I think you're making pretty good sense for someone wrapping their brain around this as we speak. What's in me feeds off rage, fury, vengeance. But it also knows loyalty, fairness, justice, amongst other things." He leaned. "It also loves sex. So does the Beast, I might add. I'm a very sexual creature."

And I had to laugh. "Okay, well that part doesn't sound bad."

"Mm. It's not, except for the part where I can't keep a steady girlfriend, see."

"Which you're about to explain."

"I just can't keep a *nice* girl. I tend to scare them off, for one thing."

"You said before that you were a beast in bed. I think I'm *just* beginning to get the picture. But still. Don't some other vampires like that? I have a slight idea that Michel and Gabriel do."

"Yeah, but they have that middle ground. I'm not so good with holding a middle ground."

I set my elbow on the back of the sofa and leaned on my hand. Geoff, meanwhile, snuggled even closer, though he was intent on the discussion. "Okay, just lay it out for me, will you?"

"Let's talk about my sex life?"

"Could be a new favorite subject," I said with all seriousness.

Travis grinned. "All right, it's like this. The ones that can handle me in bed, the Fierce Dominants, as they're called, well I don't really want to date them. They want me to be beastly all the time, not just in bed. They act like I'm a pussy when I'm nice. The thing is, I like being a nice guy. I'm a nice guy, aren't I?"

"Absolutely," I said and Geoff nodded.

"Right," continued Travis. "So I find a *nice* girl. They end up being too docile." He shook his head. "You'd think they'd run far away from me when they sensed I wasn't such a kitten after all, but no. Really, I must have a blood red, flashing pheromone sign over my head that says *freak*." He shrugged. "I think they believe they can tame me, or something." He shook his head again. "But I admit, even if I could, I don't want to be a kitten all the time, either. So...away they go. Better off anyway, because I end up hurting them in ways they don't like. I really don't like to hurt people who aren't asking for it."

I took a breath and let it out slowly, not feeling as casual about this, suddenly, as he seemed to feel. Or maybe it was resignation on his part, which bummed me out.

"You're *that* fierce?" I asked.

He paused, looking at Geoff, as if gauging how well Geoff was taking all of this.

Satisfied, he continued. "I can be terribly fierce and not know when to stop."

"Damn," I breathed out.

"I know. Even when I'm calm for a while and a nice girl sticks around, they end up thinking I'm a freak when they find out some of the things I've done, or do, and have to do."

I could only shake my head, not sure what to say.

"On top of that, I haven't found one I feel comfortable sharing my secret with, so maybe they'd understand." He took a deep breath. "Admittedly, I can also be a bastard when things are building inside me." Beat. "Though I'm always direct to a fault, either way. I have to be."

Questions, questions. "Okay, wait. They think you're a freak why? What is it you have to do?"

He turned a serious expression on me. "When things builds up too much, I have to purge it."

"Purge it how?"

"Algeria helped take the edge off. Killing a few vampires, that's always good, a nice battle. Killing that vamp at the Fall Out, that sort of thing helps."

I sat up. "And if you can't get that? Or if it's not enough?"

He gazed at Geoff again. Geoff, in turn, held Travis' gaze. Those amber eyes returned to me.

"I get shackled, chained, and other vampires whip the living hell out of me. The Beast unleashes, and off we go. Purging."

I sat up even more. "You're serious."

"I never kid about these things."

"You're in restraints so—"

"So I won't kill them, though sometimes I break through the chains. All part of the show. Sometimes the punishers get hurt, but they know what they're signing up for." He spread his hands. "I'm quite popular."

Mental shake, mental shake. "Show?"

He started smiling that sultry smile, except this time wickedness curved its edges. "At the Fall Out. It was mostly my idea. Special audience, and whoever gets the lucky draw that night, they get to participate."

"I...dude."

He started laughing. "I know. Freakish, ay?"

I looked at him a minute, then shrugged. "Well if you gotta do what you gotta do, have some fun with it I guess. Do you enjoy it? Or is it only a function?"

"I get something out of it beyond purging."

I held up my hands. "Then who am I to judge?"

Sharp brow arch from him. "Maybe you'd like to watch some time."

I thought about it. "Uh, I'll get back to you on that." I gave him a square look. "I'm not sure I'd like seeing you hurt. You must get hurt."

"Yes I do. But I'm a good healer."

I shook my head. "Still, I'm only human. I think I like you too much to see you hurt that way."

His smile, bright. "Aren't you a darl?"

I pointed a finger at him. "That's not an Aussie way of saying I'm a girl, is it?"

"Nah. Well..." he lifted a brow. "You have to admit, you really are kinda spunky." He tossed a wink to Geoff, who giggled.

"Shut up." I grinned. "I'm not as pretty as the twins."

"You have your own thing going on." His eyes sparked with humor.

"I," shut my mouth. Then I chuckled with Geoff.

"Feel free to fantasize all you like, mate."

I shot Travis a look. "Like I need you to say that."

He laughed, then spread his hands. "I might not have said that when I was human."

I considered that. "I guess once you're a vampire, blood is blood. As for the sex, well, live long enough and maybe anyone's tendencies can shift."

"I reckon so."

"I suppose I could don a skirt."

His eyes moved over me. "Shave your legs, might look nice." He grinned.

"I look great in make up."

"I don't know, I'm fancying the natural thing, there."

"Good, we got that straightened out."

"Always good to suss things out up front, and speaking of." He sat up straight. "Michel supervises when I purge at the Fall Out. He's the only one who can bring me down. So no worries on me getting hurt beyond my limits." He waggled his brows. "I kinda like pain, anyway."

"Uh...kinda getting that now, yup." I nodded. "Mmm hmm."

"Seriously now, Trey. You took that pretty well."

"Let me guess. No wonder Michel likes me."

"There's that, but no wonder *I* like you. No wonder they *all* like you. You're pretty cool, mate."

I kinda shrugged. "I'm just me."

"Like I said, pretty cool."

"Like knows like."

He turned a full smile on me.

Geoff surprised me, and spoke up. "Is there more like you?"

Travis leaned back. "I've never met another one like me, and Michel hadn't seen or heard of someone like me for a very long time. He said that we were rare. He's the one told me everything. Though sometimes I have these, I guess you'd call them race memories."

"Does he know why you're so rare?" I asked.

"For one thing, creatures like me were sought after by other vampires. We make very good fighters. Problem is, as those who sought our services found out, we won't willingly serve a master we feel no honest loyalty towards. So, they tried various ways of achieving our submission, like torture."

I could imagine what kind of torture a vampire might dish out.

Geoff shuddered.

"We'd rather die than serve without loyalty. We'd rather choose," Travis said.

Go down fighting.

"And for another thing?" I prompted.

"Others of my kind were killed because they couldn't reproduce one like themselves. The gene has to be present to begin with. And more of my kind died because others would drink and drink from them, hoping they could gain this mysterious power. When that proved useless, they drained them anyway."

God, it was monstrous. "Why?"

"Our blood tastes very sweet to others. Intoxicating. So when all else failed, my kind were highly prized on their menus. We'll take everyone we can down with us, though. Not so easily captured, us."

My eyes moved over his face. "Made nearly extinct by your own species."

"People are people and always have been. How many animal species gone, because of man, as well?"

I couldn't stop the shaking of my head. "Somehow it's so much more awful when it's brothers killing brothers."

"Yes. Like the Holocaust. Genocide."

"Yes. The technology's just different now." I squeezed Geoff's hand, because this had saddened him. "Our worlds aren't really so separate. You just live it on a larger scale."

His expression softened. "You really *don't* see us as so different, do you? I mean on a *personal* scale."

"I know you have gifts I don't have. So? Some people are faster, stronger, smarter, whatever—than others. I know your moralities might be different. But then again, you know very well that human morality is subjective. And okay, I don't have a demon gene that I know of, and I don't live on blood, but— well Vampires were once human."

He lifted from the sofa, came around the coffee table, squatted, and took my hand.

And then—

Darkness slid through his eyes. Not just darkness. Blackness.

Like an eclipse. It was like an eclipse of his irises, and for a second, two, there was—

Moon-kissed blackness.

Geoff gasped, but it didn't seem like fright.

"Your heart is larger than your chest," Travis said, while I fixated on this phenomenon.

And then his eyes were shades of amber that held light, once again.

"You're not a freak," I blurted. "You shouldn't confine yourself to someone else's labels, and I hope you find the right girl."

He laughed with little sound. "It would be nice to have just one. I always have to bounce from lover to lover, because I'm too much for one girl. One nice girl, anyway."

"She's got to be out there."

"It's best I stay away, really," he said.

"If you do that, you won't find her. You've just been meeting the wrong ones."

"It starts to get depressing, Trey. Every hope dashed is another knick in my heart."

My eyes dropped.

"But in the meantime, I still get laid, remember? Even if some of them are bitches on wheels."

My eyes lifted and I had to smile. "Looking at the bright side again."

"It's better than being celibate. That I can't abide, and it would send me right off as well."

"Yeah, that definitely sucks."

He arched a brow. "Would you know this first hand?"

I felt a grin growing. "Not anymore."

We both looked at Geoff, who, yes, blushed.

"It's likely I shouldn't say I thought so, but I thought so."
Travis winked at Geoff.

Who, yes, got redder.

Travis looked at me. "Good on ya, mate."

I adopted a smug expression. "I'm sure it was a good show, too."

Grin from Travis. "Well. There you have it, any rate. My secret."

Geoff made a small sound. Might have been trying to clear his throat. "It very special, you share."

Travis touched his hand. "It feels good, sharing it with you."

Geoff said, "It sad, no others like you for you to know."

Travis squeezed his hand. "That's all right, precious. I have family, don't you worry about me."

Geoff smiled.

I smiled.

Travis smiled as he stood, and went back to sitting on the other sofa.

Another question popped into my head. "How did Michel

know it was a special gene?"

"Over the centuries, it's been deduced." Travis studied me intently a moment. "There was, also, a human once found, who during the course of some testing displayed anomalies in his genes. Vampires are everywhere, mate, and some have medical backgrounds."

Dayum. "What happened to the human?" I whispered.

"He died, during *testing*."

"Oh!" Geoff's reaction.

"Damn." Mine.

"Yeah." Travis. "There are rumors there were others. Never confirmed, but I'm betting it's not just a rumor."

Shake of my head. "To this day, you're still coveted."

"Some still think they can gain the power, if they could ever find one of us."

"I will never let anyone get your secret out of me," I said.

"Me, too," Geoff said.

Travis smiled. "I told you, which displays my trust, guys. No worries."

"Well." I glanced at Geoff. "We just had to say it."

"I know," said Travis. "Don't worry about anyone plucking it from you, either. No one knows there's one of us about in France, so no one's looking. Got it?"

Geoff and I both nodded.

A lighter thought popped into my head. "Hey. Dane called you Uncle Travis," I said. "Why?"

"Because they both consider me an uncle, you think?"

Eye roll and laugh. "Fine, fine. You said something about their dad wanting a report."

"Yes," he said, waiting.

Yeah, for me to ask an actual question, right. "Who's Dad?"

"Kar's their Maker."

Ahah. "Uncle makes more sense, now."

"Why is that?" Travis asked.

"Because even with what was going on at the time, it seemed

to me Kar treated you like a little brother."

Travis' smile unfurled. "We do think of each other that way. But let me tell you this. Shane and Dane chose to think of me as an uncle, same as Kar and I chose each other as brothers. There's a difference."

I understood what he meant, and returned his smile. "It's nice to be chosen like that."

"You would know as well as me."

Fuller smile. "Yeah. So. There has to be a heck of a story behind twin vampires. They were made at the same time, or close, yeah?"

Travis nodded. "The same time, and they're the only ones I've ever met."

"Mmhmm. Some kinda story for sure."

"Ask Kar sometime, mate. It's his story to tell."

Chapter Thirteen

JULY 31

BRUGES

Gabriel

My Michel strolled across the mezzanine, leaving the business with Miles behind and smiling in a way that could break the darkest clouds.

"That was an interesting conversation." His comment was light, and he reached for my hands, which immediately found themselves a home in his.

"By the sparkle in your eyes alone I would know that you are quite pleased," I replied. "Bruges, then, was not a waste of time?"

He bestowed my brow with a kiss, his head turning as Kar approached.

"All is ready when you are, my Lord," did Kar say.

"Splendid. We should like to leave at once." My love's

dancing eyes returned to me. "Shouldn't we?"

I gave him the gift of my smile, easily enough offered. "If only there were quicker ways than at once."

"My Lord, this was delivered to the hotel while you were meeting with Miles." Kar handed a plain white envelope to *mon lion*, which he took, giving it a short glance.

"From whom?"

"A messenger in the service of someone bearing the name Dracul."

My angel, he snorted. "How original." I observed the knitting of his metallic brows. "Dracul." He came to my side, his arm finding its customary place about my waist. "Carry on, Kar, I'll read it on the way."

We began to follow Kar as he escorted us to the automobile, Michel speaking no more of the missive, and I feeling a desire to let it pass for the time being, as his mood seemed to indicate.

"To answer your question, my darling one, Bruges was not a waste of time, no," my love said to me.

"What have you learned that has you in, dare I say, such impish spirits?"

"It would seem Elise has been more careless with her assets than even she knows, and," he paused to place a kiss to my cheek, "someone missed correcting a mistake in one of *Vicont's* contracts, so the intel goes."

A brow, I felt one arching. "A mistake?"

Michel laughed, the sound waves dancing *en pointe* up my spine. "An attorney who never got to finish what he started, in the way of double cross."

"How intriguing."

"Indeed, how intriguing."

"You will have Trey looking into this as well?" I inquired, a swift and sudden pang of doubt striking my gut.

"Not to worry, dove. Most can be done without leaving a trail, and furthermore, should Trey feel uncomfortable with it all when I present my idea, I'll simply find another way."

With this reassurance, I found myself refocusing on the missive in his hand. "Dracul. As we know without doubt who it is not, pray tell me, do you know who it is?"

"No, I don't."

"Would this be what caused your brows to crease?"

We reached the Mercedes, and he removed his arm from my waist so that he might open the envelope. "What caused my brows to crease was surely a ridiculous thought."

I watched as he removed the plain white paper that was within the envelope. I watched his eyes move with swiftness over the words, and I observed the drawing together of his brows once more.

"*Mon ange d'or*, what is it?"

"If I am to believe this, it's from Vicont." He thrust the missive at me. "It is not, however, his handwriting."

I took it, skimming the printed words. My eyes leapt to his. "He wishes to see you. He has something important to tell you. Isn't that *nice*."

His generous mouth, for a moment it set in a scowl. "What he could possibly have to tell me is anyone's guess, not to mention I am not interested in his bullshit. If it were true, that is."

"Games." I made to tear the note, but suddenly stopped, thinking to save it after all. "Someone is playing games."

"He's extending an olive branch; surely you didn't miss that part."

"If this were truly relayed from Vicont, his dictated words are not worth the paper that they have been printed upon."

"Of course not." His eyes moved to Kar. "Let's go, I tire of Bruges."

Kar bowed his head and took his place behind the steering wheel. Michel opened the rear door and stepped back, a gentleman bidding I enter first.

I paused. "Who here would taunt you so, other than Elise?"

"At the moment I really don't care, my love, as long as they fuck off after one note."

I situated myself in the back seat, knowing quite well that the subject was off the table, which was well enough with me for the moment, as I touched the smile which returned to his lips.

PARIS

Trey

Geoff had the day off. He, Scott and I had spent some of the day just sitting around talking about any subject that came up. Scott got to know a lot more about Geoff, asking him about Carmona, his parents, and what he liked to do.

Geoff loves to skateboard; I don't think I mentioned that. Well, I haven't known that long.

No, I didn't find out just *today*. Anyway, that set me to thinking about the next thing I was going to buy for Geoff. Especially after Scott said something about snapping some shots of Geoff in action, and Geoff commented that he'd broken his last board and hadn't gotten another one yet. I definitely wanted to see him in a little beanie or something, skater clothes, rolling along and no doubt, rosy cheeked with excitement.

Yes, I could picture it, especially considering how excited he got just talking about it.

Scott and Geoff were getting along very well, and I was feeling very good about things, so after sitting around a while, we headed out since it was such a nice day. Geoff wanted ice cream, so Berthillion's it was. By the time we made it through the line, more than an hour had passed. Geoff had his usual chocolate, I got my lemon sorbet, and Scott fell hard for a caramel and strawberry confection. We strolled around the islands, we hung out in the park behind Notre Dame, and then we decided to hit up Polly's shop.

Scott decided, we agreed.

Eventually, when it was clear to me that since Polly and he didn't get (totally) freaky the other night, that tonight was definitely the night, I took Scott off to the side and asked if he'd mind if I left with Geoff. You know, to show him that little section of the catacombs, maybe.

Scott had grinned and said he didn't have a problem keeping Polly company.

Duh.

So I told him and Polly we'd see them later (maybe) and Geoff and I left.

I told Geoff my idea as we strolled through the neighborhood. He was a little nervous, but also excited by the prospect, so we stopped at my apartment and gathered two flashlights. It wasn't dark yet, but it would be where I was taking him.

The place I'd taken Scott wasn't *terribly* far, so we walked all the way there, me thinking the dwindle of daylight along the way could only help. As we walked I told him more about the catacombs, and told him about Marc's explorations, because back up or not, Marc hadn't been lying about being a cataphile. I'd visited his website. The photographs were amazing, and he even had a video of one exploration.

Geoff ate this up with much interest and said he wanted to see the pictures. Also, the ones Scott had taken.

Once reaching our destination, I did a thorough look around, making certain no one was close, that no one would see us slip through the innocuous looking crack, which was just wide enough for a slender person to squick sideways through. It led to a narrow tunnel that widened as it descended down to the open underground room. Squeezing, squeezing through that long crack was almost enough to make me claustrophobic, but it was worth it, so I sucked it up. The tunnel wasn't short, though it wasn't horribly long, either, and it winded back and forth a couple of times, but we wouldn't get lost because it didn't lead anywhere else that we could follow.

Anywhere we *should* follow, I should say, without a map or guide, and better preparation, probably.

We had to go in single file for a time. I would have beamed the flashlight on Geoff's sweet ass as he walked, but since he'd never been here, he took rear, possibly directing his beam at my ass, the thought of which made me grin.

Other thoughts came and went as we walked in the quiet flash-lit glow of the tunnel, which had nothing to do with the tunnel.

Was I still afraid? Geoff wasn't Sean, even if he were only the second angel I'd ever known. I wasn't the same man that drained the light little by little from that first angel, even from a distance.

Was I?

Yes, but then again, no, and in Geoff's presence I shouldn't be afraid. Was finding it less and less fearful with each step we took. In his presence, I was the man he saw through the outer shell from the very first day. The man he knew I was, even when I thought I wasn't.

The man I wanted to be.

I looked back, he smiled at me, and I knew.

Like Gabriel, I was more afraid of not having him to love than loving him, and I definitely loved him, I knew I did; I couldn't talk myself out of it.

I didn't want to.

I reached back and found his hand, and he moved up beside me as we spilled out into the tomb of a room.

"Wow, this is so cool," he said, looking around, following the beams of both our lights.

"P.K. told me about it. We're underneath the church, now."

"You sure we don't get in trouble?" he asked in a bare whisper. It was the third time he'd asked tonight.

"No one saw us go through, and no one else is down here to see us now."

"All alone, dark scary place." I saw his smile, the beam of

his flashlight making him look like a jack-o-lantern and giving his teeth an evil slant. "But I not scared with you here."

I squeezed his hand, returning his smile ten-fold.

"Listen," I whispered. "Listen, it's just like P.K. said, somehow the sounds funnel through."

Geoff's eyes moved up in the direction the voices were falling from, though we couldn't actually see people, only the cracked limestone and perfectly laid concrete bricks. "Wow," he whispered back. "I can hear them up there. Neat."

"Imagine the eavesdropping we could do."

"Hee." He looked at me. "I didn't know about all these places that you could get inside."

I gave him a smile. "I'm glad we're seeing it together, your first time."

"Me too. There are many caves in Spain; maybe sometime we can see those together."

I ran a finger over one of his fine, thick brows. "I'd love to."

He caught his lip between his teeth, then planted a soft, soft kiss on me. I wrapped my arms around him, hugging him tight while kissing him back.

"And I love you," I said into his ear. "*Te amo, mi pequeño gorrión.*"

He made a little sound. His head drew back and wet brown eyes found mine. A smile that could have lit the darkest place illuminated his face.

"Now I always remember this place," he said.

My own smile followed. "Me, too."

"*Te amo,*" he said, quietly, and kissed me again. "Oh... listen."

I did, and I heard something so appropriate it made me laugh a little, it made my chest a little warmer than it already was.

Someone above was speaking words of love, too.

"Perfect," I said.

He nodded.

I took his hand again, and we started walking around the area. "Maybe we'll just hang out down here a little longer. I'm sure we could get all kinds of freaky and no one will ever know."

He giggled. "But we're on holy ground."

"Correction, we're under it."

"Around us."

"Technicality. Besides, I'm not exactly Catholic." I glanced at him. "And you're a lapsed one, right?"

"I don't know…"

"Well, until you figure it out, we'll say yes."

He giggled again and let go of my hand, taking a few steps ahead. "What this over here? Ooo, mural."

Before I could answer, his body jerked away from my beam.

It moved in excruciating slow motion, at least in the replay in my mind seconds after it happened.

Geoff's body jerks.
I stumble as I reach for him.
Reach for him because he is falling.

And nothing else exists.

"Geoff!" Frantic, hoarse.
He doesn't reply.

"Geoff, Geoff, Geoff!"

I pull him back into my chest, moving back against a wall. I slide down and sit back, cradling him to me.

Lump in my throat. "Geoff, talk to me, talk to me please, Geoff…" what just happened "Geoff," what the fuck just happened, "Geoff, what's wrong?" What's happening?

Blood.

There's blood.

A flower of black is blossoming on his chest, painting his tunic like modern art, hideous flashes of crumpled black rose blooming in a spinning light.

My hand comes away from him, I gape.

It's black, too. It's sticky wet black, red, black-red.

"Oh God, oh God, oh God, Geoff?"

His face is so still.

He is so still.

Shaking him. "Geoff!"

So deathly still.

"Geoff," I can barely speak, "*bonito*, please, *please*." I can't feel his heart. "Talk to me," hugging him to me, "Please, please," I choke, "Geoff, *pleeease*."

I can't feel his heart.

A shudder, a shimmer and glow.

Absolute stillness. I reach for his face.

The fluttering of little wings.

I reach for his serene face, cast in the harsh glow of false light.

It moves through me and a void grows.

I hold him closer, closer. "No!" I think I yell. "No, don't leave me, ooGghod."

I see the darkness and hear the whisperings. Louder, closer, louder.

All becomes silence. Nothing but the silence where his breath and heart beat should be and I am paralyzed.

It has paralyzed me where I sit, but another world sucks me down.

I run towards the Cross Roads, heart thumping in my chest. "Papa. Where is he! Is he here? No, he can't be here."

I can't speak, can't even cry, and my chest feels empty, so empty of where he just was.

My chest bears a ton of iron. Papa turns. "He gots ta Cross, chile."

I am choking on further words and can only shake my head.

I look down at his face. His eyes won't open.

I see him ahead, he turns. His velvet brown eyes hold so much love, along with a tear. He waves at me. "Te amo, angel."

I can't even cry.

"Geoff! Papa, don't let him Cross. You can't! I say no! It's not time! I'm the Roads, you said, and I say no!" I can say no, I can say no, can't I, can't I?

I see nothing.

"Te amo, angel. Always." I see Geoff begin to turn away, and Papa is holding me back. "I's sorry, chile. He passed through you already."

I grab the Old Man and shake him. "It can't be time! Don't take him away from me now, please. I'll take him back, give him back."

"Give him back," a mere whisper the limestone absorbs.

"Give him back! It can't be time, no not again; this was supposed to be different!"

I think I see a shadow; it flits through the yellow laser of light.

"He Crossing, chile. Destine to come back."

"In a life where I don't know him!" I cry. "Right?!"

"He crosses."

"Then...I'll go with him! I'll go with him!"

I think I see a shadow; it flits through the dead yellow casting of light on stone.

"Go ahead; kill me." I don't care anymore.

"Ain'chore time."

"It's not his time, it can't be!" I almost go to my knees.

Papa grasps my shoulders "You'd die with him?"

Tears sting, they sting my eyes, the emotion dangerously fierce. "I'll die slowly without him; he can't leave me now, please." No I lost Sean, I killed Sean, don't take Geoff away from me, please. I lose him, everyone else loses me, too...I will lose my mind.

Papa smiles. "Den you got ta choose."

"Choose...choose?"

I see a shadow.

I close my eyes.

"Someone gots ta take his place. Death a callin'. If not him, who you goin choose take his place?"

Geoff is so utterly still in my arms.

Geoff is getting farther and farther away. "Geoff!"

I'm shaking.

Choose.

Choose.

Choose.

Oh God.

Oh God.

Oh God.

I straighten my shoulders. "I...I have to trade?"

"Dis da price. Hurry nah, if ya goin ta keep him. He ain't stayin' here on dis side. If you die, you be lookin' for him in da next life. He ain't stayin', he destine to move on, like I said."

Geoff looks over his shoulder. "Te amo, angel."

I close my eyes and tears flow and flow. "No, I can't let you leave me! Don't leave me!"

I open my eyes.

The shadow is close.

Closer.

"Pardonez-moi?" The shadow spins a woman's voice and my eyes roll up to see a face forming in it, looming closer, until I see a woman's face, closer, until I see concern through the knife slashings of light.

She asks if we need help. French, in French she asks what's wrong, what happened, do we need help?

I close my eyes. "Forgive me."

I hear her say, *"Pourquoi?* Let me help you, something is wrong?"

"I can't live without him. I can't. I can't. Forgive me." I can't let another one go, not when I can save him, this time I can *save* him, not kill him.

I open my eyes. "Help me. Yes, yous can help me lil girl."

I hear...feel...her drop.
I see Geoff turn back toward me.
I see her lying there.
I hold out my hand.
I touch his face.
He walks to me. He takes my hand.
There is the fluttering of little wings in my chest.
I embrace him so tightly.
There is a warm glow.
"I can't let you go."
I feel his heart make a beat.
"Geoff, I can't let you go, I can't."
He kisses me.
Breath moves through him.
I kiss him harder.
His lashes flutter. "Angel..."
I hold him tight. "Ooogh God. Geoff..."

And I can't speak another word. I shift him to kiss him, my face wet. It's then something slips from between us and tinkles across the concrete.

Bullet. I know it's a bullet. I now know that I felt it leave him. I just know.

I can't look. I know where it's going. I just know.

I made the trade, I know.

I feel her move through me and I shudder.

There is another shadow and I look up. I feel outside of myself. What I'm seeing, I'm seeing it from somewhere else. It's happening to someone else.

Travis. Staring at us. His brows furrow. I see him look to the now dead woman.

The sacrifice.

His head tilts. He glances around, sniffs the air.

His eyes move over the woman once more before returning

to me. He looks confused, he looks to contemplate, and then his eyes soften.

"Let me get you home," he quietly says, leaning, holding out is hand.

I don't think I can move.

Geoff takes his hand before I can move.

I can't move, because it's not happening to me. But I feel Travis pull me to my feet. I feel him touch my face. I see him gaze at Geoff, and then caress his face.

He glances at the sacrifice one more time, then to us.

I think we start walking.

Yes.

We do.

I think I'm in shock.

I have my arm around Geoff, and I can feel it, and I know I'm moving, and Oh, God.

I can smell him.

Geoff.

I can smell him all over me and I think I want to cry, but I can't seem to cry.

Chapter Fourteen

We must have walked, but I don't remember getting home. I know that when we got there, I realized Geoff was swimming in a jacket far too big, and that it belonged to Travis.

I just didn't know when Travis had given it to him.

I know that Travis might have said something about being too late, and I might have said something about it being daylight and as he could see, it wasn't too late after all.

I knew it was dark when we were walking home.

We walked, right?

I think Travis started to say something about being too late again, but he dropped it. I think he was the one who covered us in a blanket, Geoff and I, when we sat on the sofa.

I think Travis is the one that took the bloody shirt from Geoff, too, and gazed at it a moment in silence, not asking a damned thing about what had happened.

Probably because I was still in shock.

I think I'm still in shock. Travis excused himself a little bit ago, though he said he'd have his eye on us, so not to worry.

I'm sitting here, holding Geoff, who is dozing, but there's no sleep for me, no, no sleep for me. I'm watching him breathe. My still-breathing Geoff, my once-again-breathing Geoff. I can feel him breathing, but I have to watch, too. Every time I think of closing my eyes, I panic.

He'd fallen asleep in my arms after Travis left, because I just couldn't speak, so he didn't speak, and that's okay, because my little sparrow, he's born to understand, so I'm sure he understands why I can't speak. I'm sure he understands what I'm feeling and what I don't even know I'm feeling, and I have no doubt he knows exactly what happened.

That he died.

He died in my arms.

He died in my arms and moved through me and I chose someone to take his place.

What.

Have.

I.

Done?

But I couldn't let him go! I love him, I love him, and I just found him, I couldn't let him go!

What happened, what happened, we were alone and then...

I gazed and gazed at his face.

How could I be sorry he was here? How could I be sorry he was alive, warm and alive in my arms?

I'm not.

But I am. I'm sorry about that girl. That girl, she just wanted to help. They're going to find her eventually and think someone shot her, and she has a family that's going to grieve, and they'll wonder why, why?

Will they find her? Is that where Travis went? No, they have to find her so they know.

Did he go to find the shooter? It wasn't her; somehow I'm sure it wasn't her. I don't even know who, why, I didn't even hear it. I didn't even hear it I just saw him falling, falling, my—

Soul, his soul moved through me. He was all over me, I

realized. He was under my skin, in my pores, in my—
    Soul.
    How could I be sorry?
    I can't be sorry.
    Gift. This is a gift. I saved his life!

    But I killed that girl.

    Two...sides...of the same...coin...the disc.
    The disc balanced on its edge.
    A spinning coin and I flipped her tails, didn't I?
    A curse and a gift...

Chapter Fifteen

Michel

"Thank God you're back," Travis said, striding across the front room to me.

"We just arrived." I embraced him, sensing something was terribly amiss. He was quite agitated and quite upset about something. "What is it, darling?"

Conflicted eyes with slit pupils met mine. "I failed you. I failed."

"Now now, how could you possibly have done this?"

He turned away and started pacing, circling in that very feline way of his.

"David, I shouldn't have given him the shift. He just fucked off."

"Travis, I can see you're very upset, but please, slow down if you can and explain," I said.

He turned to me. "David left his post. He was supposed to be watching Trey and Geoff."

I had been doing my best to remain calm and not let his

agitation feed my emotions, but it was becoming very difficult. "What happened to Trey? To Geoff?"

It was then his expression fell to the floor and confusion took lead in his eyes. "I don't understand it. Someone shot Geoff, but he's alive. There's not a scratch on him."

Thank the gods he added the last part, not just for me, but also for Gabriel, who had just entered the room.

"Shot?" he asked, looking to Travis.

Travis deflated and sank into a chair. "It wasn't quite sunset yet. It was before I got there. I don't understand." He looked up at me with seeking eyes. "I got snatches from Trey's mind that confirmed what I'd seen from a distance. Blood, a bullet. Geoff falling. There was blood all over Geoff's shirt and he *died*, Michel, but there's not a scratch on him now. He's perfectly fine."

"Where are they now?" Gabriel asked, for this was his first concern. He could well know himself, but he wished to hear it confirmed by Travis. Something I understood most completely.

Travis looked to him. "At Trey's, and Trey was still in shock when I left."

I moved closer to Travis and knelt, taking his hands. "What else can you tell me?"

"There was a girl, dead there on the ground." His eyes moved between Gabriel and I. "She was shot. The strange thing is, I could have sworn..." he shook his head.

"Sworn what? Speak it," Gabriel interjected.

Travis looked between us again. "She was breathing when I got there. She seemed unharmed when I got there, but I swear the bullet just, well it just found her and..." he rubbed his forehead. "It makes no sense. It found a home in her heart without aid of a gun. I don't know how else to put it." He spread his hands. "Trey's human, Geoff's human, she was human. I don't understand. It was like some strange magic."

Gabriel and I exchanged a look.

I returned to gazing at Travis. "Where is this girl now?"

"I left her there. It merely looks as if someone shot her, nothing strange." He spread his hands again. "And well, I was a bit fucked off at David, so that's where I went after leaving Trey and Geoff."

A bit fucked off. This surely meant that David was dead.

"It's perhaps proper she be found," I assured Travis. "And you did not fail, David did."

"I shouldn't have trusted him. I should have—"

"Your instincts are fine. Perhaps something *took* David away."

Travis shook his head.

"Then it was snap decision you couldn't have anticipated."

"Still, I should have—"

"What," I interrupted. "Done it yourself? You couldn't go out in the sun."

His gaze dropped to our hands. "I could see some of it happening and I couldn't do a damned thing. I ran out anyway, but I was still too late."

I stroked his cheek and commenced seeking signs of damage from the sun, which, I then told myself, was ridiculous. Some time had already passed and Travis was an exceptional healer.

But he was my son, how I could not? My son, who placed himself in peril and yet insisted that he had failed me.

"You were there for them afterward, this is what matters. They live, this matters," Gabriel said, attempting to sooth him.

Still Travis did not lift his eyes. When next he spoke, it was in a gentle whisper. "Geoff touches a tender place inside me. I want to protect him. What good is all this power if I still fail?"

The emotion that moved through him, I recognized it. From his past, some of this, a past that included a little brother who had died at a young age, a little brother Travis felt that he had failed.

"*Mon fils*, what matters here is that they are whole." I rose so that I might stroke his hair. "They are shaken, yes, and I know that you would have liked to spare them the tragedy, but they are whole, my darling."

He nodded somewhat. Meanwhile I grasped for logic to soothe my nerves.

"As for how it was possible," I began, "my only thought is it must be connected to Trey's gift. No one else was there, correct?"

"No. Certainly no vampires," Travis replied.

"I can think of no other explanation, then."

Gabriel, now at my side, concurred. "This would be my first assumption, that it is connected to Trey."

Travis' eyes lifted. "He can bring back the dead?"

"What you've been able convey to me, it seems that yes, Trey has some power in this area," I replied. "For if not..."

"Thank God, whatever the case may be," Gabriel said quietly. I wrapped my arms about him, knowing that his very core shook with the idea of losing either of them.

"It was more than that," Travis said. "The girl. The bullet."

I had no idea what mechanics would be involved in such a thing, and now certainly didn't seem the time to ask Trey. It was, however, a matter of importance, seeing him immediately.

We had to see with our own eyes, after all.

"I lost the bastard that did it," Travis said then. "Trey was so shaken, I wanted to get him home, and I wanted them safe."

"You did the right thing," I said. "We'll track the wielder of the gun one way or another."

Travis rose. "Damned right I will."

I could not help but smile. Travis who was so loyal, who was at times so loving, was also someone you dare not cross.

"He must have been human. This will make it easier, I should think." I laid a hand on his shoulder. "You may begin now. We'll go see to Geoff and Trey." I knew it would help distract him, amongst other things.

Travis nodded and wasted no time in leaving. He was on a mission and no one would be able to stop him.

I had no prayers to offer the one he was tracking. I was quite fine with the idea of Travis unleashing on said human.

Chapter Sixteen

I tapped on the door, and when there was no immediate response, I could not help but open it, slowly stepping inside.

A few more steps brought to me the vision of Trey's haunted face, his eyes burning holes through Geoff's eyelids.

Gabriel breezed past me as Geoff's lashes fluttered, his eyes opened, and his head lifted.

"Little Angel." Gabriel leaned, placing his hands on that precious little face, and placed a tender kiss to Geoff's forehead.

Geoff lifted completely, though Trey had a death grip on him, at first. When Trey's eyes found focus on Gabriel, his arms fell away.

They were soon pinned to his sides by Gabriel's embrace, Trey remaining silent. By this time, I had embraced Geoff, unable to stop myself from scanning him, and I let out a sigh of relief that he was indeed without scratch.

The velvet of his brown eyes shimmered when they lifted to meet mine. They then moved to Trey, who was now situated beside my Gabriel on the couch. After pressing a palm to Geoff's cheek, I moved to sit on the other side of Trey.

"Beloved?"

"He died," Trey blurted, his shock bringing flatness to the words.

I took one of his hands in both of mine. "He lives and breathes even now."

"He died," Trey repeated, as if no other thought could form.

I glanced at Gabriel, but he had room only for his grandson in that emerald gaze. Trey's eyes, they remained on Geoff, as if he would disappear should he so much as blink. After a kiss to Trey's cheek, I relinquished my seat to Geoff, which eased Trey immediately. My eyes closed of their own accord as I took a few steps away.

Geoff's scent, it saturated Trey completely. It seemed a true part of his being, as if Geoff had literally passed through him.

I began to understand how literal this truly was. Geoff as well, he scented of Trey, and together their scents merged into something new, something uniquely their own.

I desperately wished to know what had happened beneath that chapel, desperately wished to know the nature of the miracle that was Geoff, there in Trey's arms, alive and well. I desperately wished for the blanks in Travis' understanding of the event, to be filled. I was admittedly, desperately curious.

Yet I was desperate for Trey's mind to stop folding in on itself, desperate for him to breathe normally again, and desperate for him to have some peace.

I could ask not a single question in these moments. I could not pry; I would not pry into his mind.

I wished to channel these feelings into anger at the one who Travis hunted even now, but this would do no good, and Trey was not ready to move toward anger, no, it would not do well to become angry.

What does one say after such an event? Long I have lived, yet even so, it has not prepared me for every situation; bringing someone over to immortality was not the same as this. There was no joy in the reason for the resurrection, though Trey would find the beauty in it eventually.

This was not the time to push him to see the beauty of the side effect of such a horrific ordeal.

Nor was it a time for me to apologize for bringing him into all of this, and nor was it the time for me to touch upon guilt. It was too late and I knew what Trey would later say about being in my world.

Although he may always change his mind.

I shook myself of these selfish thoughts and looked to Trey when I felt his gaze upon me.

"Did you see Travis?" he asked.

"Yes," I replied.

"He brought us here."

I nodded. Simple seemed best while Trey's mind reached for a calm center in other details.

"Where is he now?"

I contemplated Trey's question a moment. I decided he wanted the truth, that perhaps he did wish to latch onto who, why, when. Logic was his retreat, so like Gabriel.

"Seeking the one that caused such distress," I answered, careful not to speak of death.

"What will he do when he finds him?" His eyes, their stare was level.

"After learning the reason, he will kill him."

At this, his cheek went to Gabriel's shoulder. "Good," he said with little enthusiasm.

Geoff snuggled ever closer to Trey, and Gabriel ran his fingers through Trey's hair.

"I missed you," Trey then said.

"As we missed you," my angel replied.

"There was a girl," Trey said.

Gabriel looked to me. "Likely she will be found," he said, and I affirmed this with a nod.

"There was no time."

Gabriel and I both looked to Trey then, uncertain what this meant.

"No time," he repeated.

Gabriel's question was gentle. "No time for what, *cher*?"

"She was just there," Trey whispered.

My gaze moved over the three of them, resting at last on Geoff, who returned my look, the epitome of compassionate understanding in that gaze.

To choose, it said to me.

To choose. Dawning wished to creep over me in degrees, but just then, I sensed a presence outside Trey's door, and this presence soon filled the apartment.

My eyes moved to Scott, as did Gabriel's eyes. Geoff's did as well. Only Trey seemed not to notice.

Clear blue eyes took in the sum of us, stumbling for a moment upon seeing Gabriel, before fixing on Trey. "Did someone die or something?" When no reply came, Scott's features creased. "Oh damn, I'm sorry. What happened?"

I moved to Scott, capturing his eyes. For one moment while I held him there, transfixed, I considered shifting the details of what he'd walked into. I considered letting him believe everything was fine, however I just as quickly realized this would not do. There would be signs of the distress in Trey for days to follow, and unless I was going to arrange Scott's memories several times, glossing it now just would not do.

I opted for a lie that wasn't terribly far from the truth. "There was a close call this evening. Geoff and Trey were in a car accident, though miraculously both are well. The event has shaken them, as you can well imagine, however. We've just brought them here, after dealing with the reports and such."

I released Scott. His eyes immediately darted to Trey. "Oh man, are you sure you're okay?"

Gabriel resumed the thread. "He is somewhat still in shock, but otherwise unharmed."

Trey lifted his head, and no doubt with a gentle mental push from Gabriel, was able to speak.

"I'm, yeah, I'm okay. We're okay."

"What happened?" Scott asked.

Trey looked at me. "It...was so fast, it happened so fast, I'm not really sure."

This did not seem terribly far from the truth, either.

Geoff, blessed little angel, took up the slack. "A taxi hit us hard, bam! From the side, and all the airbags puff out, and I got scared, feel like, like, suffocating!" He touched Trey's face. "But worse for Trey. He don't like to be pinned. What word, claus...claus..."

"Claustrophobic," Gabriel provided.

"Yes that word." Geoff nodded and returned to looking at Scott. "He no like to be pinned. It freaks him out."

Scott nodded, the expression on his face and taste of his emotion, speaking to me of knowledge of this phobia.

I had knowledge of Trey's phobia. In this emotional situation, and as wretched as was the cause of this phobia, I was still able to spare a thought to Geoff's brilliance, choosing something that indeed would freak out Trey, as he put it.

Also for the fact that Geoff, dead and resurrected, was so calm, did I marvel.

Scott moved closer to the three on the couch. "Well it's all over now," he assured Trey. You're home and you're safe."

Trey looked up at him, able only to nod.

"Do you need some scotch?" Scott asked.

Trey nodded again.

"In the kitchen, right? We left it there, didn't we?"

"Yes," Trey said.

"I'll be right back."

I watched Scott leave the room, grateful for his love of Trey. I could feel it, taste it, and touch it.

"Perhaps we'll leave you in Scott's good care." My eyes moved to Trey. Neither Gabriel nor I truly wished to leave, however I did not want to complicate matters as Scott had no idea what world Trey was now part of, in truth, and I wanted news of the one Travis tracked the moment it arrived.

Trey's eyes held mine a moment. "I'll...I'll be okay. You'll come back though, right?"

"But of course, my darling."

"Yes, of course," Gabriel agreed.

Scott returned with a bottle and a glass just as Gabriel rose.

"Are you guys leaving?" He looked between us as Gabriel made his way to me, and then could not stop staring in awe at my Gabriel.

"Yes," I said. "We know he's in good hands with you here."

A bit of a smile found Scott after a moment. "Well, thanks for seeing them home, making sure they were okay."

"No need to thank us for what we cannot help but do, yet, you are welcome," Gabriel said.

Scott, mesmerized yet again for several seconds, and several seconds more by Gabriel, at last managed to return to himself. "You seem like good people. Um, see you again, I hope. Under better circumstances, of course."

I presented him with a smile. "I'm certain we will see you again, yes. Good night, everyone, and do take care."

"Night," we heard Geoff say as we walked to the door, and just before closing it behind us, heard Scott assuring Trey once again that he was safe.

I took Gabriel's hand as we walked down the hall. "Scott will take good care of him."

"The girl, Michel. She has something to do with this, you heard him."

"To choose," I replied. "I got this from Geoff."

Gabriel's scrutiny of my face demanded I look at him. "To choose who would go in Geoff's stead?" he asked.

My gaze shifted ahead. "I'm beginning to think so."

When Trey mentioned the girl, I had gleaned a measure of guilt.

"It seems logical, what with Travis' mention of the bullet," my angel did say.

My attention shifted from Gabriel when first her scent,

then the picture of Polly drifted down the hall in our direction. Dressed in a gauzy cotton halter dress made of sweet cream butter, her steps quickened when she spotted us.

"Is Trey home?" she asked before coming to a stop.

"Yes," I replied. "Judging from your demeanor, I don't have to tell you that something happened."

Her head made to shake.

I reached and took her hands, then proceeded to explain as best I could what I understood of the evening's events.

Absently, one of her hands lifted, her fingertips coming to rest on her lower lip a moment before she spoke.

"Goddess. Geoff crossed the veil, and Trey brought him back...?" Her hand slowly lowered. "Geoff's all right, you said."

"He seems perfectly well, yes."

"Trey?"

I took a breath. "Trey is still in shock."

She made to nod.

"Scott is with them," I continued, then proceeded to fill her in on our little story.

"It is my understanding that Scott does not yet know of us, or of Trey's gift, and so I reached for the first thing available in my mind," I concluded.

"Right. All right, car wreck, air bags...got it," she said. "Oh, he must be so shaken."

I gave her hand a squeeze. "Go see to him, I know you wish to more than anything at this moment."

She looked deeply into my eyes before bestowing a soft kiss to my lips. "Thank you."

It gave me a moment's pause, this, before I shook myself of darker thoughts. "But of course," I replied. "Go on now."

She looked to Gabriel, her expression soft, and gave him a nod before going on her way.

Once she was out of hearing range and Gabriel and I began once more to walk, upon reaching the stairs, he said to me, "Short of locking him in a room with no windows or doors, you can never truly keep him from harm, from life."

I met his gaze. As shaken as Gabriel himself was, he was also the practical sort when it mattered most. "No...we cannot keep him from life."

"He will not blame you," he added, speaking to my unspoken thought of before.

"Perhaps he should," I whispered before descending ahead of him.

Chapter Seventeen

AUGUST 1

Trey

Breaking the surface with a cry.

Hands on my chest, on my face, and soothing, honeyed words.

It took me a moment to realize it was Geoff and that he was with me in my bed.

"Angel, angel, just a dream."

I finally managed to focus on him.

He was alive, he was speaking and breathing, his heart was beating, he was alive.

"Dream..." I shook my head. But it wasn't just a dream. I crushed him to me.

"It okay, I'm here."

I tried to speak past the sandpaper and lump of an Adam's apple, but couldn't.

Warm and breathing in my arms, and I could feel his heart.

I could *literally* feel it, it beat insistently in my own chest, it seemed like.

"I couldn't let you go," the words scraped through my throat.

"I didn't want to go," he said.

"I," didn't want to let him go now, but my bladder was also being quite insistent. "Damn it."

I plundered his lips before finally giving in, unable to ignore it any longer. "I have to get up. Don't go anywhere."

"I not going anywhere," he reassured me.

I glanced at the clock. "God, it's not even four a.m. Go back to sleep. I'm...it's okay."

He gave a little shake of his head. "I stay up."

"I can't go back to sleep, Geoff. Really, just rest. For me, okay?" I traced his brow, then gave it a kiss.

"Okay, I'll try."

I gave him another kiss, and after making sure he settled back onto the bed, managed to tear myself away. Once shutting up my screaming bladder, I stared at myself in the bathroom mirror for a bit, though what I saw wasn't my face.

It was the blood on my hands, Geoff's blood, the blood on his tunic.

After splashing ice-cold water on my face, I headed for the kitchen, thinking *coffee, coffee*, I can't go back to sleep, I won't go back to sleep, even if it doesn't matter because I can still see it and I'm awake.

While going through the automatic motions of getting the coffee ready, it was still so clear.

Bang!

Jerk.

He falls.

Blood red flower blooming under my hands.

Bang!

Jerk, he falls.

Blood petals on my hands.

Except I never heard a bang. My brain was more than happy to betray me with the imaginary detail that should have accompanied the scene. Silencers are for assassins.

Hot sweat.

Assassins.

Next I knew, I was gripping the counter.

Next I knew, I couldn't breathe.

Next I knew, there was a voice, a sleepy voice.

"Trey?"

I can't breathe.

I'm getting dizzy.

"Whoa, whoa, hey," I heard. Then I felt hands, arms, someone holding me up. "Slow down, you're hyperventilating." I heard a barely-breathed curse word. "Paper bag, let me see if you have one."

Gasp of words. "I'm...I'll be..."

"Slow down, man, ohh, deep breath."

I'm trying, I'm trying.

Hand, rubbing my back. Scott's hand, right.

"There you go, that's it."

Inhale; inhale....Geoff...inside me, in my nostrils.

It started to soothe me.

But just when I stopped breathing too fast, the tears that wouldn't show last night exploded, and I thought I'd faint.

Next, I was sitting at the breakfast table in the kitchen and Scott was sitting in the chair beside me, pulled up as close as he could get.

After a too-furious rubbing of my eyes and a wiping of my nose with a kitchen towel, I looked into Scott's gaze and waited for the spots to fade. As they did, I saw the questions there that he wasn't yet asking.

"I had a nightmare," I offered. "I'm fine now."

I am full of shit, and he'll know it.

"Musta been a fucker," he said low.

I nodded, saying the next thing to come to mind. "They usually are."

He made himself glance in the direction of the counter. "Let me get that coffee going." He'd been about to say something else, I just knew it, but I was fine with what he did say.

Scott often knew when to let something slide, and I loved him for it.

"Yeah, I could really use some," I said, pressing the heel of my hand to my forehead.

"So could I." He got up and set about finishing what I'd started.

Some more of my wits returned. "I woke you up, didn't I?"

He looked at me over his shoulder. "Well, I needed the bathroom, actually, and then I heard you. Took me a groggy minute to realize it really was you and that you didn't sound okay." The pot started perking and he turned, facing my direction. "Was it, um, the wreck? Your nightmare, I mean."

Wreck...wreck. I ransacked my brain.

Last night, Michel and Gabriel, right. Polly, too. All going on about a car wreck.

Even Geoff. Geoff said something about a car wreck.

"Yeah," I said, and it took me a beat too long, because it looked to me like he didn't believe me, quite.

"You said it happened fast. Your brain's dumping all the details now, huh."

"Guess so." Did he believe me last night? Wracking my brain, I seemed to remember that he did. Except I couldn't lie for shit. He believed me why?

No—he believed *them*.

Right.

"It'll pass soon enough, I bet," he said, looking at the coffee pot again. "Smells good. Wish it would brew faster." He looked back to me, giving me a smile.

"No shit," I breathed out, pushing my hair back.

His eyes rested on me a time before he started talking again. "I remember when we lived together, that you had nightmares."

Of course he remembers that. "Those were—well those were

about the rape, usually."

His eyes made it halfway to the floor. "Yeah, I was figuring that, now." His eyes lifted. "Geoff said the air bags freaked you out. It's really bad for you, being pinned."

Swallow. "Yes."

Wait. How did Geoff know that?

My brain is too rattled for a mental shake.

"Um, my face was planted in the ground part of the time when they—so anyway, the airbag fucked me up." I ventured if we'd really had a wreck, it would no doubt be true.

He cleared his throat. "I don't want to make you freak out again, so I'll shut up now."

I leaned on my hand, trying to feel less out of sorts. "It's okay," I said, quietly. "You come in here, I'm about to pass out or something, and you just want to understand."

"And make sure you're okay," he said.

"That too." I tried to give him a smile. "You don't have to stay up, though. It's way early."

He glanced at the pot, again. "Ah, it's almost done, and it smells too good to ignore. How can I go back to bed now?" He looked at me. "Besides, if talking about it will help, I'm still here to listen."

But I couldn't. I couldn't *really* talk about the current issue. Would he even believe me? Do I even believe me? It's all so surreal, a scene in a movie and I can't turn the T.V. off.

Did that really happen last night?

Denial, such a friend and sometimes bastard.

"I know you are." I managed a real smile, small as it was. "I will sometime." Someday, maybe. Vampires, Marks, and Geoff—can't even think it, oh my.

"It's cool," he said. "Just remember I'm here for you."

This time. He didn't say it but I heard it, whether he was thinking it or not. I'm here this time. Don't you go running off this time, Trey.

"And I'm glad." And I meant it, I really did.

"No coffee without breakfast." Scott and I turned our heads at the sound of Geoff's voice.

"Breakfast you're gonna cook?" Scott smiled at Geoff, who smiled back.

"Who else do it?" Geoff walked by the table and planted a kiss on me before heading for the small fridge. "Maybe have to go to market."

I couldn't take my eyes from him, walking and talking. "Oh baby, it's so early, you don't have to do that. Besides, is anyone open?"

He waved me off. "I can so do that, and I can think of place maybe, open soon." He started rummaging in the cupboards. "Have first course, and then I go."

How could I stop the smile? Everything's fine, his words and actions said. Everything's normal. I'm perfectly healthy and everything's going to be just all right, Trey, and I'll take care of you.

I wanted to cry again, but just managed not going there again so soon.

"Well hey, we're all up," Scott said. "And first course, this sounds promising. Is there something I can help you with, Geoff?"

Geoff waved him off, intent on condiments I didn't remember buying.

Probably because he did.

Scott laughed. "I think I got it. Only one cook in this room."

"That right," Geoff said, tossing him a smile. "But okay, maybe you can go to market for me."

"Sure, just tell me where, and what you need." Scott's eyes travelled to me. "If it takes me longer than thirty minutes, send the search party."

Geoff giggled.

It was the most beautiful sound I'd ever heard, next to the beating of his heart.

Chapter Eighteen

Michel

I met Travis at point zero in front of Notre Dame. I could scent the human's blood that stained his black jacket, though he had already reversed it when he finished, and he was free, visually, of any lingering traces on his flesh or hair.

To mortal eyes, in any event.

"What did you learn?" I asked.

"The assassin came through one of the other arteries. Trey and Geoff never had a chance to see him coming; he wasn't in the same area as they were. Sniper with a rifle, a real professional. He targeted Geoff through a crack in the wall."

I studied the crease his expression left between his eyes while digesting the words *a real professional.*

"Vicont's involved," he continued, anticipating my next question.

"He told you this?"

"More or less." His following smile was sinister on its edges. He was still riding slightly on the thrill of the kill, which was certainly better than the gutted feeling he'd had when telling me that he failed, a feeling that would no doubt return.

More or less, he said. This meant he had ripped it from the human's mind, or literally scared it out of said human, and I could not help but return his smile.

I was soon frowning, however.

"Vicont may be a lot of things, but stupid he isn't," I said.

"I was suspicious of it myself, but I couldn't sense a lie, or that he was hiding anything. However..."

A lift of my brows indicated my wish for him to continue.

"I'm not as good with this as you by far, but I had the impression his mind may have been tampered with."

I became aware of the tilting of my head, as I viewed him from a slightly different angle, Travis. "What gave the impression?"

"It seemed as if sections were missing." He offered a shrug. "But you know how I am. It could be I scared him blank."

"Minds do to tend to scramble around you when you're in certain moods."

He laughed somewhat and then offered me one of his most contrite expressions, one rarely seen on his face. "This is important, and I might have gotten carried away too quickly. I was straining on my leash already."

"My dearest darling, if I had found him first, I would have peeled the skin from his body, thrilled in his screams, and watched with glee whilst he twitched. And that's only the beginning."

His laugh, warm and breathy. "You still would've gotten more information, I'm sure."

I pushed the fringe of hair that had fallen near to his nose back into place. "You're my best, and often enough, I neglect to ask questions when I'm angry. Now then, tell me more of these missing parts. Where were the gaps?"

"I clearly saw Vicont's face, but I didn't find all the words to go with the visual, this apparent meeting."

I offered a nod.

"I got the visual of the assassin being shown a photograph of the mark, but I couldn't see who handed it to him." He made to shake his head. "I heard Vicont somewhere in there giving orders, but it's murky."

"Someone who knows Vicont, who has the talent, could place him in a memory."

"You don't think it was him, do you?"

"Do you think it was, regardless of the splintered memories?"

"I'm not certain. I know there are people willing to pin things on him, hoping you'd do something about it," he said.

"Exactly." I stepped two paces to the left, crossing my arms over my chest. "He's not in a position to be fucking with me so blatantly." I gazed at him in my peripheral. "Vicont has the talent to erase and place whatever memories he likes." I paused. "Though he is weakened, such a gift he could still accomplish well enough, especially in a human mind."

I reclaimed those steps, facing Travis once more. "Even were he not able, he would certainly find someone who was. He'd not leave such a blatant trail."

"I don't disagree with you, but on the other hand, maybe that's what he wants you to think."

I took two steps to the right. "Yes, there's always this. Make it so obvious I couldn't possibly believe he'd done it." I made a swift turn back. "You saw nothing else?"

"I'm sorry to say that I didn't." His brows furrowed. "Hang on. There was one face I didn't recognize, popped into the middle of the rest. It didn't make sense; I figured it was just random brain dumping."

I stepped back to the left, and stepped closer to him. "What did this person look like?"

His eyes closed, more out of habit than necessity, as he conjured the image in his mind. "Sandy haired female, plain but pretty, with light brown eyes."

His eyelids lifted; meanwhile, I was gleaning the image, his mind opened to me, for he knew I'd wish to view it myself.

"I don't recognize this person," I said at length.

And yet…it seemed something about her should be familiar.

"What else can I do, Michel? Is there anything you'd like me to follow up on?"

My smile to him was warm. He cared for Trey and Geoff and had a desire for his own justice.

"Not at this moment. I won't hesitate to call, should I require anything of you later."

My thoughts were turning and turning, deciding what, exactly, I would do next, concerning Trey and Geoff.

Deciding as well, whether or not I truly wished to see Vicont in person again, and so soon, if only, perhaps, to draw out whomever it was that was hiding behind him with notes and implied guilt.

"Do you think it's connected, Michel?" I heard Travis ask of me. "The note, this shooting?"

I lifted my eyes, which had drifted to the cathedral. "I was musing on such. Perhaps I should spring the trap, if there is one."

"If you want me to track him down, I'll begin."

"So loyal, you." I graced him with a smile. "The note bore instructions for getting in touch with him, however, and," I reached out, touching his chin, "you are still guarding my mortal loves."

"Hopefully I do a better job of it from here on out," he said, nearly sans voice.

"My darling, my darling, you are doing your best, which is far above most people's best. David obviously lost his bleeding mind that night," I finished, mimicking Travis.

This brought to him a genuine laugh, just as I had hoped, and I moved to embrace him.

"Thank you," he said, embracing me in return. "I love you, you bastard."

An endearment, this, and it was I who laughed. "I quite

literally am, yes." I stepped back after dropping a kiss on his cheek. "You have my love as well, always. I'll see you later. Gabriel awaits me."

"I'll get back to doing what I do." He presented me with a genuine smile.

"And how I do love all the things you do." I offered one more smile in return before strolling away, several and several thoughts swimming around in the darkest confines of my brain.

Trey

There was just no fixing my mood the rest of the day. I declined every offer of distraction, not that Scott or Geoff called them distractions, the ideas for something to do.

Nope, I begged off and said I should do some work. Lose myself in files; I thought maybe that would help. I would have gone to the office, except I couldn't let Geoff out of my sight yet.

I wouldn't say I accomplished much on the computer at home, but I kept trying, between the times I went to the bathroom to splash my face with water, or just sit on the closed toilet seat, trying to get a grip on my thoughts.

They kept going back to that girl. They kept going to the moment Geoff fell, to the blood, and to the moments before, when Geoff said he'd always remember that place, because that's where I first told him I loved him.

I'd finally said it. Now it was tainted, and the completely psychotic part of my mind was saying *see, see?* You said it, and you lost him.

Except we didn't lose him, I said.

It killed him, it said.

But I saved him, I said.

If not the girl, who would you have taken, huh?

Shut up, I said.

Travis maybe? He was the only other one there, wasn't he? If he'd walked up first...

Shut UP.

I'm not sure I could even do that anyway; he's a vampire, I said.

Geoff's clearly in danger because of you, it said.

SHUT UP!

I wanted to cut myself.

I couldn't cut myself.

I wasn't alone.

Wasn't alone, couldn't do that to Geoff. I wouldn't do it to him; I wouldn't do what I did to Sean.

That was my day. Arguing with myself and trying not to cut.

Eventually a knock came on the door. Geoff and Scott were in the kitchen, talking about dinner and giving me space.

So I answered the door.

It was Travis.

Not a second or two after I opened the door and saw him, I was in the hall, shutting the door behind me.

"What the fuck are you doing here?"

He paused before answering. "I wanted to make sure that you were okay."

"Sure, I'm fine, we're fine, everything's fine."

He took a step back. "I can see this isn't a good time. I'll go on, then."

"Where were they?"

His gaze didn't waver from mine.

"Where was Marc, or whoever? Where were they?"

"David left his post," he quietly said.

"I thought you didn't hire anyone less than stellar."

His lashes dropped.

I moved forward and grabbed the lapels of his jacket. "You

said no worries, no worries." I realized I was starting to gasp for air. "You said no worries."

I felt his hands cover mine. The touch was terribly gentle, and some of my steam leaked out, the pressure of needing to take it out on someone lessening.

But only a little.

"I watched him bleed. I felt him die. His heart stopped, he died!" Gasp. "You said no worries, you said..." can't go on.

Want to cut.

"I did say that, yes. I'm so sorry, Trey."

The tone of his voice sapped more of my steam.

"I couldn't get there in time. I wish I could have gotten there in time, saved you the shock, the entire ordeal, Trey."

The look in his eyes—I sagged against him. "If I hadn't been there..."

"At least you were *there*, and whatever you did, thank God."

He sounded so full of remorse. It was also the first time I'd heard him sound lacking in confidence. Completely lacking.

I pressed my forehead to his shoulder. "It's not your fault; it was still light and..." Raspy breath. "It's not your fault. I'm messed up, and I'm taking it out on you." I found his darkened eyes. "I'm sorry."

"I'm the last person you ever need to apologize to for an *honest feeling*. I understand, Trey. I did fail you, though, and I'll always be sorry about that."

I wasn't sure what I saw in his eyes, then. It wasn't just regret. Not over Geoff. There was more. There was something much deeper there, and that something was working its way into his voice.

"You didn't fail. David did."

His lashes dropped again, this time with a dry, barely heard laugh. "That's what Michel said." His lashes lifted. "That's what my parents said, that I didn't fail."

I searched and searched his eyes.

He hadn't meant to say that last part, I thought. But

sometimes we stumble precisely so we can talk about it. "You lost someone before."

His eyes shot to the side. His jaw clenched. "Another time."

And sometimes we still don't want to talk about it. I knew that feeling very well.

I nodded.

He found my eyes again. "Thank you."

I took a cleansing breath. "Geoff's alive, that's what matters, right?"

He found a bit of a smile. "Yes, and Michel said that, too."

"Well, don't beat yourself up. That's my department."

He found a bit more of a smile, a sympathetic one. "You should turn that over to someone else, at least for while."

I found a much smaller smile. "So I've heard."

He then inhaled deeply, and his lashes fluttered with it.

Moon-kissed black eyes replaced amber eyes. This time it wasn't just an eclipse.

"He is in you. I can smell it, taste it. You are one."

His voice, it had gotten deeper, richer.

"There is beauty even in tragedy. Always remember this, Trey du Bois."

Falling into the abyss of his gaze, I couldn't speak, and the air seemed to crackle, just a bit, it crackled, electric.

Amber suddenly shattered the darkness, freeing me.

Travis smiled.

"I," blink and blink, mental shake. "Did you want to come inside? You know, see him for yourself again?"

Tenderness touched his eyes. "Very much so."

"I think I cleared my system for now. I'll try not to be a brat. Oh, and Scott's here, too."

He nodded. "Michel filled me in on the story that was told, so I've got that straight."

"I hate lying to Scott."

"I don't much care for lies myself, but this is your truth to tell, if you do."

I rubbed my face. "He's not buying it anyway, I'm sure."

"Let's go in and I'll help you with that, Trey. Not with tricks, mind you."

I turned and opened the door. "I could use some help, yeah."

Once inside, Travis made his way directly to the kitchen, me following. Scott gave him a *hey*, which Travis returned.

Then Geoff turned, giving Travis a cheery smile.

Travis? He went straight to Geoff, and gently, sweetly, folded him into his strong arms, his eyes closing as he did.

"Precious angel. I'm so relieved you're well."

Geoff, his voice as sweet as the embrace, said, "Everything is okay, it's all okay."

Comforting. He was comforting Travis. I couldn't take my eyes away, eyes that were misting for the sweetness of the moment.

Travis stepped back, if slightly, and took Geoff's face between his hands, smiling down at him. "You remind me of someone I once knew, in ways. I loved him dearly."

The smile Geoff shined up at Travis was beatific. "Such a thing to say to me. Thank you. You're special, too."

Travis' smile widened, and then he let go, reluctantly it seemed, of my angel's face, and turned toward me and Scott, who—I realized after the spell was broken— had been just as caught up in it.

"It wasn't important at the time, but Michel wanted me to tell you not to worry about the car. It wasn't your fault, after all," said Travis.

Car. Right, the car. I guess in the lie we were driving one of Michel's cars.

"That's nice of him. It's such an expensive car." What kind of car?

"He has other Mercedes. The two of you are far more important."

Mercedes. Got it.

Scott said, "They seem like really good people, Michel and Gabriel. They brought Geoff and Trey home after the wreck."

Travis looked to Scott. "They are, and quite generous, too."

Scott smiled. "I'm sure you mean more than material generosity, but I gotta say the perks Trey gets with his job sound damned good."

Travis gave him a warm smile. "They're generous with good employees. Trey's the best attorney they've ever had."

Well, gee. If they were going to talk about me right in front of me, at least it was good stuff.

Scott looked at me. "Yeah, he's a sharp one. So they let you drive their cars, too."

I turned my eyes to him. "Another perk, yeah." My car, that ridiculously expensive but damned sweet present from them, suddenly popped into my mind. I hadn't told Scott about it.

Right. Explain *that* gift. Shit, I was lying left and right, wasn't I?

Omitting. I was omitting certain details.

Close enough, damn it.

"So, Travis," Scott said then. "Trey said that you work for them, too."

"Yes." Travis answered.

Geoff came to my side, listening to the back and forth. I put my arm around him, wondering if Scott was just being conversational to help lighten things, as he had all day, or—

Guilty conscience. I had it. It was making me suspicious for no good reason.

"What do you do for them, exactly?" Scott asked.

"Security." Travis kept it simple.

"Security. They need much of that?" Scott asked.

"They own a lot of properties. I oversee security in some of them around Paris. Set up crews, that sort of thing. Occasionally I do the same thing for them in other countries."

"I get it. Sounds kind of cool," Scott said.

"I like it," Travis said.

I just kept gazing at Travis. He didn't have to lie, and he wasn't. All he had to do was offer just the right details. Scott probably wouldn't ask a question that would make Travis need to lie, anyway.

Wished I could say the same.

During the lull, Geoff did the polite thing, even though he knew about Travis.

"I was getting ready to make dinner. You want to stay? There is room, and much food."

Travis shifted his gaze to Geoff, a smile easily forming. "Thanks precious, but I'm afraid I can't. I just stopped by to make certain you were both okay. There's some property I need to check and your place wasn't too far out of the way."

"You work late hours," Scott said.

Travis' eyes shot to Scott. "Sometimes all hours. Any rate, it was good to see you again, Scott." He took in all of us. "Sorry to dash in and out, but I have a schedule to keep."

"It was nice of you to check on them," Scott offered. "Hope I catch you again sometime. Don't work too hard."

"I always work hard. It's the way I like it," Travis offered a wink to Scott, who chuckled. "I'm sure I'll catch you again sometime, though, yes." He nodded in Geoff's direction and mine. "I'll leave you to dine in peace."

"Hey, uh, I'll walk you out," I said.

"If you like." Another look to Geoff and then Scott. "Night, all."

"Bye," from Geoff.

"Yeah, later man," from Scott.

I walked Travis to the door. Went outside the door with him, shutting it.

"So I was driving a Mercedes. I was driving, right?"

He gave me a sympathetic look and placed a hand on my shoulder. "It'll work out mate, I'm sure of it. Scott there, he really cares about you."

I sighed and leaned back against the door. "This is why I hate *lying* to him."

"When you figure out the best time and the best way, you'll tell him." He leaned in. "Polite omissions aren't the same as lies."

"You caught that. I wasn't thinking polite, though."

He shook his head. "I didn't literally read your thoughts. I can scent changes in your body chemistry, though, and I've been around you enough it's even easier to guess what you're thinking."

"Oh. Nifty trick, I guess."

"Fair enough. I'll shut it."

I'm a heel. "It's okay. You're just trying to help. I know this, I really do."

He somewhat smiled. "Then I'll say it wasn't a difficult guess anyway. You hate lying, we've established this. You've certainly had to leave things out when talking to Scott. Dance around the truth." He replaced his hand on my shoulder. "I said *polite* omissions, because some things are best left unsaid, for the sake of the other person."

Half grunt. "I've been dancing around the truth for years now, really."

His hand moved to the side of my neck. "I don't know all the secrets that burden you, but I do know that you have them. That can be a lot of weight to carry, Trey."

"Having secrets gets lonely," I whispered. Travis had said that.

"Yet some are difficult to verbalize."

I looked into his eyes. "Very. I finally shared with someone, but I still feel weird about it, and there I was telling him not to feel weird about it. It's me, not him." I rubbed my forehead. "And shit, I haven't seen him for two and half years, but I asked Polly to distract him. You know, since I'm being weird."

And since I can't tell him everything about my new life, yet.

If I was cryptic, Travis went right by it, giving me a soft

smile. "The scariest time isn't in the telling. It's in the minutes after."

I didn't exactly laugh. It was more an expulsion of air. "Yeah. I think you nailed that." I sighed. "God, and then this happens and it's one more thing to hide. I feel so guilty about…" I shut my mouth and looked away.

"That girl," I heard him say low.

My eyes snapped back to him. "I killed her."

"You didn't pull the trigger." His eyes, searching mine.

"No, but I may as well have."

"I don't exactly understand what happened, but it's right that Geoff's here."

I tipped my head back against the door, closing my eyes. "I know. I mean I want him here, I couldn't let him go, I— but all she did was offer help. Some innocent girl that somehow happened along and it ended up the worst place for her to be." I opened my eyes in time to see his head tilt.

"Happened along at just the right time."

"Wrong time, she was there at the wrong time, what did she ever do to me?" I pushed a hand through my hair. "Shit. I'm not sure I understand, either, I just know I made a trade." I held my hand up, staring at my palm. "I mean, what's this power?" I dropped my hand. "Who am I to choose?"

He shook his head. "I don't know about that. But I'm still thinking she showed up at the right time."

I closed my eyes again. "You almost sound like P.K. Almost." Opening my eyes. "You believe in fate?"

"The older I get, the more I wonder. I don't think everything is mere coincidence in the world." He absorbed my expression. "You tell *me* how it is that she just happened along you in a hole in the ground you snuck into, at that precise moment."

"Speaking of, how'd you get in there?" I asked, not ready to think about what he said.

"There's another way round, a longer way. She fit through the other entrance, the one you went through. I don't. I took you out the long way, but you were in shock. I'm not surprised you don't remember."

I ran a hand over my face. "I can't...I can't talk about this right now."

I want to cut.

But I can't. I can't, I can't.

Travis studied me.

Finally, he spoke just as I was wondering what else he could smell in me. "I understand. But I'll be around if you get tired of carrying every secret that you hold."

His expression gave me nothing to read but friendly support.

Slight nod. "I'd better get back inside."

"I won't be far."

Bigger nod. "Okay. Hey, and I really am sorry about before. I'm tense."

"No worries, mate. I would be, too." He gave me a warm smile. "Go on; go hold him in your arms."

"Exactly what I want to do. See you." I turned to open the door. Paused. Looked over my shoulder. "Travis?"

He'd taken a few steps. He turned back, reclaiming the distance. "Yes?"

"The person that," —bang, blood—,"shot Geoff." That felt like gravel, clear throat, Trey. "Did you find him? Her?"

"Yes."

Good of him not to offer more than I asked, I thought.

Still, I asked another question. "What did you do?"

"Ripped him in half."

Swallow.

Twinge of darkness. "Good."

"Anything else you wanted to know, Trey?"

Was there?

Maybe so.

"Did someone send him?"

"Yes."

Assassin. *Assassin.*

"Who?"

"On the surface, we've been led to believe it was Vicont. However, considering the position Vicont's in and other discrepancies, Michel's not convinced."

Gritting my teeth.

"So maybe it's someone wanting to pin it on him? Someone who knew Geoff was special to Michel," I said.

His face smoothed, then softened. "If it's about pinning this on Vicont, it's likely it was someone who knew that Geoff was even more special to you, and that Michel would do most anything for you."

My breath hitched for two reasons—dating me was dangerous. My knowing Michel was definitely dangerous. My Adam's apple lodged on the lump next to it for one reason.

Michel loves me that much.

"Vicont learned in that mountain that Michel truly loves you. He learned, possibly, just how much. But as you once said, news spreads amongst us like poison ivy. We'll get to the bottom of it one way or another, I swear."

I was still trying to swallow.

I felt the touch of his hand to my face. "Yes, Michel loves you that much. It's a reason I was happy to be the one looking after you."

I managed to peek at him through my lashes.

He leaned close. "When I felt the love he had for you, and then Gabriel's certainly, I knew I'd like you. I already liked you for the happiness in Gabriel's heart. I've already grown rather fond of you myself, Trey."

I managed to croak out, "Enough to tell me your secret."

His lips curved. "You're good people. I'm less alone now that I told you, little brother. Though I'm sorry for the extra burden. Give me one to carry in return, and I'll carry it forever, if you need."

I wanted to swipe at my eyes, but he was too close. His thumbs, they did it for me, moving across the flesh beneath.

Too much to feel, I grasped at something else. "I think I'd be more like your grand nephew or something."

"Nah. You don't belong to Kar." He grinned.

"Yeah you're right."

"So little brother it is, since I'm not your dad, either."

Cleared my throat. "I'll take that."

He moved back. "Speaking of little brothers, you were going inside to hold Geoff. That's good therapy, mate."

Deep breath. "Yeah." I found a smile. "You think of him that way, too?"

It took him a moment. It was as if he just realized that what I said was true. "Reckon I do now, yes." After a beat, he quietly continued. "He reminds me of my own little brother. Keegan was his name."

With that, he turned and strode down the hall, and I would have bet that when he lifted his hand, he was wiping his own eyes.

Chapter Nineteen

AUGUST 2

Here I was, back at the office. It was difficult to leave Geoff, but he said he was going to work, anyway. I didn't like that either, even though Michel had made a point of calling very early this morning to inform me that we were well watched, that there were extra eyes.

This didn't stop me from wanting to sit at Le Parvis and stare at Geoff through his entire shift.

Normalcy, though. There needed to be some normalcy. Geoff had said this not so much in words, but with his actions, and he was right. It was likely to help me. He was alive, damn it. I needed to stop thinking about the forever-minute he was dead. He was alive *now*.

At least my reason for being at the office was pleasant enough. Renaud had requested another meeting with me. Marcus wasn't with him this time, either. Renaud admitted he'd also just wanted to see me before he left Paris. I couldn't say no to that plus business.

"Yes, I believe *Monsieur* Lecureaux might be interested in-"

Blink.

"—your proposal. I can't, of course, state this definitively without speaking to him."

What was that?

"Which I can do this evening, I believe."

Renaud's eyes paused in their searching of my face.

Focus, Trey.

"It would be wonderful, meeting with him myself, at some point," he said.

I offered a smile. "You know how elusive he can be."

Lilt of a laugh, his. "I do, yet I continue to hope."

"I'll extend your—"

Again. There.

"—invitation, and let you know—"

Blink blink.

"Let you—"

No.

"Trey, is something amiss?"

Blink.

"Pardon me," I said. "I'm—"

Distracted.

No. Can't be.

"I'm uh—"

"You don't seem well, Trey."

Can be.

Pardonez-moi.

I tried to focus on Renaud's concerned features. "I'm sorry; I'm feeling a little—"

Hazel eyes.

"—dizzy…"

Forgive me. *Pourquoi?*

"Gracious, my boy, you've blanched. Come, sit." I feel Renaud take my arm.

I see her smile turn into a scowl. She's standing just behind him, just behind and to the left, and she's scowling at me.

What did you do?

I back away from him, hand flying to my forehead.

"Excuse me, I feel...sick. Excuse me."

I couldn't get out of the room fast enough, down the hall fast enough, into the bathroom fast enough, couldn't lock the door behind me securely enough.

Leaning back against it, I found some slower breathing.

What did you do?

My eyes dart to every corner of the bathroom and between, while my heart thumps toward my stomach.

I don't see her.

Where am I?

But I hear her.

Why am I here?

My hands cover my ears in vain.

You did this, didn't you?

My heart rattles towards my knees when she appears, leaking, bulging through the wall opposite, but solid, so solid to my eyes once she's fully occupying the same space as me.

"You did something. Forgive me, I think you said."

I think I begin a slow slide down the door.

"Why?" she asks, her voice sweetly innocent, sweetly young. Sliding.

"Why?" Her eyes, sweetly innocent, taken over by confusion.

"Oh God. I'm sorry," I think I say.

"You're sorry. Forgive you. What did you do?"

"I..." she's drifting closer.

"What is happening to me?" She's reaching for me.

I shiver. I shiver because I'm a bit frightened and she feels terribly cold, her touch chills my flesh.

Her touch. I can feel it. She's so solid.

I jump through my skin when someone knocks on the door.

"Trey, pardon, but are you in there?"

You're sorry.

Tap tap. "Sweets?"

The girl with auburn hair, she begins to fade, particles dispersing like water vapor in a breeze.

Knock knock, more insistent. "Do you need assistance? *Monsieur* Chomette said that you weren't well. You almost run me down coming from the room."

Slide up, up, answer, answer.

"I'm okay, doll. Tell...tell *Monsieur* I'll be right out."

"You are certain that I cannot do something for you?"

Pull it together, man. "Thanks, but it's okay doll. I just need a minute."

"Okay. I don't mean to bother you, I am merely concerned."

"Thank you, really."

"Okay."

Ear to door.

Click click click, her heels.

Visual search of every nook and cranny.

Nothing.

Half a gallon of warm water on my face measured in handfuls.

All right now, leave the damn bathroom, Trey. Go on. Get out.

It's not as if you can hide anyway.

Take a breath, open the door, and walk back to that meeting room before everyone thinks you've fallen and can't get up, and don't think about the ghost of the girl you—

Murdered.

****

Outside their house. *Their* house. I wasn't entirely certain why. My feet just carried me there once I got off the Metro.

The ride on the Metro proved interesting, if only because

the moment, okay, moments of paranoia that came and went were complete with real sound.

At least I thought the sound was real. Truth is I wasn't sure. I kept hearing her on a loop. On a loop, asking if we needed help. For what? Forgive me for what?

Rewind, play. Rewind, play.

I'd managed to get out of the office after convincing Renaud it was a blood sugar thing, then assuaging Odette by eating something, and then being able to hold it together well enough, long enough to satisfy her.

Sweet girl, really she is. But I had to get out of there. Especially before I made a bigger fool of myself in front of the client.

For one thing.

Also, so no one would start to think I'd lost my marbles out in the street. So no one would ask me one more damned question.

Yet here I was, in front of their house, giving Loki a good chin scratching. It made me feel better, really, and Loki didn't ask questions I couldn't answer.

I did want to see them. Just Michel, if Gabriel was asleep, that would be good, too. I just wanted to see them. I wasn't sure I could talk about the shit that went down underground, but maybe they'd let it slide.

Yeah. Sure they would, I told myself.

Or maybe they'd remind me, too, that Geoff was alive, so let's focus on that.

Sure. Let's focus on that, no problem. While I'm focusing on that, maybe I'll forget about the innocent girl I murdered in order to purchase his soul.

I plopped down on my ass in front of the gate.

Everything has its opposite, that's what P.K. said. Geoff alive on this side, there had to be an opposite on the other side. Right?

Right. Like that made it okay.

"Fuck." I raked my hair back. "I'm not sorry he's here, I'm not."

Loki gazed quizzically at me. I looked into his intelligent doggy eyes.

"Why couldn't I at least have more time?" I asked Loki, whose head tilted. "Maybe...maybe I could have come up with a bad guy or something." Humorless laugh. "Who am I to judge? How fast *could* I find some murdering rapist or something, anyway?"

Loki's head tilted the other way.

I narrowed my eyes. "Pretty fast, at least in my head, actually. I happen to know some rapists. Maybe they're murders by now, too. Too bad they're far away." Too bad I was too stunned, freaked and frantic to think of them. Maybe—

As if I had a clue whether or not that would have worked. "But I'd feel a lot less guilty."

I stood up and paced. "Hey, Lucien. Where the fuck were you, by the way, huh?" I let my eyes roam the greenery. "Thanks for the fucking warning, asshole."

I turned back toward the gate. "Not going to talk to me now, huh? Worthless fuck."

I turned a circle, arms out. "C'mon, where were you, *grandpa*?" Turning, turning. "No answer? Well fuck you, too. Fuck you!"

I put my face into my hands and stopped. "Jesus, Trey. Stop it. Just stop it. Get a grip." I dropped my hands and looked to the front of their house. "Just rant on like some psycho out here, accomplishing what?" Pause. "Yeah, exactly."

I turned away. "Just go by Le Parvis, or something, Trey. Then find Scott, and see if you can convince him you're fine."

Sure. Not a problem.

Michel

"Where did *this* one come from?" Gabriel sneered as he

looked over the note.

"It was delivered to Shane at the Fall Out. He was at the door."

"Are you going to call this number?"

I took the note from him, comparing it to the one he had thought better of shredding. "Dialing a number won't kill me. This is the same handwriting."

"How kind of them to be consistent." Gabriel's sigh was languid. He draped both of his sinuous legs over the chair arm. "We shall see if this amounts to anything more than a trite annoyance."

I set the notes on the side table and flowed to the floor to lean against his chair. His hand dropped so that his nimble fingers might comb through my hair.

"When are you going to make this call, *mon lion*?"

I reached up and rested my hand on his glass smooth thigh. "This evening, I think."

"After visiting Trey? I have missed him and should like to see how he fares."

"Travis told me that Trey was as well as could be expected." I looked up at my dark angel. "I do wish to see him. I merely haven't wanted to complicate matters concerning Scott."

"Then we shall invite him here."

I traced a network of fragile blue veins. "Splendid idea, yes, I was thinking on it. He could inform Scott he had business to attend, perhaps."

"Perhaps Geoff will be free as well," said my darling.

"That would be lovely." I directed a smile up at him.

"Then call Trey now, leave him a message if you must."

I offered up another smile. "Post haste." I rose to make my way to the telephone. I paused at the prickling of my senses. Someone was now outside our gate.

"Never mind," Gabriel said.

I trained my senses on Trey.

He was not faring so well, it seemed.

I observed him for a time, as it also seemed he needed to work a thing or two from his system. I felt Gabriel's movement, and soon the length of him pressed against my back. Soon his chin rested itself upon my shoulder.

"Poor boy," I said, frowning.

"Let him in."

"He hasn't yet ceased to debate this."

My backside cooled with Gabriel's absence. I further observed Trey, attempting to calm himself down.

Soon Gabriel had returned wearing one of my black velvet robes. To me he handed one in sapphire. I began slipping into it immediately.

"I'll fetch him now before he retraces the circles of his thoughts," I whispered, placing a kiss on Gabriel's cheek. "Don't fret. He'll work through this."

"I do hope so." His eyes, they had darkened.

After a caress to his cheek, I made for the front door, mentally opening the gate along the way.

Trey

The gate opened.

Too late to walk away now. Not that I *really* wanted to.

The door opened a bit and I saw a golden-tanned arm, its hand beckoning me.

Ah hell.

I headed through the gate, closing it behind me, and then toward the house. Michel opened the door wider as I approached, and when I was close enough, he grabbed my arm, pulled me in, and hugged me.

For I second I wanted to protest and move away.

Less than a second.

I gratefully hugged him back, then sagged in his arms, letting my cheek find his broad shoulder.

"I'm glad you don't always sleep during the day," I mumbled.

"*Mon cher, mon cher.*" Strong fingers slid through my hair and I sighed. "Gabriel is awake as well. Come inside." He moved back, taking my hand and leading me into his living room. Shortly after that, I was in Gabriel's arms. A purr rolled through him, lulling me, comforting me, and as far as I was concerned just then, he could have kept me there all day.

Well not all day, unless Geoff were here, too.

Gabriel then let go and took one of my hands. "Come, sit, grandson. You are torn and weary."

Those were some words for what I was. I let him lead me to the antique velvet sofa. Sat beside him. Michel took up the space on my other side. Together they made a safe little bubble for me to sit in.

"Sorry to bother you," I said. "Really. I don't know why…I just…my feet led me here." I glanced at Michel. "Not that I didn't want to see you."

"You apologize where there isn't a need to apologize," he said.

I studied my hands. Now that I was in the house, I had no words. Maybe just sitting here was all I needed. Hell if I really knew.

I decided I didn't want to think about the incident. In an attempt not to, I asked Michel a question.

"So how was Belgium?" I found his eyes.

He knew what I was doing. Thankfully, he let me do it.

"Interesting might be a word for it."

"As interesting as politics can be, right?"

He smiled a little. "Occasionally they're quite interesting. There was a subject or two of interest on this trip."

"Well if you need any legal advice…" I grasped for a smile.

"You'd be the first I look up."

I looked at Gabriel. "Did you have any fun at all?"

"Outside of Michel's arms? *Non.*"

I reached for a laugh. Not finding it, I planted my face in my hands. "Shit."

"Shit," Trey said into his hands. Poor boy, trying so hard to avoid his own mind, which is of course, an exercise in futility.

"If it's quiet you seek, you may have it here. If it's something else, you have only to say, and we'll give it to you if we can," I said, smoothing his hair.

He lifted his face to find my eyes. "Right now I feel about five things, at least."

My only reply was to nod, to let him go on as he would.

"I feel like I'm avoiding Scott, and it's shitty, because it's been so long since I've seen him. It's shitty, but I can't pretend nothing's wrong."

My Gabriel took one of Trey's hands. "One day he will come to understand. One day."

Trey's eyes moved to my love. "And I yelled at Travis. It's my fault, my fault. I shouldn't have taken Geoff down there."

"If David had been doing his job, you would have been safe," I offered.

Trey's eyes moved to me. "Do you know this for a fact?"

In all honesty, I could not say yes. "Perhaps no, but the odds would have been far more favorable."

He sighed. "I just...it was romantic, I thought, and..." he sighed again. "Now it's a nightmare."

I looked away, several of those selfish thoughts of mine returning.

"You will reclaim the romance of it again," I heard my dark angel tell Trey. "The more that you see Geoff smiling at you, the more you will remember the moments of happiness before the darkness."

It was not Gabriel Trey replied to, however. "Michel, what are you thinking about?"

I returned my gaze to him. "You're in my world. This is why

Geoff was shot."

He searched my face. "This is true." Before I could look away yet again, he touched my hand. "But I don't know. If I wasn't here, I'd probably still be alone in New York, still be burying myself deeper and deeper in the past, and I wouldn't even have Geoff to lose."

A smile twitched at my lips. "In a job you hate?"

"Yeah."

My eyes dropped to our hands, his still atop mine. "Thirty minutes," I whispered.

"Except thirty wasn't enough for me. It isn't enough."

My eyes flew to his. His that were so conflicted, so deeply troubled. "It was within your power to save him. I would have done the same. Right or wrong, the same."

"Would you have to kill someone for it?"

"I *have* killed others for it," my gaze shifted to Gabriel. "Many others."

"I mean...I'm not like you, and you don't have to kill one person to make another live."

My gaze returned to Trey. It was the same, and yet it wasn't; he was correct. "I couldn't save someone who was already dead. You have a gift even I don't possess."

He raked his fingers through his hair. His guilt wound through my senses. Guilt over the girl, guilt for even thinking to feel guilty as it meant Geoff was alive.

So much guilt. So torn, was he.

"I don't know if I like this gift. But then Geoff wouldn't be here and, fuck, I can't stop dancing this circle."

I slipped an arm across his shoulders. "We are all grateful that Geoff is still here. You think yourself a murderer; here you sit in murderous company, at least. If you're selfish, then we are all selfish."

I caught Gabriel's somber expression. I caught his quietly intense studying of Trey.

"But then you knew this about me, didn't you?" I continued.

"I had to have *you*, after all."

I managed to bring a small smile to Trey, with this statement.

"I chose," he said.

"I'm a force of nature. Are you so certain that you chose?"

This brought to him a somewhat larger smile.

"We chose each other."

I was touched, and I was pleased I'd gotten the smile from him. Unfortunately, it was soon lost.

"She didn't get to choose," he said.

Gabriel, at last, broke his silence. "But you did?"

Trey looked to Gabriel. "Papa said that I had to choose." His hand moved over his face. "I could see Geoff leaving, leaving me. He was getting farther away and—and there was no time. I had no time."

Gabriel took up both of Trey's hands. "Papa said. Then there is a reason, no? For if Papa gave you a choice, there must have been a reason."

Trey's emotions shifted and tumbled. The logical part of his brain knew Gabriel was correct, but logic was not yet ready to save him.

Or he was not yet ready to be saved by logic.

"But she was just some innocent girl," said Trey.

"You also said that you had no time. Who would you choose with more time?"

"Not an innocent girl, Gabriel."

"You do not know how innocent she was or was not, do you?" inquired Gabriel.

Trey's brows knitted. "That's the problem. I don't, and all she did was offer help."

"*Oui*, she offered help," affirmed Gabriel.

"I'm sure she wasn't counting on dying for him," Trey snapped.

Gabriel, unperturbed and understanding, said nothing, only stroked Trey's hair.

"I'm sorry," Trey quietly said. "I didn't mean to snap at you."

"You are still shaken," I said. "We understand."

He looked to me. "Why haven't you come by?" he asked, shifting the subject slightly.

"I thought it might complicate matters with Scott," I replied. "We were just speaking of inviting you over when we sensed you outside, however. We've been desperate to see you, believe me."

Of a sudden, he rested his head on my shoulder. "I believe you. I'll...I'll figure it out eventually. You're not leaving again anytime soon, are you?"

Gabriel's eyes captured mine, asking of me the same question.

"We may be leaving again, yes."

Trey's head leapt from my shoulder. "Where now? More business?"

My heart, he squeezed it. Like a small boy, hating the idea of his parents leaving, that's what it felt like, this is what lanced through him.

"Don't worry, beloved. A short trip, likely shorter than the one before, I promise."

"But why?"

Breaking my heart, the pleading of his eyes. He was so unsteady, now.

"I need to speak with Vicont," I replied, answering both him and Gabriel, truthfully.

"Will you be safe?"

My eyes moved over his face. "Yes."

"Why do you need to see him?"

I glanced at Gabriel. "To get to the bottom of a few things."

"Travis said you didn't really think he was the one who sent the assassin." Trey stumbled on the last word, whilst my heart seized on the last word.

"I am not convinced, no. But we also have personal business." I searched his eyes again, deciding to give him more information; deciding it may help him focus on something else as he so wished to do, something other than Geoff falling, bleeding, dying.

Oh yes, I could see the images, images I didn't want to see, in truth.

"The woman I met with in Belgium," I continued. "She's someone both Vicont and I knew. Let us say I'm on a fact finding mission."

This piqued his interest. "Is she on his side?"

Gabriel interjected. "She is on her own side, generally."

Trey's eyes moved to Gabriel after his icily spoken words. "You don't like her."

"This would be an understatement, my disliking Elise."

"Elise," Trey repeated, the diversion working at the moment, the visions of Geoff receding. "You don't like her, but you went to see her after she asked for help. Travis said something about it."

I picked up the thread. "This was also a fact finding mission." I could not help but to add, as I thought of my last conversation with Elise, the next words, "It's time I pay her back somewhat properly."

Trey's eyes snapped to me. "What did she do?"

I considered what I actually wanted to say. As I looked into his eyes and saw that the diversion was working even better than I had hoped, I decided I would not let him down, now.

"She performed a metaphorical vivisection on my heart."

At first, he merely blinked at me. "You were close once."

"Yes."

"What did she do to you?"

"She betrayed me, and…" I paused.

"And?"

I found that I had need of looking away. So much for my not letting him down.

"Michel?"

My gaze shifted back, yet I could not speak it.

Trey's face set in grim lines, and I tasted the shifting of his emotion. He did not press further, instead asking, "How are you going to pay her back?"

I found Gabriel's eyes once more. "Take everything she owns, for a start."

"Do you mean businesses, or more?" Trey asked.

I continued to hold Gabriel's gaze. "Businesses and then some."

"I'm a damned good attorney, you know."

I nearly smiled. I then felt a twinge of guilt. Now was not the time. Then again, perhaps it was; after all, he still wasn't currently wallowing in his own guilt.

I found Trey's eyes. "You may be able to help me, yes."

"Tell me how."

Distraction or not, I knew that he would have said this regardless. How I loved him and his loyalty.

"Once I gather more information, I'll lay it out for you. Do keep in mind there is a slight risk involved."

He shrugged. "When isn't there?"

I marveled at his range of emotions, how each was genuine in feeling whenever they occurred. One could never say that Trey did things half way. Gabriel would say the same of me.

"We may leave this very evening to gather more information. I shall keep you informed," I said.

"Good." He paused, his thoughts shifting yet again. "Michel, P.K. told me about the ransom note, by the way." His gaze became level. "What did Vicont want from you when he took me?"

I directed my gaze to Gabriel.

"I need to understand, Michel," I heard Trey continue. "If it *is* him that sent the assassin, if it *is* him that's still fucking with me, I want to know the real reason. I need to know…please."

I did Trey the courtesy of meeting his gaze. "He wanted us to be one happy family," I stated with little humor. "He wanted me to return to him, combine our power. He went so far as to say Gabriel was part of the family as well, that he conceded this. This is utter bullshit, for when I first met with Vicont while you looked after my husband, he threatened with all sincerity to kill him. This is why I spent the night; it was Vicont's condition at the time."

Trey's brows furrowed deeply. "Could he...could he really do it?"

I tasted, then, Trey's fear.

"There was just enough doubt that I couldn't bear risking it. Vicont does have his allies," I replied.

"But you came back the next day. Daylight." His brows made a slow ascent. "My God. You felt it, didn't you? Gabriel's distress, from that far away. Did you feel it?"

"Yes. And then Vicont began to use you against me in earnest. I was only to stay the night and speak with him, which I did. He left Gabriel alone, but then, well, then there was you."

His eyes dropped to his hands. "But you couldn't give him what he wanted."

"I'm sorry, but no."

His eyes were quick to lift. "Don't be sorry. I don't know a drop of your history, but what you *have* told me is terrible, and I feel so much from you when you talk about it. Things I hate." He touched my hand. "I wouldn't have wanted you to do it for me, to be under his thumb. Besides, he started talking about me hanging around, too. I think he's full of shit."

This moved me to caress his face as a light laugh discovered me. "You are so extraordinary to me, Trey."

A manner of incredulous laugh found him. "I'm extraordinary to vampires. Ironic. But I'm certain that's one of the reasons I love you." He smiled, yet his brows then re-knit themselves. "Does he still want you to come back to him?"

I let go with a sigh. "I believe he may understand at last that we're not about joining houses, at the very least. Gabriel made certain of that, I'd say."

"So what *does* he want?"

"Truce. So I am led to believe, if the missives we've recently received are truly from him."

Again did I taste his fear. "Notes. You've gotten notes and you're going there when you don't even know whether it's someone else fucking with you?"

"I must get to the bottom of this, Trey. If I am to claim all of France, there is no backing down now."

"All of France?" His brows made a swift ascent.

"All of France, beloved. Protect the borders and cut off the enemies before they even reach Paris. Power. Others of our kind respect *power*, Trey, for some this is *all* they respect. If we are to have any semblance of peace down the road, I must gather all my allies and truly become keeper of France. This will also show the fence sitters that I am not afraid of Vicont, that I am serious, and that I will protect them from him and his minions."

He took a breath. "Gaining you more allies." He shook his head. "Wow. King of France, at least to vampires."

I inclined my head. "As you like. King fits, I rather suppose. Vicont has fancied himself King of France and beyond, for far too long. I must finish dethroning him."

"Well, they already call you the Prince. God, but this all sounds like the lead up to a war."

"This is a reason I should attack their resources. The less they have, the weaker the threat of war, well, at least on certain fronts. Vampires do not require weapons, generally— though some are rather fond of them. But it will give them less advantage when it comes to purchasing allies and the like, and display a weakness on their part. Power—as I said."

"Money is power," Trey said. "Yeah, I get it." His attention turned to Gabriel. "*Their* resources. Elise is part of the bigger picture too, right?"

"Elise was, and is, partner in several of Vicont's business affairs," Gabriel replied.

"You've been planning this for a while," Trey said.

"Not terribly long," I offered.

Trey considered a few things before next speaking. "You're

planning to double cross them." He looked to me.

I merely nodded.

"In the process you get your revenge on her." Deeply, he searched my eyes. "What she did to you, was it something Vicont was in on, too?"

I found I had to retreat from Trey's scrutiny, and in the process my gaze found Gabriel. His eyes, they darkened, and he then rose. He rose and he walked away.

Trey was quick to apologize. "I have no idea what I'm talking about, I'm sorry. Just forget what I said."

I looked once more to Gabriel, who had turned again towards Trey and I. He silenced any words I might have had with his expression, choosing to reply to Trey himself.

"Vicont could not abide the fact that I would never see his way of things, and eventually gave up in his attempts to sway me. Elise was enlisted to tear us apart." I stiffened a bit as Gabriel's eyes drifted, as his thoughts became darker and darker, this reflected in his tone. "She is the reason that I was drifting. She is the reason that I found myself in Louisiana."

I both felt and heard Trey's sudden intake of breath. For my part, I could not help but think that Gabriel was being kind in his explanation. I truly caused him to depart, a thought that still would not leave me regardless of the way he forgave me, regardless of his reasoning. Yet the thought itself brought me guilt, for did it not display that I was again incapable of believing what was truly in his heart?

"I wondered," Trey whispered. "You met Lucien, you saw me. It wasn't that long ago that you got back together, then."

Gabriel continued in near monotone. "That time is yet fragmented in my mind. I was not always in Louisiana, this I know. Other places did I wander." He turned yet distant eyes in our direction. "I saw Michel more than once during the last years of my wandering, this I remember quite well, every meeting, each that led to our reconciliation."

"What did she do?" Trey was loath to ask, yet he dearly

wished to know. "How could she possibly get between the two of you?"

Gabriel snapped fully back to the present, seeking my gaze, searching my eyes. I nearly shrank from his scrutiny, knowing he wished me not to blame myself any longer, knowing that he wished me to be the one to tell Trey, and to do so without berating myself in the process.

It, therefore, took me a bit too long to find a voice.

"She lied. She manipulated. She played on my insecurities. She was...an accomplished actress," I managed to say. It had not merely been her convincing me Gabriel no longer desired me, no. She had convinced me that he tired of my impotency regarding Vicont, and would just as soon I fester and die with my Sire.

How I had believed this, I still could not explain to myself in any way that excused a damned bit of it, though Gabriel had given me reasons, had offered the very ones I had just spoken to Trey, amongst others.

A wisp of sadness moved through my dark angel's eyes, for of course, he could detect everything another couldn't in the sound of me, in the vibrations along our bond.

"She was as a sister to me," I said. "A dear friend." A phantom of a lover in my blind pain. "She was quite thorough in her plans, enlisting others in her scheme, others who were very good at connecting fake dots and presenting convincing evidence of Gabriel's supposed plans to undermine me even in business and..."

I could not continue. How long I had known Gabriel by this time. I should have known better. The very idea of him spurning me caused me instant and deep pain, yet I did not immediately believe it, my only saving grace in the situation, if I had one. They were so thorough, yes, it was all so compelling, yes, and there were things that he was fully capable of doing, presented to me, true.

But I should have known better. I should not have lost faith.

I held his heart and I should have known better. Pain and anger had blinded me.

I was devastated, yet I should have looked beyond this. I should have held tighter to my initial reaction. That we were destined, that I was the one thing in the world he loved, and that he had not given up on me in all the centuries we'd been together thus far.

Ah, but the one you love more than your own life knows best how to wound you, and I was capable of believing he had tired of it all at last, for I had not made things easy over the years. Perhaps he had lost his patience at last, I said to myself then. Perhaps he wished to leave me in the dark place he sometimes visited over those years, I reasoned, or not reasoned, as the case may be.

I then felt the warmth of Trey's hand on my face and heard him speak, pulling me somewhat from the dark place I was visiting even now. "Whatever you want to do, I'm in," he stated quietly, yet with even more conviction than previously. "I want to help you. I want you to win."

My vision lightly blurred red. He wanted to help me. He wanted me to win...

He wanted me to find some peace in *revenge*. Yes, I was certain he had his own thoughts of such things. "How I love you, Trey du Bois." I pressed a kiss to his cheek. "You have your own things to attend to as well, yes? As soon as I have more details, as soon as *you're* ready, I shall come to you with said details."

He returned my kiss, the warmth of his lips lingering on my cheek long after he moved away.

"I should probably—yeah, I should find Scott. I have to stay calm in front of him, starting now. And I won't be any good to you later if I don't get my shit together."

I offered him a gentle smile. "As I said. When you're ready. Not one moment before, beloved."

He nodded.

I extended my will, my mind's eye, in the direction of Trey's apartment. "Scott is in your shower."

Trey took this in stride. "Well. That takes care of that. Thanks."

"He's in possession of a rather nice build," I added, wishing to end on a much lighter note.

A beautiful sound followed. Trey's laugh. "He still jogs and does sits ups, all that."

"He wears it well."

"Speaking of, I was supposed to ask you if he could lense you."

I arched a brow. "I'm not certain Gabriel would approve of such things," I said, knowing Trey would catch my undertone, for I had caught his.

"It does sound dirty, doesn't it? That's why I love hearing him say it."

I laughed; even Gabriel laughed. We were both happy to see Trey relax. I was pleased to see my Gabriel relax – this as well, certainly.

"I may have to add this word to my repertoire," I said.

"I believe that you have *lensed* me well enough over the centuries," my dark angel said.

"I'm more than certain he has," said Trey.

I touched Trey's face. "I should like to pose for Scott," I told him. "Tell him that I said yes, as soon as we've both time."

He offered a nod and then said, "I can't stand it anymore. I have to see Geoff."

I placed yet another kiss to his cheek. "But of course. Give him our love, will you?"

"I will." He stood and found his way to Gabriel, who also kissed his cheek. "See you soon, right?"

"But of course," Gabriel assured him.

Trey looked between us. "Thanks for—just thanks."

"You are most welcome, beloved," I said.

He closed his eyes, speaking very quietly. "You can smell

him too, right? Geoff...I know you can."

"Yes," I confirmed.

"He passed through me both ways."

My eyes moved over him, as if I might see the place they joined, and in a sense, I could. Trey's aura, for lack of a better term – it too had changed, along with his scent.

He opened his eyes. He did not say what he had been about to say, when he opened his mouth, however. "I'll see myself out."

And so he did. For a moment I dwelled on what he had been about to say before he left.

That he was sorry, so sorry, that Gabriel and I had ever suffered each other's absence. These were not the exact words in his mind, but it was the sentiment within him.

It had further burdened him, knowing this part of our past. It was a burden that he wanted to share, however, and I loved him still more for this.

I slid closer to Gabriel after he returned to his seat, and voiced the question I'd had when tracing Trey's aura.

"Did you see the dark spot?"

"*Oui.*"

We looked at each other a moment in silence. Gabriel was the first to voice the next thought.

"It seems something that does not belong there. It was not there before, in any case."

I made to shake my head. "No, it wasn't. But I know nothing of his situation, do you? What the effects of bringing someone back from the dead might be."

"*Non.* Perhaps it is normal."

We gazed at each other another long moment.

"Somehow I don't think so," I said at last. "It reminds me of disease, yet he is not diseased."

"Not physically," did my angel say.

I prompted with a lift of my brow.

"Perhaps something from there, it touched him," he said.

"It came back with him when he retrieved Geoff. Polly said that Trey crossed the veil."

"Such as? A ghost? Ghosts do not infect auras that I have ever seen."

"As neither have I, yet perhaps it is so." He rested his chin on my shoulder. "I know nothing of crossing veils. We are walking death, some say, but that is a place we cannot go, as we cheated Death."

I tipped my head against his, of a sudden more worried about Trey than I had been. Gabriel then prompted me to recline with my head in his lap, and when I looked up, the eyes gazing back at me were swimming with emotion.

"I have *always* loved you completely, and I will *always* love you completely, my own."

I closed my eyes, the weight of his more than I could bear in my guilt, the weight of his words asphyxiating me, rendering me speechless.

Chapter Twenty

Trey

Somehow, I managed to make it through the rest of the day, hanging out with Scott. It didn't hurt that I was still thinking about this woman named Elise, and this proposition Michel had for me. It hadn't hurt that just sitting with them, even, had soothed me and carried itself over for a while. Gabriel, particularly Gabriel, he could just do that. He could just say nothing and emit a vibe that made things better. Like he had in Baton Rouge.

Even though it had hurt, them talking a little about the time they were apart and why, it didn't hurt that it kindled anger inside me, a bright anger for a woman I hadn't even met, and solidified more my hatred of Vicont.

It gave me something else to focus on, someone to imagine hurting that deserved it, someone I could actually help them get revenge on, in some way.

Revenge, yes. There needed to be vengeance. Never mind that Michel sounded guilty in some way for a moment when he was talking about it. I couldn't fathom someone being able to sway him away from Gabriel, it was true, but I only had a surface view. I knew I had my own vision of them, but I also knew they could feel things on levels I couldn't comprehend, and I knew there was a hell of a lot more to the story, but they were together now, so...

Fucking with my dark fairytale, my Gothic Romance. No. I couldn't stand it. I could still hear Michel's words when he told me about meeting Gabriel as a child, then again when they were older. I could still hear the two of them on the yacht, talking about the first time they spoke as adults. That was fate. It was. They belonged together, they did.

Sure, I knew Michel had probably made his own mistakes with Gabriel over the years, and that Gabriel had, too. Who wouldn't in all that time, no matter how much they loved each other? I *knew* they weren't actually perfect. I *knew* that no relationship was perfect, but someone had exploited an imperfection, and that was worse; it had made them both suffer horribly.

I was certain of that. For fuck's sake, I'd seen how Gabriel was with Michel gone only twenty-four hours. Years? I couldn't imagine years, and he stood right there and said he couldn't even remember all of it. I knew what that meant. Michel told me about Gabriel's mind blocking things out, and I had seen what happened when memories jumped Gabriel.

Tip of the iceberg. I hoped to God that he'd never remember all the days they were apart. He remembered me, that was enough. God. And what did Michel do when they were separated? I probably didn't want to know.

But something like that, what they had – it was worth fighting for.

I still wished they weren't going anywhere. I tried not to think of them being gone again. They wouldn't be gone that long, they said. It would be fine. I'd be fine. And I wanted Michel to get the information he needed. The look in his eyes when he'd said what she did was worse than his words. The sooner we brought them down, the better. He'd suffered long enough. They'd suffered long enough.

It didn't hurt, either, that I didn't see a ghost the rest of the day, and it didn't hurt that Scott was in a good mood, and I knew I had P.K. to thank for that. Except, I think I'd been avoiding her. Why? Because I wasn't ready to talk about it yet, not really, not in any detail. She'd know, she'd probably not push, but she had this way of getting me to talk without pushing.

Avoidance, yeah, I'm real good at it, sometimes. Stating the obvious at this point, again.

It didn't hurt that Geoff came over about two hours after I'd seen him at Le Parvis, that he cooked us yet another wonderful meal, or that he kept on as though everything were just the way it was supposed to be.

Everything is as it should be, and everything will be as it should, Trey du Bois.

Oh, Dad. Did you ever imagine all this? I could probably ask you, but I don't want to go there yet. I know you're there. That's good enough for now.

Finally, yet importantly, it didn't hurt that I had Geoff snuggled up to me now, in my bed, or that he was making patterns on my chest with his soft little fingers.

I didn't want to talk about him dying, but I got the guts to ask him about something else.

"Geoff?"

"Mmm?"

"When you told Scott about the airbags, how did you know that?"

"Some it just come to my mind." He shifted, his chin coming to the dip in my chest, and looked at me. "Um, and you don't like blankets on your legs so much."

Hadn't taken him long to notice that.

"In Baton Rouge, you keep kicking them away in your

sleep. I stop putting them back."

Oh.

"You have bad dreams. Not always wake up, I mean."

"I have for a long time," I whispered.

He traced some imaginary circle on my pec. "You talk."

Shit.

"What do I say?"

"You say *no* a lot."

I kinda figured that.

"You say a name."

I bet I could guess. "What's the name?"

"Billy."

Yeah. I *could* guess.

"What else do I say?"

He suddenly broke into tears.

"Oh baby, what's wrong?" I was thinking I might actually know, and now I was sorry I had asked anything at all, as I stroked his hair.

"You keep asking him to stop."

Shit. Shit and shit. This didn't need to go any further. His tears killed me, and if I told him, he'd probably cry more, wouldn't he?

"It's just a dream."

"I no think it just a dream."

I closed my eyes tight.

"You sound scared and hurt."

I hugged him to me, tight.

"You not asking, you begging."

Lump. My throat. Lump. He was going to know sooner or later.

If he didn't already know.

"Something happen to you?" he asked, yet didn't ask.

"Yes," I managed. I was not going to lie to anyone else, damn it, whether I could get away with it or not.

"This Billy, he did it."

Swallow. "Yes...and some of his friends."

Hands on my face. Drip on my face. A warm drip.

I opened my eyes. His I could see in the candlelit glow of the room. It didn't hide their sadness.

"What they do?"

Don't say it.

Don't say it.

Look at those eyes. Don't say it.

Look at those eyes...

...Say it.

He already knows.

"They raped me."

He kissed me, hard. Then he said, "I thought so. I see into you more, now. I see other things."

I took his face in my hands. "You see into me?"

"Since I die."

Damn that word falling from his lips. Yet he said it so calmly.

Not to mention, now that I'd said the filthy words, he'd stopped crying.

"I feel like you always with me," he said.

I gazed and gazed at him. "Me, too."

"You the one."

"The one?"

"I tell you *mi abuelo* say I would find the other soul. You're the other soul and you don't have to have all the secrets alone, now. You don't even have to explain."

Lump. A very different lump in my throat.

"No more worry, now. You are *not* dirty or spoiled or any of those things. You are beautiful. You are special, and you are here so we can show you. So you remember."

I almost crushed him. "Geoff...I love you so much."

Drip.

Mine.

"So much."

"I know. I love you." He wrapped himself around me, basically, and then said. "Sleep. No dreams tonight."

Chapter Twenty-One

No dreams.

He was right. I didn't have any nightmares. I woke slowly, to the sweet scent and feel of Geoff.

I smiled, and then I smiled some more. I didn't know if he'd somehow had something to do with my not dreaming, but whatever the reason, I felt rested for a change.

There wasn't much light, I noticed. I glanced at the bedside clock. 5:30 a.m. I may not have slept long, but it'd been a peaceful sleep.

I ran a finger through his hair, then reluctantly disentangled myself from his warm body as carefully as I could so as not to wake him, and made my way to the bathroom, cursing my bladder yet again. Of course, I could always climb back into bed.

After finishing, I gazed at him there on the bed. He looked so peaceful. He looked so beautiful. I decided I'd let him sleep, and that since I was wide awake, I'd go make coffee; that way I'd be less tempted to wake him up. I also decided maybe I'd try my hand at breakfast and surprise him. I could do omelets. They weren't that difficult. They wouldn't be like his, but it's the thought that counts, I told myself.

Maybe I'd try some of his spices.

I slipped on some track pants and left the bedroom.

After I got to the kitchen and set the coffee to brewing, I realized, as I was standing there, maybe it'd be better if I didn't touch the spices. After all, I didn't know what several of them were best for, when it got down to it.

I opened the fridge. Good, we still had eggs. I looked to see what else was in there.

A noise made me jump. I listened and realized it sounded like the T.V. I made my way to the living room, thinking Scott must have woken up.

But no one was there. I stood and listened, hearing nothing but the T.V. Sounded like a news broadcast.

"Weird," I said to myself and grabbed the remote off the coffee table.

I shut it off. I set the remote down, and started for the kitchen.

The T.V. came on again.

"What the?"

I turned back. Grabbed the remote and shut it off.

Again.

Stood and waited.

Nothing.

Yet again started for the kitchen.

Froze in my tracks when—

The damned thing turned itself on again.

I was a lot slower in going back to the living room as I thought to myself—

Turned *itself* on?

But we know there's other things in this world, now don't we, Trey.

I stared at the television screen. It *was* a news broadcast. Breaking news.

Body found in...

Body of a girl found in...

"Fuck." I covered my eyes. This didn't make the sound go away, the French I understood too well.

Female, aged early twenties, found in restricted section of the catacombs beneath—

I shut it off.

It clicked back on.

Name withheld pending notification of the family.

Off.

On.

It appears she was shot—

"Stop it." I shut it off.

Since I have your attention and you already know what happened, all right. Do you want to know my name, Trey?

Oh. God.

I'll tell you anyway. It's Adele, that's my name. Well, it was my name. Is it still my name?

"Y-yes."

"Oh good," she said, appearing five steps away from me.

Bullet hole in her red shirt, not red enough to hide the darker red bloodstain.

"What...do you want...Adele?"

"Why did you do that?" She gestured to the television. "Why me, I should ask. I think I understand what you did, but why me?"

Breathe, Trey, breathe. "There was no one else there." What a horrible thing to say, Trey.

"So it's my fault for being there?"

"No, no. I-I didn't have time."

"Time for what?"

Oh. God.

"To...to..."

"To?"

"Choose."

"So you did trade for something. The other, well I guess they're ghosts, too, they were whispering about it. How you made a deal. You're the master or something?"

I grabbed my head. "I don't know what I am."

She laughed. It didn't sound very nice, that laugh. "But you are allowed to decide who lives and dies?"

I started shaking my head.

"But you did. You decided."

"I'm sorry; I didn't want to do it."

"You didn't want him? The one who's in your bed?"

"Yes, I mean, not that way."

"What way?"

I had to sit down. "I didn't want to take you."

"But you wanted him to stay."

I covered my face. I just couldn't look at her. "Yes."

"What makes him so special?"

I can't do this, I can't do this.

But she—she needs to understand. Right?

"I love him."

"People loved me, too. And so?"

I can't do this. I don't know what to say.

"What makes him so special?"

"I couldn't let him go," I said into my hands, being an absolute coward.

"What?"

I dropped my hands. "I couldn't let him go."

"You mean you couldn't kill him, like you did the other."

I lost my breath.

"What was his name?"

I still had no breath and gaped at her.

"Sean, isn't that his name?"

"How do you know that?" I stood, if shakily. "How do you know that?"

298

She laughed again. "Oh, I find out more about you every day."

"Have you...have you seen him?" I asked, incredulous and freaked.

"Do you want to? I'm sure that we could find him."

I moved around the sofa. "No."

"Why?"

I said nothing.

"Did you kill him, too?" She asked oh so sweetly.

I started backing away.

"You did, didn't you?" She pointed an accusing finger at me.

"Listen I know you're upset, but please..." I backed up more.

"Who are you talking to?" I whirled and there was Scott, stifling a yawn.

I glanced behind me.

She was gone.

I almost grabbed my chest to keep my heart inside it.

"Trey?" Scott was waking up more and more.

"Uh, myself. I do that. You remember."

He rubbed his eyes. "Yeah, kinda. Sounded like you were having a total conversation, though."

"I do that sometimes, too. Practice for a meeting."

"Oh." He looked up at me. "Sounds like a weird meeting you're gonna have, then. But whatever, I think I'm still half-asleep. Mmm, but I smell coffee."

I forced myself not to look over my shoulder again. Forced myself to breathe. "Should almost be done."

"You okay?"

"Yeah." Not. "Sure."

He started heading for the kitchen, scratching as he went. "I'll pour, c'mon."

"Right behind you."

Right behind you.

When I looked, she wasn't, thank God.

"So you're up early," I said as I padded into the kitchen, hoping to God that she'd leave me alone. At least, while Scott was with me. So I wouldn't seem insane.

"I think I'm still messed up over time changes," he said as he filled two cups.

How did she know about Sean? How did she know?

"You're up earlier than me." He headed for the table and sat across from me, setting a steaming cup in front of me.

"Yeah. I don't always sleep much." I gulped some coffee.

"Damn, how do you do that and not burn yourself?"

Shrug. "I like it hot." I swigged some more.

"Did you always do that?"

I shrugged again.

How did she *know*?

"You have another nightmare or something?"

She passed through me.

"Huh? Oh, no. Actually, I didn't."

He slowly sipped his own coffee.

I got up to refill my cup, trying to reason with myself. Lucien knew things about me. Had she been inside my head?

But wouldn't I know it, now, if she had?

I gulped some more coffee. Geoff said he could see into me more, now...

"Trey, uh, what's got you so distracted?"

Mental slap. Pay attention, Trey, don't make him worry more, Trey.

Turn, look. "Sorry. Business, big investor."

"Oh. That meeting you had. Did it go okay?"

"Yeah, yeah it was fine." Except for Adele, the bathroom, and all that jazz. Change the subject, Trey, redirect. "By the way, I forgot to tell you that I saw Michel yesterday and he said he'd pose for you."

"Cool. When?"

"Soon as he takes care of some business. He's going out of town for a while." Damn it, with me so ready to hide in their house with Geoff. Or something. "Soon as he's back he'll tell me what works," I said.

Hiding would not help me. Stop it, Trey. Maybe you should tell P.K. about this. Maybe she could help.

"Do you think Gabriel would pose with him?" Scott asked.

"If Michel asked him to." Of this, I was certain. There. Something certain. Gabriel would do it for Michel.

"He's...amazing."

For a moment, the look on Scott's face snapped me from other thoughts. I found a smile, a real smile. "I doubt there's anyone in the world remotely like him."

Scott leaned on his hand. "So do I. Who looks like that, y'know?"

Yeah. I knew. Wished in a way I could tell you why, Scott. Why he looks like that. Then I realized I didn't even know if he'd seen Gabriel full on, no filters, though his comment suggested it. Still, even with filters, I was betting Gabriel was one of a kind.

"His eyes are amazing," Scott said. "Something about them, besides the color."

Another smile found me. "Emeralds."

He came out of the reverie he was losing himself in. "Yeah. Emeralds. And he's so pale. Startled me at first, but somehow it works, even with that hair. He almost doesn't look real, though."

No filters, I thought. Then I realized, duh, the first time he saw Gabriel was the night of my supposed car wreck. I doubted either of them was thinking about glamours.

"How does someone that's not albino get that pale?"

"He's a night person. Doesn't go out during the day, really." Truth. I could tell him some of the truth.

"Still..."

"And he wears make-up." Lie. Well, he did wear eyeliner and shadow sometimes. Michel told me that when I was recovering from the last fucked up mess.

"Oh." Scott shrugged. "Hey, whatever pushes his pedals."
Slurp coffee. "It pushes Michel's pedals."

"Ah." He grinned. "Do you still Ziggy out sometimes?"

"Sure do."

"Does Geoff like it?"

Chuckle. "Yes."

"Cool. He still here?"

"Sleeping, yeah."

He nodded. "They like him a lot, too, I could tell. Michel and Gabriel."

"Very much. He knew them before I did."

"Travis too. He must have known Travis. There was something special there when he came over the other night. Travis was beyond relieved to see he was okay after the wreck."

I looked into my cup. "Yes. Geoff reminds Travis of his little brother." Truth. What a wonderful thing.

"Is his brother in Paris?"

I drank the last swallow of coffee in my cup. "He's dead." Unfortunately, that was a damned safe bet, and I had a feeling it wasn't from old age.

"Oh, shit." Scott cleared his throat. "What he said to Geoff was extra cool, then."

I lifted my eyes. Nodded. Felt like a heel again, for yelling at Travis, because I flashed on his comment about his parents telling him he didn't fail.

Damn. It had something to do with his brother. I was feeling confident in that assessment.

"What's on that mind of yours, Trey?"

Turn, pour more coffee. "I'm just a little worried about this business of Michel's." Not a lie.

"How come you didn't go as his attorney?"

Turn back. "It's more personal, this particular business of his."

"Oh."

Swallow coffee. "The guy he's going to see, they haven't

gotten along over the years." Understated truth. "But anyway, he needs some information on something, and unfortunately this guy is the only one that has it." Hey, more truth. Nearly all I knew of it myself, in fact. "That's all I know, really."

He contemplated this. "Why so worried?"

"Because the guy is a fucker and he upsets Michel." Ehem. Back off, Trey.

Scott held up a hand. "Okay, dude, okay."

"Sorry. I've met this guy and believe me, he's a real piece of work. I really like Michel, so I'm just hoping it all works out and he doesn't end up totally aggravated." Or I don't know what.

Scott gazed at me quietly, then finally said, "I think you more than like him."

I set my cup down with a clink. Faced him again, crossed my arms. "Yes, I do."

"What about Geoff? What about Gabriel?"

"I more than like Gabriel, too. In fact, I love him. He and Michel, and Geoff knows it."

He held up both hands. "Hey, that's cool. Why didn't you just say so in the first place?"

Deep breath.

And sigh.

"Jesus, I'm being a shit," I said aloud. Scott just stared at me. "I love them like family."

His brows knit. "Okay, then yeah. You're definitely being a shit. There's nothing wrong with them being like family, you know. Did you think I'd tell you it was weird or something?"

I'm being a shit because I can't tell you everything and because Adele's creeped me out and made me—a little angry, I think.

"I mean, why not just say they're like family in the first place? Why sound so seriously smart assed and defensive – because you were, you know. You weren't teasing me." Scott carried on.

I pressed my hands to my eyes. "I'm not a morning person."

"Lame, Trey. Really lame."

"I know." I dropped my hands and looked at him. "Lame and fucked up, that's me."

He got out of his chair and walked toward me. "What's eating you? Seriously, just tell me."

I wish I could.

"You can, I'm listening."

Shit. I said that out loud, too.

I started shaking my head. "I'm not feeling that well. I didn't mean to be so cranky."

His eyes narrowed.

"Please, Scott, let it go. Please."

"You're starting to worry me, dude."

I grabbed his shoulders. "Please."

He looked back into my eyes. After a long moment, he said, "For now."

I sighed. "I'll take that."

He did me another favor, and shifted the subject back. "It's nice you have people here that feel like family already. I could tell they really care about you. So does Polly. She really, really cares about you."

I leaned back against the counter, trying to relax. "Yeah. I seem to have hit the jackpot." And I'm still not sure how, sometimes.

"I'll feel a lot better when I go back to New York now that I know that."

I met his gaze. "You'll come back though, right?"

His smile to me, gentle. Assuring. "You bet. You'll visit there too, won't you?"

Will I? New York City? That damned City I love and hate?

"To see you, yes, Scott."

"No hotels, like Geoff said. Bring him along." He smiled.

I finally found another of my own smiles. "He'd probably like that. He's never been there." I had a sudden, very strong need. "Speaking of Geoff, I'm gonna crawl back in bed with him, if that's all right."

"Your home, your boyfriend, 'course it's all right. I'll just finish the coffee."

"Great. More hyper Scott."

"By the time you come out, I'll probably have lost the high."

A chuckle found me.

"Go on, don't leave him in there by his lonesome." He patted my shoulder. "Maybe try some more sleep, huh? You'll feel better."

I had felt good when I woke up the first time. I wasn't so sure a second was going to be better as I left the kitchen, and heard her in my head.

Isn't that precious.

If I did go back to sleep, that is.

Geoff, he was still asleep, thank goodness. I gazed at him some more.

What makes him so special?

"He's the one."

The one. Wasn't Sean the one?

I closed my eyes.

Will there be another one when this one is gone? Or will you always be there to kill for him?

Stop. Please. Stop.

You can't always be there, right?

Why won't you go away? I could make you go away.

No, I can't. You deserve...

Go ahead and cuddle up. I can wait.

I climbed into bed and tried not tremble or pull the blankets all the way over my head. He murmured something in his sleep, his body fitted itself against mine, and I knew—

I knew I'd do it again if I had to.

I'd take my punishment, because I would do the same thing if I had it to do over.

****

Two black rubber bracelets sitting on a paper, a neatly written note. Just a few words and they say:
I'm sorry, Trey.
It's not your fault. Don't follow me, angel, please.
I will always love you.
            Sean

Two 'sex bracelets' on a note, not far from his cold stiff hand, his face pale, angelic, surrounded by a wave of light blond hair.

I'm sorry, Trey.
It's not your fault. Don't follow me, angel, please.
I will always love you.
            Sean

A needle. A spoon. A lighter.
A needle. A tourniquet. A vein.
A needle. A speedball. A stab.
Jack back. Plunge. Dive.
Poison flooding veins, poison winding, winding, flowing, numbing, lifting, dazing, swirling, floating, seducing, freeing, loving, damning, soothing, hating, caressing, dropping, fucking, adoring, raping, killing—
Heart races. Heart slows.
Freeing. Euphoria. Freeing—

I'm sorry, Trey.
It's not your fault. Don't follow me, angel, please.
I will always love you.
            Sean

Salt. And water. And smack. And salt. Water. Smack. Salt.

Water. Salt water. Snot. Fuck it. Shoot it. Can't snort through snot. Shoot it. Smoke it. Shoot some more. Chase the dragon, then shoot some more.

~~~~~~~~~~~~~~

He jerks. He falls. Red flower blooming.
You cheated.
He jerks. He falls. Blood blossom flower.
Cheated.
Waves of light blond hair surrounding a pale sleeping face. Forever sleep.
Murderer.
Blood flower blooming, with light blond hair.
Cheat. Murderer. You didn't even value your own life, why should you choose? You should have finished it the second time. I loved my life.
Light blond hair trailing through my blood. Leaving blood trails, the veins beneath bruised skin. My skin.
Abuser. Killer.

Sudden chest expansion, so much air.

"Angel. Angel?"

Zoom in, velvet brown eyes.

"Angel? It okay, I'm here."

I can taste the heroin. I can taste the blood. I can—

"Angel, say something."

—Taste my tears. Dream tears.

"Angel?"

"S-something."

A cold cheek on my burning chest.

"I was leaving for work, but then you were dreaming."

He sounded so concerned, but I was still in some strange dream-shock. I could just, just, touch that black tar high, that place I died and resurrected.

Feeling rushed back, then, reality came crashing back, that place that makes you tap another vein.

"Oh Angel, you so heavy in your heart."

I couldn't say anything. A dream? It was a dream. I'd never had a dream exactly like that. Not just exactly like that. A dream with her voice, a dream of my own overdose, my own overdose layered through—

Her voice. Adele's voice. I heard her in the dream. I heard her in the—memory.

"Do you want to tell me?" I heard Geoff ask.

You already know, don't you? I found some of my voice. "I was dreaming about Sean. His suicide." My suicide. The very thing he asked me not to do. One last time, begged me not to do. "And you, in a way."

"So sorry, angel." I felt his hand touch my face.

"So am I." Asked me not to follow him, but I tried, I did, I tried in earnest the last time, no more lying to yourself, Trey.

By what miracle was I breathing now?

Destiny?

...Sean?

Geoff lifted his head to find my eyes again, the room filled with late afternoon light. "You dream of this often, too?"

God, I'd been under a while.

Under?

"No. Not like this," I said. He'd know anyway. "I think it's because of what happened to you."

His eyes searched mine. I suddenly felt so strangely calm, I realized.

"Much death in your life," he said, soft.

Too much. "Yes, but you're here. I'm not sorry you're here, you know that, right?"

"I know." He touched my face again. "Something else is wrong."

"I can see her."

He didn't even ask. "Hear her too?"

"I have. I can," I whispered. I could feel her. "I think she's angry. She was confused, but I'm not sure she's so confused anymore. Not about some things."

"Angry. You…you can make it stop, no? Or tell Polly she haunt you."

I felt my head roll back and forth on the pillow. "She deserves to understand all of it. I don't think I should shove her away. It's part of my function. I think."

"No, no running. But you say she is angry."

"She can't hurt me."

Right?

"Mostly confused. She deserves," her revenge, "her time with me," I said.

Geoff's brows tightly knit. "Angel."

"I'd be angry too, wouldn't you?"

He thought about this. "Maybe so."

"I need to help her move on." If I said I thought I deserved it too, well that wouldn't fly, and I didn't want him to think I was sorry for saving him.

Which he'd probably understand, but still.

He nodded in response to my previous statement.

"You should go on to work, baby. You'll be late, if you aren't already."

He gazed and gazed at me.

"It'll be okay." She deserves a little revenge, and maybe I deserve a little punishment. Part of the price to pay. Small price for his soul, wasn't it? "I just need to talk to her."

He quite unconvincingly said, "Okay." And then, "I tell Scott you need rest. That you are not feeling so well."

I kissed him. My lips to his, I told him that I loved him.

He kissed me back. He reluctantly left.

I laid there for a few minutes, working up the nerve, maybe. Wondering what, exactly, I should say. Do.

What was right?

All the while hating myself in some way, which was an emotion I was very accustomed to feeling.

Finally, I got up, went to the door, and poked my head out.

"Scott?"

There was no immediate answer. I said his name again.

No answer.

I ventured out, down the half hall, and through the living room. No sign of Scott, I ventured into the kitchen. There was something on the breakfast table. A note. I crossed the room to the table and picked it up.

His handwriting.

I thought I'd give you some peace and quiet, let you have your apartment to yourself for a while. Geoff said you were coming down with something, and you sure didn't seem well earlier. I'm a little restless anyway. I'll be back in a while. Give me a call if you need anything, though. I have my cell on me. I think I'll stop by Poe to see Polly, so I won't be far anyway.

Hope you're feeling better later on, buddy.

Scott

That took care of that. At least for now.

I set the note down and made my way back to my bedroom, locking the door once I was inside. Stared at my bed. Finally went to it and lay down.

It would only take a little while, right? A little while and then I'd know how to send her on. Or something. I wasn't certain. But I had to learn one way or the other and Papa and Lucien had been completely silent.

I figured it was for a reason. Though maybe it was that internal defense mechanism as well, along with me being a little upset with them.

I was. I was upset with them for being in this position in the first place.

And I had bitched about not having control, not having a choice, when I was in Baton Rouge. I'd insulted Lucien, too. Maybe he was ticked off at me and that's why he'd been leaving me alone. But damn it, I just wanted some control.

Like everything else, I'd have to get over it eventually. The cards were already dealt, all bets were off. I was whatever I was and I'd show my hand right now.

"Okay Adele. Do what you need to do. Let's do what we need to do."

That's all I was waiting for, Trey. For you to give me permission.

Chapter Twenty-Two

GERMANY

Michel

Only one guard met us at the entrance. Kar exchanged the proper words with him, and then led we were, through a grand foyer with marble flooring in rose, down a long hall in shades of rich gold and crimson, to a double-wide door of cherry wood with ornate golden handles.

Even in exile, he enjoyed his comforts.

The doors opened to us. I bid Kar remain just there as Gabriel and I entered the large room. I mused that it was quite arrogant, brave, or an attempt to show trust, Vicont having merely one guard visible for our arrival, as we walked.

Of a certainty, it was a grand room, but my taking in of details did not go far, once my eyes reached a specific point. Antiques and leather chairs, sculptures and paintings, they lost their interest.

My approach, it slowed, slowed more still, the closer I came to the figure in silhouette near the far corner of the den. As if walking through water steadily rising, it was; water and sand, yes, I recalled this sort of feeling, the literal feeling as a mortal, and this is what it resembled.

Anger, resentment, these I carried with me, yet remorse, pity, some sliver of each wished to splinter from within to work their way without, for I could taste it upon the very air, his weakness.

Impatiently I shoved these things aside, plucked them free, and reached the spot I designated as close enough.

He turned. He turned in his chair, toward me, he turned there in his plush circular chair of somber green, and I, at first, near recoiled.

His skin, never as radiant as Gabriel's, nonetheless having owned a milky light, now—now it was the pallor of a corpse a week in its tomb.

Sallow, the cast of his skin, and lines not before present now finely etched themselves upon his cheeks, and in delicate webbings around his eyes.

His eyes, they struck some deeply buried fear within me, the look of his eyes, the once coldly gleaming grey now as if struck by cataracts, and watery, liken more to those of a human awake too long and having indulged far too freely.

Aged. He appeared aged, and waves of his weakness created a grimly dull aura about him, an aura fed with mental strain.

Even his hair had dulled and taken on a sickly yellowish cast; yet worse, the worst of all, it was his heart.

I could touch the strain, I could feel the throb, and I could nearly taste the blood.

I would prefer dying to such a state, I thought. The idea sent a thin finger of fear through my spinal cord.

Beneath my fear, pity stirred once more.

"Michel," his spoken word, at least here there still be some manner of strength.

His look to Gabriel contained an ounce of respect with a

dash of wariness. Referring, no doubt, to his own impression of Gabriel's nature, Vicont said, "The silence often, of pure innocence persuades, when speaking fails."

Gabriel offered the barest of nods and a wry half smile to accompany his dryly-performed return quote. "I hear, yet say not much, yet hear the *more*."

"Yes," countered Vicont. "Tis better to be brief than tedious."

"More of your conversation would infect my brain," Gabriel said, and then reclaimed his silence. Vicont thought better of continuing. False hope manifested in those watery grey eyes when next they sought me, false on how many counts, I was suddenly uncertain.

"You agreed to meet," said Vicont. "I scarce believed it until seeing you arrive."

I gathered myself to reply, remembering why I was truly here. "I'm not here to listen to your false words of apology and truce."

Decidedly weary, his response. "Then why have you come, Michel?"

"The truth, if such a thing exists within you. In your current state, I may find it at last."

A brief smile moved across his dry lips. I had made an admission that, unsurprisingly, pleased him. That, under other circumstances, I could not easily tell the difference between his lies and his truths. It was something he knew, but to hear me say it aloud, yes, it pleased him.

Unfortunately for me he could often read, if not my mind— everything else. Gabriel had never had this problem with Vicont; Gabriel, with his deeply ingrained, iron-fisted control over everything necessary, when he desired.

"What truth do you seek?" Vicont asked.

"I want to know what game you dare to play now."

"Game? I am at a loss. Did we reset the chess board?"

I moved closer by a step. "Don't mock me, or I'll finish what

Gabriel started earlier than you'll find pleasing."

His sigh, it rattled quietly. "I'm not mocking you, Michel. Be more specific, perhaps I'll have an answer."

I studied closely his eyes. "Someone important was shot. Did you or did you not send the assassin?"

His brows made a slow ascent. "It wasn't your Trey, was it?"

Another few inches between us were lost. "You evade, so often a sign of guilt."

With his reply, one of his hands drifted upward. "I have sent no assassins, Michel. To do such certainly wouldn't add to your confidence in my offer."

"It certainly wouldn't, but this would be nothing new."

"I swear to you that I have not moved against any of your people."

I gazed and gazed into his eyes, looking for the sign, a sign he was lying.

Such was not to be found, yet bold honesty was not something I was certain of, either. Not by his word, in any case. Yet I had my own doubts before agreeing to the meeting, of his involvement.

I longed for the ability of separating completely my thoughts from the vision before me.

He studied me in return, and in my silence, chose to speak words that agitated, yet piqued an interest that I longed to subdue.

"I very well might have an idea who would do such a thing, however."

"You didn't do it," I scoffed, "but you were aware of the plot, would this be the case? Is this what your offer of information was?"

"I did not know of the incident until you told me."

I turned halfway, folding my arms. A glance to Gabriel gave me his smooth expression, the cold gleam of his green eyes fixed on Vicont.

I turned back. "Say what you have to say. It should prove

amusing, if nothing else."

"You've met with Elise somewhat recently, correct?"

"Obviously you're still spying. What does this have to do with anything?"

He handed me a patient look. "I'll get to it."

I ground my teeth.

He continued. "Did she offer you a song and dance, as is said, about companies and contracts, etcetera, etcetera?"

For a moment, I merely stared him down.

"I do have a point in all of this, Michel," he offered. "If you'll bear with me."

I inhaled quite slowly. "I've had to bear with you for centuries. I suppose another moment or two won't kill me."

I needed to know. I came for answers, any that I could get. I needed to find out if there were still contracts on any of my beloveds, and I needed, much as I hated needing it, to know exactly what he was after saying of Elise.

Curiosity, damn the large cat.

His gaze rested on me as he waited.

"Yes. She sang about companies and contracts, and wanting me to either finish you, help her to finish you, or give her the leverage to do harm to you herself." It did not pain me one bit to tell him what she was after. After all, I left her home detesting her more than when I had arrived.

And that was a lie, damn me.

He contemplated this but for a moment. "Hardly surprising," he said, calm as ever. "You didn't agree to it?"

What was this softening in me?

Yet another item added to the list of detestable things.

"You know I didn't," I managed to whisper, and then to add, "I'm currently enjoying the state you're in far too much."

For this he only smiled, and I—I glanced away and back.

His expression became as somber as the chair in which he sat. "Gabriel, whom I underestimated indeed, would not have the same compunction, so worry not. I'm still at your mercy."

I took another breath. No words followed.

I had not expected to be moved in so many directions upon seeing him this way. Upon sensing, scenting him this way.

I had not expected sincerity to taste so real, coming from him.

"I'll get closer to my point and the information that I wished to share with you, Michel," said Petrov. "For it does touch upon the information I offer in part, as remuneration for harming your Trey before."

I could not help but glance at Gabriel once more, and still he was a statue carved from glaciers.

"And in its other part?" I inquired.

"Admittedly, to put Elise in her place. Also, so that you might come closer to believing I regret our last chess game."

At this, I snorted. "I'm all a-twitter. Do carry on."

"Did you ever wonder how it was that I knew Trey was in New York? Where to send my men?"

"What a ridiculous question," I replied. "Your spies, of course it was your spies."

Yet another patient look from him. "Did you not wonder who the spy was?"

"Stupid question." I waved my hand. "Of course I did, as would you."

"I'll hand you the spy, Michel."

My focus narrowed sharply on his pupils. His steady gaze. "Tell me and I'll allow you to live a while longer if it turns out you offered the truth," I hissed. I wanted nothing more than to eviscerate the one that gave up Trey. If I could not yet have Vicont, I would have the spy I had not yet flushed out.

"The table just there," he motioned toward Gabriel's right. "In the drawer there are photographs."

My dark angel came to life and moved toward this cherry wood side table, and opened the small drawer, retrieving a small manila envelope. He brought it to me. I took it from his hand, and looked to Vicont.

"Open it, Michel. Tell me if you see anyone familiar there."

I did so. I opened it, thinking it would turn into a joke, that there would be no one I recognized, or conversely, someone I did, someone I knew, someone I'd not believe could be the one.

I freed the contents. I began to laugh, fanning the pictures in my hand. "This is Elise. She's in several of them." I lifted my eyes, finding his face. "What are you after doing?"

"Keep looking, Michel. The one you seek is in the photographs, and I will tell you which one."

"Why? To further prove that you wish to use me, just as she did?" I nearly threw the photographs on the floor, but one caught my eye. "To…" I plucked a single photograph free, the rest, along with the envelope, cascading to the floor.

A girl. Light brown eyes and sandy hair

The girl. The image of the girl I'd seen in Travis' mind, the girl he gleaned from the assassin's mind, and she was with Elise.

In Elise's *home* in Brussels. It was then I understood why I felt she should seem familiar.

A painting. A painting there was in Elise's home of this girl.

"It seems you may recognize the one already," I heard Petrov say.

My head began to shake. "You're trying to use me." My head made to shake more. "It's all a scheme to get me to play a different game, to play on your side, to give you the satisfaction of me doing something you want." I flung the photograph at him. "No. I will not fall for it."

His brows lightly knitted as he glanced at the photograph there in his lap, and then back to me. "She's the one that relayed Trey's plans; I swear it to you, Michel. She's the one that spied on him."

My teeth ground together, hard, harder.

"Where have you seen her before?" he asked.

I whirled away. "Enough."

Of a sudden, Gabriel touched my mind.

He is telling the truth of the girl.

I spun to look at Gabriel. His eyes were yet on Vicont.

I looked to Vicont. I closed my eyes, willing the shudder of anger and near shock, away. My breath was deep. "She was plucked from the assassin's mind. The one that shot one of my beloveds."

His brows, their starlit sparkle damped, swiftly lifted. "This, I didn't know of, as I said before. What further proof do you need?"

Anger returned. "It tells me nothing of Elise! This girl was in your employ when your thugs took Trey, drugged him and flew him to Algeria!"

I made a near lunge at him, my hands finding his throat, my fangs bursting free and baring themselves in his face. "Give me one damned good reason why I shouldn't kill you now."

The emotion that set up house in his eyes told me what I already knew.

I could do it. I could kill him this instant, a too tight wire had snapped within me, *ping ping*; it set off others.

I could *do* it this time.

"I did not hire her, I swear it." The fear lacing itself through his words was immensely satisfying.

"You lie," I growled and squeezed his neck.

"Chrétien." I felt him touch one of my hands. "My love, I did not hire her," he rasped, for I was squeezing harder, more tightly still. "The information was given to me on a silver platter, unasked for."

A growl coiled, slithered and rattled from my chest, clawed up my throat, and escaped fully, through my drawn back lips.

I felt his hand come to my cheek. "Chrétien, you have every reason to doubt me, but this is the truth, I swear it."

I then felt hands upon my shoulders. Firm, yet gentle, the grasp.

"*Mon lion.*"

My fingers, they trembled. They convulsed.

I shuddered with the frustrated howl and shoved back, knocking Gabriel away. I turned a red-hazed stare on him. "You stop me?" I advanced on him. He did not move, and so chest to chest, nose to nose we became. "You stop me?"

"My love," he smoothed my hair. "In this he states, I scent no lie."

My jaw wished to fall. Yet my teeth begged to gnash. And still, my heart wanted to ache, it wanted to bleed from a freshly opened wound, a new wound directly above the old wound Elise had left behind.

I then found myself having taken steps back, found my hands covering my face, and found myself, most absurdly, wishing to cry, and very near to it.

Therefore, in its stead I raged.

"Salope! Je vais lui faire la peau!"

I was intent on leaving the room, leaving the damned country and making for Belgium faster than immediately.

"Michel!" I heard from Vicont.

Strangely, or perhaps annoyingly, or, perhaps, much to my damnation, his tone gave me pause. I looked over my shoulder in his direction, still there in his chair.

"Don't believe her lies."

So desperate. He sounded entirely too desperate. I'd never heard such from him; his words had bathed themselves in *desperation*.

I felt the surge of sympathy impale me, and as this just wouldn't do, said my mind, I tore my eyes away with a roar of words. "She won't live long enough to lie!"

"Will you return?" he pleaded.

Pleaded.

I felt the surge of tenderness spike my gut, trying to make its way closer to my torn heart.

As this just wouldn't do right now, my mind said; I left without another word.

And that is another lie.

Perhaps. Perhaps, I said.

It was then I left, with Gabriel and Kar not far behind.

Chapter Twenty-Three

Trey

Hours. Was it hours?

Or days. Was it days?

Slipping away, little by little. Slipping away, while she told me about her life.

I killed her on her birthday. She was supposed to meet her boyfriend later for a birthday party with him and his parents, but she liked sneaking into that place where she had found us, and she went there first. Just a peek, just a quick peek at something she was proud of and sometimes showed others.

She was the one that painted the mural, the Patrick-Nagel-looking modern art mural of a woman with a shock of black hair, and peach and white skin, the woman with wide and tilted ice blue eyes and red, red lips wearing a lizard skin jacket.

Twenty-two. She had just turned twenty-two, and was attending the Parsons Paris School of Design. She had a bright, bright future, and the mural in that section of the catacombs was something she had done when she was nineteen.

It was a beautiful piece of work, I agreed.

She was going to be famous one day, she said. But I robbed her of that. I robbed her of everything, and why? All because she wanted to peek at her art, commune in that dark and quiet place. All because she saw someone on the ground and became concerned, offered help instead of sneaking back out, because she was certain we needed help.

All because she was a nice girl who just wanted to help.

Slipping away, I was slipping away, while she tormented me with questions, the same questions over and again, because my answers weren't good enough, of course they weren't, because they didn't change the fact that she was dead.

What makes him so special? He was supposed to die, right? What makes him so special? How did you do it? Why can you do it? Do you think it's fair? What makes you so special? Why me? Do you even deserve him? Do you deserve him?

Do you?

Deeper and deeper. She got deeper and deeper. She could see everything in me. She could play it over and again.

Deeper and deeper. She found my secrets.

And then she got serious.

Chapter Twenty-Four

BRUSSELS

Michel

From yet several feet away I issued the command. "Get out of my way."

Her servant didn't move. "She's not accepting visitors," said he.

"Is that so," I snarled. "We'll simply have to remedy that." By the time I'd uttered the last word, I'd grasped his arm.

A twist, a turn and a duck beneath his arm with another twist, and he howled in pain behind me. I made a slow turn in his direction, tossing his arm at him.

"Now be a good boy and run along, before I have my emissary rip out the other one. And for God's sake see if you can reattach that one. You look a *mess*."

He let go of his shoulder socket to snatch up his dismembered limb, and I spared a smile for the gush of blood.

Gabriel was approaching just as I turned and strode through

the front door and headed for the salon, where I sensed her to be.

Behind me, Kar made certain no one else arrived with such a misguided idea as trying to stop me.

She met me close to the entryway. "Michel, what are you doing? You can't just—"

There must have been quite the look in my eye, for she stumbled back and away from me, her hands out as if to shield herself.

"Tut. Do I frighten you, Elise? Shame on me. Not only have I barged in, but I've made you uncomfortable in your own home." I devoured the distance between us. "I'm about to make it worse, I'm afraid."

My arm shot out, hand finding her throat. Her feet lost contact with the floor. She clawed desperately at my hand in vain. I was assuredly not of a mood to let go; a few scratches were not about deterring me.

"M-Michel—" my name came on squeaked syllables. "M-Michel—s-stop."

"No." I pulled her close, my face in her face, my breath where hers wasn't. "You gave him up. *You!*"

Her eyes gone wild, she grasped for more words. "Wh-who...I don't...didn't..."

I may have squeezed harder, my anger having become a deep freeze for the moment.

Yes, I certainly did squeeze, and certainly grinned at the crackling sound. "Trey. Need I say more?"

Her legs flinging themselves at my shins of their own accord, she attempted to plead her case. "Vi-Vi-cont."

"He told me," I spat. "For once, he told me the truth."

She became still, she forced her struggle to abate, and she leveled my eyes with hers. "He did-n't tell y-you everything... then."

I gazed hard into her dilated eyes. "You don't even know what he *did* tell me, *salope*." I launched her across the room. She rocketed into a large mirror, which shattered, glass showering her before she finished hitting the floor.

I yanked her up by her hair before she'd had time to settle there.

She grasped my wrist with both of her hands. "Wait, wait!"

"Allow me to consider." I launched her again, this time toward the iron-hooded hearth, which she hit with a satisfying clang. "That would be a no."

Her arms thrust out in time for her hands to press to my chest, but to no avail. I was once again lifting her, quite enjoying the idea of breaking everything in the room with her body.

"Spy, I have a spy, yes, yes, okay, but—"

Her words gave way to a shriek when I shot her toward a glass partition by the stairway. At the last second, she twisted, and like a cat, landed on her paws. Glaring up at me as I approached, she reached yet again for speech.

I wasn't exactly interested in talking, if she hadn't noticed, the bitch.

"I'll give her to you!"

"I already know what she looks like," I fired back, reaching for her yet again. She sprang and kicked at my chest. I caught her ankle, taking her legs out from beneath her, her head hitting the floor with a delightful whack.

A foot on either side of her, I bent and hissed in her face, gums itching, and fangs longing to rip into her flesh. "The only reason I don't flay you first is that Geoff's alive, though I'm beginning to rethink my position."

"Who!" Her eyes widened more.

A roar and a slice to her cheek. "Don't bother pretending."

Her words raced to beat my next move. "Michel! I don't know a Geoff! I thought this was about Trey!"

"Of course you know of Geoff!" I snatched her by the shoulders. She kicked me in the groin. I was too angry, the freeze becoming lava once more, to care, truly to feel it, and she found herself skidding on her ass to a stop near to Gabriel's feet.

Her eyes rolled up, finding him. "I don't know a Geoff, I swear, I swear it."

"Go ahead, beg him," I said. "Throw yourself on his mercy, the Left Hand of God. See where it will get you." I laughed a devil's laugh. "Would you like to join in, my love?" I looked to him. "You deserve your vengeance, after all."

She began to weep, which irritated me to no end.

"Spare me," I said, looking still to Gabriel.

A gem-cold and hard gaze dropped to the woman at his feet. "You admit to the spy. What precisely did she do for you?"

I folded my arms, not much in the mood for her lies, yet held my tongue, certain he would dazzle me with his finishing moves eventually.

Her hand clutching at her throat, she lifted slightly, hesitantly. "To follow your new attorney." She became less hesitant when he remained frozen. "In July. It was in July."

"To what end?" Gabriel inquired next.

Myself, I snorted fire.

"I was," she risked a quick glance at me, and just as quickly returned her eyes to my archangel, "I was angry. Spiteful, yes. Neither of you would speak to me, not even after years and years. She already was my eyes in Paris many times before, and she told me about this Trey."

"You then came to know Vicont was interested?" Gabriel continued his interrogation, much to my impatience.

"I didn't know exactly, but I knew he had liked to get under Michel's skin through others before."

"Yes, you should know well, you hussy," I snapped.

Yet on he went, my Gabriel. "So you offered him information."

She made with a short nod. "I sent her to him. I did, I admit it. I didn't know what he would do, but yes, I sent her."

"What else were you about achieving in this?"

She hesitated.

"Gabriel is not in the habit of asking questions he doesn't

want an answer to," I said. "Answer before he finishes it or I do."

Her eyes darted between us. They settled once again for the one who wasn't currently seething, so it appeared.

"It's true about our business contracts. I thought if I did something for him, perhaps he'd relent."

Another burning snort from me.

Her head snapped in my direction. "I know. I know what you think. Stupid hope. Well I had to try."

I gazed at Gabriel. "Are we finished yet? We might catch a movie before returning to France, one of those torture flicks, mmm." I arched a brow.

He did not reply, nor did he take his eyes from Elise. "Is she still spying for you?"

Elise never shook her head so fast, I thought. "After giving Vicont information on Trey last month, she left me."

"You have no idea where she is?"

"I've been looking for her, thinking to kill her myself."

"And why would this be?"

She slapped the floor. "She betrayed me! She told Vicont's people about my plans for assuming his companies!"

My laugh echoed in my ears. "Do you believe this tripe?"

She fired me a look. "It's true! And if you had asked me before throwing a tantrum, I would have told you then!"

My fangs, they pierced my lower lip. "Sure. You'd have confessed to sending assassins to France."

"I know nothing of assassins."

She turned her eyes up to Gabriel once more. "I know *nothing* of assassins. I'm spiteful, yes. I'm trying to get my own revenge, yes. But not against the two of you. I have never brought harm to any of your companions and I wouldn't. I'm not Vicont!"

"Yet he taught you so well, did he not?" I moved a step closer. "Didn't he?" I began to tremble. "He taught you so well that I fell for it."

She rose from the floor, Gabriel making no move to stop her, and faced me. "You never allowed me to tell you why I did it. You wouldn't hear a word before you left me, and you wouldn't hear a word of it in all the years since."

I was yet again in her face. Yet again, her coppery hair wound in my fist. "I. Don't. Care."

"Michel."

My gazed shifted to Gabriel, his tone asking me to pause, and this was incredulous to me.

"Don't tell me that you want to hear this," I said.

"I do not."

"Then what? What?" *Twice you have stopped me*, was my thought.

"She had no hand in Geoff's trauma."

Incredulous. I let go of her. I shoved her out of the way, and in a moment of déjà vu, Gabriel and I were chest to chest, nose to nose. "You believe her?"

"*Oui.*"

"You believed him, too!"

He made with a slow motion blink.

"This doesn't change what happened to Trey because of her spy," I spoke low and felt far too dangerous, speaking to him this way.

"*Non*, it does not. Though I believe that she had no idea of Vicont's plans."

"Grrrah!" I found the closest thing and threw it. The vase exploded against a wall. I stared him down, literally biting my tongue. "How is it they're both telling the truth, my *love*?"

"Neither of them sent the assassin. Vicont did not directly speak of Elise concerning the assassin, nor offer reasons. Only that the girl in the photograph was the spy. You were not wont to waste time, and too soon we had taken our leave of Vicont, else I would have bid you wait before making for Brussels. I believed that we might gather more information here, in any event, and now we have."

Simple. As. That.

Frustrated, I turned away, reaching for the next closest thing. "How can you care? I thought you hated her. What does it matter?"

I did not fling this vase, however. Instead, it slowly cracked, then burst, in my grip.

I would not make the mistake of doubting him again. I would not. There was a reason for his pause. A reason and he was right in his words. He was always right.

Simple as that, yes. It had been someone else. Entirely possible. Entirely possible she truly didn't know what Vicont would do with the information, yes, this as well.

Don't believe her lies, Vicont had said.

Gabriel had no reason to believe her lies, however.

I would not doubt him. Certainly not because of she and Vicont, not ever again, and he was most certainly correct in that I hadn't lingered with Vicont, no, I had fled in a rage.

I pivoted slowly back, finding my beloved's face. I yet loathed that believing in Gabriel meant also that I must believe her, in this instance.

My shoulders, previously so tense, sagged with the realization that perhaps I didn't loath it as much as I ought.

I turned my eyes to her, proud yet shaken, standing there in her regal blue blouse and torn navy Capri pants. "Why did you do it?" I asked with barest volume, internally damning my own question. "Those years ago. Why?"

Her hands came together, the fingers worrying each other. "I..." she stole a view of Gabriel before continuing. "I loved you both. Gabriel and you. But I couldn't have him, and certainly not both of you. Gabriel was never interested that way."

Ire flared brighter within me once more.

She held up her hands. "I didn't do it just to be with you, Michel, though I wanted that. I wanted to touch more closely the feeling between you and him." Her eyes dropped. "Which I still have never known, I know this." Her eyes lifted. "I know I was only a distraction from your pain. I know the bond the two of you have can't be repeated with another."

My teeth, gritting. "Then why?"

"Vicont told me that he was going to kill Gabriel. I believed him. It frightened me. He wanted you out from under Gabriel's influence."

I saw her through a pinpoint of light. "You are not suggesting—"

"I didn't want him to die, Michel. I did it thinking it might save him, save the both of you. I told Vicont what I was going to do, hoping he'd back off. I told him if he killed Gabriel you'd be so devastated you'd be worthless to him."

I was either going to vomit, or to sink to my knees. Or, find myself shoving my heart back into my chest, telling it to shut the hell up.

"And it worked too well," she swiftly added. "Maybe Vicont lied to me all along. I'm no savior, I'm not asking you to thank me. I know for you that the separation was likely *worse* than death. But if Gabriel died, I think too so would you."

I felt her move. Toward me, perhaps. An army of feelings warring within me, kept me paralyzed.

"I say this not to hurt you. I was still certain I'd fail, but I thought that at least it would buy time. I didn't think you'd believe my lies about Gabriel. I gave it my all, and I swear to you it hurt me to do it."

Yes, she had moved closer.

"You were so conflicted at the time. So hurt, so confused. I wanted to be both happy with my apparent prize, and weep that you stayed with me."

I near crushed myself with my own arms.

"If you don't believe me, it's what I'd expect. But I've said it, now. I've wanted to say it, that is; when I found the courage to face you, I wanted to say it. I knew you wouldn't reply to my letters right away. I knew it might take years. I admit to growing spiteful and impatient when more and more time passed, when I was ready to tell you, but you wouldn't so much as sneeze in my direction. Then you came here last week, for such a flimsy request. I was stunned, but thought perhaps... just perhaps."

I pivoted, finding my dark angel's face. What I found in his eyes further strangled words before they could reach my lips.

It appeared he believed her, and he was gazing with less coldness at her than before, he was gazing at her with some manner of pity mixed with sorrow.

He asked of her one question. "Why did you not merely tell Michel and myself of Vicont's threat?"

"Fear. Fear that you'd confront him and that he'd then kill others I loved to punish me. Fear that then he'd devise some other plan I wouldn't be privy to, and I would have no way to warn you, help you. Fear that he'd kill you immediately, and I know. I know you're strong, both of you, but he has so many willing to do his dirty work."

I looked at her. Truly looked at her.

She spread her hands, a self-depreciating expression stealing her beauty. "My logic isn't always so logical to others, I know." She looked to me. "You may never forgive me, I know. I'm not sorry you're both still here. I'm not sorry if what I did made that possible. I can't be, because you're alive and together again. I also have admitted my own selfish desires. But I *am* sorry for the pain, and I'm so sorry about what happened to Trey because of me. I didn't know how much you loved him. I didn't know how special he was." She took yet another step closer. "My emotions lead me, as often do yours. I may not have been the most rational person all these years, but what can I say? I'm a Gemini woman."

She offered me a tentative smile. Gemini woman, a play on something I used to say of her split personality, a jest, an affectionate jest.

I sucked air. "Elise...I..."

No. I cannot do this right now. I cannot forget. I cannot...

I cannot grasp...
I fled the room, having once more, that absurd urge to weep.

Gabriel

My Michel exited the room, moving beyond me and well beyond Kar, who remained in his position, knowing better than to follow, particularly uninvited, when Michel was of a certain mood.

Even I did not follow, although in the pool beneath my detached view of the situation, the desire began to swim. Beneath the thick sheet of ice that covered the pool another creature lurked, but for now it too remained detached, numbed.

It and I looked out through my eyes, studying Elise as she stood before me. Elise, a woman that I had come once to care for, and the beast within me had come to detest. I did not flounder in the same rush of emotion my beloved Michel now did, he who had been closest, he who had been the child molded, manipulated and abused time and again, emotionally, by those who coveted each what they saw within him. His potential, one thought. His fire, his passion, his charm and his ever-inquisitive nature, time never dulling it. His inner child, this is what Vicont knew that he could use, could bend. Michel's capacity to love, this he could twist, and then his unique power could he direct.

So Vicont thought when he came upon Michel, who was at the time, nearly eighteen. Michel who was not completely naïve, but of certain things in the world he had been sheltered, and this too Vicont played upon, for Michel had been convinced there was far more to the world and its workings, the machinations of its people, than he had ever glimpsed. He was certain that there were wonders and terrors in this world that he simply must see.

Much like Trey, I thought.

Vicont was one of those wonders who also, as it happened,

was one of its terrors. A young Michel, some part of him knew that the terror lurked, but this was thrilling, this was something not mundane, not the boring existence of a bastard child pampered and protected. Pampered and protected in part so that the secret of his father would not come to the wrong people and thus place Michel in danger of being used or kidnapped or killed, any of these things.

Yet he was used, kidnapped, and in a sense killed all the same, my beloved.

Vicont admired Michel's strong will. This, naturally, became the thorn in Vicont's side when he found that he had not molded Michel as completely as he once thought. When he could not mold him as easily as he once thought. When that stubborn streak of Michel's was in opposition of Vicont's desires, naturally it became something that Vicont despised.

Michel's capacity for love soon became a thorn in Vicont's side as well.

I have always said that Vicont should have known better, for it was everything that he coveted in Michel that made his plan fail in the end. But of course, we often desire what we cannot truly have, such as the magnificent creature in the wild. We cannot claim it, we can only hope it deigns to give us another glimpse; we can only in our wildest dreams, hope that it deigns to share our company a while, just a little while.

When that glorious untamed creature that is my Michel deigned to share *my* company for more than just a little while, this, of course, drove Vicont mad with jealousy. Yes, jealousy was the seed from which all other emotions sprouted, their fine tendrils lacing, tangling themselves in Vicont's body.

His prize was not his prize. It had given itself to me.

I looked at this creature before me, Elise, and knew that it was not the same jealousy. I looked into her eyes and I knew that she had never deluded herself into thinking she could own the lion or the panther, as my love sometimes referred to me.

But though I understood, even believed her motives,

forgiveness was not within me, not now, and I did not know if ever. Though I knew that she was more a child than Michel was, manipulated and molded as well, the block of ice blanketing the space that she had held in my heart, it would not melt. Not now, if ever. The pain of mine and Michel's separation, the pain of his disbelief, the pain of watching him once more become someone I thought I did not know, it had been too great. The pain that it had caused him, that also was too great.

I realized I could not now say it never would melt, however. This revelation peeled away one of the layers separating me from the situation, my detachment shimmering.

I could not say that it never would, for I understood doing anything for love, and in her eyes, I recognized the desperation of love.

The worst pain is always inflicted or felt when it reaches through love. Only with those we love, who love us in return, can such pain devastate us; otherwise, it simply does not matter.

"You did not speak of this to him on our last visit," I said at last. "You yet danced."

"It wasn't something he wanted to discuss, and I didn't think he'd believe me at that point. I couldn't just bring it up out of nowhere." She took a hesitant footstep closer. "I admit I became spiteful, baiting him, when I felt he had only come to refuse me." She gave off a sigh. "I was stunned when he struck me and so I struck back. He'd never once hit me before. Verbal lashing, this I expected." She smiled at this. "I've never faulted him for *that*. It's one of his beautiful traits that he still bursts with emotion no matter how long in the world." Her eyes, they lowered. "But you know this."

I knew it well and loved him for it, yes, even finding the ugliness in some of his outbursts beautiful; for it only solidified that he was a fully *feeling* creature. Something that I sometimes clung to when I myself was too detached, and he in turn at times reached for my distance when he needed it.

"I often thought, since our reconciliation, that you must have been a stupendous actress," I said. "Need I say that I did not reflect on this in a positive manner?"

A shake of her head and a lifting of her eyes. "Of course not. Why you seem to believe me now, I'm not certain. Why you don't appear ready to finish what Michel started, I'm really not certain."

"I am and yet I am not, for my part."

She, for her part, nearly smiled. "I actually understand this."

I found myself near to smiling as well, something I could do when detached, just enough, detached. "I rather suppose you would."

Her smile did find her at last, yet, she again lowered her eyes, the smile fleeing. "There aren't enough apologies I can offer for the past." Her eyes, they made to slowly lift as she continued. "Perhaps not for Trey, either, but in this, please know that if I'd realized how special he was I never would have done it. A terrible excuse, maybe; surely you'll say I shouldn't have done it, regardless."

I contemplated this. I contemplated her.

"You no doubt heard of Stefan. As we didn't much care for him, I rather suppose it is not the worst excuse you could offer."

Hope. It sprang in the depths of her eyes. "You're being generous. I should stop while I've still got that."

I merely gave off a light shrug.

She began to say more. She instead took in a lungful of air, then one more after releasing the first.

"If you have more to say, best now to say it while I am still being generous." Though I would not of a necessity term it generosity just then, no. Distance. It was yet my detachment.

Something she likely knew, I realized.

"I'm beyond surprised that you're still standing there, talking to me," she said at length. "I didn't think you'd be the one still standing there. If nothing else, I thought Michel would still be railing at me if he did remain."

"I am merely assessing the situation."

She made with a slight nod. "A retreat in logic. I often envied your ability to do so."

"It at times serves me well."

Yet another nod of her head. "This is why you believe me. You're able to step outside the situation after all this time."

I did not voice the thought that, often enough, it was a defense mechanism as well, which sometimes clicked into place of its own accord, whether I liked it or not.

She spread her hands. "I told the truth to Michel during his last visit. What I wanted to do to Vicont. I didn't hide it. I could have."

"He knows."

"Then perhaps he'll believe what I've told him tonight...in time."

He already did, thus his inability to remain in the room. This I did not give voice to, either.

There was a slight clearing of her throat. "This Geoff. I'm very sorry, truly I am. Even in his anger I could sense the love when he said the name."

"Geoff is well."

Her brows crept higher on her forehead. "This is good. I'm glad. Really I am." She touched the phantom marks on her throat, marks having healed during our discussion. "I'll give you the spy. I said I would, not merely in hopes of saving my skin."

I merely gazed at her.

"Her name is Vita. The last lead I had was that she might be in London." Her eyes narrowed themselves. "Wily for a human."

One of my brows felt to arch. "Lover scorned, were you?"

Her focus returned outward, to me. "Fitting, isn't it?"

A smile, one did find me. "It is a start."

Her smile to me was wry. "That's fair enough." In a sudden

move, she was yet closer to my person. "Think on this, if you can see your way to it. You want to bring Vicont down more than me. I'm certain you do. I can help you do it."

My own vision narrowed. "And you would ask what in return?"

"Nothing. Nothing at all. I would have the satisfaction of him being brought low, and—"

"And?"

She inhaled, gathering herself. "It's another offer of apology for what I did. Nothing can erase it, but it's something I can offer right now."

"An offer of apology, whilst having what *you* need to carry it out, for you cannot do it alone."

She took a step back, for my detachment was lessening as my mind focused on thoughts of Michel once again becoming someone's means to an end.

"If I could do it myself, I would. I would give this to you. You know as well as I that I can't do it alone, no. But I have information, I have had spies in place, I have allies."

"This Vita, you stated that she had already betrayed you to Vicont."

"Yes, but I regrouped, and she didn't know everything. I'm sometimes daft, but not completely stupid."

A laugh, a dry laugh, worked its way through me.

I took a step away, contemplating. "I should like to know why it is that we would trust you, in your mind."

"I don't know how to prove that to you, other than to give you access to everyone and everything I have concerning the matter. Keep me locked up, keep a guard on me, whatever it is you need to determine that I won't cross you."

I gazed across my shoulder in her direction. "Keep you in shackles and chains; this seems something that might entertain me."

Her chin lifted. "If you will it, I will suffer it."

"You do not know the half of suffering." I took another step away, another layer of detachment peeling itself free.

"In comparison to yours...no," were her quietly spoken words. "To his, no. I witnessed his."

I made a sharp turn in her direction. "And you allowed him to keep suffering."

Her hands, they found her chest. "If you believe one more thing, believe this. In the end, I urged him to find you. Right before Vicont told him the partial version of my deception and Michel confronted me, leaving me too paralyzed to even think of explaining, I told him to scour the earth for you."

My blood, it was ice in my veins, and yet I said nothing.

"Ask him, Gabriel, as it appears he never told you. Ask him," she pled.

Still, I said nothing. For what did it matter if she had? What did it truly matter?

Did it matter?

"He was never with me, you were right. He never betrayed you deep in his heart. Nothing assuaged his pain. He was prisoner to a broken heart that yet wanted you more than anything in the world, and prisoner to the doubts that grew and grew, prisoner to the idea he'd made a mistake after all, and so afraid that if he found you, the pain of you turning him away would be greater still." She reached a trembling hand in my direction.

My vision, of a sudden it misted deep crimson.

"He never could hide an emotion, Gabriel," she continued. "But you know this. And these emotions I don't think anyone could have hidden. They bled from his heart and through his skin."

I then realized that she had moved more than her hand, and that this hand was now lightly resting upon my arm. "He wasn't really with me so often. And he used to hurt himself as if trying to cut out the pain," she whispered. "I couldn't stand it. I told him to look for you. I told him you were meant to be together and your Fate could be salvaged."

Deepest crimson must have thieved its way through my lashes, for I felt a sting to my cheeks.

I swallowed thickly.

"If...if I'd not been so cowardly, so afraid to brave what I'd done and told him before, told Michel that you'd never spurned him, never thought to leave him, never in your life wanted anyone but him, I...if I'd had the other man confess..."

Her hand slipped away as I walked away.

"Oh Gabriel, I hate myself. I hate your pain. I'm so sorry," she cried.

Her own tears, she cried, while mine seeped through my chest.

"I shall," I began. I began again. "I'll..."

I continued on my path, passing Kar, where I paused as his hand lifted as if to touch my face.

Slowly he lowered it, and after an inclination of his head, led me, who was blind with too many things, having lost my distance, out of the house of pain.

Though the house remained within me.

****

I found him standing at the edge of the river, having bid Kar to leave me to walk in peace.

His velvet-adorned arms were tight about his waist, his fingers digging into maroon velvet sides.

"Michel."

He turned, his cheeks adorned with rubies black and bloodied, still spilling from his jeweled eyes, breaking my heart, bursting there in my chest.

"I'm a fool," he said, tears coloring his voice. "I want to believe in the good in people, I believe in the good, and for that I'm so easily duped, so then I reach for the worst, and for this I'm duped as well."

I moved closer to him. "You are no fool, *mon amour*."

"Yes I am." He threw out his arms. "I should live with you in a cave far, far away from the world. You're the only one I can trust, the only one I should ever believe in. Damn the rest of the world. I wish I was like you, Gabriel, oh, how I wish it."

My throat became tight. I reached for his hands and tightly did I grasp them. "No you don't. Nor do I."

He averted his gaze. "All the pain."

"Is worth it," I said. "Your ability to love, your ability to look for the best in people rather than assume the worst, like me, is one of the things I most love about you. You're my salvation."

His eyes made a slow return to me, searching mine.

"My dearest love," I said. "What would I be without you to shine this light upon my life?" I pulled him into my arms. "I'll tell you. A man so far removed, so hardened, it would be worse than death. It's only through you I see hope for this world I so long despised."

He near choked on his breath. "In what is there hope? It all comes to no good end."

I captured his face between my hands. "You don't believe this. You're upset, and so you say these things. You know where the hope lies."

The face of the child I had first beheld so long ago looked back at me.

"It's in Trey's eyes. In Geoff's breath. In Travis' touch. You wouldn't have these things if you were like me. *I* wouldn't have them without you. They are proof there is something yet in this world to love," I said.

His hands covered mine as his lashes fluttered, flirting with the tops of his cheeks. "They will die because of me. Trey and Geoff, I'll be the death of them."

"I can't say they will or won't. But I know this, Michel. It is right that they are in your life, our life, and if they die too soon, it was their choice to be in it, and *this* is a reason they are so beautiful...a reason that you love them."

He made to take a step back, yet I held him firm.

"You would waste away, not embracing life as you always have, the risks it entails. I would lose you, then. You wouldn't be Michel."

His forehead tipped forward, meeting mine. "No," he whispered. "I wouldn't be me. But it's dangerous for them, having my love, and I have been selfish in this, always."

I shook my head against his. "You who are so fond now of telling me how similar Trey and I are, of basking in this connection, that you forget how strongly you and he are alike sometimes."

His lashes fluttered upwards, his stained glass, stained eyes meeting mine.

"Your hearts, so generous. Your ability to love, so complete. Yet you fear the damage your love may cause another and you wonder that you're being selfish, however ill informed this belief may be. You fear, but you're too alive to walk away, so desirous of touching just one perfect moment, you and he. He chose to remain, Michel, for several of the same reasons you chose to claim him. *This* is beautiful. That you each punish yourself is not."

Briefly, I thought of Elise's words of cutting out the pain.

"I guess we're both selfish, Trey and I." He attempted to smile and failed.

"All love is selfish. Does this make it less real?"

He did not reply.

"Yet all love can be selfless. You each struggle with the correct definition. Neither of you is selfish."

His forehead returned to mine and he sighed. "I must again wonder why fortune smiled so brightly upon me when it came to you."

"It wasn't your fortune. It was mine, and ours."

"Gabriel—"

"So like Trey when he first arrived, not understanding why anyone should so freely offer him their love."

Michel, at last he returned my embrace, melting into me, and I ran my fingers through and through his hair.

"Gabriel...if I ever forgive her..."

I felt the skirting of fear in his heart. "I will not hate you for it. Forgiveness is most often for our own sake." I caressed his neck. "Your capacity for such is yet another thing that I love about you, and something that I wish I had more of. You are the light to my dark, as always. The sun to my moon."

His hands moved over my back. "I've spent years believing one thing about her that I didn't want to believe. In less than one hour, it's tumbled like a house of cards, and now," he gazed deeply into my eyes, "Now I don't know what to feel. I don't know what to think of Vicont, either."

"In this we are even."

"It's good he yet lives, however. Because I want to get to the bottom of this."

"As do I," I whispered. "A reason I stopped you."

"It's good you stopped me from killing her, too. However fucked up it is."

"Fucked up, yes," I whispered yet again, and thought not of her reasons for doing as she did all those years ago, but her words on encouraging Michel to seek me. I wondered if there were more words, yet also despised in some way this desire to know, for we had already reconciled.

Her words on his self-mutilation, this is what had most compelled me from her presence. I wished to know how bad it truly was, yet despised the idea of knowing.

"Gabriel?"

I had drifted away and concern wound through his gaze.

"Home, Michel. Let's go home."

Whatever he had been about to say then, other words replaced. "Yes. I'm still worried about Trey. The rest can wait."

I merely nodded. Yes, there was Trey. Yet there was also the feeling of being in a place that was only Michel's and mine, our house.

Of a sudden, I desperately needed it.

His lips caressing mine, he spoke, his words warm breathy and tickling trails. "How I love you, *ma vie*."

"How I adore you, *mon ange d'or*."

Chapter Twenty-Five

Trey

How long had I slept? Dreams, there were dreams, some beautiful before they became tainted and turned uglier and uglier. Full of blood and pain and sorrow, in mangled snatches that made sense only to me because I knew the pieces of the twisted puzzle.

I gazed at Geoff. Except it didn't feel like my own vision, and her voice was buzzing in my head just as it had been every other moment I was awake. I reached to touch his face.

Except he wasn't actually there.

I wasn't really dreaming, either.

Is he worth it?

"Yes." The word barely made sound, but that didn't matter.

Why wasn't Sean?

I pressed my hands to my eyes and got out of bed.

So many images of Sean. Sean who was haunting me whether he knew it or not. She was using him to haunt me more.

"Enough. Leave him out of it now, please."

Why? Didn't he grieve and grieve over you so many times that he finally took his own life? Why leave him out of it?

Speaking was becoming difficult. More difficult. "It has nothing to do with this."

Then you don't deny it. This is part of your penance. This is part of the deal. I thought you already knew that.

I stumbled from my bedroom and made my way into the attached bathroom. I looked into the mirror, and looking back were the girls that former client had raped and murdered.

I barely kept from crying out.

"No, no. Enough, isn't it enough yet? You're going too far. Adele…"

*Nothing is too far, is it? Unless **you** confess that you went too far.*

I white knuckled the counter. Was I still punishing myself, too? Was she this deep, truly this deep inside me?

Her laughter bounced in my head and wanted to drive me insane.

You don't really want me to stop. But if you face your sins, I'll go away.

"You will?"

Her voice became achingly sweet.

I promise. Just a little more and then I can rest. I'll believe that you're sorry and I'll go away. Isn't that why you let me in? So I could move on?

I stared at the stranger in the mirror. "You'll be able to move on? Will you really go?"

What do you say? Cross my heart and—well, cross my heart.

I could see her face where my face should be.

I felt so weak.

"How much more, Adele? How much?"

Just a little more, Trey.

"It's too much," I nearly sobbed.

You said that he was worth it.

My eyes squeezed shut. "Yes."

Oh, Trey. I can make it easier. We know how to make it stop hurting for a while, now don't we?"

I started trembling. "No...yes...no."

I stared into my hazel colored eyes. "Yes, we do."

There was then a razor blade in my left hand, my trembling hand.

I watched myself shake my head even as I brought it closer to my arm.

"This will help for a little while."

"No."

"It always did."

"...yes."

"Yes, this and other things."

I watched my reflection nod.

"A little relief from your penance, Trey, however slight. Besides. I want you to bleed for me. I bled for you."

"Please..."

"Just a little blood for me, Trey, and you'll feel so much better for it."

I felt the tears rolling down my face as I made the first cut.

And then struggled not to make the second.

And failed.

Struggled not to make the third.

Failed.

"You know what works even better?"

I watched myself nod.

"I bet we can score some easy, so I tell you what. Forget this razor, let's go."

I didn't...

Want...

I want...

...it to go away.

The images of them. Black piping. Strangled. Bruised. Cut. Violated. Wide vacant eyes.

The images of Sean's tears, the note, and the way he looked when I found him.

The images of my parent's faces when I woke up in the hospital.

The image of Geoff falling. Bleeding. Again. Again. Again.

Adele's innocent face, asking if I needed help.

Her lifeless form, the bullet making its way toward her.

"I need help," I whispered while I still had something of myself in my grasp. A sliver from the increasingly dark and darker place I was sinking.
"Yes, and we're going to get some, Trey."
Scott?
Geoff?
I think I've gone too far.
But she said just a little more, and then...
Did I hear banging at a door?
"We're not going to let him stop us. Let's go, Trey."
Did I hear Scott?
"I'll take care of it."

I think I heard knocking at my bedroom door.

I hear banging at my bedroom door. I feel myself walking toward the door. I think I do.

Except I don't seem to have much control over me, anymore.

"Trey?" I hear Scott. Knock knock. "Trey, are you okay?"

I—

She—

We?

Open the door and give him a smile.

I could see him. Except I felt far away. I felt like I was—

The veil. Was I on the other side? Straddling?

Desperately trying to hold on, not even straddling.

"Hey," he said. "I just wanted to see if you needed anything. You've been in there forever."

"I'm feeling much better," I—she said.

Through me.

He stared at my

Were they my eyes?

"Yeah? I've been back for a while and I thought you were still asleep. But just now I thought I heard you crying or something when I walked by your door."

He kept peering at my eyes with knitted brows.

I feel so far away.

"I threw up," we said. "But it made me feel better."

He stared. "I thought I heard you talking."

"I still do that, yes, Scott."

He stared some more.

"What is it, Scott?"

"Are you wearing contacts?"

No, I tried to say. "Yes," she said. "How do I look?"

"It's weird. I'm used to the blue. You're, uh, you're not going out or something, are you? I mean, why the contacts?"

No! I tried to say. "Yes, I thought I would."

"But you just threw up, and you don't exactly sound like yourself."

I'm not! "I'm sure. Something didn't settle in my stomach, that's all."

He stared.

"Couldn't have been Geoff's cooking."

I think we only smiled. She smiled with my face.

"Well if you're intent on going out, I'll go with you. Polly was asking about you. She had to help a friend with something, but maybe we could hook up with her later."

Yes, I wanted to say. Stay with me, Scott. "If you don't mind, I'd rather go alone."

His expression fought falling. I was watching a movie, from a very different seat.

Glued to my seat. Chained to my seat.

"There's a little something I have to do," she said for me.

"Oh, well. I guess I could watch a movie until you get back."

NO! Don't let her take me!

"Help yourself." She must have made me smile.

What have I done?

I watched his brows knit as his eyes drilled a hole through my skull.

Then I watched his eyes suddenly drop. "Jesus, Trey." He grabbed my arm. I felt it, but not enough. "Christ, what did you do?" He searched—her eyes. "Jesus. Let me clean this up. You have something in the apartment, right?"

My arm, yanked back. I was a puppet. Just a marionette and she was pulling the strings. "Just a little accident."

"That doesn't look like an accident, Trey." So concerned, he was so concerned. "You cut yourself on purpose."

"Well, maybe just a little," she conceded.

"Let me help you, Trey." He reached.

Yes. Help me.

She pulled the strings. Moved me around him. "I don't need your help."

"Trey, stop. Wait." His hand, on my shoulder.

My hand, it pushed his away. "Let it go, Scott." Marionette, moved away.

God! I'm not in my skin, am I? I see it, I see it happening but I don't feel it the way I should be feeling it.

Oh God!

"No," he said, following. "You're not okay at all. Let me help you."

Yes! Help me, Scott, please!

He grabbed me. My hands shoved him away. "I don't need your damned help," she made me say.

No. No. No.

"Trey..."

"I never needed or wanted your help, got it? Why don't you go back home already."

No! No please, don't say that to Scott. Please, no, please, no. Don't twist it. Don't use that against him. It's me you want, Adele. Me.

He's in our way.

I could see the hurt lashing his eyes.

I didn't say it, Scott! I didn't say it! I'm sorry, I'm sorry!

"Now get out of my way."

No. No! I want my skin. I want to feel the pain of the cuts. I want to feel!

Walking way. I'm walking way even though I'm suddenly in a haze of...haze of...

Ohhh. I can taste it.

Black tar.

"Trey."

No! I don't want it. No! I don't do that anymore, I want to feel the pain! I need to feel the pain!

"Trey, wait!"

I'm scared. I'm so scared, Scott. I've lost control. Oh God. I can't stop. I can't stop, and she's letting me see all of it, all of it.

"No. Not this time, Trey."

Cold. I'm so cold.

Scott! Don't let me walk away. Don't let her walk away with me. Don't let her do it.

Halfway through the living room. Halfway. We're halfway.

"I'm not letting you leave this time…and you promised," I heard him say.

Then he tackled me.

Yes!

I wanted to hug him, to hug him tight.

Instead, we were grappling.

I was grappling in my own way, straddling—

No. Getting farther away.

Lucien. Lucien! I'm sorry! Help me. Help me! I don't want this! I can't do this!

You're mine, now.

Lucien! Papa! This can't be right, it can't be. Help me, I'm not strong enough!

"I'm not letting you go, damn it," Scott nearly cried. I could hear the edge of frustrated and hurt tears.

I could hear the fear.

Don't let go, Scott. Don't let go. I'm all alone here. Don't let go, please don't let go.

Life for a life, right Trey?

Adele no! Leave him alone. Don't make me do this. Don't make me hurt him, please.

I don't mean him.

Oh…

God.

I said I'd die for him. I said I'd die for Geoff.

Whisper. Rustle. Whisper.

Cain't…

…work dat…

Sa spun ya missed…

Lucien? Is that you?

She means ta…

…but it…

"I'm not letting you go. Do you hear me, Trey? Stop fighting me! I'm not letting you go this time. If I have to knock you out, I will, damn it!"

I hear you, Scott. I hear you! Hit me harder. Make me feel it, damn it. Make me FEEL. Knock me out, do it, do it, and "don't let me go."

"Trey?"

Was that—did he—did I say it? Scott, don't let me go, please don't "let me go." It's so cold I'm so cold I'm so scared I'm so cold and far away.

No. Life for a life. You owe me.

"I'm not letting go Trey! I'm trying to help you!"

She think…

…her life

Lucien, I can't make you out! What?

You're mine. You let me in. You trade, I trade.

So. Cold.

So cold with understanding flashing bright in my eyes on the Other Side.

I don't need to hear Lucien. I know what she wants. I think I know what she wants.

I struggle. Not with Scott. I struggle to get to Scott. I struggle to reach for Scott and my reward for this is bloody visions.

Visions of me covered in blood, blood and Sean's frantic eyes.

"Trey, can you hear me? Oh Jesus, Trey?"

Is he shaking me? Or am I just shaking?

"Trey!"

Assault. Assaulting me. So many visions.

Feelings.

Visions.

Feelings.

I can feel. I can feel.

All the wrong things.

"Trey!"

Oh.

God.

"Trey, come on, talk to me. Oh Jesus, talk to me!"

Lucien! Papa!

Scott!

Oh God!

Make it stop, I can't take it!

Life for a life. One way or the other. Thank you so much for the freedom to run through
your mind.

Screaming, screaming, with no one to hear me.

Too much. Too much.

It hurts. It hurts.

I want to die.

I'm going to die for him.

I'm going to die for him.

You said that you would.

But ...

You said that you would, and you're learning a lesson.

L-Lucien? Adele? I can't—I can't tell. I can't tell. My brain is white with the brand of a hundred hot irons.

Will you take it back now? You said that he was worth it.

No. No. Will he die if I don't?

You said that you would.

No. Don't take him. Don't take him.

Take me. Make it stop. Make my eyes stop bleeding, make my chest stop ripping, make my heart stop exploding, make my intestines stop knotting, make it stop.

Make their faces go away, make their suffering go away, make my—

Soon, now.

Geoff...

I will always love you.

Chapter Twenty-Six

Michel

"How much longer, *mon lion?*"

I smoothed the hair away from his face and let my palm rest upon his cheek. His other, it was on my shoulder.

"We'll be landing in just a few more minutes, dove."

"I am feeling anxious."

So I could feel as well. For him to state it was more disconcerting. "You need to be home."

"I wish to see Trey first."

"I would like this as well, Gabriel."

Though the flight in our jet was short enough coming from Brussels to Paris, I too had begun to feel a manner of my own anxiousness, separate from his, though it was often difficult to separate, about getting to Paris. More precisely, getting to Paris to check on Trey.

But then, this was the same feeling Gabriel was having.

He stiffened under my arm before the thought had fully moved through me.

"How much longer?"

My brows came together. More still, when he sat up and quickly leaned to the window, looking out. "How much longer?" he asked again.

"Only a few moments." A few moments too long, apparently. There was then a vibration in my pocket. My cellular. Gabriel's attention snapped to me.

"Answer it."

Yes, I was all about answering, my love. Fishing it from my pocket, I flipped it open and slapped it to my ear. "*Oui?*"

Travis was the caller on the line. "Michel, are you still in Belgium?"

"No, we are nearly on the ground in Paris." And as I had immediately detected something off in his tone, I asked, "Is there a problem?"

"Something's wrong with Trey."

It was I that stiffened and sat up straighter. "How so?"

"I don't know, exactly. Geoff is heading that way. I have him in my mind."

"Follow." I dropped my mental shields, reaching first toward Travis. Gabriel's nails were digging into the velvet over my shoulder.

"On my way," Travis said.

He was seconds away from their building. "Stay with me. We'll be there two minutes after this damned jet touches pavement." I mentally reached for rue chapon. For Trey's apartment.

"Trey's fighting with Scott. Do you see?"

I closed my eyes, for I did see. "Stay in my mind." I snapped the phone shut.

I felt Gabriel's gaze.

"Perhaps something did get hold of him after all," I said, and the sudden flash of fear made it seem far too ominous.

Gabriel's nails punctured fabric and found flesh.

****

Less than two minutes after the jet touched pavement, Gabriel and I were at Trey's door, letting ourselves in without hesitation.

The scene that presented itself to me, to us, was far worse than the live action movie that had been in my mind. As vivid and complete as such could be, as realistic as the images are, they still paled in comparison to live and in person.

Scents, they had come to me even before opening the door, and they were an assault after this before my eyes found a single one of those assembled in Trey's living room.

Blood. Blood scent I immediately detected, and it began to flood my nostrils. Trey's blood, and as my senses separated and tested each layer, the scent of blood foreign to me came to my attention.

Not completely foreign, this my receptors processed soon enough, no not completely foreign. Only a few days ago I had scented the blushing of this blood in the flesh of Scott O'Neil, he of the clear blue eyes, and it was now more pungent, free of his flesh.

Confusion, fear, anxiety. These assaulted me, merging and separating, catalogued, merging again, and beneath this, something—someone? Yes someone, foreign to me indeed.

This all happened in a manner of seconds, physical sight taking its notes in the next few seconds.

Scott's blood, it was trickling from his nose while he sat, there in a corner on the floor, his knees drawn to his chest, his eyes a convoluted tangle of emotion.

Trey's blood was running from fresh cuts on the inside of his right forearm. They were clean cuts. They were clean, but they were deep, and it welled and ran, pooled, and ran, it ran and stained his cream shirt red-brown, it stained his lounging pants maroon-black, and it splashed, drip drop, onto the floor, finding its way between the varnish to tarnish the wood grain forever.

Trey's blood was on Scott. Scott's blood was on Trey. Trey's blood was on Travis, who was holding Trey by the arms to keep him from struggling, for Trey was struggling, but Travis was not exerting much force for fear of harming him, for fear of making the situation worse, in fear of frightening Trey.

Geoff—Geoff was two paces from Trey, his hands clutched and to his chest, appearing just rebuked. As if he had been shoved aside. Rebuked and concerned and fearful.

So much fear there was in the room. Geoff's and Scott's, mostly Scott's, fear.

Trey, fear within Trey as well—but Trey's confused me. It ran deep, but it did not flow freely. It was there, I could sense it, but it was suppressed. Suppressed? It was—blocked. He was—blocked.

Seconds, mere seconds passed as these details and more assaulted me, merging, separating, filing, merging and separating again.

I then saw Trey's eyes, and they were not Trey's eyes.

They were not my darling boy's eyes, and his aura, which had catalogued itself during the previous seconds, was not his aura.

The black spot had grown. It had grown, and now engulfed him, engulfed the once bright colors of his being.

I had seen *this* before.

This was the aura of Death. This is what enveloped those just after I drained them to the point of dying as their souls broke free and left the body completely void, all its light fading, fading, the last spark leaving, fading until nothing at all was left, until even the blackness disappeared and left the body cooling. Then the shimmering heat, this I would observe as it slowly dissipated in waves.

He was alive, assuredly, every other sense told me that he was alive, most assuredly he was. This aura wished to baffle my other senses, for it could not be, he was not dying, bleeding or not, it was not fatal, no, and even were it, he should yet be filled with light. He should be a spectrum through a prism, the colors split through yet another prism, and yet a third, and so on, to my eyes, and were he dying, I would be watching the colors lose their vibrancy. I would see them dulling, fading and winking out.

Gabriel now had Geoff in his arms.

I had now taken a step toward Trey, focusing on this that simply should not be.

There. There, just beneath the yet smoky blackness, there were his colors. Faint, but they were there. They were not gone but the blackness was smothering them.

The blackness did not completely engulf the color of pain flaring scarlet, however.

Words, words were spoken in the seconds I focused on this, in the seconds it took Gabriel to make his own assessment and move to comfort Geoff.

These words came to me, filling in the spaces before the ones spoken now. Trey's words *Let me go, damn it. Let me go, you brute.*

It was not my darling Trey's voice. The timbre was off.

Travis' words, "I'm trying to help you, Trey." These came to me.

Several things attempted to click into place in my mind. I was utterly certain of one detail.

"That's not Trey," I said, taking another step closer. "It's not Trey you're speaking to."

A set of multi-faceted amber eyes and a set of hazel eyes moved to me.

"Call Polly," I heard Gabriel say to Geoff. "Tell her that we need her."

"No, he's definitely not himself," Travis said to me. "I'm trying to reach him."

His thoughts then brushed against me and found their way in, my shields dropped.

He was near dying, convulsing when I arrived. Geoff, his touch, his presence, this seemed to—to reach Trey in some way.

I felt my own hand fly to my chest.

This Shade was trying to kill Trey. She was trying to kill my Trey.

"What the hell are all you people doing in my apartment?" The girl demanded through Trey. Travis allowed him to break free.

No. I would not lose him to an icy hand reaching beyond the grave.

"This is not your apartment," I said, closing the distance and grabbing his wrist. "And this is *not* your blood to spill."

"It's my body, it's my blood."

I looked hard into the stranger's eyes. "No. This is *Trey's* blood. *My* blood. *Gabriel's* blood. It doesn't belong to you, *wraith*."

Focused, yet still aware of my surroundings, I heard Scott's strangled intake of air, and very much wished someone could, would, comfort him, poor confused boy, yet I did not at the moment think one of us vampires was the one to do it.

"It is too mine," the dead girl said. "I'm just doing what he did."

Gabriel, you understand these things better than I do. She's possessed him.

He seems completely taken over.

But she can't take his life, can she?

If he allows her.

But he's marked. He's the Master.

"You wish to kill him? Is this your revenge?" I asked.

"He took my life. I want it back."

This gave me pause.

Gabriel, I'm not so certain she means to kill him, exactly.

Polly is moments away. She was already on her way...and I think she means to live through him.

Can this wraith do this?

I am out of my realm. I do not remember Mathilde speaking of such things. But if for some reason he has surrendered completely, I think perhaps so. I think perhaps there is something she said of such things.

Gabriel's last thought danced with sorrow, and beneath this, irritation.

He couldn't remember because there were yet black spots in his mind.

I will stall best I can, I silently told him.

Geoff attempted to comfort Scott. I silently thanked him for that, thanked his nature that he could do this while the man he loved suffered in what manner of hell, I could not imagine.

Or could too easily imagine, being the creature of vivid imagination that I was, who was also a creature that courted Death before I was resurrected in the Night. But Trey needed me, and I would not give over to fear and despair.

I would not let him go. I would not allow him to leave me. Us.

I gazed into the eyes that didn't belong to my Trey. "How will you get it back?"

"A fair trade."

"You think it fair, stealing his body?"

"He stole my life."

"But what have you offered him in trade?"

At this, she hesitated, and all I could think in that moment was how strange Trey looked to my eyes, how very wrong it was, the color of his, how very wrong, the expression.

Her answer should have startled me. More succinctly, I wish that it would have startled me, but given what I knew of Trey, it did not.

"He agreed to trade places."

Though it did not startle me, I still had the feeling that he had not known exactly what he was trading when he agreed, and to this, I clung. I clung to this, because my Trey, our Trey, he would not leave us unless he had no choice. Unless he thought that he had no choice.

I could not believe otherwise. He could not leave Geoff, no. He would not leave the very one whose soul he bargained for.

"But did you tell him *exactly* what you meant to do?" I asked her.

She gazed at me the longest time...

Trey

"What the hell are all you people doing in my apartment?"
I can't—
I'm not—
Michel?
"This is not your apartment."
Travis. Travis was here.
Geoff—that was Geoff before. Where am I?

Cypresses. Moss. Roads.
The Dead.

"And this is *not* your blood to spill."
Michel?
Michel! I can see you!
You know. You know! Travis...Travis knows.
What do they know? Why don't they leave us alone?
"It's my body, it's my blood."
You've cut before, after all.
The pain. It's gone.
"No. This is *Trey's* blood. *My* blood. *Gabriel's* blood. It doesn't belong to you, *wraith*."
Why isn't this working, Trey!
Because—because they *know* me.
Help me. Help me, Michel. I can see you, I can hear you, but I can't reach you.

Well, since they know—and they can't help you. No. They can't.

"It is too mine. I'm just doing what he did."

No, you're not.

Are you.

"You wish to kill him? Is this your revenge?"

Revenge. She's…revenge. Yes.

No, Trey. You said that you'd die for him.

"He took my life. I want it back."

Wait. Wait. Want it back.

The Dead. Closer. Reaching.

Stop confusing me. Stop confusing me!

"How will you get it back?"

"A fair trade."

Wait. Wait! I didn't trade for this! You said you'd move on, that it would help you.

Do you want him to die? After all this, you'll let him die?

No!

"You think it fair, stealing his body?"

Stealing my body, yes she's stolen my body.

It's not my fault that you're confused. You're not half as confused as I was, murderer!

"He stole my life."

I did…

I did.

"But what have you offered him in trade?"

A tremor. I feel a tremor in the air around me. No, in the— Veil.

She's hesitating. Hesitating.

Michel! Michel, can you hear me?

"He agreed to trade places."

No! I didn't! I didn't!

It's not my fault that you didn't understand.

"But did you tell him *exactly* what you meant to do?"

No—

No! She tricked me!

Here, Trey. Have another look at your past while I deal with these people.

Michel

A ripple, there was a rippling in his aura as she spoke. "He knew what he was doing. It's what he's supposed to do."

Another, there, another ripple. A gossamer webbing flash of purple and orange.

Fighting. He was somewhere, fighting, I suddenly tasted it, at first faint, then stronger.

Yet so far away.

Trey's hand made a blind and stressful bid for my shoulder. I caught him as his body shuddered with effort that I could feel sparking my nerve endings, my flesh.

In the same moment, I sensed the shifting within Travis, and without looking, knew his eyes were changing, sliding from amber towards a black abyss.

In the same moment that a hand with hard, polished and lengthening jet claws, reached for Trey's face—Polly burst into the apartment.

As she reached them, Travis had already turned Trey, capturing his face between two clawed hands, and the abyss of that gaze did bear down on those startled hazel-hued eyes that looked back into the endless void.

Everyone, including myself, froze when Travis, his voice also having shifted, spoke in a tone thick with metallic baritones.

"His life is not yours to have. This is not the right path."

It took a moment for that poor, tortured soul of a girl to reply.

"I offered them help, I didn't offer to die!"

"The sacrifice you made gave meaning to your death. Do not taint it now, this noble purpose."

The Demon. The Demon within Travis held sway, in an aspect that touched ancient blood wisdom, and I was as awed as I always was, whenever Aeshma—as those few of us who knew had taken to calling Travis in such moments—surged forth, caressing chord within me.

"He… murdered me."

Polly, coming out of her own stunned and awed moment, stepped in.

"No. It was your path. If there had been another road for you to travel, Trey couldn't have taken you from it. If Geoff had been meant to walk the road of Death, Trey couldn't have saved him," Polly said.

Hazel eyes widened and then narrowed in a flash of anger. "He cheated!"

"I'm sorry that you're lost, but Trey can't bend the roads. Not even Papa can give Trey the power to tilt the balance, because Trey *is* the balance. He is the balance between Life and Death, and he can't violate that." Polly moved closer. "Can you hear me, Trey? All roads led to this conclusion; otherwise Papa wouldn't have given you the choice. You can't cheat Death, Trey. You didn't cheat. Let go of your guilt, she's using it."

Another rippling did I see in Trey's aura, and suddenly he grasped Travis' arms, his knees buckling, struggling to speak.

"Help…I can't…I'm sorry…"

"Hold on, Death Dancer. Reach." Travis held him up, bringing him closer. "Let her go and reach for me. Honor her sacrifice and let her go. Reach for your family, here. Reach for the one in your Soul."

When stormy blue flashed pinpoint dots in the hazel of Trey's irises, hope came to me on a sharp intake of breath.

When the blue disappeared, that breath began to escape me.

I then became aware of the soft, droning chant of thoughts in my beloved Gabriel's mind.

Let her go. Let him go. Let her go. Let him go.

Aeshma, he did not let go. "You cannot take from him what

Death took from you. It was the only viable path and he was merely the way through. It is his function."

I became aware of Geoff, holding still to Scott, who remained frozen in shocked disbelief, utterly confused and unable to grasp what was before his eyes.

But Geoff, it was Geoff I felt most in that moment, reaching—that movement of soul than can only be described as mystical.

But then Travis-Aeshma said, "He is slipping from me."

The girl then said, "You lie, you lie."

And Polly said, "I know you're lost and confused, but if you look deeper, look within Trey beyond your anger at leaving this world, you'll know he never wished to harm you. You'll know he was merely the Road, and that there is no lie. Please don't use his guilt against him. He's suffered so much, and so have you. Help him to let you go. You can move on if you let go. You can go where this is no pain and confusion, sweet girl."

My darling Trey, he did shudder—and Geoff reached.

Trey

T-Travis?

Travis?

"Help...I can't...I'm sorry..." Abyss. An abyss.

Darkness dotted suddenly with thousands upon thousands of fireflies.

"Hold on Death Dancer. Reach."

Words, words drifted in and out, but mostly I heard Adele. *Who are these people! They lie, lie, lie. I shouldn't be here!*

Reach. Death Dancer, reach. What was this swell, this warmth, this electric purple warmth? This pregnant celestial breath?

No. No, you're mine now!

Words, words...P.K.? P.K. is that you?

My...family.

My....Soul.

You haven't paid in full yet. You haven't paid.

Assaulted with visions, I cry out, but only the Dead hear me, I think.

Presence, looming. Closer. Closer.

Sucked, sucked down, and trying to hold onto the tendril of purple heat.

But my hands, they're so weak and the pull is so strong.

"Chile, you done let her in too far. Let go nah."

L-Lucien?

"You let him go nah, girl. Messenger cain't be punish dis way. It doan work dis way. His life ain'chore's ta have."

I lost the energy rope.

But I don't disappear into a black hole. My feet hit earth. Soft, musky earth.

I turn. I see him. "Lucien!"

"You's stronger, chile. She gots to move on, help her move on. You's stronger than you know."

I see Adele. I feel Adele. Her hands clutching me. "No...this can't be right. It can't be right."

"She said she'd move on if I... I said I'd die for him."

Lucien shakes his head. "You been tricked in yore guilt and love fo' dat boy. Trade been made. She died for him already, it cain't be took back, done is done. Touch da Sparrow, move her on."

"Trey...Trey I'm scared." I see Adele's eyes dart back and forth.

Wing beats. I hear wing beats. She hears them, too, I realize. That's why her eyes are darting.

Something moves through me.

No. It's already within me, and it moves, fluxes, shimmers.

His scent bathes me. His warmth floods me.

All the words come to me, all the words spoken in my apartment.

Then Lucien speaks. "Doan sully her sacrifice by holding onto her, chile. Separate, let her go, 'member her well."

Then he speaks to Adele. "Doan torture you self no more. You cain't have his life, but you can have another. Dis boy ain't no murderer. He da Road."

She stares and stares at him.

She stares at me. Confusion spreading on her face.

Words. Words.

Feeling. My own feeling. I can feel. I can feel Geoff.

Finding myself. Finding her, the real her.

Her soul. It passed through me before. Now I know it, see it clearly. I remember what I didn't understand that I already knew before. It was waiting there all along for me to remember, if only I'd let go of the guilt.

"Adele." I take a step toward her. "Adele, I'm sorry your time was so short. But you have a beautiful Soul. You'll go forward into an even more beautiful life. A longer life."

She starts shaking her head.

Wings...wings, the flutter, fluttering in my chest.

He gave me strength. The beat of his heart, it gave me strength. He was meant to live.

She was meant to die.

We were meant to join.

"Don't be afraid, Adele. You'll have a beautiful life."

"But I had a good one here!" She's so scared, and I'm sorry for it, but I'm going to help her.

I am. It's part of my function in this. I know it. Just not the way I thought before.

"It'll be even better. You won't miss this one. You won't remember it."

Her hands went to her chest. "But...where am I going?"

"I don't know. But a Soul like yours is destined for beauty." I took another step, spreading my hands. "You'll do great things. You'll find great love."

"How...how do you know?" She lowered her hands.

"Your Soul moved through me before. I've touched it. Your death paved the way for a life meant to continue. What you have

given me is priceless, because you've given me the other half of my own Soul. For this, you'll be gifted in the next life, I promise you."

She searched and searched my eyes and I took another step, holding out my hand. "Such a gift must be repaid, Adele."

"I'm...still scared. Are you sure?"

I gave her a gentle smile. "There's no pain in the transition. Your death itself was only a transition, one with no pain. There was no pain, was there Adele?"

"N-no."

"Such a gift could not come with pain and such a Soul will not pass with pain."

She looked at my hand, took it. "It didn't seem fair. So much I still wanted to do."

I squeezed her hand. "It was sudden, you didn't understand. I know. You felt ripped from the world, lost and confused."

She nodded. "Then I-I saw you. I remembered you."

"I was the last person you saw and the one you clung to, and you could see into me. I let you see even deeper."

She lifted tear-filled eyes to mine. "I thought I could take your place and I hurt you. I found your secrets."

"Yes...you found my secrets."

"But it really wasn't your fault, was it."

Something moved between us, through our touch.

My heart. I poured my heart into that touch.

"It wasn't your fault, Trey. I'm sorry. So much pain inside you. I used your pain, I used your pain, I'm not that kind of person, I'm really not."

"I forgive you."

"You forgive me and say that I'll still have a beautiful new life after what I did?"

I lifted a hand, touched her face. "You aren't to be blamed for what you did in death. Just one thing, though, one thing I ask of you."

She searched my eyes. "What?"

"Forgive me, too."

She closed her eyes. "I...forgive you."

"Now I can let you go, Adele. Now I can let you go."

"Your touch...I'm not afraid now."

I smiled. "No pain. Nothing to fear. You have an entire life ahead of you."

"Will you forget me?"

"Never. Some part of you will always be with me."

She hugged me hard. "But I'll forget you."

I stroked her hair. "As it should be."

I felt her nod. "I can almost see it. A new life. Because of you, I see it."

And the final string snapped.

She backed away.

"Maybe...one day...you'll see me again, Trey."

"I'll know you if I do."

"You will?"

I didn't have an explanation, but I knew that if I ever saw her, felt her again, no matter how old I was...I'd recognize that soul. Gender and time meant nothing to the Soul.

"I will," I said.

Farther and farther away she drifted.

"Good bye, Trey."

"Until we meet again, Adele."

"Trey?"

"Yes?"

"Forgive yourself. You need to forgive yourself."

The last thing I saw was her genuine and soft smile, and then she disappeared, first enveloped in a thick blanket of blackness, then outlined in a shimmer of fire opal light.

"Now reach, boy," I heard Lucien say. "Dey waitin' fer ya."

"Reach," I heard again, the voice richer, deeper and wiser.

Papa. I could see Papa. "You suffer too much. You take da hard road. But you learn well, yes'm you learn well and is even stronger for it. Cross back. Take da thread. Breathe in da Sparrow. Your Soul."

*Purple streak of energy falling from a pregnant, celestial sky.
I reached. I inhaled. I grasped. I inhaled the golden light that
outlined the sparrow's beating wings.*

And then I was looking into an abyss of darkness—
Kissed by silvery moonlight at its edges.

Michel

"Travis?"

One word, one word falling from Trey's lips, one word and
it was the most stunningly beautiful thing I had heard to date.

His voice it was, and his eyes they were, that stunningly
beautiful, twilight-time Mediterranean flooding my gaze when
his lashes lifted.

Travis smiled broadly. "That's me, mate." A universe of
black gave way to amber lights as he gazed back at Trey.

Geoff let go of Scott and swiftly came to be hugging Trey
from behind, prompting Polly's hands to both of their faces.

Gabriel, in the meantime, found his way to me. Arms around
each other, we could not help but sigh in relief, all manner of
things swirling in our minds.

"Geoff," Trey said his name softly. "Geoff, I felt you. You
were there with me. Even there, you were with me."

"I feel you, too. Everything right, now."

"I'm sorry I scared you," Trey's eyes found Polly. "Oh God."
They flicked to Gabriel and me. "All of you. I'm sorry, I—"

Geoff and Polly both hushed him at the same time, and
Polly said, "We can talk about it later."

Trey looked into Travis' eyes. "You. I heard you. And I
saw—" he stopped himself, Trey, and his head whipped about.
"Scott?"

We all looked to Scott, then, still huddled on the floor,
speechless.

Trey, disentangling himself from the others, moved toward

Scott and reached for him. My heart sank when Scott flinched, and I registered the flash of emotion in Trey's eyes as he backed away from Scott, not knowing what to say.

Scott's eyes flicked to Travis. To us and back to Travis, then Trey, before once more travelling to Gabriel and I.

He slid up the wall, and keeping his eyes on all of us, seemed intent on making a retreat.

Trey longed deeply to go to him. The feeling sat heavily upon my tongue and weighted my heart at its center.

"Scott…" Trey spoke his name from a distance he couldn't bear.

"I'm glad you're okay," Scott stammered and bolted for the door.

I reached Trey before he took the second step in that direction, gently grabbing his shoulder. "Let him go."

Trey turned, tears in his eyes, eyes that his hands swiftly covered.

"He needs time," I whispered. "Just some time." I took his hands and kissed the soft flesh on the backs of his knuckles.

"He saw me shift," Travis said. "I couldn't help it. It called to the demon, this part of Trey called to it."

"Not your fault," was Trey's automatic response, though he was uncertain precisely what Scott had seen. "I let her in." His watery eyes moved to Travis. "You helped me."

"I'm grateful for that. I'm sorry to have startled Scott, but I'm grateful," Travis said.

Trey barely nodded; a bundle of emotions, he was.

"Just some time, Trey," Polly gently stated. "He can't process it just yet."

Trey looked into my eyes. "I…" He did not complete his thought aloud. Instead, he sank against me, his cheek finding my shoulder.

"It will look different in the morning," I said into his ear. "It will look different in the morning, my dear sweet boy." I ran my fingers through and through his hair, trying not to dwell too much on that unspoken thought of his.

Chapter Twenty-Seven

AUGUST 4

Slowly waking, waking surrounded in warmth, his warm honeyed skin, his warm breath tickling a nipple.

I had fallen asleep in a warm cocoon, and I was now waking in a warm, full bodied embrace. Embraced by his entire being.

His Soul. My Soul. Our Soul. Priceless, precious gift.

Death was only a transition.

I'd embraced this more and more as I'd sat with my family in my living room after finding my way back, after finding the beauty in Adele, and fully understanding just how lost she was. A lost, frightened Soul, clinging to all she knew and desperately trying to change it.

I could not fault her for that, and never had. Not even the things she'd done to me, I couldn't be angry with her for that. I found my peace in her finding peace.

I found peace in the haven of Michel and Gabriel's arms. In Polly's arms. In Travis' arms, even Travis stayed.

No one had asked a word. They each knew I couldn't yet explain. They each knew I'd tell them when I could.

They each understood in their own ways, understood enough until I could find my own words, and they each understood that I felt drained, and that the one thing burning in my hazy thoughts, the thoughts I could spare through the draining of emotions, were for Scott.

There had to be some way to explain that he would understand. There had to be.

But even this, my family's presence soothed. In even this, they exuded quiet confidence.

All would be well.

His Soul. This spoke to me most of all. It told me not to worry. It told me Scott would always love me. It told me Scott would find his way through it.

Gift. Such a gift. Everything else started to fall away. His dying. The grief. The terror of it.

Oh, it was still there, but it started seeping into the background while his heart thumped a beat in my chest.

But—this was morning, and other thoughts returned. Geoff was asleep. I could taste him, smell him, feel him, but thoughts are powerful things, and all I could think was how am I going to explain this to Scott? Of all the ways to come into my new world, the atomic bomb last night certainly was wasn't it.

Maybe not an atom bomb. It could have been worse. But then I didn't know exactly what he saw. Felt. Heard.

How do I explain this?

If Scott were here, I suddenly thought, and the thought of him being gone struck a chord of panic that vibrated from my guts to my lungs to my brain, and back.

Geoff stirred. I touched his face, stroked his hair. Willed him to settle.

He did.

I took in a lungful, a nervous lungful of air, and carefully moved his arms, carefully slid away from him, quietly left the bed.

Slipped into the first thing I grabbed, velvet drawstring pants, and quietly, very quietly, left the bedroom.

And listened.

Kitchen. A sound in the kitchen.

I slowly went in that direction, praying I'd next smell coffee. Hear it spit, spit, cough, perk.

That didn't happen, but I heard water start running, and as I made my way into the kitchen, I saw him, his back to me, filling the coffee pot with water.

Here. Scott was here, he'd come back.

I stopped a few feet away, remembering how he flinched away last night. Remembering that he looked frightened.

I lightly cleared my throat and he jumped. Turned.

"Oh…I didn't hear you coming," he said.

Wearily. He sounded so tired. So very tired. As I gazed at his face, I could see he hadn't slept. Probably hadn't slept. His eyes were bloodshot and the skin beneath was dark.

"Didn't mean to startle you," I said. Not last night, not ever.

He chewed his lip, winced with it, and my mood sank more. I'd split his lip, apparently.

My mood sank even more when I studied his nose.

I decked him more than once, apparently.

"You, um, look a lot better," he said, glancing at my arm and quickly looking away—avoiding it.

Gabriel had healed the cuts. They were nothing but lines of shiny pink new skin. Another thing to explain.

"You…look terrible," I stated the obvious, sad truth.

He pushed his hair back, turned, and headed for the coffee maker. "Yeah, well. I didn't sleep, really."

Awkward. Awkward, awkward. What do I say? Sorry my fist hit you. It was literally possessed.

I *was*. I was so *fucking* sorry. But not sorry he wouldn't give up. Not sorry for that. I remembered that.

He saved my life, I think.

"Scott, I…" I what? "I'm…I didn't want to hurt you. I swear I didn't."

He poured the water into the maker, set the coffee pot in place.

Flipped the switch.

"Yeah," he said, terribly quiet.

"I'm sorry. Really fucking sorry."

He nodded.

Hiss, spit, hiss.

"I was…" possessed. "I wasn't myself."

"No shit."

Cough cough, perk perk.

I found the floor with my eyes.

"I sincerely wasn't," I whispered. "I didn't mean to hurt you."

He slowly turned. He leaned back against the counter, coffee pot spitting behind him, room flooding with the scent.

"What was wrong with you? It's as if you lost your fucking mind. It was like—like I was looking at Trey, but that wasn't Trey. Hearing you, but that wasn't you. Not the Trey I know. Knew." He folded his arms, lowered his eyes. "Freaked me out. I was losing you, or something."

"You have no idea how right you are," I said.

His eyes lifted. "What haven't you told me? What's wrong with you?"

I almost nodded. Of course. He thought something in my brain had blown while I was gone from his life, and that I hadn't told him.

"I um, I briefly lost my mind." That's not going to help, Trey. But how else do I ease into it?

It was true, in manner of speaking.

His arms tightened across his chest. "Are you…have you…" he grasped for what to say. How to say it.

"I'm not insane," I said.

"No…course you're…" he forgot about the cut on his lip. It reminded him of its presence when his habit tried to kick in. He touched his mouth, then refolded his arms. "You had a seizure, too. I really thought I was losing you. I didn't," his hands went to his face, "I didn't…"

And I was there. I had closed the distance. I was pulling his hands away from his face. "Before this goes any further, I want you to know that you saved me."

His eyes lifted and found mine. "How—I did?"

"Yes." I gripped his hands. "You didn't let me go. You didn't let me walk out that door, and because of that, I'm standing here now. Because of you, the others reached me in time."

"I don't…I don't understand, Trey. I don't understand what happened last night." His eyes pleaded, they were pleading with mine.

"I'm going to explain. I'm not sure how, but I will. I don't know if you'll believe me, but I need you to believe me, no matter how crazy it sounds."

His eyes moved back and forth between mine.

I sucked in a breath. "Geoff and I weren't in a car wreck. That's not what happened that night."

Confusion registered in darkening blue eyes.

Bear with me, Scottie, bear with me.

"I took Geoff to see that mural. Remember that place?"

He nodded.

"I took him there, and…" ah dear God, just say it, it's all fricking insane no matter where I start. "Someone shot him."

He blinked, blinked and blinked. "Shot…but…"

"A girl happened along, and I…I traded her life for his." Yes. I sound like a lunatic.

He pulled his hands away from mine. "You're not making any sense."

I pushed at my hair. "I know, I know it doesn't yet. I'm trying to get there, give me a minute Please, Scott, I want to tell you the truth."

He gazed at me in silence. His nod, slight.

At least he was willing to listen.

I sucked in another breath, searching for words. "Voodoo,

Scott, you've read about it. Well I'm a voodoo child," I just refrained from wincing when I realized what I'd said, and carried on, "I have…I can…" Frustrated sound.

"I'm listening," he whispered.

"I speak to dead people. I see dead people. I…it's my realm. It's my domain."

Staring at me.

"I'm a pathway. I'm the Cross Roads."

Staring.

Staring.

"Geoff died. Papa Legba, he said I could choose. Could bring Geoff back."

"…choose…what?"

"Someone to take his place."

Stare.

I rubbed my face. "A girl happened along."

"And what, you, you…killed her?"

I looked away.

Back. "It was her time. I was the path. She died. Geoff lived."

He turned away, moved away, shaking his head. "Oh man, oh man." He turned back. "Either your sense of humor has gotten totally bent, or I've already lost you."

"No!" Hand through my hair. "I wouldn't joke about Geoff that way. Never. He died in my arms, Scott. He died in my arms, and I brought him back."

"It's still not fucking funny, dude."

I refrained from striding to him and grabbing his shoulders. "I would not joke about Geoff dying. I love him, and believe me, I don't think it's funny, either."

He closed the distance, grabbed my arms, and shook me. "Jesus, listen to you." Concern flooded his eyes. "I need to get you help."

"Do any of the others act like I'm crazy, Scott? Don't you think they'd know?"

His mouth opened. Closed. Opened. "I don't really know them." He pressed his hand to his mouth, then dropped it. "I'm sorry. But last night, now this. I'm scared for you, Trey. I'm scared."

"No. No. Listen. Geoff and Polly. You think they'd let me run around bat shit crazy? I'm not crazy, Scott. I'm not sick." Desperation was creeping through me.

Fear. My own fear.

His other hand dropped, releasing my arm. "It's not like I want you to be crazy! Not you, not now, not my best friend." He turned a circle. "What—okay, okay. What does this have to do with last night?"

So torn.

For me.

So torn.

"The girl that took Geoff's place. She possessed me. She said those things to you. She had control of me. She made me cut myself. She wanted my life, for the one she thought I stole from her."

Gaping. At me.

An expulsion of air, and then, "Next you'll tell me Travis is a...a..."

"You saw." I reached for him. He backed away, running into the counter.

"You saw," I said again, though I backed up, giving him space. No one wants to be cornered by the possibly dangerously crazy person in the room.

"I don't know what I saw. I didn't see anything," he amended.

"No, you saw something, didn't you," I pressed.

He started shaking his head. "I don't know what I saw. You were...you were..."

"I was what? What, Scott?"

"Out of your mind!" Tears fled his eyes.

He moved around me. I pivoted in time to see him leaving the kitchen.

Nearly ran after him.

"Scott, wait," my voice cracked. "Don't leave me. You're the only one left, please don't leave. I know I sound crazy, but I'm not. I'm not lying, and I'm not trying to shut you out either, I swear."

He stopped so suddenly I nearly ran into him. I stumbled back.

"I'm not crazy, Scott. Please don't walk away."

He turned to look at me while I stood there, feeling increasingly frantic.

"You said that if I'd stayed with you in New York, you wouldn't have left me. Please don't leave me now. I asking you this time, Scott. I'm *begging* you, please."

He reached for me.

He reached for me and then hugged me. "I'm not leaving you, okay. It's okay, calm down; I won't leave. I'm freaked and confused and I don't want you to be sick and I'm not sure—not sure what to do."

"You're the only one left from then that I loved. Still love. I need you to believe me; I *need* you to believe me."

I was sobbing.

I was. I was sobbing. I was petrified.

He held me tighter. "Okay, okay. Take a breath, take a breath and—I promise I'll listen."

I hugged him hard. I didn't let go.

I didn't want to let go.

"I wanted to tell you. I didn't know how to tell you. I'd already told you so much, and then this happened and—"

"Slow down. Slow down, partner. Slow down." I felt him rubbing my back. "I'm not leaving. Take your time, Gabe."

Gabe.

He called me Gabe.

He called me Gabe and the fear let go of me.

He only called me Gabe twice before that I could remember. Once when I told him about the case.

Once the night I left him.

Gabe. He was soothing me. Reassuring me.

And he was deeply worried about me.

Mom had sometimes called me Gabe and I flashed back to the first time Scott said it, having picked it up from her. Subconsciously, probably. She said it when I was upset about something, tense or stressed, or just plain pissy.

Or when she was worried about me.

She infused it with love and tenderness, and he must have noticed what it did to me, when she called me Gabe, which is what she called my father.

Scott said it in his own tender way, and like the other times, I was certain he didn't even know he'd done it.

It meant that much more that he didn't.

But though my fear might have fled, the other emotions stayed.

"You didn't let me go this time, and you saved me," I said, hunched over him. "You were here this time and you didn't let me go, and I'm asking you to help me again right *now*. I'm asking you to try to believe me. I only lied to you once before this and you knew it. You'll know if I'm lying now. I'll never lie to you again, I swear."

"Take a breath. Don't say anything until you can take a breath, Gabe. I'll still be here."

****

Me on one sofa.

Scott on the sofa right next to me.

After I'd calmed down more, I took it slow. I told him as best I could. First I told him about the voices, and going to Louisiana, and how I was still learning about this Mark myself. I told him about Lucien and Papa, and that P.K. had been trying to help me.

I told him about the moments before, during, and after Geoff died. Told him about Adele. Tried to explain as best I could what it was like seeing him from outside my body, and how I was begging him to help me though he couldn't hear me.

How I wanted him to do whatever it took to keep me in this apartment.

I told him without the lurid details, the horrifying details, about how she'd found the darkest things in my mind, things that had already haunted me and were easily used to torment me, weaken me, and that I had done it just as much to myself as she had.

She couldn't have done it without my help. My letting her in. My guilt, my need for punishment, it let her sink her claws deep.

I told him how we made peace, her and I. I told him how she moved on.

I told him that out of all of this, there was a gift.

Something beautiful even in the midst of tragedy—Travis had said that, his eyes eclipsed when he did.

But no, not once did I mention vampires. Not yet.

I told him that Geoff was in my Soul and I was in his. I told him that I realized even his dying was a gift; that had I lost him forever, at least I would have felt him go, held him in my arms and he would know how much I loved him when he left me.

Not many people could say that, I thought. Not everyone got to say goodbye, especially not like that. I'd have grieved and grieved, but I'd of had his last moments with me forever.

But he didn't leave me, and I also had the gift of his first breath, the first beat of his heart, as if witnessing his birth.

Rebirth, in a way.

He'd passed through me twice and we were like—one.

Gabriel and Michel, they were like one. I didn't know if they went through something like that to achieve it, but they'd gone through a lot, and maybe—just maybe this was my own dark fairytale.

How many humans knew this feeling? This feeling I coveted in Gabriel and Michel, this feeling when they kissed. A feeling that drew me repeatedly and enraptured me. The beauty of their bond, so tangible and engulfing.

If Geoff and I possessed even half of that, it was more than enough for a human body and lifetime.

The pain was worth it.

I finished my story.

Scott had sat silently the entire time. Now, he looked at his hand, there on his cotton-covered knees. He let out, slowly, a lungful of air.

He finally looked at me again. "So Polly…she understands?"

"She's like a Mambo. Though even some of this was outside anything she'd witnessed."

"Mambo. I know that word."

"I remember. You read a book or two."

He rubbed his knee. "Yeah." He rubbed his other knee. "Michel and Gabriel, do they know about this stuff, too?"

"They know a lot of things." Do you believe me now, Scott?

Absent sounding.. "And Travis…"

I think I held my breath.

"Travis helped you. After Geoff." he nodded. "Geoff, when Geoff got here you calmed down. Stopped seizing. I thought, God. I thought you were dying. You— maybe you felt him…" another absent nod.

He'd like to believe me.

"But Travis…"

Travis…?

"Travis…"

Travis?

"I don't know what he did."

Since I'm not positive myself, we can leave it at that for now, Scott.

Vampires and ghosts and marks—oh my.

"I don't blame you for thinking I'm crazy," I said. "I don't.

I want you to know that."

He picked at his navy blue pajama bottoms. "Well if you're crazy, then I guess they all are."

He...

"Maybe I am, too."

Almost...

"I don't think you're *lying* to me."

Believes me.

"I mean, who could make up a story like that? I don't remember you being that imaginative."

I wasn't quite ready to smile.

"Damn." He planted his face in his hands, elbows to his knees.

He believes that *I* believe it. He's trying to catch up.

"You wouldn't make up a story like that. You wouldn't make up a story where Geoff dies." He lifted his head. "No, you love him, you wouldn't."

He's nearly catching up.

"I love you," I had to say.

Sheepish look from him. His face relaxed. "I sure as hell saw some things I couldn't explain. But I haven't wrapped my brain around this, yet. I'm not sure what I think, yet."

"I still love you."

He shook his head, but then he smiled. It was tentative, but it was there. "As long as you're still here and you're okay now, I guess I'm okay with not grasping it yet."

"I really, really love you, Scott."

He smiled a little more. "I'll even deal with you being crazy, if that's the case."

I felt my smile widen, relief giving way to happiness. "You're a beautiful human being."

He shook his head, again, a soft laugh leaving him. "I love you, too, you spooky, crazy fuck."

I gave him a serious look. "Thank you for tackling me. I was too lost to stop her myself. But I knew you were here."

His eyes dropped. "I wasn't going to watch you walk out a second time." His eyes lifted. "No way."

"That's a reason I love you."

"I'd better not have to do it again. Goddamn, dude." He pressed a hand to his chest.

"No. Way."

"Are you—are you so sure?"

Emphatic nod of my head. "I learned something important. I won't repeat that mistake." And by God, no one else was going to die on me and make me choose. "I'm in control. I am always in control unless I give it away, and I'm not giving it away again."

"If you're sure." He touched his lip. "You've got a wicked left hook, and I don't need you clocking me again." He held up a hand. "I'd have to kick you in the balls, next time, and I don't wanna do that. That's just mean."

He grinned, and I laughed.

But then his expression smoothed. "But...so okay, if Geoff was shot, what about that? Are the police looking for this fucker?"

Uh...

"It okay I come in now?"

We both turned our heads and there was Geoff, adorable in white cotton drawstring pants and a white tunic.

Angelic. And just in time.

"Of course it's okay, *bonito*."

"Yeah, yeah, get in here, Geoff," Scott said. "Here." He got up and moved to the other sofa.

Geoff walked over and snuggled up beside me.

Scott gazed at us. His eyes then riveted on Geoff.

"It didn't hurt. I wasn't scared. Angel was with me."

Scott's brows shot up.

"He knows things. He's meant to understand things," I said.

Scott refocused on Geoff. "Um...I'm glad you're here, Geoff. I'm confused, but you're here, Trey's here, and...yeah, I think there's something special between you."

I looked at Geoff. He smiled at Scott. "I am happy you're still here. I am happy you helped Trey."

Scott's fingers fiddled with each other. "You're meant to understand things? Would you explain that to me? I'm in this far, might as well keep going."

Geoff beamed at him again. "I try."

"I'll try to follow it," Scott offered.

Geoff giggled.

Scott couldn't help but smile.

"Scott's half Inuit. His mother taught him some things. Told him the stories. I think he'll understand you more than he does me," I said.

"Inuit. *Abuelo* tell me about them." Geoff studied Scott. "Maybe you tell me a story after."

"Good idea." I looked at Scott. "Like Whale and the Raven. I always liked that one."

"Story for a story," Scott said. "But before I forget, though maybe I don't want to ask, but I'm gonna ask anyway, seems like..." Scott gave me a pointed look. "You cut yourself, but now you're—there's no cuts. Did I imagine that part, Trey?"

Geoff and I exchanged a look.

I looked at Scott. "Well..."

Epilogue

Scott was here five more days after the ordeal.

Because I promised I would never lie to him again, and because I'd promised myself I wasn't making any "polite" omissions unless I absolutely had to, I'd answered his question about the cuts that had magically disappeared from my right forearm.

I took it in steps, mind you, but it came out eventually.

I told him Gabriel healed them.

He asked if he knew some special medicine.

I said: define special.

Scott said: like special potions.

Me: yes, you could say that.

Scott: Mom knows herbs. None of them works that fucking fast.

Me: Blood does.

Scott: Huh?

Me: Vamp blood.

Yeah right, Trey.

To make a long story short, vampires were the cherry that

rolled off the sundae. Vampires were too much for him to contemplate, so he pretended, for the next five days, that I'd never mentioned blood, and that I'd never said the V word.

I was more than happy to cut my dear friend some slack. We even pretended that maybe I hadn't cut myself after all. We were both hallucinating.

Although, he did start asking more questions about Gabriel and Michel, and he said something about the red stone in my bracelet moving.

Also, he said something about Travis having weird eyes.

But mostly we skipped that stuff.

He asked about the shooter again, of course, and I managed honesty with a polite omission or two. I told him that since Geoff was living and breathing, there wasn't a murder to investigate, at least, not one that involved us, because Adele was the only body left in the catacombs.

He agreed with me when I said that even though I'd love to help the police find whoever was waving that gun around (not a lie), I couldn't, because they sure as hell weren't going to believe my story, and I'd end up a suspect for sure if I told that story. (Still not a lie. That's exactly what would happen.)

Naturally, I *didn't* tell him that I knew someone was most certainly looking for the murderer, and I let him assume it was random violence when I said I had no idea who it was (true). This worked well, because with full disclosure on my part, he'd wonder what kind of dangerous pricks I was hanging out with.

Parisian mafia, Scott, yeah. I'm with the Parisian Vampire Mafia.

Sort of.

He was still mostly in denial over vampires when I took him to the airport, but that was okay. A shit-load of bricks had already buried him on this trip, and then the steamroller had made a pancake out of him.

But, he promised to come back. I promised to see him in NYC. I promised to keep in touch. After a long, tight hug, he let me go and boarded the plane.

While Scott slept during those five nights, I'd seen my vampire family. It had been explained to me what happened to Travis in those moments I was somewhere else and couldn't see across that side of the veil. Those moments when I dealt with Adele one on one.

Demon. I had seen "the Demon." I had glimpsed it before, in fact.

However, I was told there was a lot more to it, and that it wasn't always—so helpful.

I was told I really did see what I thought I saw. Those eyes. Black claws.

I learned this wasn't the only shift he sometimes literally made. I learned that when he Beasted out—my term—the cat had its own claws that weren't quite as long, and that they had a stronger curve to them and were a different color.

I'd already figured that, in retrospect. Those claws ripped into the other vampire at the Fall Out.

I learned he really did have four fangs and that the bottom ones really did curve inward, and during a bite they hooked into a person's flesh, trapping them. If they struggled, flesh came away in a chunk.

Shudder.

Sounds like a pit bull, the description of the way he locks his jaws.

Thank God he's on my side. Though, I also learned he could grow those claws in less violent circumstances. His fangs could lengthen in less violent circumstances—of course.

But I also learned it could be worse.

Oh, yes. It could be worse. Gabriel and Michel had *eight* fangs apiece, I now had confirmation. I don't even want to *talk* about the bottom ones right now, even though it fascinates me, too.

I explained my side of things with Adele, to them. After they were assured I was going to be fine, just fine, they were fascinated.

You haven't *lived* until you've seen three completely fascinated vampires staring at you, completely rapt in every word you're saying. Three vampires that think you're exceptional, and not just for a human.

Those night meetings also gave me the opportunity to learn more about Michel and Gabriel's plans. Because I asked, of course. Because I still want to help, of course. They are family, they are taking over, and I've had it up to *here* with stalkers, and I am *not* going to sit by and do nothing.

No more fucking with Trey. This is *my* movie.

I did, of course, see Polly during those five days, too. Once she was done checking...I don't know, psychically, checking my...I don't know, aura or something, she asked me what it was like.

For posterity, all that. I wasn't having a difficult time talking about it any longer. I was getting lots of practice.

She was happy that I'd found some beauty in the tragedy.

Then she proceeded to bash my ears a little for not asking her to help, which is okay, because...yeah.

My big sister.

I explained about Scott, too. She said she could not wait to see him again, because he was special.

And cute. Very cute.

Now I find myself heading for the meeting Michel asked me to attend. A meeting with, he says, a new ally. Someone who will help us access Vicont's records, someone with lots of information and their own personal grudge with Vicont.

He would not give me a name. I don't suppose the name would mean anything to me anyway, but it seemed he was keeping a secret regardless.

Oh well. I was about to find out.

I made my way to the elegant old building. It could have housed anything from apartments to stores. So many of Paris' buildings were aged works of art.

Actually, this building reminded me of an embassy in a way, and it did house offices.

Michel's *private* offices that no one entered, except those he invited.

I reached the front door and someone buzzed me inside.

Someone met me at the bottom of the spiraling marble stairway with highly polished ebony banister.

Kar.

"Good evening, Master Trey. Allow me to escort you."

God, but he looked elegant. His suit, black silk, a modern interpretation of an Asian staple.

Mandarin collar. Black embroidery. Frog clasps. His silk trousers were sharply white, his shoes black slippers.

His eyes, glittering black stones.

He was an elegant specimen of a Japanese – hmm, and maybe Chinese? – male.

Survival of the fittest and prettiest. (Except for that one, eh?) I was intensely curious about his background, since Travis told me how old Kar was, but now was not the time. There was business to discuss.

"Good evening, Kar. Lead the way."

He executed a perfect bow before turning and heading up the stairs.

I followed him up, studying his hair. It was black, certainly, but not quite the black of Gabriel's. It was longer than Gabriel's was, though. Even tied back, so slickly smoothed and tied back high on his head, that ponytail nearly reached his ass.

Three flights up and he led me to a set of gleaming ebony doors with large golden handles.

Lion heads. There were lion heads at the tops of these handles, their stretched bodies the part he grasped and pulled to open the doors for me.

"Master Trey," he said into the room, then turned to me and executed another perfect bow. "Enter."

I had to bow in return. The respectable thing to do, and it

was contagious anyway.

I caught his smile as I straightened and walked through the doors. He shut them behind us.

I saw Travis. He was standing to Michel's left, and God but he looked elegant, too, in his chocolate suit, milk to dark, his jacket reaching his ankles.

He gave me a smile.

I was glad I'd dressed well, very well, because Michel was in Armani, black, with a silvery shirt and blood red tie. All immaculately tailored.

He crossed to me, his hands outstretched. I took them and he kissed each of my cheeks twice.

"My darling, you cut a fine figure this evening."

"I'm still lost in the middle of the rest of you."

"Ahahah. Hardly, my beauty." He released my hands. "But we may discuss this later. As you and I prefer, shall we just get to it?"

"Yes."

His eyes moved to the doors, and he gestured with a nod to Kar, who opened them as I turned. Two men walked in, dressed in a way that made them look like secret service.

Make those vampires.

They parted, standing one to each side of the doors, and in walked a forties screen siren with red hair, complete with evening gown.

I ripped my eyes away from her promise of a smile, and looked at Michel.

"Trey, meet Elise."

He *so* did not say that name.

"Elise, meet Trey."

He *did* say that name. *Elise*?

"What's *she* doing here?" I couldn't help but bristle.

"Ohhh. Not much of a welcome. What did you tell him, Michel?"

I refused to look at her after she spoke, still staring at Michel.

"Elise is the ally I spoke of," he said.

No. Fucking. Way. "I thought you hated her, Michel."

"He did. He likely still does," I heard her say. "But we have a common goal."

I watched his gaze move to her. I wouldn't have called it friendly.

I wouldn't have called it unfriendly, either.

"Did you bring it?" he asked her. "Your peace offering for Trey and your buy in for me?"

Peace offering for me? What the hell is going on?

I turned at the sound of snapping fingers to see a much too pleased smile on her face, followed by two more secret service Mickey Mouse mofo's coming through the door, hauling along with them a dirty blond who didn't look happy about the shackles.

Or bruises.

Gee, wonder why. But she still managed to look arrogant when she looked at me.

I looked back to Michel, brow arching.

"Trey. Allow me to introduce to you the spy that led Vicont's men to New York," he said.

Both of my brows lifted. "The spy. The one that gave me to him?"

"Indeed. Elise is offering her to you."

Stunned—but pissed off all over again—I looked at the girl.

I took a step, and then another, closer to this spy, and she smiled in a way that made me want to slap her.

But I *don't* hit girls.

"She also," I heard Michel say, "had some hand in leading the would be assassin to Geoff."

I decked her before I could think twice, my reaction so visceral.

Someone else already bruised her anyway. Her mouth was already a blood crusted pie hole in her ugly face

My not being able to stop the surge of anger from springing

didn't leave me feeling none too guilty. Go ahead. Hate me. I was compelled to do it.

I heard a woman laugh. Must have been Elise.

My glaring eyes moved to Michel. "What're you going to do with her?"

"She is yours. What would you *like* me to do, Trey? Would you *like* me to do something to her?"

Darkness wound through my brain in thick tendrils. The tendrils infested my insides, coiling in my guts. "Use your imagination. After she's dead, she's *mine*."

I was wickedly angry, beauty in tragedy or not. Besides, they were going to kill her anyway. I'm not stupid.

Michel's smile was the very definition of evil. "I'll see to it with *great* pleasure." With a gesture of his head, they dragged the bitch away.

"Mmm. I think I like him, Michel," said Elise.

Michel's look grew impossibly more evil, and it fed my own darkness. "You may witness the torture if you like, Trey."

"Nice to know." Though to be honest, I wasn't certain that I could stomach it. Maybe I'm not such a badass after all.

"Yes, I do think I like him," I heard Elise say, while Michel laughed a dark laugh.

I turned on Elise. "I'm assuming she wasn't spying on Geoff for *you*. If she was, you wouldn't be standing there, I don't think."

She shook her head, slightly.

"Fine. Enough of this," I said. "Business." I looked between her and Michel. "Tell me the plan so I can get started." I pointed at Elise. "If you cross us, I'll figure out a way to kill you *myself*. I am done being fucked around, and this is my family you're looking at."

Her smile, slow to spread, came all the same. "Ooh. *Meow*." She licked her lips. "No wonder you love him, Michel."

"Get this straight: I don't like you, and I'm not bluffing. If you sleep, I'll find you, and I'll kill you in your sleep. I'll set your fucking house on fire right after I fasten you to the floor with a nail gun. So don't fuck with me," I said.

Well, fuck me. I just threatened the *vampire*. I've retrieved my balls.

She lifted her chin. "*Monsieur* du Bois; the only idea of fucking with you that may ever cross my mind, carries a different definition." Her golden-green eyes flared brighter.

"I suppose a girl's gotta have a dream."

Her smile, saucy. "Given enough time, perhaps you could learn to like me."

"You can just keep holding your breath, toots. I know about you."

I turned to Michel as he chuckled, low. "Oh my. This is going to be interesting, indeed," he said.

A glance to Travis showed me his ghost of a smile and the brief eclipsing of his eyes. "Gentlemen," Travis left out the lady. "This way," he said.

I made my way to Michel's side and whispered, "You're going to explain later, right? Explain how it is you can stand her being here after what you told me?"

He slipped an arm across my shoulders. "It's complicated... but yes."

We followed Travis through a side door.

"Complicated. Well that's nothing new."

Acknowledgements

Fam'House and Alex Greff. Melissa. My online pals— for listening and talking me through things. Fans—for your wonderful words. taliesinttlg.blogspot.com. lovevampires.com.